Mary read

THEY HARDLY KNEW EACH OTHER.
AND YET THEY KNEW THEY HAD MADE
THE RIGHT CHOICE.

She was Ada Wilder, escaping the confining life of a
school teacher in a small town in Michigan.
He was Emmett Newcomb, escaping a Boston marriage and generations of stifling family tradition.
Together they were fleeing all the follies that bind
people to a life that is smaller than they deserve.
Together, so long as they both lived, they would
fight valiantly, side by side, to win a stake in the new
American frontier.

THAT WILDER WOMAN

A stirring saga of early California

D0775794

That Wilder Woman

Barry Jay Kaplan

GOLDEN APPLE PUBLISHERS

THAT WILDER WOMAN

A Golden Apple Publication / June 1985

*The author gratefully acknowledges the support of Nessa
Rapoport, Kitty Sprague and the contribution of Stanford W.
Blum, whose research into certain historical materials
helped initiate the writing of this book.*

''Developed by Stan Blum, based on a story by Nicholas Hordern in
Los Angeles Magazine and a screenplay by Nicholas Hordern
and Kendrew Lascelles''

All rights reserved.
Copyright © 1982 by Bantam Books, Inc.
Cover art copyright © 1982 by Heidi Oberheidi.
Cover copyright © 1985 by Golden Apple Publishers.
Book Designed by Cathy Marinaccio
This book may not be reproduced in whole or in part, by
mimeograph or any other means, without permission.
For information address: Golden Apple Publishers,
666 Fifth Avenue, New York, N.Y. 10103.

ISBN 0-553-19844-0

PRINTED IN THE UNITED STATES OF AMERICA

0   0 9 8 7 6 5 4 3 2 1

for
Adele Shefrin
and
Ron Van Lieu

Part 1

The Promised Land always lies on the other side of a wilderness.

—Havelock Ellis, *The Dance of Life*

Chapter 1

Desideer, Michigan, on an early autumn day in 1890, was enough like all other home towns to make its inhabitants proud of belonging to the mainstream of American life, and different enough to satisfy the new American creed of individual glorification. It was Methodist. It had streets Main and First to Fifth, it ran by a river. Autumn and spring were brief and dramatic, summer and winter attenuated and dull. Its society ranked a minister above a banker in public, but only above a tanner in private, its fascination with money more compelling than its reverence for God: at a New Year's Eve celebration the previous winter, a baritone had begun the festivities with "Nearer My God to Thee" and ended them with "The Man Who Broke the Bank at Monte Carlo."

Desideer lay in a flat plain, far from hills or mountains or valleys. Served and scolded by the Orenoke River, a distant tributary of the Mississippi out of the Ohio, Desideer's citizens felt a nice sense of history flowing through their town. The river, a major means of transportation—rafts and barges mostly—was also a place where people cooled off in nearby summer promenades. Boys would leave their britches behind a log and dive in bare-rumped and shrieking, their excitement heightened by the sure knowledge of being watched. Girls hid in the blueberry bushes that grew deep and tall along the stone wall built during Pontiac's Rebellion and giggled at the flashes of flesh sailing through the air.

The classroom where Ada Wilder taught school was located on the Orenoke at the south end of River Street, past the blacksmith's, in what was once a storehouse for grain. That location proved too damp, being but ten yards from the water, and the grain went to mildew; the sour smell drove away the ladies from Tye's Ice Cream Parlour, opened just the year before when rock salt started being shipped in bulk from Chicago and refrigeration was no longer only of the moment. But the warehouse was considered dry enough to accommo-

3

date a maiden schoolteacher and a classroom full of ignorant children.

A half-hour before the children were to arrive, Ada Wilder flung open the high double doors of the schoolroom; a breeze circled leaves around her ankles, lifted the edges of her dark blue dress, and set them down with a sigh when she closed the door. With her wide gray eyes, chin tilted forward and lips parted, her hair swept back in deep waves, Ada conveyed a sense of implacable movement, like the generously sculpted women on the prows of seagoing ships.

She regarded the room critically for a moment: the ceilings of the former malt storehouse were high—there had been a loft once—and windows were built into the walls where there had been none before, windows almost as high as the room itself, arched at the top and giving out onto a view of the river and a dock that was, even at this early year in the history of Desideer, already rotting in disuse. Ada moved quickly to arrange the room for her pupils: music sheets placed on desk tops; the floor swept of the remains of yesterday's experiments with the age of Orenoke sediment; "There is no frigate like a book" scrawled on the slate board; and a carefully hung facsimile of Mr. Grey's drawing of the human leg.

She had just begun to erase the slate of yesterday's lesson—"Heard melodies are sweet, but those unheard are sweeter . . ."—when the doors opened. Expecting an early pupil, she was surprised to find the Reverend Dr. Blaisdell standing in the open doorway, sharp-shouldered and angular as a stork; his unlined, embryonic face belied his twenty chilly winters at the pulpit of Desideer's Methodist Church. Since it was Dr. Blaisdell's long-held practice to remain ensconced in the church building and receive, Ada thought it curious for him to pay a visit without the requisite, at least, of an impending death.

He walked slowly, following the chalk-dusted slate around the four walls, nodding and murmuring. "Always admired Miss Webster's work here," he said, indicating the border of alphabet in the meticulous style of the Spencer penmanship book, painted by Ada's predecessor. "Quite fascinating," he muttered as he passed "there is no frigate like a book," and came to a full stop to examine Ada's drawing of human leg musculature. "Oh!" he piped, lifting its corner to reveal a scowling likeness of President Benjamin Harrison. Nervous fingers behind his back fanned in and out like a carnivorous plant.

Finally the reverend turned from his perusal of the classroom to a survey of Ada herself, nodded, nodded again, then gestured beneficently for Ada to be at ease. She remained at the slate board while the reverend proceeded to recircle the room.

"I wanted to have a few words with you about your classroom activities," he said finally, removing his coat as he went, with not a small struggle at the sleeves. "I'm sure it's something that can be cleared up and dismissed in just a few moments." His quick nervous glance at the walls of the room suggested that this might not be so. "I know your young charges will be here soon," he added, and looked apprehensively at the high doors as if tiny demanding souls were about to break them down. Unused to these forays into the world outside the church building, the classroom diminished his own sense of significance, he looked itchy in the worst places. "Let me get to the point straight off," he said; his lips had turned quite dry. "Certain parents of... certain pupils have complained about all the questions their children have been asking."

"What kind of questions?" Ada asked.

Dr. Blaisdell stopped walking and shook his head. "No, no, no, child," he replied. "You miss the point. They said you have been encouraging the children to... ask questions in general. About anything."

"Children have inquisitive minds, Dr. Blaisdell," she said.

Dr. Blaisdell bowed his head, thought for a moment, then looked up at her. "Let me put it another way," he said, and continued his walk as he spoke. "Compulsory education is sweeping the nation like a... commandment." He looked at Ada for acknowledgment of the aptness of this metaphor, and made an automatic adjustment in his planned Sunday sermon. "It's an unmistakable sign of progress, don't you see?" He gave special emphasis to the word "progress," and seemed genuinely moved simply to say it. "As head of the school board I want Desideer to assume its rightful place in the future of America. We want our city to move forward into a position of importance in the twentieth century. Your job is to educate our young people so they may be the leaders of that movement. Now do you see?"

"I've wanted to talk to the school board about this very

thing," Ada said. "I don't think children ought to learn by
rote. They don't really learn anything that way except to act
like mechanical dolls."

"Discipline is always a problem with children," the reverend agreed. "You have a willow rod expressly for that purpose."

"Fear of pain's no way to teach anybody," she said.

Dr. Blaisdell pursed his thin lips and made a small whistling sound. "I am certainly not one to espouse corporal
punishment," he said, then took Ada by the arm and led her
to a child's desk in the first row, while he sat himself at the
teacher's desk in front of her. The inequity of their relative
positions did not escape Ada's ironic eye, and she regarded
him now with open skepticism.

The reverend spread his hands in front of him and gripped
the edges of the desk, elbows locked, shoulders to his ears.
"There is a tested method for everything we teach our
young," he intoned. "Penmanship, for example, has been
standardized nationally by Mr. Platt Rogers Spencer. You
have the approved curriculum. You have only to follow it. You
see there on the wall your 'Mechanics of Mathematics'?" The
chart was illustrated with proliferating watermelons and radishes
and beets, with pecks and bushels, with pint, quart, and
gallon water pitchers, and the final exhortation, stenciled
along the borders of the chart: drill! drill! drill!

"It pains me to be the one responsible for forcing information into their heads," Ada declared.

"Really, Miss Wilder!" Dr. Blaisdell said. "We are not
concerned with personal feelings and ideas, but with what
your students learn!" His eyes and mouth drew toward his
nose in consternation. He walked to the slate board and
stared at the lines of Keats which Ada had copied out, 'Heard
melodies are sweet, but those unheard are sweeter.' "Of what
use is this to them?"

"It stimulates their imaginations," Ada said. "It lifts the
spirit!"

"We have the church for that," he said and pointed a long
white finger to a needlepoint canvas hanging on the wall. "'In
the training of children,'" he read aloud, "'it is better to do
one thing one hundred times than one hundred things one
time.'" He looked at Ada expectantly. "That is your credo."

Ada jumped to her feet. "That's not learning!"

"You may resume your seat," the reverend said.

The room was suddenly hot; Ada felt as though he had

strapped her arms to her sides. "You treat me like one of the children," she replied.

"Because you act like one," Dr. Blaisdell said, reddening. "You are a grown woman, Miss Wilder. You must set an example worthy of your charges, and obey your elders. Now sit down and calm yourself."

"Learning by repetition only makes them incapable of thinking for themselves," Ada said. "Children need to ask questions. Yes, I encourage that. They need to know how things work. To learn why things are the way they are."

"Children are required only to learn the facts, and you are required only to teach them," Dr. Blaisdell said. "These are children, Miss Wilder. I think you credit them with more than they merit."

"When they grow up is soon enough for them to start accepting their limitations," she replied severely.

"I am shocked by your cynicism!" Dr. Blaisdell said. He rose from his chair and glared at her. "If you are so opposed to the very essence of the American educational system, perhaps you should not be teaching in our school."

Ada was silent for a long moment. He was right, she thought, but for one thing: There was no other job, there was no other way to live. She hated the Reverend Dr. Blaisdell for showing her the implacability of her situation. "I don't want to lose my position," she said finally, looking defiantly into his eyes.

Dr. Blaisdell hesitated, began walking again, then stopped and regarded Ada. Her place in the town was not without its sympathetic aspect; a schoolteacher's job fell by default to the bright but plain girl in town, in charge of the children she would, sadly, never bear. He knew, too, that Ada was likely to remain at her post only until she married, and that would be soon; she seemed, even to Dr. Blaisdell, who by nature eschewed such observations of the flesh, too . . . full to be a spinster. He breathed deeply, then nodded, a satisfied sigh restoring his color, and extended his hand to her. Ada took it with some reluctance, and allowed him to lead her to her own seat at her own desk. Dr. Blaisdell touched her arm gently: a lamb returned to his flock. Though she had retained her position, Ada feared that under his benevolence she might lose something far more important. Like Dr. Blaisdell, Ada knew that she was not to be long at this post; not now.

"Young Ed Kraemer was asking after you just the other

day," the reverend said as he pulled on his coat. "Came to my office after his Sunday-school class. He teaches the youngest boys, you know."

"I know," Ada said, head down, flushing with shame, knowing that if he could begin to arrange her private life in this way, she was already losing herself.

"Very fine fellow, young Ed. Stands to take over his father's milk delivery service when the old gentleman retires. A regular churchgoer, too. Seems he and you might—"

"Excuse me, Dr. Blaisdell." Ada stood, and went to the slate board where she erased the line of Keats. "But I don't see that my life outside this classroom is your concern."

The reverend stiffened; he clutched at his coat as if Ada's remark had whipped it like strong wind. Her students rushed in then, a cacophony of children's screams and shouts, scarves flapping like banners. Their high spirits were abruptly subdued at the sight of their minister; they dropped their arms to their sides, and huddled near the front door, frightened by their own sudden silence. The girls curtsied and the boys doffed caps as Dr. Blaisdell walked by them with scarcely a nod their way.

This is what he would call respectful good manners, Ada thought sardonically, knowing it for a rote lesson drummed into their heads by parents equally badgered into believing what was right.

Two of the older boys detached themselves from the group and rang the eight-o'clock bell as the others took their seats and unstrapped their books; Ada watched them all through a haze of anger and humiliation. Once again it had been demonstrated that nothing was safe, that nothing was truly hers. Dr. Blaisdell's presence remained in the room as an overheated pressure on her chest. She appointed the bell-ringers to lead the class in daily calisthenics, an innovation Ada hoped the school board, from their headquarters in the church basement, would not now disallow.

She walked to the arched windows that faced the river; a cloud momentarily covered the sun. The river was brown under an early autumn sky which presaged the steel-gray winter to come. A printed box rode by on the swift current; a green apple bobbed in its wake. The sun glistened on the muddy bank near the unused dock. "I do not want to lose my position"—a new wave of rage washed over her.

A tapping on the window startled her. Her brother's eager

face appeared on the other side of the glass, his red hair an exotic flower against the mud-gray sky. He made a praying sign with his long bony hands then knotted them into fists and Ada knew he had witnessed her encounter with Dr. Blaisdell. She shook her head, never comfortable with his watchful protectiveness. It was different once, when they were students themselves in this very classroom. In the years after the Civil War they used to play on the battlements and on that very dock when it was still a place to load the rafts that brought the grain downriver to Pilophilos where they made the beer...

Ada and Obie—for Obidiah—were glad they didn't live in Pilophilos, because the smell of brewing was so strong that on summer days women and weak men had to wrap their faces in handkerchiefs splashed with lilac water. Old folks even fainted. Desideer, once the malt storehouse was gone, smelled most like apples, especially in the fall, when they dotted the ground in the orchards. And there was the smell of hay in the rain, and of horses, too. That was a smell that Obie liked particularly, but Ada held her nose against it, especially in the summer, and he laughed at her for it, called her a girl. If they were near the river she'd chase him into it and show him who was who. Swimming was never something that separated them, even though grown-ups cared very much about the differences between the sexes and what was proper for one to do accompanied by the other. The town mothers accused Cornelia Wilder of moral laxity—"Letting them go about just any way they please," said Mrs. Garnett; "Why, you'd think she'd want to keep them out of sight altogether," agreed Mrs. Fry—and never called her the Widow Wilder, though they might have if she'd gone out of her way to curry favor. But that manless home was too ambiguous for their comfort; her existence was an affront to theirs.

Cornelia Elizabeth Reef had been a pretty, small-faced girl from Oxtail, Missouri, when Felix Wilder brought her back home to Desideer after he had had a hand shot off at the battle of Spider's Wail. She had abundant chestnut-colored hair; she had a light step which gave her a reputation for being birdlike, and she loved her new husband like mad. But more than Felix's finger had been undone in battle. He was apologetic, and often sweet, but a fallen angel whose only successful act was to leave town before he undid himself and his family any worse. Cornelia soon went bulky and gray, sewing and laundering for the very people who'd once been charmed by her birdlike step. She took long walks at night, sometimes didn't come home until the next day, and no one knew from where. Town loyalties went to their native son—to memories of him pre-war, at least—and against the woman who'd driven him to his sorry end. It made Cornelia tie red ribbons around her throat and snort with derisive laughter at Dr. Blaisdell's sermons; it made her refuse church donations of clothes for her children, but accept offers to sew.

"Corn whiskey'll come next," Mrs. Sewall said, "then henna'd hair and who knows what. Men?"

Cornelia kept her back straight and tied big bows in her hair when she took Ada and Obie into town, chin held high against the wind, holding on to her children for support. "Just once let them say it to my face," she muttered as they walked up Main Street hauling a sack of corn meal for chicken feed and enough cornmeal bread to last a month. By the time they got home, the sun was a quivering arrow in the pond across the road. Cornelia warmed herself in the rocker by the wood stove. Ada set to braiding a rag rug at the kitchen table. Obie sat on the floor near his sister's feet, leaning against her chair.

"I was in Moss and Getchell's while you was getting the corn meal," he said. "Heard Mrs. Sewall telling Mrs. Garnett how sorry she felt for us having to live in such a poor place."

"I hope you told them to mind their own bees' wax," Cornelia said, settling a shawl around her shoulders.

"Bees' wax," Ada whispered to herself, and smiled.

"I told 'em we was fixing to move soon as Papa come back," Obie said.

"Next time you tell them we like it here just fine," Cornelia said.

"Mrs. Garnett said that in her opinion—"

"Devil take her opinion!" Cornelia said and twisted in the rocker.

"Mama, that's bad!" Obie said.

"What they said's worse," Cornelia told him.

"I wish we was nice like Mrs. Sewall," Obie said.

"Can't be nobody but yourself," Cornelia said, staring at the fire in the wood stove. Ada heard in her voice for the first time the terrible weight of being Cornelia.

"We're different, Obie," Ada said and threaded her fingers through his hair, her fingers feeling the heat of the stove.

Obie listened carefully—he was three years younger than Ada, who always seemed to know what would bring his feelings out—but he was still trying to find a hole in this reasoning that would widen so better things could rush in.

Cornelia had her head turned up now, as if seeing something far off down the road. "Can't waste your life trying to please people, or make 'em like you if they don't. When your daddy left like he did...well, that just put us out with the town. It's what's called circumstances. You see?"

"I see, Mama," Ada said, and Obie, a wild hammering in his chest, repeated quietly, wetly: "I see."

Neither Ada nor Obie liked being the poorest of the poor but as long as the other kids—like their parents—insisted on assigning that position to someone, Ada and Obie were destined to fill it. They mostly stayed away, to find pleasures for themselves before they had to go home to their chores: making slip whistles from green willow twigs, fishing with a bit of string and wire and maybe catching a catfish; or searching for hickory nuts they could store to roast in the winter; finding treasures like a solid wedge of colored glass from the heel of a bottle of patent medicine, nails and screws and chipped marbles they kept in a cigar box they found in the old Bellevue place before all the other kids ransacked it; poring over newspaper accounts of the great Centennial Exposition in Philadelphia—a favorite pastime of Obie's—and marvel at American technology: imagine a steam-powered thresher! imagine printed wallpaper! On long winter afternoons they huddled behind huge picture books in the town library. It was too cold to go home, because firewood was so hard to come by, there being no extra pennies to buy it by the cord the way the church ladies could do, and no man to chop. The very notion of a man had assumed an ephemeral shapelessness in Ada's mind.

More and more, Cornelia seemed to be looking at some message in the distance, and Obie clung more to Ada. Both felt the fingers of difference stroke them against the grain; only Obie saw no privilege in it. More than one night they wrapped themselves in a quilt and slept on the roof of the house, afraid to stay inside until Cornelia returned. The dark would settle on top of them, them so high and it so low it seemed a blue-gray cloud could touch their shoulders, and Obie huddled close to his sister.

"There's this place where orphans go to live, and ladies come dressed pretty and give big presents and let the orphans kiss their cheeks."

"Don't be silly, Obie," Ada said quietly. "We got a mother, so we're not orphans."

Obie peeled a piece of shingle, and threw it into the road. Ada watched the shingle glisten and fade with each blink of her eye, as night came deeper. She kept her eyes on it; at some moment Cornelia would have to cross it.

"Haven't got a father, though, have we?" Obie said.

"Felix," Ada replied, mimicking her mother's disgust. "He just gave mama us two babies, took a swipe at her whenever he was sober, and drank corn whiskey the rest of the time."

"He worked at the blacksmith," Obie said, and clutched her hand. "And people liked him."

"I'm glad he's gone," Ada said. They were silent a moment, listening for Cornelia's singing to rise up out of the darkness, hearing the wind moaning in the apple orchards instead.

"Is mama a widow?" Obie asked.

"Can't say," Ada replied. "A widow's only if your husband's dead, and... papa just..."

"Widows are supposed to wear black dresses and have a sad expression," Obie said hopefully. "I think people'd like us more if mama had a sad expression."

And when Cornelia did come home from these excursions to God knew where, she was mean-tempered and sharp, and often as not she'd hit one or the other of them and then cry far into the morning till she'd come and wake up her two babies—as she called them at those times—and all three would huddle close and cry and cry, and the feeling Ada mostly got then was that they were the Wilder family together, and to hell with everybody.

School was a relief and a torment. It separated them for the first time, Ada being three years older, and put both into the official life of the town; no longer could they so righteously be ignored. When Obie started school he demanded to sit near Ada, though that would mean displacing Ada's new friend Katherine Fry. But separation made Obie so quiet and dreamy the teacher didn't know how to bring him to his lessons except with that willow switch in the corner. Katherine Fry was moved next to Irma Blaine, and they became best friends.

Once, it was the separateness from the respectable life of the town that kept Ada from having a friend and then it was because of Obie; his very loyalty mocked her and made her unacceptable. No one dared come too close—not Mrs. Sewall's Karen, or Mrs. Garnett's Monica, or Katherine Fry either— nor invite her to an afternoon party or a cake and punch social except that one time when Karen Sewall did and then in front of all the girls dared to make a careless remark about Ada's family being dressed in "sackcloth and ashes." Then: "Oh, Ada!" she'd exclaimed in a perfect imitation of her own mother, "not you, of course," and gave Ada room to agree. "Rather be dressed in ashes than have 'em spilling out of my mouth," Ada replied.

Boys didn't feel the same way about her, though; Ada suspected this stemmed less from acceptance than from sheer male opportunism, and she viewed their attentions with a cool eye. The summer she was thirteen she went to a Sunday box lunch picnic at Lake MacBride with Jason Hawkins, called "the mule" because he was "stubborn as one when it comes to taking no for an answer," Katherine Fry had warned. "And what about those ears!" ten-year-old Obie said, disgruntled that Ada would not join him in storming the picnic with rotten apples as usual. But Ada found she liked walking with Jason along the edges of the lake, away from her mother and brother; she liked someone paying attention just to her. When it began to rain she and Jason took shelter in that deserted Bellevue house, where the old lady had died in that funny awful way.

"Bet no one could ever find us here," Jason said.

"Bet anyone could," Ada said with a laugh.

Jason watched her, pushing his wet, dark hair off his face, and hunching his shoulders the way she'd observed salesmen around the drugstore doing before barreling up to a likely customer. "Bet no one will."

"Oh, listen to the rain!" Ada said. "I wish we could build a fire or something. Did you know how old lady Bellevue died? Her dog—" Jason grabbed her hand and looked at her, hopeful, expecting the worst, but Ada let her hand stay in his. "House like this has such funny sounds. I wonder . . . You look like you caught a chill. Want to head back?"

Jason swallowed hard and shook his head, hair falling in his eyes again and Ada laughed in a way that twisted a shy smile out of him. He pulled her hand, drawing her closer, his face looming over hers, his mouth set.

He smelled like pine-tar soap up close; Ada noticed little beads of water under his closed eyes where the skin was faintly blue. He was aiming blindly, and Ada touched one ear to guide him and let him kiss her on the lips. Oh, we'll be friends now, she thought, I just know we'll be friends. They stayed like that for a moment, then Ada heard a scraping sound, looked to the side, and something enormous flew at Jason, and knocked him to the ground.

Ada screamed at the sight of her brother, knees clamped on Jason's back, kicking his ribs and pounding his head on the floor. "Obie, stop it! Stop!" She pulled at his shirt; a piece came off in her hand. She slapped his back, and pushed until he tumbled off Jason and fell to the floor, where he crawled up against the wall, staring up at her, his eyes filling with tears.

"You slapped me!" he cried, holding his hands to his face.

"Spying on me!" Ada screamed at him. "Following me and spying on me! Why can't you leave me be?"

Ada helped Jason crawl to his knees, and saw blood on her dress. Jason rose to his feet and backed away to the front door, holding a handkerchief to his bloody face, his wet hair hanging down like a curtain which shut her out. He glanced at Obie, and shrugged. "Guess I believe it now," he said, "what everyone says," then ran out. Ada watched him disappear down the road. She turned to Obie, still crouched against the wall, and the anger drained right out of her.

"You ruined it." She shook her head slowly and walked out into the rain; she did not have to turn around to know that Obie was following.

It was their first fight which wasn't to be resolved by a tussle in the dirt. They didn't talk it out either, and Ada could never quite get to the bottom of the feeling she had about her brother after that; something about it seemed like forever. They squared off, and stayed distant for a few weeks; then Obie lobbed an apple at her from a tree in the orchard a mile down the road from their house, and she looked at it, hesitated, then threw it back up at him, and it was all right. At least, it was as all right as Ada thought it ever might be. Obie didn't interfere with her anymore, but Ada knew he followed. "For protection," he said once, and there was nothing more to say.

The weight of this protection increased as the school years drew to a close—he quit permanently when Ada was graduated—and Cornelia's place in their lives dwindled. Ada felt her mother's death approaching long before she died, the daughter a nightly witness to her mother's concentration on that distant spot in the road; during the winter of '85 she went out and met it.

The cemetery overlooked the Orenoke River from the top of Capachonic Hill, named for the Indian tribe that had settled the region and was wiped off the face of it when the first settlers arrived by boat a hundred years before. Ada stared at the pale gray stone with only her mother's name and dates dug in; she had found Cornelia's body a half-mile from the house, stretched out on her belly in a final embrace of the road. Ada had agreed to Dr. Blaisdell's presiding at the funeral because of the teaching post he'd offered, but this yielding to the forces of town propriety frightened her; the murky bottom of such easy acceptance surely presaged a place in Desideer she never wanted to assume.

The stone was wedged deep in the earth. An earthworm folded and unfolded itself along the top; Ada squashed it with the heel of her hand. Behind her, Obie stifled a choke and moved restlessly.

". . . ashes . . . dust . . ."

God rest you, Mother, she thought, and God help me from being buried next to you. Her gaze lifted as Dr. Blaisdell patted her shoulder and walked off. Ada stared fiercely at the town below the cemetery, slabs of gray houses and brown roads, and the quick heavy pulsing of the Orenoke. Obie moved among the tombstones, beckoning to her; his red hair made him seem a wild flower tormented by winds. The burden of his need for her was suddenly intolerable.

"This town don't need misfits upsetting the balance of things," a voice said. "Fitting in's what's important. I know."

A few yards away stood a stout, middle-aged woman dressed in lumpy dark clothes, men's boots and thick gloves, next to a large black box balanced on three wooden legs. The woman saluted her and came forward, leaning the contraption on a slab of stone. "'Course, that's the thing I always liked about your mama," the woman said. She had a full, round face, a

second chin propped up on a black muffler, and eyes that
seemed pinned to her nose. "She didn't fit in, and had a right
nice contempt for the ones who did, like they was the ones
who was strange."

"I didn't know she ever spoke to anyone," Ada said.

"Far as I know she never did," the woman said and they
both looked at Cornelia's tombstone. "I just watched her
from my parlor window. Never talked to her, myself. Wouldn't've
wanted to intrude."

Miss Harriette Austin was something of a curiosity herself
in Desideer, not a married lady, not a cook or a scullery girl,
neither, or a maid or a teacher or a ribbon clerk, but a
military man's daughter, who lived alone in the finest house
in Desideer and practiced the burgeoning craft of photography.

"General Austin built this house for my mama in 1847,"
she told Ada on one of what became their regular Sunday
afternoons together, Miss Harriette often elbow-deep in silver nitrate and smelling of developing baths, Ada leafing
through photographs Miss Harriette had had printed in newspapers as far away as Chicago and Boston, always under the
name Harry Austin. "They were married in this house, and
my mama died in it, too, the night I was born. They had to
cut me out of her, like . . ."

"MacDuff," Ada said.

Miss Harriette nodded. "And you can imagine how my
daddy prized me after that. The people in Desideer loved my
daddy—he was a great hero. They took me as part of his
baggage. All the old ladies of the town wouldn't hear a bad
word said about me now. Oh, I bet the younger ones're eager,
though. Lady photographer: I don't know what'll happen
when they get the power. The only difference between me
and your mama, you see, was circumstances."

"She said the same kind of thing herself once," Ada said.

"I remember when Felix Wilder left her and run off," Miss
Harriette said. "Rage makes a face real alive. You looked like
that back there at the cemetery that day she was buried. Like
you wanted just to leap into the Orenoke and let it take you
away."

"Did you ever try getting away from Desideer?" Ada
asked.

Miss Harriette thought for a moment, her eyes tracing a
path along the mantelpiece filled with framed photographs.
She picked up a few as she spoke. "I see the whole world

right here in Desideer," she said. "Every face tells me
something I didn't know before. Just when I think I know all
there is to know about venality and greed, or kindness and
beauty, too, why someone is born in Desideer, or someone
dies, and joy and grief bloom all over again and transform
faces. I could stay here forever and take photographs." She
put down a small picture of her father, and smiled shyly at
Ada. "Oh, maybe Paris," she admitted, and added quickly,
"but I'd always come back here. Desideer's my home, like it
or not."

"If I was a man," Ada said, taking long strides around Miss
Harriette's overfurnished parlor, "it'd be easy. A man can go
away to college. He can get a job on the railroad, or take a
raft downriver. He can join up with a band of traveling actors,
or become a salesman or a writer, and go all over the country.
A girl can't do a thing but marry up, and quick." She paced
nervously in front of the bay window, looking out at River
Street. An old dray pulled a wagon in and out of sight.

"This town, this town, they make it impossible to breathe.
And the boys who want to marry me—like my mother used
to say, dull as the Orenoke's bottom in November. The girls I
went to school with, they're married, they have kids of their
own, they do needlework for church socials. They're just
becoming their mothers all over again, and pleased as punch
about it, too. I would like to accomplish something in my life.
Be a wonderful teacher in my own school somewhere. Is that
wanting too much? I can't hardly wait. I'm itchy. But I'm
scared that one of these days I'm going to fling myself onto
someone out of sheer frustration. One of these poor boys that
keeps bobbing around me . . . tugging at his hat . . . asking me
to walk with him . . ." She stopped, clutching the window
curtain. "And I'll make us both miserable. Stuck here, stuck
in Desideer. But I won't just go home to a little room over the
dressmaker's, either," Ada said, "like poor Miss Webster at the
school, until I die some night like she did, with a shawl around
my shoulders and the next day's lesson in my lap. I won't!"

"You know," Miss Harriette said, "a woman doesn't have to
be a man's wife. Never saw the great appeal in men, myself.
Always found women more to my liking; don't seem so
strange as men do. Seems most of the women in Desideer
don't even like their men. Just happen to need 'em, is all."

* * *

Ada watched the river flowing by outside the classroom window, thinking, as she often did, that the river would be her transport, then walked toward the front of the room and the high double doors that had never been changed from the days of the old malt storehouse when buckboards were pulled into the building to load up. The children continued their calisthenics as Ada paced; she thought with shame of what Dr. Blaisdell had brought her to.

She looked through the front window and saw that Obie was waiting for her now on the oak-tree swing, the sun at his back. As he swung toward her the sun lit up his face; Ada straightened, then leaned closer to the glass: it was not Obie, but a man she had never seen before. She backed away, wondering if he'd seen her, then inched her way toward him again. No, he hadn't seen her, and she watched him swing in and out of the sunlight. His face was lean and fine-boned, hollowed and curved by sculpting thumbs. She would have remembered that face if she had only seen it for the instant that lightning tears across the sky, so different was it from the faces she had seen her whole life in Desideer.

She turned to the children. "Lesson twenty-four," she said quietly and waited until they opened their McGuffey's before turning back to the window. A black serge suit, a faint gray stripe in the trousers, freckled hands and long blunt fingers and those boots! a deep, deep red, hand-tooled, and not at all in keeping with the conservative Eastern-looking serge. Ada lifted her chin and looked at him with curiosity. His eyes widened on the shaded down-swing, with an expression of just having opened to something startling. She was not at all sure that she trusted such a display of male beauty, though she knew that women were not even supposed to notice such things. She ran her hands over her hair, tucking in loose wisps, then looked back at him.

He looked like no one else in Desideer: too handsome, too well-dressed, his silk four-in-hand so loose and smart, his serge suit fit so snugly, the vest so well-tailored, and not bulging out at the waistline like the suits of the young men in town that were bought from the Sears Roebuck catalogue and shipped postpaid from the factory, then stitched up by their mothers, quickly shiny from too much sitting at desks and leaning on counters. And those red boots! She was drifting off, just looking at him on the swing sent her thoughts out of the room. What's he doing here? Probably lost, she thought, or visiting a cousin.

She forced her attention back to the children, and taught to the very last minute of the class but restlessly, her eyes repeatedly glancing out the window to see if he was still there. Waiting for one of the children, maybe. Or visiting a cousin. Or selling something. But what could he be selling, dressed like that and swinging in that swing?

Chapter 2

Emmett Newcomb's doctor would not have approved of this behavior, swinging from an old oak in a cold yard twenty yards from a river, waiting for a young lady he knew only from a photograph. It was this same doctor who suggested that childhood bouts with scarlet fever, chilblains, and rheumatic fever had resulted in a thinness of blood, a weakness in the heart and lungs and a concomitant lack of vigor. The doctor confided to the chastened parents that young Emmett would not in all likelihood continue life much past two decades and a half and those would best be done quietly. For a brief period Emmett enjoyed brooding on his fate, but life in a third-floor Boston sickroom was clearly not a poetic languishing on an English moor or a swoon in the Italian Alps or a painless bloody cough on a beach in North Africa and brooding was put behind him. He would not waste what life he had; he dreamed of a full one, and the doctor did not reckon on the strength of this dream.

The physical beauty which eluded his sister was bestowed generously upon Emmett, alternately a blessing and a curse, for he was praised and petted and admonished on the same account. His bearing was proud and, as his health improved, youthfully confident. By the time of his graduation from Harvard College, however, he was having a recurring nightmare of crawling stealthily along the floors of a vast dark cavern, and finally coming into the light only to realize he was encased inside his late father's body like a suit of armor, seeing the world through those eyes and reflecting that corpulent self-satisfied image he so despised in the gilt mirror over a mantelpiece draped in cobwebs and dotted with ancestors in miniature, cackling at him in tiny horrible voices. He invariably awoke with a pounding heart and a growing determination to escape the particular fate that awaited him if he remained where he was.

"I never said the city of Boston contained all that the world holds in store for a young man," Mrs. Newcomb said, knowing that to oppose her son would be to court his rebellion.

"But it's the only city in America that is justified in calling itself civilized."

"I think Boston civilization's about as stimulating as a year-old copy of the *Globe*," Emmett replied sulkily.

"It's been a perfectly fine city for generations of Newcombs, who have never felt the slightest need to leave it," his mother said. "I see no reason why you shouldn't be proud to have your portrait hanging in the family gallery along with your ancestors."

"Mother, I don't feel like an ancestor!" Emmett said with a shiver. "I feel like a... predecessor."

"That's because you're young," she said and pursed her lips fretfully. "All that changes around when you get older."

"It's frustrating to sit put when you know the rest of the world—the real world—is going on somewhere else," he declared.

"And where is this real world, I'd like to know?"

"I'm not sure," he replied. "But it's not in Europe, I know that. There's no room for me with all the past they've got stored up there."

"Europe is an essential part of a young man's education," his mother replied. "I don't want to hear another word of denial. You're going and that's settled."

She stopped herself, fearing she'd gone too far, and heaved a dramatic sigh of mock defeat. "Promise me one thing, will you?"

"What is it?" Emmett asked, and took her hand.

"That you'll come back home before you make any important decisions about your future."

"All right," Emmett said. "I promise. Anything else? Shall I bring back a duke for you?"

"Don't be sarcastic," she said, and thought for a moment. "Promise me... that you won't marry a woman with an accent. There, I've said it and I'm glad."

And so, Baedeker in hand, dressed in knickers and tweeds, binoculars slung about his neck, Emmett gawked dutifully at Windsor Castle and Oxford University, at the Tate, at Chartres, at the Prado, at the Vatican, murmuring appreciatively and making tiny xs in his guidebook next to paintings and monuments which had been paid homage to, until he determined that a decent amount of time had been spent at this honorable pursuit, then shucked like a heavy coat History and Art Appreciation for more contemporary and sensual avenues of pleasure. His letters to his mother and sister became, of necessity, brief and evasive.

There were many adventurous women in Europe, so he had heard, and if he was not too hopelessly off the mark, he finally found himself gazing at one across the terrace of the Hôtel des Artistes in Cannes. He fixed the moment clearly in his mind—silver gleaming in the candlelight, his own face above a white silk tie upside down in a spoon, a peal of laughter on the beach below—when he understood that the woman's smile was an invitation. He caught his breath, and followed her into the lobby of the hotel, where, after a wait of several moments spent fingering the fronds of potted palms and several more of anticipation as she arranged herself at the stairwell, Emmett and the lady—an impudent Alsatian named Cheri who was just a bit down on her luck, though such could not be discerned by her jauntiness of manner or dress—retired to his rooms. With the curtains lifted by the ocean breeze, and the sound of a string orchestra coming faintly from the ballroom several floors below the bed, Emmett tasted female flesh for the first delirious time. The woman was attentive, unembarrassed, and, most unexpected of all, responsive to his caress. To his post-love query of mutual pleasure, she replied *"Pourquoi pas?"* and fell asleep. In the morning she was gone, her only traces the scent of gardenias, a hastily scrawled *"merci"* on a hotel envelope, and the grin of concupiscence on the face of this proper Bostonian come to a fine European debauch.

The weather in Cannes being clear and bright, Emmett hired a carriage and driver, and told the man to drive, drive, drive, he cared not where. The driver, surmising quite correctly the source of such *élan*, drove into the hills and stopped at the crest of the highest. He hauled out a picnic basket and lap robe for his young charge, but, eschewing such woolen coddlings, Emmett sat down on the grass itself, buttered a brioche, and looked at what there was to see.

The sight was too overwhelming to take in all at once: the sea and the sky and the long stretch of sandy beach and the hills rising to meet him; a sense of endless horizon. He closed his eyes and began again, detail by detail. The Atlantic he had crossed was not so blue nor so nearly translucent as this sea—too deep to rest the eye or the soul upon, too vast and threatening for comfort; one lost oneself there—but here the blue was of a clarity that suggested gentle life and an aid to thought and contemplation. The air smelled of... lilac and ginger and brine; sea air borne to him on the gentlest of breezes. He stood, a sweet roll in hand, butter making his fingers slippery... comical, and felt enormous and free. He breathed deeply, thinking mockingly of doctors. A man could live forever in this beauty.

He traveled to other places on the Mediterranean, and found beauty and peace wherever he went. With his moody eyes and olive skin burnished by the sun, he could have been Italian. If he had exchanged his tweed knickers and walking shoes for the animal skins of a sheepherder, he could have been a peasant herding his flock up rocky slopes above the green sea of Greece. Time did not exist here, the nineteenth century had made no mark on the land or the sea or the people. The North African sky was gold; sea waves tumbled rust over blue at dusk. He observed each place as though memorizing it for future reference. For these places were what he found the most exciting about Europe and not, as he had assumed, the museums, the cathedrals, not even the women—they seemed to know something he could never know, they were overbred, inbred, they were so serious—but the land! the sea! the air!

A foreign wife? No, Europe was the past. And the future, Emmett knew—and he would hold it out in front of him with an excitement all the more delicious now, for his sense of its inevitability—would occur with a woman of the future, an American, in a wild and beautiful place with a view to the horizon. Naturally, then, Boston could never again be home for him.

Emmett returned there in time to give away his sister Elizabeth in marriage, and promptly contracted pneumonia. His mother, now scolding, now smug, blamed it on Paris. Yielding to prolonged bed rest, Emmett thought no more of Europe but of Europe-in-America, transposing treasured images of sky and sea to native shores. In 1889, American land went on forever, her resources very much available to the dreams of rich young men. His plans called for decent health to begin with, then a place to settle that would give him what the Mediterranean had given him: peace, sun, the sea, an atmosphere of contemplation and sensual pleasure.

He read travel books eagerly, tossing aside paeans to Florida and Louisiana and the Gulf Coast of Texas. He was

determined to discover for himself American land to equal
what he'd seen in the Mediterranean. No, to surpass it.

Then he came to a book which actually compared a place in
America to the Mediterranean with no prompting from him: a
place of healthfulness and longevity, cornucopias of fruit and
flower; vineyards and head-high mustard and rows of cypress;
pastures of buckwheat, clover, sage and wild mint; shepherds
and horses and sheep and the sea, even the sea. Emmett felt
he was reading a description of a place he had already
experienced; he was not so much surprised as relieved at last
to have his fantasy recognized.

He wrote letters and received prospectus upon prospectus,
railroad timetables and rates—it was the first time in history
that land was being settled to accommodate the rapid growth
of the rail system—artist's renderings of a landscape which
could have been Sicily or Hydra, projections of cities to rival
any in Europe but new and modern; American! He estab-
lished postal contact with a young lawyer. His mind was made
up: as soon as he was completely well, he would emigrate to
Southern California.

Having encouraged his European adventure, his mother
began to pull in the reins. Women of marriageable years, in
an age when marriage was all a girl dreamed of, planned for,
and lived and died within the blessed state of, were now
paraded before him. Emmett, though not adverse to the sight
of an amber-stockinged ankle extending from the voluminous
satins and brocades of the day, or a fair set of hazel eyes
peering from beneath wisps of hair come artfully astray from
the elaborate coiffures so much a part of each young woman's
equipment, or a comment intended to please with its
appropriateness, was singularly unmoved. After what he'd
seen of European women—though their essential decadence
was ultimately too rich for Emmett, who was Beacon Hill-
born and -bred—he was not impressed by the contemporary
Boston variety.

"Ruined by foreign hussies," his mother sniffed.

Emmett remained tactfully silent on this subject, but
defended his ideas just the same. "The reason I won't marry
Dessie Flynn or Ethel Moody is because I don't want a
woman who reveres etiquette second only to God. Or do I
have it the wrong way around?"

"Emmett!"

"I want a woman who isn't afraid to say what's on her

mind," he continued reasonably, articulating it perhaps to himself as well as his mother. "A woman who *has* a mind. Of her own. Who won't hesitate in fear of what I'll think of her, or what anyone else'll think of her, either."

His mother drew herself up straight in her chair. "And *I* think you dramatize yourself and your life. You're really quite like other boys, but you won't admit it. It's all that reading you did when you were ill. It's spoiled you for your place in the real world. And you'll never get a nice Boston girl to take a trip to California with you!" she added with cautionary righteousness.

Her rage pickled in the next weeks into hurt and contempt. When she showed him a photograph printed in the rotogravure section of the Boston *Globe* she had already adopted a scathing tone. "Is this what you're going out west for?" she asked, grimacing at the photograph. "Here's your example of an 'American' girl. A nasty-looking beast in a poor pathetic dress."

Emmett looked at the picture. "I wonder what's made her so angry," he murmured.

"She does look like she'd just as soon bite a man as curtsy," his mother said, warming to Emmett's agreement.

"Oh curtsies!" he exclaimed. "As if curtsying were the sum of a woman's accomplishments." He held the photograph under the light. "Photographed in Desideer, Michigan, by Harry Austin, it says. Hmm. She makes the girls in Boston look piggy and stupid, with their tiny little noses and 'adorable' smiles."

"Emmett! She's coarse!"

Emmett continued to look at the photograph; the woman's face intrigued him more and more. "She's not beautiful..."

"'Not beautiful'?" his mother said. "You're being kind."

"And yet there's something exciting in her face," he said. He imagined her voice would be deep and reedy; he imagined her laugh would be—"I wonder who she is, if she's real or..."

"You're being contrary for no good reason but to spite me," his mother said. "Now give me that picture."

"I'm intrigued, Mother," he said, not taking his eyes from the photograph even as Mrs. Newcomb attempted to wrest it from him.

"I will not encourage this!" she wailed. "I will not!"

After an exchange of letters with Mr. Harry Austin, Emmett

ascertained the identity of the girl in the photograph, and began to spend odd moments staring at it, imagining it coming to life, imagining conversations with this Ada Wilder, the lifting of a hand from the invisibilities beyond the edges of the frame, a wind ruffling her hair, a sharp noise startling her eyes. Emmett altered his westbound railroad ticket to include a stopover in Desideer, Michigan. His mother, apprised of this, could not restrain her indignation.

"Are you thinking of picking up this wretched girl on the way?" she challenged. "You might just as well. You've already compromised yourself by writing to that photographer."

"Maybe I will," Emmett said seriously, then took a deep breath and went on. "You see . . . well, I wasn't going to tell you at first, but—"

"What?" his mother piped. "Tell me what?"

"You see, the trip is more than a . . . trip," he said. "It's going to be permanent. I mean, I plan to stay in Southern California."

His mother merely stared at him for a moment, waiting for the grin to broaden and signal the jest. But the seconds broadened instead, and her mouth started to work. "But . . . but . . . it's the edge of the continent!" she exclaimed. "You can't live there!" Her voice rang the appropriate toll of the doomsday bell.

"The land is rich and fertile," Emmett declared, waving brochures and pamphlets dog-eared with use. "'Pacific breezes blow, valleys produce tender grapes,'" he read from one. "The climate is warm; health blooms," he added, hand to chest in sincerity. "Why, there's even a bill bouncing around the California state assembly to call it officially 'the sunshine state.'"

To his mother, however, the idea of losing her son to a place so far from the centers of civilization and society—and incidentally her own bosom—was an outrage. "It's a deadly waste," she declared.

"The land is there for the taking, Mother!" Emmett exclaimed.

Mrs. Newcomb was not convinced. "Yes, you gain land, I suppose, but you lose just about everything else that matters! And just what is so special about land?" she demanded of her son, even as she watched him draw long red marks on a huge map of Southern California he'd tacked to the wall of his study. "What is all this land for? Isn't a house enough? I should think a person would get lonely on all that land, for goodness sake. You're not a farmer, you know."

"Maybe not now," Emmett said. The horror of what he suggested his future might hold quieted her for the moment.

As the weeks passed, she pursued him from library to parlor, trailing heavy skirts and the scent of Mme. Gris, but none of her lines of attack produced any halt in his plans. He bought a new Gladstone bag and two sturdy trunks. He instructed his Southern California lawyer to hire realtors to scout suitable houses near the ocean. Mrs. Newcomb reminded him of his poor health, and warned of the paucity of trained doctors in his wonderful west. She threatened never to visit, to disown him, and ran out of possibilities only as she bid him goodbye at the train.

The school doors flew open, and the children poured out. Emmett stood and held on to the rope of the swing as he watched her dismissing her charges, turning to help this one with a jacket, bending to help another with a shoelace, but remaining within the shadows of the classroom. His hands ran up and down the rope impatiently; come out, come out; he felt close to shouting her name. Finally she emerged from the building and closed the doors behind her, then stood, head down, and fussed with her cloak. Emmett clung to the ropes to keep from rushing up to her and taking her face in his hands. Then she raised her head, eyes half-closed, as if testing the air, and walked toward him.

It was the photograph becoming life right before his eyes. Her high, smooth forehead was unencumbered by curls, as her mouth was free of the paints and smirks of fashion; her very features—prominent nose, high cheekbones, eyes set wide and deep under humorously arched brows—appeared swept clean of extravagance, and made her face seem direct, even gallant, as though she were walking into the wind. How amazing to see this face in animation after having grown accustomed to Harry Austin's photograph of it.

She stopped a few feet in front of him and, without dropping her gaze shyly or peering coyly from beneath lowered lids—her eyes were enormous, her face broad at the cheeks and so frank in expression—nodded her head in greeting.

Their eyes met for a moment. "Miss Wilder?" he managed to say.

He tipped his hat; its tightness, Ada noticed, had not quite tamped down the black, curly hair. He bowed slightly from the waist, one hand behind his back in a manner so formal that the children shouted with laughter. His mouth widened in a generous smile at this; he bowed to them, too. He certainly is handsome, Ada thought, but she had to admit that bow was just the slightest bit absurd. "They've never seen real manners, I'm afraid," she said with a slight catch in her throat, thinking that she had never seen them, either. She watched his eyes—gold-flecked, reflecting a crescent of blue sky—seeing something that obviously pleased him.

Emmett felt himself blush under the frankness of her gaze. "Please forgive my appearance," he said. "I'm afraid I didn't have time . . . that is, I didn't want to waste any time changing. You see, I've just got off the train from Boston and . . ." He paused, breathless and began again. "Your photograph doesn't do you justice." To her look of query, he removed it from the inside of his coat. When carefully extricated from a glassine envelope, Ada recognized the portrait of her Miss Harriette had taken by the river bank. Ada had worn her white graduation dress, though she knew her anger at its poorness would show up on her face.

"But how did you get this?" Ada asked.

"My name is Emmett Newcomb, by the way. I'm from Boston, Massachusetts. This photograph of you appeared in the rotogravure section of the Boston *Globe*. The article was called *Visions of Our Middle Western States*. I was sort of . . . taken with it and I wrote to the photographer, Harry Austin—"

"You mean Harriette Austin," Ada said.

"I do?" Emmett inquired. "I thought it was Mister Austin. You see, I wrote him a letter . . ."

Ada was shaking her head, curious that Miss Harriette had never mentioned sending her photograph to the Boston *Globe*, or getting a letter from this man inquiring after the subject herself.

". . . and Mister Austin . . . I mean, Miss Austin, of course . . . wrote back and said you were the school teacher in Desideer. Said you were full of pepper, and Lord knows that's what I've been after, been talking about it ever since I got back from Europe. Even before I went I was—"

So he'd been to Europe too! Not just from Boston, but from Boston to Europe. She drew her head back to look at him; close proximity did not afford the proper perspective to take in such a sight as a man this handsome who had even been to Europe. He was getting larger, growing and growing until he was too big to fit under the shadow of a grain-house-*cum*-schoolroom in Desideer. Suddenly the image of Dr. Blaisdell filled her inner eye. "I do not want to lose my position." This man—his eagerness, his optimism—made her feel ashamed.

She was staring at a spot just below his mouth where his morning shave had missed a few dark hairs. As she saw his mouth widen and relax, she realized that her earlier assumption that he was lost was incorrect; he had found something, instead. She looked about her as the children squealed and shouted, scattering for home in pairs and trios, looking back at her and laughing, now that they were free of her rule. "This is quite improper," she said, pulling on her black gloves and buttoning them. "The whole town will be talking about your visit for weeks to come."

Emmett toyed nervously with the rope that held the swing. "Something tells me that you don't care very much what people might say."

"Oh, I care," Ada said, looking away then back into his eyes. So Miss Harriette had sent him . . . lured him was a better word. Ada shrugged. "I just don't care enough."

"I hoped you'd say that," he said and laughed, his teeth the white of a red apple bite.

Ada, used to embarrassing people with her frankness, was disarmed by his laughter; without either saying another word, they began to walk together along River Street toward town. The sun filtered down through the overhang of leaves, and turned houses and faces gold and secretive.

"It'll be winter soon," she said, and Emmett heard a note of sadness in her voice.

"There are some places," he said, "where you don't mind winter at all."

The remark, calculated to arouse her curiosity, only made her regard him with suspicion. "I take it you've never been to Desideer before?"

He stared at her for a moment and stopped walking. "You see, I've just come from Boston especially to . . . well . . . to get right to the point . . . What I want . . . what I want is to . . . Should we be standing here like this?" he asked, indicating with his head the faces peering at them from the windows of the dressmaker's house.

"Let them stare," she said, and they continued to walk.

The trees ended as they came to the beginning of the town's center. Here carriages vied for passage with pedestrians, the right of way going to the bolder. Ada and Emmett did not speak as they went slowly through the town. Ada, out of the vulnerability she always felt when on public display; Emmett, for his part, was prolonging his silence with a delicious perversity, as a thirsty man ambles circuitously to the bar now that it has opened for the day and relief is plainly his. He put off the moment when he would tell this newly met woman that he had interrupted his trip to California to stop off in Desideer expressly, exclusively, to see her.

They passed Anderman and Aucoin's Plumbing and Heating, Schulsky's Haberdasher, Frazetti's Undertaking Parlor, Strebel and Meyers Produce. Each store brought new faces to stare. Greetings hailed them from corners, arms waved, and mouths flapped in false and real conviviality, Emmett Newcomb tipping his hat now to the equine lady clerk adjusting a bit of ribbon in the window of Moss and Getchell's, now to Farmer Ed Willis unloading a cart of carrots at Miss Roberta's restaurant.

"Desideer," Ada remarked dryly when they had passed the town's five long blocks in silence.

They walked alongside the river, the dirt road marked with wagon tracks, horse hooves and boot heels. A man-made waterfall for the paper mill roared in the distance; there was the smell of burning wood and a fresh mistiness from the river itself. A man and woman sat under a white umbrella in a rowboat on the river. As Ada and Emmett crossed a footbridge over the water, they approached a group of young boys smoking cigarettes. One of them ran into the trees and disappeared. Farther down the river, someone played a flute. It was late afternoon, the time of long shadows and whispered confidences. Emmett and Ada sat on the grass under the deep, feathery coolness of a tall willow tree. Ada looked at leaves swept along the current. Emmett watched her; her skin was clear; he thought of snow melting on apple trees on Beacon Hill.

"This is as pretty a river as any I saw in Europe," he was saying. "Though I have to say that the Tiber was special. Oh, Europe's really something, Miss Wilder. You should see it. Just full of great old stuff. And the people there are so

unusual. Not at all like the folks back home. Much more...
'civilized', my mother'd say. Well, I guess they'd have to be,
seeing as they're from a part of the world that practically
invented civilization. We're a new country, don't you see?
Our people are still learning about things. Though in Boston
they're just trying to imitate Europe, and what they've got
themselves into is a social paralysis—that's how I see it. Very
rigid, very strict on what you can and can't do. Not that
Europeans don't have strict rules, only for the life of me I
could never figure them out. Their women especially. Fancy
free! Oh, not immoral, don't let me give the wrong impression. But I think an American man is looking for a different
sort of woman. Leastways I am, and I'm an American. We've
got the chance here to be really ourselves, don't you see? I
picked California as the place to settle down because it's as
grand as the Mediterranean countries; grander, I hear. And
that's where people are going just to start things right, don't
you see? Just to—"

"Well, that's all very nice for you," Ada said, her shoulders
up hard and her lips pressed together and whitish. "And I
suppose it's very impressive, too, and I'm very impressed.
But I am also sick and tired of hearing men talk this way, with
this freedom. It's very well for you to roam the world, seeing
things and meeting people and doing what you like, then
picking up and moving on and doing something else you like.
And what are we women allowed to do? Nothing, that's what!
Nothing but sit and wait for one of you men to come along
and tell us we're the lucky one."

Emmett had never seen a woman display such frank temper. Always before this, such displays had been shot through
with female petulance or a kind of sinuous importuning that
left a man not exactly weak, but defenseless and exhausted. It
was not that Ada spoke like a man—men were far from
frank—but that she spoke like someone not concerned with
maintaining the niceties of her sex. It was better than he had
imagined she might behave.

"I've made you angry!" he exclaimed, rising, surprised and
delighted to have elicited such real emotion from her. "In
Boston this'd take a wedding and six children at least."

Ada broke off a cluster of fading hydrangeas, and took
several deep breaths of them, embarrassed now to look at
him, having revealed so much, and surprised, too, that she
had allowed herself to see just how discontent she was.

"I think it's wonderful that you speak your mind so freely," he said.

She stared at him for a moment and stood up. "Don't think I'm grateful for that. I don't need your approval. I think you're conceited."

Ada's steps took her out of the shade of the willow and onto the soft loamy banks, where the smell of damp earth was rich and doughy. Emmett laughed with genuine pleasure as he skipped alongside her.

"I'm sorry," he said though he did not put aside his obvious pleasure. Ada slowed down and dropped the flowers into the river. She was intrigued by his acceptance of her; her anger spent, she returned the smile.

That they liked each other with such openness made them both suddenly shy, as if they had already a sense of their own destiny. They continued to walk in silence along the river bank; long reddish shadows from the setting sun dappled their faces and hands.

Ada's spirits rose, and she pointed out to Emmett all the places she had touched as a little girl in the town of Desideer. "That place there, just below the graveyard, we had a may-pole every spring. Jimmy Juleson used to live in that old house; he had that birthday party me and Obie had to watch through the windows. We used to collect maple syrup from that tree, right there," she said, pointing to a maple already going red and gold with the fall. "And Obie skinned a rabbit, his first one, right by that tree stump, there. Oh, he was sick for a week, don't think he ever forgot it. And this apple orchard belongs to Seth Kemper and his wife. They're real accommodating about letting us have as many apples as we like. Lord, I'm sick of apples. I guess . . . I guess you can leave me off here."

Emmett had hardly spoken during their walk, but for a murmur of appreciation at the appropriate moments. He sensed that Ada was speaking out of some sorrow that he'd best give room and respect to. Having half fallen in love with the idea of Ada Wilder before he had even met her, and hoping she was in reality like the spirit he saw in her photograph, he glanced shyly at her now, her profile etched cleanly against the apple trees: she was more. And here they were together, they had argued, they had apologized, they had smiled. His chest swelled, he had for the first time since that hilltop in Cannes a sense of the fullness of his life and the possibilities he and a woman afforded each other. He put his hand out to her now, and she shook it with a hearty laugh, as a boy might before it comes natural.

"Tomorrow?" he asked.

"Aren't you going to California?"

Emmett smiled and shook his head. "Not just yet."

Obidiah Wilder was six when his father left home for parts unknown; town rumors, spread from Addison's Barber Shop to O'Steen's Billiard Parlor to Jack Byron's Smoke Shop, led the boy to believe that a woman with yellow hair was involved. At first Obie could only imagine that she was a circus performer because he'd never seen a real person with yellow hair. For years after that, Obie would beg his mother for the few pennies to get into the circus if it ever came to town. Cornelia never had the extra pennies, and the circus never came to Desideer, she said, comes only as close as Cashman and that's too far for such a little thing like you to get to on your own, son.

By the time he had grown he knew yellow-haired women didn't mean the circus, and he felt he'd been played the fool. He tore up a treasured likeness of his father, then wept in remorse and conducted a funeral for the pieces; a shred of an eye reproached him in dreams. He blamed his father's desertion on his mother's plainness; if she'd been that kind of yellow-haired woman, his father wouldn't have left. The certainty of "when papa comes home" became a tentative "is papa coming home?" As papa remained gone it became "don't care if he never comes home," and, finally, a silence on the subject, though the hurt remained, deep inside him in a private cave of feeling, an emotion with arms crossed, from which nightmare demons flew at his eyes and in daytime made him jumpy and mean without knowing who to hit.

Animals soothed him; he got quiet and still at the sight of a horse in the meadow near his house, and would work at the town stables after school, or smile shyly at a collie dog like the one his schoolmate Judah Blessed had on a long leash. Even lazy house cats like Katherine Fry's fat tom Brindle filled him with peace. The only pet he ever had was a scrawny rooster, who nipped his face when he held him, and whom Obie accidentally hugged to death one cold afternoon waiting to find out if his mother was dead or alive. That afternoon a woman's body was discovered face down in the river near the dock at the schoolhouse. As it was dragged out, Obie thought he recognized the shoes. He ran home, found Cornelia and her shoes not there, and, terrified, waited on the roof. Ada wasn't there either, but Obie could not, did not dare, leave his own house until he discovered his mother's fate. When she did come home, she found him pressing his face to the stiff feathers of the dead rooster.

Afterward he clung to Ada for protection, both parents having failed him, Felix by desertion, Cornelia because she needed protecting herself. In her independence, Ada seemed able to supply it to both of them. Obie loved her with a wild indiscrimination, unaware that he burdened her. By the time he was ten she had come to define home for him.

He was a skinny boy, red-headed, with small green eyes always narrowed to a squint, whether at the sun or at something he saw that was just too much for looking at wide-eyed. He approached life sideways—slinking down alleys in town, listening in the dark to grownup gossip, following people who for one reason or another piqued his curiosity— as if a head-on meeting could only bring the pain of uncontrolled revelation. The demons that haunted him, his quietness, the secret life he led inside himself, kept him a child apart. The world moved very fast indeed: a rushing rhythm he could pick out in the river. He sought solace in the smells around his house: of gravy and vegetables in a stew, of alkali soap, of the copperish smell of his own hands. Town folk thought it strange that he was so little affected by Cornelia's wintery death; not Ada, though. But it was long ago that he had killed his rooster; Cornelia's waywardness banished her from his circle after that.

When Ada strolled down Main Street with Emmett Newcomb, Obie was drinking a lemon phosphate at Tye's Ice Cream Parlour on a break from his work at the stable and after his morning check-in at the schoolhouse. As he walked back up Main to the stable, he passed Jack Byron's Smoke Shop, where some older boys and young men were itching to get into any kind of trouble there was before settling down to the lives of respectable burghers. There were boys of Obie's age and a bit older wearing vests and bowlers and tight checkered suits, patent-medicine salesmen and feed-and-grain salesmen, a dandy or two from out of town in a straw boater, though the season for them was nearly over, one or two with spats or a gold chain slung across their vest pockets, a handlebar moustache on one. Obie greeted them with a reluctantly mumbled hello—the ladies of Desideer took it for shyness, the men for surliness, while Obie pined for invisibility—and was greeted in return with muffled laughter. Obie looked up in surprise, his eyes squinting against this unexpected assault. He held his elbows into his body and pressed his lips together in sort of a smile that didn't have to be taken one way or another.

Eugene Chase hunkered up to him, twirling his moustache like the villain in illustrated books. "Ferdy here was just reciting a new poem, huh, Ferdy? Go on, Ferd. Tell it for Obie. Go on."

Ferd Kinnan, his scrawny neck flecked pink with heat rash, detached himself reluctantly from the small group and pulled at his collar. Then, clasping his hands together like an orator, he began:

"There once was a girl with a blister
Who didn't much bother who kissed her.
I gave her a buss
And caused lots more fuss,
Till she screamed: 'Please! I'm somebody's sister!'"

The boys didn't laugh this time, but stared expectantly at Obie, who clenched his fists in his pockets but showed nothing on his face.

"Speaking of sisters," Eugene Chase said, and this set the boys off sniggering again, "we just seen Ada strolling by. Isn't it so, fellas?"

Obie's mind was rattled in front of all these boys, his hands feeling huge, skittish as a never-ridden colt.

"She was walking with a fella, too, isn't that so?" Eugene added, undaunted by Obie's lack of response.

Obie felt licks of fire in his stomach. He wanted to take Eugene's words out of the air and force them back into his mouth.

"An Easterner he seemed to be, in a black suit and fancy manners," Eugene said. "Just the two of them. Very cozy."

Obie's eyes darted from one squawking face to another, then he spun on his heel and half walked, half ran back to the stable, knowing this was just what they wanted him to do but unable to bear their mockery.

He stood in the cool shadows for a moment, catching his breath, taking in the high, ripe smell of hay and manure. Then, with a movement so sudden it startled even himself, he jumped on a horse, whipped the reins around, and, before his boss Jake Whittier even knew he'd been back, he was out, galloping down Main Street, eyes half shut, heels dug into the chestnut mare's smooth flanks, slapping her on the rump with a hand, calling out to her. As he rounded a corner, he and his horse unsettled a wagon load of bricks into the street. Obie kept going, hearing the shouts that followed him but paying them no mind.

Who was this man? Who was this man? Whoo? The wind called it to him, the question rode outside and inside, whooshing through all his secret places. What could a stranger know about Ada? He'd want something from her, want her to do things for him, and then he'd leave her off somewhere with a streak of sorrow running down her face.

He rode the horse along the banks of the river, and saw them in the distance walking toward the setting sun—he could recognize Ada from anywhere at any angle; even the haloed edge of her hair was familiar to him. He reared the horse back, and it slowed to a halt. Ada and the man walked slowly, their heads bowed in intense talk. Obie watched, walking the horse slowly after them now, humming to himself or the horse, a keening sound close to a cry. Then he stopped, dismounted, and tied the horse's reins to a tree, shushing her still. Crossing the river at the shallows before the paper mill's waterfall, he squatted and watched them from behind a willow trunk.

Ada was nodding. The man was describing something, his hands moving geometrically in the air. Ada bent down and picked up a leaf from the ground: she twirled it between her fingers. They were headed for the footbridge. A group of younger boys was standing at Obie's end of it, rolling cigarettes and smoking. Leaping from behind the willow, he joined them.

But when Ada and the man started across the bridge the courage to confront them failed him. Tossing the cigarette in the river, he ducked into the bushes. With half-closed eyes he watched them walk farther along the river bank. His fluttering lashes made the couple appear dreamlike and hazy as they sat on the bank. Then Ada was standing and waving her arms in anger. Obie narrowed his eyes further, clenching and unclenching his fists, ready to spring at the man if he made an attempt to hurt her—hoping for a good reason—but nothing more happened.

Obie followed them to his house, where the man saw Ada in, and then, curiously, watched the house for a long while, alternately smiling and knitting his brows. This drove Obie wild with anger, such emotion spent on Ada. Then the visitor took a deep breath and turned back to town.

Obie watched him walk into the twilight and disappear around a bend in the road. He sighed deeply and crawled to the ground outside the kitchen window where he rolled an apple between his palms and watched Ada. Wind rustled the trees. Ada glanced at the window; Obie ducked and held his hands over his ears. When he looked again, Ada was bending over to light the stove. The kindling caught, and in the burst of flame Obie saw how much like Cornelia she looked, like she did just near the end. "Have to help her very hard," he whispered.

He waited, crouched down on his haunches, ready to spring, the apple warm between his palms, until Ada fell asleep in the wicker rocker, then crept into the house and covered her with an old patchwork coverlet. She stirred as he kissed both her hands. He added a few sticks to the fire, then moved to his cot in the corner of the room. Obie fell asleep with the image of Ada right before his eyes.

He woke up with a start to the sound of her moving around, and the smell of chicory simmering on the stove. He curled inside the covers, feeling warm and small. Ada passed him— he smelled apples now—and he opened his eyes to little slits, watching her move across the room in that white dress with little lilac flowers on it; he liked how those lilacs all bunched together and came apart when she walked. She left his view, and then the kitchen door opened and clicked closed. Obie opened his eyes wide but it wasn't until he heard voices outside that he jumped out of bed and ran to the window.

"What business he got calling at my house?" Obie said when he saw Ada and that same man walking off down the road. There on the pine table was a big bunch of flowers which he lost no time stuffing into the belly of the stove. He pulled his boots on, then moved across the road into the apple orchard, keeping his eye out for Ada and the man on the road until he found them fishing in just the spot upriver

where he and Ada used to swim, and settled himself behind a
maple tree. "Made her take him to our place," he whispered,
moving his lips against rough bark. After a few minutes, Ada
caught a catfish, and the man laughed so hard he had to sit
down on a tree stump, only he fell off the back of it, then Ada
laughed so hard the catfish wriggled off the line and flopped
back into the river. "Damn fools," Obie said pressing himself
into the tree. "Laughing like damn idiot fools."

He followed them across the footbridge and along the far
bank of the river, past the blacksmith's and the laundry, then
up the hill to the cemetery. Obie crouched low behind
General Austin's eagle-carved stone. Ada was standing at
Cornelia's grave, pressing her hands to her chest then to her
mouth. Then she looked up and pointed down at the river.
Obie watched the man watching Ada; what's he looking so
serious for? What's he know about it?

He cooled his face on General Austin's tombstone until
Ada and the man passed him, then followed them down the
hill. Bells rang out just as they turned from River Street
onto Main, and the street came rumbling alive with the
volunteer firefighters galloping off to a blaze in the mill.
Obie ducked behind a buckboard filled with sacks of potatoes; all he could see through clouds of dust was the man's
right hand pressing into Ada's arm flesh to keep her out of
the path of the fire wagon. If she calls me I'm right here,
but Ada didn't move the hand away, wasn't even standing up
straight now, but leaning into the fella. The fire-wagon bells
clanged so loud Obie clamped his fists to his ears. "Sounds
enough to blind someone," he muttered. The dust rose
away, and when he stood Ada turned and saw him, so he
quick dropped his head like he was counting sacks of
potatoes. He knew Ada wouldn't like it if she kept seeing
him, even though it was for her own protection, so he had
to let them walk away.

His chest hurt something fierce, though, and he sat down
on the bench outside the feed store. The street was near
empty now. A yellow dog limped across the road; a lady's
blue bonnet tumbled by in the breeze, and the dog perked
up and went after it. Obie took off for the stables where he
worked, dusting the road off himself, but the sign said
"closed on account of fire," which Obie knew meant that his
boss Jake Whittier was indulging his interest in a good blaze.
The horses were snorting and shuffling on the other side of

the stable doors. "Easy, easy," Obie said. "Don't pay them no never mind." He pressed himself against the barn door, lips at the crack, and whispered, "Just a man walking her along. I'm always around to keep her if he tries to break her up."

Chapter 3

"Of course you won't believe it, until you see it, Ada," Emmett was saying. "Why the Southern California coast is just like . . . like Italy! Or . . . Greece! It's that beautiful! Long, long sweeps of sandy beaches, and the clearest blue water, you've never seen water as clear or as peaceful." He compared California to places of antiquity—"Palestine! Crete!" It was the land where past and present prepared themselves for things that had only been dreamed, for the astonishing future; it was the last place in America—"in the world!"— where a man might truly claim a kingdom for himself. "Every other place has already got its mark made on it, any place that's worth marking, that is. I don't mean some forsaken badlands territory out of a dime novel, not that you've ever read one, of course." He eyed her with caution for a moment, not sure at all that she had not done many things he had no notion of, and Ada mischievously gave him no sign that she had or hadn't.

"It's a new society," he went on. "A new culture. My family back in Boston think it's the wildest place, and maybe it is, maybe it is. But if it is, then it's a place for a man to tame. For a woman too. Bet there's nobody like you in California, Ada."

For Ada, dreams of the future had always been mitigated by the pressures of reality. Emmett imagined the future in a different way, bright with promise and mysterious with the unknown, heady with excitement and adventure, with newness. And he was going soon.

"There's no time to waste, of course, not that I'm a hasty man, either. But time gets eaten up, you know." He did not tell Ada what his doctor had told him, for he did not believe it; or rather, he believed that not to believe it was the proper path to longevity.

He had taken her to dinner on this, his last night in town, to the finest hotel in Desideer, which had a dining room grand as any he'd seen in Europe, or so he told Ada, who disbelieved him and laughed at the extravagance.

"I'm not so innocent as you might think," she said, looking around at the elegance of the Casamassima River Room, with its gilt-trimmed hardware, oak wainscoting, deep red damask on walls and drapes, stiff white linen napkins, lustrous silver, crystal, an all over impression of splendor she'd had no idea actually existed in Desideer. "Of course, I've never been here," she added, blushing as she admitted it, then looking up and seeing Emmett's grin of amusement, and blushing even more, delighted with herself and with him, her spirits high and giddy with the excitement of this new man-woman playfulness which had something of the child in it, something of the mind and spirit, too, and something forbidden which gave a delicious edge to the atmosphere. A bubble of laughter suddenly escaped her lips.

"You've had too much pink champagne," Emmett said.

"No. Oh. Maybe so. But I was just thinking of an old friend named Jason 'the mule' Hawkins."

"What about him?"

"I don't know if I should tell you," she said, truly wondering, yet knowing, too, that this was a bit of a tease, for she fully intended to tell him, her hesitation merely a way of dangling in front of him the flower that he might in a moment press to his face.

"Jason 'the mule' Hawkins was the first boy who ever kissed me," Ada said, unable to look at him as she spoke, but raising her eyes at the last instant to see the look on his face. Emmett had never heard a woman—who was a good woman—speak openly of such things, and he feared she had gone too far, past the bounds of propriety. He wanted to place his hand over hers, so white and still on the table, nearly as white as the cloth itself but for a dab of pink at the nail. A faint blue vein pulsed on her wrist; Emmett thought he had never seen anything so tender.

In his moment of hesitation Ada drew her hand back into her lap; she, too, had a sinking sensation that she had said too much, and she used several of Cornelia's curses liberally on herself and her own forwardness. She had offended the sensibilities of this man of society. He had taken her to this fine dining room—her first meal not eaten in a person's house—and she had behaved badly, spoken of experience too personal, probably used the wrong utensils to eat, was dressed improperly, too, no doubt. She shrank in her chair, feeling acutely a sense of poverty and not belonging. But something

made her sit up straight and curse herself again. Her hand
came down hard on the table, the crystal hummed and the
silver danced and the stiff expression on Emmett's face was
shaken.

"Damnit," she said, purposely trying for shock now. "I've
had enough of this...circumspection. Oh, Emmett, can't
you see how this room makes me behave? Like some grateful
scullery maid who's never eaten with a fork! And when I
speak my mind, you get an expression on your face like the
whole evening is a terrible mistake. Well, if it is, then I think
you ought to take me home now, before I embarrass you any
further. I'm a simple girl, and I've got my ways, and it's those
ways that've kept me where I am, but I'm not about to
change them just to suit a man, not even if that man is
as...not even if that man is you."

Emmett was quiet for a moment, then signaled for the
waiter to tally their bill. While all this was being arranged,
Ada sat in stony silence. They left the dining room, finally,
walked past the gilt cages of the hotel elevator and out into
the streets. It was early Saturday evening, and the townsfolk
were out in force.

"Do you mind if I smoke?" were the first words he said to
her, and Ada shook her head.

"Why would I mind?" she asked, then added sardonically,
"I'm not a lady, am I?"

Emmett did not reply, but Ada could see by the light of the
flaring match, which painted the lower half of his face reddish
gold, that he was troubled, his mouth set in a line that
clamped tight on the cigarette he lit.

"Maybe I'm not as much of a gentleman as I think I am,"
he said faintly.

They were at the edge of the river, just past town. Half the
townsfolk had strolled down to the dock to watch the great
paddleboat grind into reverse and churn up a storm as the
captain guided the monstrous vessel to a stop alongside the
pilings. Steam poured from the tubes on the upper deck in
short, dramatic bursts of blinding white shot through with the
setting sun, then drifted away, not quite becoming clouds.
Powerful Negro stevedores dragged bales of dry goods from
the freight sections; children ran around them like flies.

"There's Dr. Blaisdell," Ada said. "Of the school board,"
she added with a hard edge to her voice. The reverend was
shaking hand after hand at the foot of the gangway as people

boarded. "That's Karen Sewall. I told you about her, didn't I? That one there being pulled by her two children. And Ed Kraemer's there, standing near Dr. Blaisdell. The one holding the prayer book. I hope he doesn't see me."

"I guess when you live in a town this size you must get to know about everyone in it," Emmett said.

"I used to be one of those children down there," Ada said, pointing to a group running circles around the stevedores loading sacks of grain into the freight sections. "Heard all the stories about gamblers and riverboat girls and men with foreign accents. It seemed like the whole of the world was happening downriver. There's Monica Garnett," she said, indicating a white-faced woman her own age, a child making curtains of her skirt, another in her arms, and behind her one of the boys who used to come around Ada with a brow full of woe. "She was in my class."

"H'lo, Ada!" Monica called to her, struggling with her brood and waving, regarding Ada as from a great distance, though she was only on the other side of the dock. Ada waved back with more enthusiasm than she had realized she felt.

"People grow old awfully fast around here," she said, half to herself, but it did not go a long way toward explaining the feeling of sadness which had come over her. The sun hung low, near to gone, rosy and gray with clouds, shimmering dots of it licking at the undulations of the river.

"I've traveled some, Ada," he said.

"To Europe, yes, I know. To Europe, to Europe." In the space of a few days, it had already become a private joke between them, but neither laughed now.

"I never met anyone like you in Europe," he said. "Or in Boston. Or in New York or . . ."

Ada shook her head and looked out at the river. "What else could I be than what I am? There's nothing admirable in just remaining yourself."

"But I would never want you to change," Emmett insisted. "This is just the way I'd want you to be."

"An odd duck," Ada said.

"I was going to say something more romantic," Emmett said.

"Don't be romantic with me," Ada said. "It only confuses things. Let's just say what we mean, you and me. Let's do that at least."

"We're so different," he sighed, as if it were simply difference itself that was the trouble, no matter what the particulars.

"Yes," she said. "You're not like anyone in Desideer, that's for sure. Any other man would already have had me scrubbing out my mouth. Any other man wouldn't have been able to look at me."

"I see you, Ada. Don't think you're invisible to me." And then he laughed himself, and pulled her into the deep shade of an old elm.

She started to speak, but he held up his hand, touched her chin with a finger, and brought her face toward his. Ada's body was rigid as their faces came closer. The side of Emmett's face near the river had a pale gauzy ribbon of reflected red running down, a tiny shot of red in the corner of his eye. A scent of tobacco and wool and, beyond that, something sweet and warm and familiar came to her and she smiled, her body relaxing. This was nothing like Jason "the mule" Hawkins, she thought as their lips touched. She felt a dry, almost harsh, heat that was soon replaced by a yielding fleshiness, a softness, a flash of sweet wet and a whimper from Emmett's throat—or was it her own—that sounded an intimacy she had never before known.

The river absorbed sounds so that all was muted and calm. A few boats drifted by with couples in them; campfires were being lit on the far shore, though the sun had not yet set. At the dock the great steamer was being readied for departure downstream.

Steam belched from the stacks on the upper deck of the boat, shot through with the rosiness of the setting sun. The paddles stirred up a surf, and there was the cry of a sharp whistle; Ada caught her breath, as if in pain. The last passengers scurried on board, and waved to those left on the dock. The ropes were undone and the boat lumbered heavily away. Ada's eyes were intent on the river while the boat was swept into the current, her eyes riveted to the boat as it was swallowed by distant darkness. The moon was coming up, its reflection making long licks on the coursings of the river; the water rushed urgently against the shore.

"It gets so tiny so fast," Ada said, shaking her head, time and distance unfathomable mysteries, only the longing to be gone comprehensible. She closed her eyes, felt the pull on her skin of the moon, the river. Emmett saw emotions play across her face, her brows together in sadness, a lifting at the corners of her mouth.

He remained silent, staring at her. Ada waited for him to continue. She felt a surge of strength and power and, despite herself, a burgeoning gratitude toward him. This was not the same thing as love, she knew, but it was close enough.

"Emmett, for God's sake!" she exclaimed, and looked at him. "If you're ever going to ask me, ask me now."

The river bank was bright with moonlight; "You mean you'd ... you'd go to California with me?"

"I'd go anywhere with you," Ada said.

Emmett smiled widely and took her hand in his. "I should say something gallant and wise right now but I'm so ..."

"I thought we agreed to just say what we mean," Ada said.

"Yes," Emmett said and pulled her close to him. "We agreed!" Ada held him tightly. She thought: I am on my way out.

The kitchen was always the heart of the house, the place where he dropped his school books and hung his coat and did his lessons with Ada at the old pine table, where the two of them cracked nuts and strung Christmas popcorn, where he watched Ada open seed catalogues that came by mail, and do her hair up in salt water curls. Ada like to sit in front of the stove to warm her feet, just like Cornelia used to, rocking in the old wicker chair she'd mended so many times now it was more cord than wicker.

The first thing he did was haul out the axe, and hack away at thick apple branches in back of the house. Ada never did complain, but he knew it was hard for her, never having enough wood for fires. The muscle line from wrist to spine was one long lick of flame, but the pain felt like it was supposed to feel when a man did what a man was supposed to do. Ada'd see that; she had a sure eye for noticing what was right.

He quit when the woodpile in the lean-to was filled waist-high. "Can always do more tomorrow," he said, nodding to himself at the soundness of his thinking. Then he filled a bucket with pump water and a cup of lye and scrubbed the kitchen floorboards with a wire brush, his eyes burning and tearing from the fumes, until he had it looking nearly raw. He ran a wet rag around the weavings of the wicker rocker, swept the ashes out of the cook stove, and stuffed some papers in

the belly alongside the crushed flowers that man'd brought
her. He set the apples he picked in Ada's favorite blue-and-
white speckled bowl, and lit a candle. Finally he washed his
face and arms, put on a clean shirt, and sat down in the
rocker to wait for her, smelling apples, thinking about Ada's
surprised face, feeling like she was holding him in her two
arms.

Dusk fell into dark, Obie breathing deeply, concentrating
on patience. The pale gray square of window turned to milky
blue, then darkened until it was black against the gray walls,
the candle flame flickering its reflection in it like a fish
darting under the surface of the river. Obie jumped up and
strode around the room, putting his hands on things, setting
this or that closer or farther away, squinting his eyes to see
what pleased. When he heard horses clopping and the clack
of buggy wheels on the dirt road, he set a fire going in the
stove and backed up against the wall.

His ears were turned to the sounds outside: the horses'
snorting breaths, the clacking of the buggy wheels slowing to
a roll then a bump as they stopped, the horses' grunting
reaction, then murmured voices, rustling, silence—the silence left his imagination too much blank space, he floundered—
then footsteps on the porch, and the door was opening. His
hands were clenched tight against her bringing the man
inside.

Ada closed the door quietly behind her—as if preserving a
mood—and, when she turned, glanced at the candle, at the
fire in the stove. Obie was breathless as he watched the slow
surprise on her face. When she had hung up her shawl on the
back of the pantry door, she touched the apples, then looked
quickly up.

"Obie?"

The sound came from outside of the horses moving again,
the light crack of a whip, the clack of the wheels taking the
man away.

"I'm right here," he said shyly, stepping away from the wall
into the light. Obie loved how the light from the candle made
Ada's face soft and dreamy. She was smiling now, too. "I
thought I'd make the place nice for you," he said.

"Well, I can see you did, Obie," Ada remarked. "I take
that kindly."

Obie nodded, and moved further into the light, bolder now
and anxious that she take note of everything he'd done. "I

picked these apples special. And the lean-to's half-filled with wood. And did you see the floor? I scrubbed near down to the ground, I bet."

Ada nodded as he continued his explanation, but Obie began to feel that he was not getting across how hard he had worked—this feeling was enormous now—and his hands began clenching and unclenching again.

"It gets pretty rangy around here sometimes. I know how hard you work at it, Ada. And I'm sometimes a lazy galoot, I guess." He paused, hoping she'd praise him, and when she said nothing he went on, trying to keep a rising desperation out of his voice. "I'd be willing to do more of my share from here on in."

Ada remained silent but when he dared to look at her he saw that she regarded him with a mournful expression. "Obie," she said finally, "you know that this can't go on much longer. Us two living here like this. It isn't right."

"I don't want to hear this," Obie said, backing away as if she meant to strike him.

Ada shook her head, but did not move toward him. "Obie, if I had to stay in this town forever, I think I'd die."

"You're looking to ditch me," he said in a voice deep and dark with hurt.

"I never said that I was," Ada replied.

"Then he's making you do it! It's him! I know it! He's behind it all!"

"Emmett isn't doing any such thing, Obie."

"Emmett," he said in disgust. "Seems to me like he can talk you into just about any foul thing he takes it in his mind to."

"Obie, listen to me. Don't you want to get out of Desideer? Isn't that what you want, too?"

"I'm going to be a cowboy, in case you forgot," he said.

"We can both go away from here," Ada said, looking around her. "This house, this town. This flatness."

"Yeah?" Obie said, brightening. "Both of us? How?"

"By me marrying Emmett Newcomb."

Obie turned and pressed his shoulder into the wall; he stole a quick glance at her. "You in love with him or something?" he asked and turned away before she could see him.

Ada lowered her head. "He's taking me out of Desideer, Obie. I'm grateful for that, and that's as good a way to start being married as any way I know." She did not mention how different Emmett was, or his handsomeness, or their kiss.

Obie leaned away from the wall, and fell back against it. "No, no, no," he moaned. "He don't want me with you. I know it. I know it." And suddenly he turned to Ada, his eyes bleary with tears. "Fire's going out," he said. Ada reached out for him but he jumped away. "Get s'more wood," he muttered, and ran out the kitchen door.

Ada rose in her chair then sat down again. Emmett Newcomb appeared in her mind, a pleased smile on his face. And why not? Here was a man who saw the possibilities of the future. She traced his movements from the moment he left her: down the road, alongside the river, under the willow and across the narrow bridge to the hotel.

She lit the kerosene lamp; bluish dusk was gone, but the lamp's meager yellow light made the kitchen look secretive and poor: the splintered pine table, the iron washbasin and chipped crocks, water stains mottling the walls, floors worn through nearly to the ground. In the shadowed corners of the room were Cornelia's rhubarb and pickled beets, on the shelves her bilberry preserves. Have to get rid of this stuff before I leave and it all goes to mold, she thought.

She poked around the stove's belly, and saw a few charred blossoms from the flowers Emmett had brought. It gave her a dark unpleasant taste in her mouth, and she listened for Obie's return a little apprehensively, going to the kitchen door where he'd left. Her shadow careened across the ceiling. The house was heavy with the quiet. The wind coming up off the river made the leaves crackle like fire. She opened the kitchen door; dark clouds moved swiftly from treetop to treetop.

"Obie!"

There was the wind in reply, but when she turned to go into the house she heard a shuffling sound above her and, with an involuntary shiver, knew that Obie was on the roof. She knotted the shawl tightly around her shoulders, and pulled herself up along the branches of the apple tree, her feet remembering just the right places, though she hadn't made the climb in years. Obie had wrapped himself in the blue patched coverlet. Ada pulled at a corner of it, but Obie held tight. She remained silent, but when Obie dared to look he saw that she regarded him with a mournful expression.

She raised her hand to touch him, but he turned his head away fast, as if she meant to strike him.

Ada wrapped her arms around her knees and faced him, talking to the back of his head. "Obie, if I had to stay here in Desideer... I'd go away even if Emmett hadn't asked me. Matter of fact, I practically asked him myself."

Obie turned his head away again, and moved further back into the shadows near the chimney.

"In two or three months from now we'll be settled in a house in California, and you'll come out and live with us."

Obie turned to her now, just his eyes visible above the patched coverlet. "'Member when we'd wait all night till Mama came home?"

Ada got up on her knees and kissed his forehead. "It's October now. We'll be spending Christmas together in California." Obie pulled open the coverlet, and let her enfold him in her arms, pulling the coverlet around both of them. The wind blew above them; he was warm. Ada held him tighter, her mouth set hard.

Obie sank deeper into the coverlet, his shoulder pressing into the chimney stack. A sharp bit of mortar dug into his flesh; he shook his head, then stole a quick glance at Ada and turned away before she could lock it, falling back against the mortar, doing it again and again, trying to get that sharp edge to make him bleed so he could get away from that heavy hot weight in his chest.

Chapter 4

The wedding took place in the parlor of Miss Harriette Austin's architecturally impressive house. Presiding was Dr. Blaisdell, whose narrow forehead was further diminished by his scowling disapproval of the task he was about to perform. "It's his duty to disapprove of things," Ada had told Emmett, "not the least of them being strangers and hasty marriages." Dr. Blaisdell had asked Ada if she was in "distress," and was no less discomfited by her abrupt laughter. He allowed as how he'd marry them, but not in the church itself, which suited Ada just fine. Accompanying Dr. Blaisdell was his wife and her daughter; both wore starched gray dresses, with matching bonnets and facial expressions.

Miss Harriette's parlor, despite the crisp autumn sunshine outdoors, retained a darkish aspect: mahogany furniture tufted in velvets and brocades, pleated and skirted, heavily carved and trimmed with studs, the windows shuttered, then draped in organza and hung over in satin; carpets on top of carpets; the mahogany wainscoting topped by portraits of Austins and Hemleys—Mrs. Austin had been a Hemley from Cashman—a pastorale here, a still life of the trompe l'oeil style, a hunt scene with a slit-necked goose, a rifle, bottle of spirits and a brass wall lamp.

Obie sat in the bay window, fingering the curtains, staring through them at the street. His Celluloid collar pinched, and he wriggled his neck as though he could crawl out of the shirt by the top. Emmett conferred with Sophie Simmons, protegée and companion to Miss Harriette, as to the musical selections.

Upstairs in Miss Harriette's bedroom, that maiden lady was telling Ada what to expect of marriage. "He will want to keep you like a pet," she said sardonically, her fingers picking and pulling at the delicate lace of the gown that had been her mother's.

"Not Emmett," Ada said. "He likes my independence; he told me so."

"That's because he isn't a husband yet. Husbands are

supposed to be brave and strong and wise," Miss Harriette
continued. "A wife need only be confident in her husband's
bravery, strength, and wisdom. Ha! I would not like to see
such a fate come your way, Ada."

"I'm not exchanging one prison for another, and he knows
it." Ada shook her head as she stared at her reflection in the
large oval glass; it would be simple to throw her life into this
man's hands, but if she did, would she have a life that she
could call her own?

"And there are wifely duties to perform," her maiden
advisor added. "I don't mean cooking and cleaning. Lord
knows your young man is rich enough to afford a housekeep-
er, and you make sure you get a good one. I'm talking
about..." Her fingers darted quickly from cuff to cuff, pulling. "Oh, I wish your mother had done some of this," she
said. "I'm talking about the... amorous duties of a wife. You
see, men... and women... Oh, never mind, you'll find out
soon enough. Just don't break over it, hear me?"

The first piano chord sounded from downstairs; the two
women looked at each other in the mirror. Ada turned to
Miss Harriette. I'll never see her again, she thought.

"Did I show you my ring?" she asked.

"Oh yes, yes." Miss Harriette took her hand, peering at
the ring. "Rubies."

Ada gripped her hand. "Oh Miss Harriette," she said. "All
the time I lived here... all the time... you were the only
one... the only real friend..."

"Nonsense, nonsense," Miss Harriette said, keeping her
eyes on their joined hands.

"I want you to promise me you'll come out to California
and visit us. Come whenever—"

The second chord came; the two women embraced.

"Don't crush the lace!" Miss Harriette warned, and Ada
left Miss Harriette's bedroom to walk down the staircase.

Her hair was piled high and off her face, but for a few stray
wisps that had escaped her nervous hands; sprigs of apple
blossom crowned her, and a veil floated from the blossoms.
Her gown—a legacy of Miss Harriette's mother which the
maiden daughter was never to use—was high-necked, heavily
embroidered with seed pearls, silk rosettes, and tiny satin
bows, layered in tiers in front and swept up in back over a
lace underskirt by a large flat bow.

She smiled nervously as she made her way down, seeing

nothing clearly. Someone was standing at the foot of the stairs. Oh my God, she thought, it's Emmett. His face swam up to her, and she was puzzled that it was this face, this man, she had chosen over all others, that it was this man she was to spend her life with. For a brief instant a shock of terror passed through her, for she had at that moment no love for him, no confidence in the rightness of her choice, no knowledge even of who he was. The pulsebeat of the music kept her from rushing headlong down the stairs and out into the street and away. Emmett held out his hand to her; she watched her own hand, as if disembodied, come to rest in his, feeling the heat of his excitement as they stood in front of Dr. Blaisdell.

Upstairs, in Miss Harriette's bedroom, a dark traveling suit was ready for her. The school board had been notifed—another reason for Dr. Blaisdell's disapproval—and a replacement found. Obie would follow them out in a few months. A buggy waited outside with their trunks, for swift transportation to the railroad station. The train left at four. And this man at her side, who was this man? Her husband...

...she had said the words, she was married, the veil was lifted, she was kissed.

Chapter 5

Ada stood on the platform alone, the westbound train a distant speck—Emmett was inside the terminal checking their luggage, Obie his reluctant aide. She looked across the tracks at the gray-brown plains stretching to the horizon, breaking crisply into the white sky; she imagined seeing through trees and around bends in the road to the house she had left for the last time early that morning. There was an enormous stirring inside her, feelings almost too large to be contained. She had to laugh or cry or run wild for a country mile. Whatever her eyes lit upon, she thought: I'll never see this again, I'll never see that again. Yet along with this sense of finality was a feeling of being truly alive for the first time, like bursting into the bloom of rosy health after having been vaguely ill for a long, long time. There was a new husband, a new land, every feeling ever held back would have room to be felt, every hope might be realized, now that she was going. Just board that train and soon—one last look, one last goodbye—on to a new life: the life I was meant to live!

Obie came up silently beside her. "Light's too bright; it hurts my eyes." He squinted at the sky in disapproval.

"It'll snow soon, if I know Desideer," Ada said. She took a deep breath: the autumn smell of potatoes just out of the ground. "Or it could rain. How I hate that icy rain. Emmett says that in California it's sunny three hundred and sixty-five days a year." She turned with a smile at Obie. "Imagine!"

Obie gripped her hand. "I hate for you to go." Ada turned away to look down the tracks for the coming train. "I know it's him taking you," Obie went on in her ear. "You don't have to say nothing. It's him." Ada turned now, but as she began to speak a denial a cry went up from the highest turret of the terminal as the train came along the straightaway. A flurry of movement swept the crowd on the platform: it undulated in waves toward the baggage as passengers made final checks and adjustments.

The train was barreling down now, black smoke belching from the smokestack, the diamond-shaped cow-catcher pointing

53

the way. More people came out onto the platform, and Ada stood on her toes to see the train over their heads. The vibrations traveled up her body and made her giddy. She held tight to Obie's hand, and then the train clattered powerfully into the station, scattering soot and cinders and live sparks over the crowd. The wind knocked Ada's bonnet onto her back, her hair came half undone, and there was Emmett emerging from the depot, tickets held above his head, chin thrust out, taller than everyone, a grin of triumph on his face.

Ada felt enormously hungry; she waved wildly. "It's ours!"

The train stopped in a screeching clatter, people got on and off, shook hands, slapped backs, embraced, wept. Emmett looked at Obie and smiled, holding out a box to him. "Seeing as how we're brothers now," he said. Obie stared at the box like something living might crawl out and claw him. Ada smiled up at Emmett—why he's done just the right thing! "Go on and open it," Ada said to Obie, and when he made no move to do so, took off the top herself.

Lying in tissue paper was a stereoscope looking like a prehistoric bird come to nest. "I seen these," Obie said; he slid the first picture in and raised the projector to his eyes. It was that picture of Ada Miss Harriette had taken tinted in light colors, her golden cheeks close enough to kiss. A little moan of longing sounded in his throat. If only everything'd stay this way, stop everything right now; she'd never leave, she'd always, always stay where she was.

Ada looked at the top of Emmett's head as he bent to pick up a shred of tissue paper, and noticed how the whorl of his hair was way off to the left side. Now isn't that something, to be married to a man whose hair you haven't even got fixed in your mind. Something stirred in the small of her back; she wax anxious to be alone with him. She touched his hair as he rose. He looked up. She laughed at her own eagerness. "I feel like I could run all the way to California pulling the train behind me!"

"These new trains are so smooth and quiet, you don't even know you're riding," Emmett said. "You might be sitting in your parlor reading a book." Their eyes met and held for a long moment; there didn't seem to be anyone else around. "I've been dreaming about you for such a long time," he said. Ada was astonished at such sweetness.

The train whistled; people jostled them to get on board.

She turned to her brother. "Christmas in California, Obie," she said a bit breathlessly, and gave him a quick, hard hug. Obie fell into her, cradled like he could break, picturing her in his mind.

"Remember me," Obie implored. "Remember me!"

Emmett shook Obie's hand, and climbed onto the first step of the train; Ada mounted just after him, facing Obie, holding onto Emmett behind her back.

"Don't miss me too much," she said.

"I know what I'm going to do," he said. The train lurched forward, jerked to a stop, lurched forward again, stopped and then began inching forward slowly. "I'm going to have Miss Harriette make lots of slide pictures of you!" He was running alongside the train now; Ada held tightly to Emmett's hand as the train gathered speed. "So whenever I'm missing you I just got to look at the slides, and you'll be there, plain as life." The train leaped past the platform with face-slapping finality.

It picked up speed, the people, the depot, the turrets and spires falling away behind it; the platform ended, the main street diminished, the plains began just up ahead. In a moment she would have left it all behind, there would be nothing that was familiar. She held her breath, already farther than she'd ever been, and going so fast! And in that last instant there was a rider on horseback following the train, riding alongside the track, and she saw that it was Obie. With Emmett holding her hand tightly, she descended a step and leaned out, her face stung by the wind, hair further undone by it. As he came closer, Ada saw the look of fierce determination on his face, as if he would stop the train himself just by grabbing tight and holding on. He rose in the saddle, squinting to see her. She waved and leaned out further; he crouched lower into the horse's neck, and drove harder until he and the horse were alongside the Pullman. As he came as close to Ada as he could without smashing himself and the horse into the train or catching the horse's hooves on the tracks, he leaned over—he's crazy, Ada thought; he's going to kill himself—extending his body full out from the horse to hold out a large bouquet of wildflowers. She stretched out as far as she could, and felt the heather and the yellow grass of the bouquet tickle her fingers. She was afraid for Obie, for his life now. Finally she was gripping the flowers in her hand, nearly touching Obie's, and as she took them he let go.

Obie wanted to freeze the moment, to hold onto her forever, but his tired horse was slowing down and he watched helplessly as Ada was sucked into the distance, the flowers crushed against her chest. He stopped riding; the wind stopped. It was still; she was gone.

The parlor car was empty but for Emmett, ear to the wall of the adjoining suite, listening impatiently to the sounds of Ada unpacking. The suite—bath, sleeper, and dressing room— was separated from the parlor section of the Pullman by a wall covered in blue brocade and hung with a mantel mirror whose frame showed smirking gilt cherubs holding celestial curtain corners aloft.

He opened his mouth to call Ada, then caught a glimpse of his flushed and eager face in the mirror and backed off, laughing at himself.

Ada faced herself in the reflection on the slick black window, her image sailing along the passing plains. Her chest rose and fell as she tied the ribbons of her nightgown; nothing she had been told or read or overheard had given her an adequate idea as to what would happen now that she was dressed for bed and Emmett was about to join her. He would be sweet, she was sure; she would follow his lead, but Ada liked to know where she was going, if not the destination, at least the direction of the road. Her eyes returned to the bed set against the wall below the window; the curtains shimmered as the train rocked swiftly through the blackness of the plains and she pulled them closed against it.

Emmett went into the dressing room, tugging at his cravat, which knotted under his fingers. There was a hot pulse in his throat. He tossed shirt and cufflinks aside; his suspenders twanged back against his knuckles and he finally struggled into a smoking jacket and slippers. So remarkable was Ada in so many other ways, he told himself—direct, independent of thought, unafraid to speak her mind—that he expected more from her now than marital accommodation. He closed his eyes and thought back to that evening by the river: Ada's response to his kiss had been more than perfunctory; satisfaction and pleasure had sounded from deep in her throat. So Emmett dared to hope. He smoothed his hands across his face, but he could not erase the smile that told him something extraordinary was going to happen.

Ada sat down on the bed and took the last pins from her

hair. Emmett knocked lightly at the door and entered, his
hands thrust deep in the pockets of a smoking jacket. He
smiled and leaned back against the door, started forward,
then sidled along the wall to the corner where he came to
rest on a chair at the foot of the bed.

"Ulysses S. Grant campaigned from this very car," he said.

"It rides so smoothly," Ada said.

"Yes, I hardly know I'm here," he replied. "I mean..." He
stopped and laughed too loudly. Ada flushed, and straightened the ribbons on her robe. Emmett took his pipe from his
pocket, paused, then held it out to her. Ada shook her head
as though he were offering her a smoke, and Emmett thrust
it back into his pocket. She found herself staring at his lips,
then, flustered, at his hands as he sat beside her on the bed.

"We'll be in California in five days," he said hoarsely.

Ada nodded, lifting the curtains to reveal the blackness of
the plains under a moody, clouded sky. "It doesn't seem like
we're going anywhere at all."

"You have to take it on faith," he said. He paused. Both
listened to the silence, then he turned the brass knob that
controlled the electricity and the room faded slowly into
semi-darkness. He moved closer to her and reached out,
finding her hands, holding them. In the moments that followed
only their breathing could be heard, the rustle of fabric, the
faint whistle of the wind. "This is all so new," he said. "We
hardly know each other." He ran his thumbs over the palms
of her hands as if testing the texture of her skin; Ada felt the
sensation all the way into her chest. "And yet... I know I've
made the right choice." He paused; Ada heard him breathe in
deeply, her own breath held. "I think... you probably don't
love me," he said.

She began to speak, surprised that her denial at that
instant felt so true, but Emmett squeezed her hands.

"Please don't. You see, I can so easily be fooled... I
suppose that right now I even want to be." His voice in the
darkness had a disembodied quality, as if his soul spoke
directly to hers. "We agreed, didn't we? Never to say anything that we don't mean." He was only his voice, only the
feel and smell of his body. Without seeing him, Ada felt she
heard his essence.

"Sometimes," she said softly, "sometimes... I felt I would
never find my way. I had ideas of how to live but..." She
raised her head; her eyes felt enormous, intense. "I just

wasn't going to let Desideer keep me." Her eyes remained wide and staring as she spoke. The scent of his tobacco, of spiced cologne, created a cloud around her. The sheets rustled as Emmett removed his smoking jacket and moved closer; his arms surrounded her, his hands came to rest on the back of her neck, lost in her hair, on the tips of her ears. She felt hot under his touch, as if the very heat of his flesh was penetrating her.

"I was escaping, too," he whispered. "Escaping a Boston marriage, escaping turning into my father. We've escaped together, haven't we? I don't think it's a bad beginning."

Before she could respond he put his mouth to hers, his lips brushing hers, guiding them, as if they would speak together, the same words. He untied the ribbons of her nightgown and parted the fabric; her flesh glowed silver, sculpted of moonlight through clouds, but soft and smooth to the touch of his lips; a tiny pulse beat from her breast to his cheek.

A wave of relief spread over Ada like soothing balm, and with relief came desire. Resistance to him—to his strangeness, his easy acceptance of her, his very maleness—fell away. He ran strong hands along her body, and moved up until he lay beside her and took her mouth in his. Their kiss deepened; the heat of his body trailed the length of hers.

She listened to the distant rhythm of the train wheels, her eyes on the dark sway of the curtains, the contours of Emmett's body as he rose above her. She felt them falling into each other, not knowing, in the darkness, in the silence, in the heat, where either began or ended.

A high whistle pierced the night as they passed through a town. Ada was exultant. I have made a better choice than I knew, she thought.

Part 2

Los Angeles...had an air of not belonging to America, though all its motley ways were American. It was a city of refugees from America; it was purely itself in a banishment partly dreamed and partly real. It rested on a crust of earth at the edge of a sea that ended a world.

—Frank Fenton, *A Place in the Sun*

Chapter 6

Was there ever a city more full of grand intentions and sprawling good times than Los Angeles, Ada wondered. As soon as they arrived at the railroad station she had this feeling of being plunked right down in the center of where America was happening, as if the whole country had been tilted west and everyone was spilling into the streets, laughing, shouting, building, buying. Me and my new husband are going to make our mark here, she felt sure of that, and Emmett practically had to hold her back from running into town on foot.

No sooner had Ada and Emmett checked into a suite in Los Angeles's Saint Elmo Hotel—"Host to Presidential wives since Mrs. Rutherford B. Hayes"—than Emmett contacted the young lawyer he'd written from Boston. A reply arrived at the Saint Elmo asking them to come into his office the next day to meet a real estate salesman.

"Now we're getting somewhere!" Ada said as she and Emmett drove downtown in a rented carriage. En route they vied with pedestrians, other carriages, men on horseback, and the new cable cars for passage. Ada noticed a high school at Spring and Fifth, the great Los Angeles Times Building at First and Broadway, and the impressive Child's Opera House on the east side of Main. Barefoot Indian women hauled sacks of meal on their backs. Mexican girls with gold earrings shouted in Spanish to merchants and farmers. Nuns collected pennies on the corner; a boy in knickerbockers hawked something called "choon gum."

I can choose what I do here, Ada thought; choose which of these people to know. I can open a shop or teach school or run a hotel or a restaurant or learn a foreign language, I can meet people from all over the world. There were no limits but the horizon. Oh, Desideer, how you have shrunk in my memory, and all your sorry people—how small you seem to me now. I can't be touched, she thought, and held Emmett's arm tight. "What a pair we are!"

Emmett tied up the carriage at the hitching post in front of the three-story brick building where Avery Benson had his office, and, arm in arm he and Ada trooped inside.

A messenger boy ran past them shouting over his shoulder: "You're the nuts, Mary!" as a red-faced stenographer in shirtwaist dress shook an inky finger at him from the top of the stairs. Two men in gartered shirtsleeves, their mouths bulging with cigars, exchanged sheets of paper as they marched upstairs in unison, shoulders hunched for battle. A husband and wife haggled over the location of a parcel of land: "The canyons," she said, and pushed him; "The valley," he replied, and pushed right back. A salesman was sprawled on the stairs, alligator display case under his heels. He tilted his hat to the back of his head—a greased curl spilled out—and whistled as they passed him. An older couple, the man in stiff collar, the woman tidy right to the tight bun in her hair, sat on a bench outside a claims adjuster's office, hands folded in their laps, determined to set an example of decorous behavior for others to follow. Ada and Emmett stepped around them and opened the frosted glass door of Avery Benson's office.

The office was a smaller, contained version of the chaos in the hallways: papers on every available surface, the smell of leather and paper, law books on shelves along every wall, a leather Chesterfield sofa, tall oak file cabinets, green window shades, and dust motes on the shafts of bright sun that slapped the floor. A small bald-headed man strode across the room, running his hands down the front of his tightly buttoned checkered suit, and made a jerky efficient bow.

"Avery Benson, attorney-at-law, at your service." His smiling, unlined face, with its wide Oriental mouth and black eyes lost in lacy pink folds made an uncertain hash of his age. Indicating the woman seated near the door, he said, "Mrs. Sweet, my secretary."

Broad-faced, wide-shouldered in purple serge, Mrs. Sweet nodded from her position at the typewriting machine, and thrust her hand up to shake Ada's. "*Bienvenido al Pueblo de Nuestra Señora la Reina de Los Angeles de Porciuncala*," she said. "In other words, welcome to the city of the queen of the angels. A little Spanish can come in real handy out here."

Ada liked her right off; the new woman, she thought, remembering magazine articles about this phenomenon—women joining the work force in unprecedented numbers.

"Hope you like the Saint Elmo," Avery said, ushering Ada

and Emmett past Mrs. Sweet to seats on the leather sofa. "Mrs. Rutherford B. Hayes stayed there, you know."

"Yes, we knew that," Emmett replied.

Mrs. Sweet gave everyone a cup of tea and resumed her place at her typewriter.

"I noticed there's a new real estate office opening across the street," Ada said. "Things are really booming these days."

"Second one opened this month, actually," Mrs. Sweet said. "The land offices on Spring Street are opening as fast as the saloons. Same customers at each, if I'm not mistaken." Ada saw Avery shoot her a disapproving glance, but she continued regardless. "For three years I've been seeing people come straight from the railroad depot to the land offices, no one satisfied till they've got that piece of California they all think they're entitled to."

"I know just how they feel," Emmett said.

"'Course, not everyone gets what he wants," she added.

"You ought to keep your eyes on the typewriting machine and off the streets," Avery said sharply.

"I expected a completely different sort of place," Emmett said as he looked out the window at the street below. "All these people, all this movement. It's not at all what I thought we'd find here." Ada was surprised to hear this; she assumed Emmett knew exactly what to expect.

"The land of milk and honey," Mrs. Sweet remarked sourly. "It's progress. It's what people come to Los Angeles for."

"I never came here for the milk and honey," Avery protested.

"No, you came because those people in the street came for it," Mrs. Sweet said.

Emmett shook his head. "Progress, progress. People move ahead, and they move back. But I don't know that I'd call it real progress. If you look at history, all you see is one long line of failure after failure of people trying to outfox their own natures. A few clever inventions is the sum of it. For the rest, people don't change." He paused and caught a glimpse of Ada's puzzled face. "Anyway, the whole point of this trip is the land. Even the brochures say that. That's why I came to California, after all, for the beauty of the land. And surely it would take away the whole beauty of it if it was filled with people. I mean, I'm all for progress, I just don't think that filling up Southern California with a lot of displaced people is necessarily progressing any."

Ada cocked an eyebrow at him. "And what are we, if not displaced people?"

But Emmett was restless now, and couldn't stop to see the humor of the truth in what she said. "I've seen cities before. Los Angeles isn't even a good example of one. Not after Paris or Venice."

"Give Los Angeles another thousand years and it will be," Mrs. Sweet remarked drily.

Emmett laughed and looked at Ada. "I'm afraid I sound just like my mother did on the day I left Boston."

Into the silence that followed this remark burst a young man clad in a voluminous white suit, and bow tie, candy-striped shirt and high-topped glossy shoes. Before Avery Benson and Clara Sweet could make a formal introduction, he was across the room and pumping Emmett's hand. From his coat he withdrew a small stack of cards, and delicately peeled off the top one, handing it to Emmett and drawing attention to the raised letters by rubbing his thumb over them. He looked to Ada like the salesmen that gathered on Desideer's Main Street, minus the Dixie Peach Hair Pomade.

"Chester Puhls," Emmett read. "Real Estate Sales."

"Hi there, cousin Clara," Chester said. He kissed Mrs. Sweet's cheek and shook Avery's reluctant hand.

"Chester," Avery said stiffly.

"Mr. Benson thinks I've got a soft spot in my head for Chester because we're cousins," Mrs. Sweet said.

"I only said that the affection people bear for members of their family tends to blur the line between real abilities and heart-held fantasies of them." Avery clamped his mouth shut; Ada could see that they had been through this before.

"At least you can trust Chester," Mrs. Sweet said. "Which is more than can be said for most of the land agents."

"Naturally, we're glad to have someone come personally recommended," Emmett said, with a quick glance at Ada, who withheld an approving nod until she could learn a bit more about Mr. Puhls. "Otherwise, well . . . how can you tell?"

"I couldn't agree more," Mrs. Sweet said.

Mrs. Sweet gave the unembarrassed cousin Chester a cup of tea and an encouraging peck on the cheek before she allowed Avery to lead her out of the office so the new business association could get under way.

"I think you ought to know, folks, that I'm a great believer in the future of California," Chester said.

"Me, too!" Emmett replied. "Isn't that right, Ada? Aren't we?"

Before Ada could reply, Chester chimed in, "The greatest place on God's good earth. And I don't believe everything I hear," he added with a wink. Ada looked at Emmett to see if he, too, saw that Chester required a closer look, but Emmett, in his enthusiasm, was obviously enthralled.

"But you've got to watch out for swindlers," Chester said. "Oh, I'm not blind to it. Not at all. Why I've seen folks lined up all night for the chance to buy property when the one advantage it had was that it was for sale. Turned out you could only get there in a hot air balloon. And when you did—Oh, Lordy, a view of the darn Mojave desert." Chester smiled at the Newcombs. "I knew of a Methodist preacher sold lots in the desert, and called it New Jerusalem. One promoter tied oranges to an acre of bare joshua trees and advertised it as Golden Groves, California. Folks have to be cautious about putting money in land. All you got to do is take a look at recent history, am I right? And Southern California is nothing but recent history. I'm right about that, too. But let me point out something to you folks. A man can't junk his faith just because there's been a little mess. A land boom's different than a boom in, say, wheat or pork or even gold, 'cause it's based on climate, on health, on the beauty of land unequaled in the United States. Now that is something that's going to continue. Confidence, confidence. That's what I tell people. The land'll be sold and settled, every last darn acre of it. You stick with me; you'll see."

"It does seem like folks back east are having a laugh at our expense," Emmett told him. "My sister Elizabeth's husband refers to California as 'the lost frontier' instead of 'the last frontier', and Los Angeles as 'Lost' Angeles."

"Why do easterners think we're lost out here?" Chester demanded. "We're the damned pioneers!" He strode from the door to the window and back again. Ada had the notion that the drama of his outrage was slightly bogus. "We're the ones making this country," he was saying. "We're the ones this whole country's looking to, seeing if we get it right. All this..." He waved his hands as if to express the inexpressible.

The great migration west was indeed unequaled in the history of America. The California Gold Rush of forty years before paled to a featherstroke under the bold iron thrust of the railroads. In the last ten years of the nineteenth century California had vowed to be the place where America would attain true greatness: not in the anemic, European East, not in the effete, eviscerated South, not in the codified, colorless Middle West, but at the very edge of the continent, where God's gifts were available in bounteous profusion to the adventurous of spirit and body. To the true Americans, a new America!

Week after week, the trains west were filled near to bursting with people lured by this promise.

Like most Americans gone west, Chester Puhls longed for economic freedom and the respectability cash could provide, for he was certain that this was how real life was endured: enormous sums of money padding the meanness of chance. He dreamed of raining silver, storm seas of cash. If only— finally, finally—someone would be smart enough to recognize how smart he really was. "You're right, Mister Puhls, absolutely," they'd say as the real estate sale of the decade was closed: a firm handshake under an easy volley of compliments, and a little smile on his face at the end because it was smart to be nice. Then a hearty masculine laugh, and "adios compadre" with a wallet lined in clover.

"Everybody's equal in Southern California," Chester said to the Newcombs. "Everyone's got a chance to succeed no matter what he's done before."

"But make no mistake, Mr. Puhls," Emmett said and held Ada's hand. "I'm looking... we're looking... for something very specific. Something I once saw in Europe. I've brought along some pictures to show you what I mean." He handed to Chester a small stack of photographs of Cannes, of Amalfi, of Crete and Lombardy. "You see? There are such places left, aren't there?"

Chester looked at the pictures, nodding thoughtfully—and again Ada felt he was feigning the intensity—and gave him back the pictures. "I think I know what you mean," he said and stood up. "Why don't you write your price on one of my little cards here, so I'll know even better."

Emmett took the card and without hesitation wrote "one hundred thousand dollars." Chester looked at the card and laughed nervously.

"I'll start drawing up a list," he said. "Bring it over to your hotel when it's ready."

"I'm in a hurry," Emmett said.

Chester ran his fingers over the card. "Me too," he said. "Me too."

The water was almost black today, a little rust, too, from the red in the trees.

Obie rocked back on his heels, the river rushing by, feeling like he could be taken away on it, floating down the river, far away. The Orenoke to the Mississippi, river to river across the prairie, and then Montana! Texas! Oklahoma! Knowing there was a direct route to the west made him feel a lot calmer. I'd know what to do out there, he thought. It'd be something to see, wouldn't it? Riding the range, a holster sitting easy on my hip, all my gear stowed in my saddlebags, hand light on the reins, all alone, with no one to bother about.

Obie hated living in his own empty house, hated everything in it that reminded him that Ada'd been taken away to that place with that man. He'd started sleeping on the roof since Ada'd gone; he just lay up there and thought and thought, and soon he was floating. Ada'll come back some night, he thought, some night, some night, and all the leaving she'd done would be wiped clean away.

The cold drove him inside on the first of November. Drafts flew through the house; he moved his cot into the kitchen to sleep near the embers glowing in the stove. He had nightmares in which he was just a tiny speck, getting smaller, out of breath. He'd waken, the walls of the house advancing, suffocating him. Once he said Ada's name out loud and was comforted, but the repeated sound of his own voice against the silence mocked him and he was more alone than before. The wind was fierce in November, howling up off the horizon and barreling toward him like it had a grudge. Two panes of isinglass blew into the house and scattered splinters and shreds across the kitchen floor. The preserves Ada had put up in August went sour, tops not on tight enough or something. Ada, Ada, you should've taken better care. He practiced holding his breath; one night his nose bled, another night he passed out. Thought he might try it for fun in front of the church on Sunday morning; let Dr. Blaisdell think it was a miracle or something.

He lingered late into the afternoon by the river, making up stories in his head about boys who went places and did things; leaned back on his elbows and felt the sun, then sighted down the length of his finger to a sparrow come to rest on a branch. "Pah! Pah! Pah!" He leaned back again and remembered Emmett giving him that present. Should've just throwed it back at him, he thought, and laughed. Should've bopped it on his head.

He spun around at the sound of his name being called, listened to hear it again, then hunched over and scooted into the bushes. Someone making fun of me, he thought. Then he listened for it again, because the voice was a dead ringer for Ada's. He leaned back into the bush, pulling leaves and twigs apart to cushion himself, and stared up through the tangle at the slivers of sky. He stayed there all day, and then went home to be alone.

Ought to take myself away, find out where it is everyone goes to when they go, and then I'll be the one who's gone. Got to leave town, and no two ways about it. Won't leave word, neither, burn my tracks and go, damnit. He laughed when he thought that he wouldn't tell Ada, just a note that says I'm going, then off and on my own. See how she likes something being taken away from her. Matter of fact, no note. Just let her wonder.

Chapter 7

Chester delivered to the Newcombs' hotel room a list of available properties, and stood at the window while Ada and Emmett eagerly read the descriptions: an orange grove two hundred miles north in the shade of the Sierra Madre range; an India rubber tree farm in Pasadena; a ranch in San Diego with going herds of hogs and sheep and cattle; another with good crops of lemons and pears and apples; a farmsite in Misericordia, nestled near the western bank of the Los Angeles River, where the sandy soils were supposedly the best in Southern California; a ranch in Monte Vista where a planned health resort made the place a potential gold mine; another in Glenrovia on the down side of an inland-facing hill.

"But none of these is what I came here for," Emmett said, exasperated. "I want land by the sea."

"I know that, Mr. Newcomb," Chester replied with a hopeful shrug at Ada. "But I thought you ought to take a good look at other kinds of land before you—"

"If I can't get what I want, why would I want something else?" Emmett said. "I'll pay what needs to be paid."

Chester adjusted his hat and tugged at his trousers. "Problem is, money isn't the problem."

"What is, then?"

"South Central Railroad's bought up all the shore land, that's what," Chester said. "They're planning to run tracks up and down the whole coast."

"Aren't they the ones running streetcar tracks all along Main Street?" Ada asked.

"They're busy, all right," Chester admitted.

"How do they expect people to live?" Emmett demanded.

"Supposed to make life better," Chester muttered, and fanned himself with his hat. "But don't you folks despair," he added, to himself as well, and drew a deep breath. "I got plenty of prospects still lined up."

"I've lived in cities all my life, Mr. Puhls," Emmett said handing the list back. "They make me tired."

"We'll be patient, Mr. Puhls," Ada said more to calm Emmett than to placate Chester. "You just do whatever you have to do to get my husband what he wants."

Emmett paced from window to window after Chester left. "Patience," he muttered. "Patience. I can't believe the government is letting the railroad get away with buying up all the coast land."

Ada pulled the shawl tight around her shoulders. "A railroad's always going to have more money than a man. That's a fact you've got to face."

"If I'd faced facts I'd never have come out here at all," Emmett said testily. "I'd never have met you if I'd faced facts."

"But we could still have a house in the city," Ada said. "On one of the hills, so we'd have a view of the ocean."

"I didn't come all the way out to Southern California for a view of the ocean. I'm tired being a tourist everywhere I go."

"We can take trips out there then," Ada said reasonably. "I heard about a train that goes out to Santa Monica—"

"I don't want to take a train to the ocean, for God's sake!" Ada had never seen this temper before and she was fascinated to watch the storm of emotion play across his face and pass.

"There's a place I see, oh, I see it so clearly." He closed his eyes and smiled. "A sweeping coastline, and golden sand. A wide, calm, blue sea, and the smell of flowers and brine." He opened his eyes to face Ada. "California's where I've come to find that place. Everything I've read about it, every book, every brochure, every pamphlet, promised me that this was the place to find it. Look, Ada. Read these!" he said, holding the pamphlets and brochures out to her the way he'd once held them out to his skeptical mother. "All of them talk about the wonderful opportunities in the sunshine, land waiting to be picked like an orange from a tree. Homes in the sun." He dropped the pamphlets on the table and looked out the window at the crowded street below. "I don't care what it takes," he said. "I'll have it one way or another."

Ada held the pamphlets in her hand and nodded at him. "I'll bet you will too," she said.

Obie put off seeing Miss Harriette; too damned full of advice, he thought, but she had the first letter for him from Ada, and that was one thing he couldn't resist, and she knew

it. He watched the oak leaves moving high up in the trees; a
few leaves fell to the ground, red ones, brown ones, yellow
ones. Have to leave here soon, and that's that, can't stay the
whole winter in that old house.

He stretched his long legs out in front of him and leaned
back on the porch glider. Inside Miss Harriette's house Miss
Sophie Simmons was playing the piano, some tune that made
him think of places far away. She was singing to herself, too,
though he could hardly make out the words, her voice was so
small and dreamy; something about little birds and little
flowers and a cool stream where a young girl died.

Then the music stopped, and she was standing in the
doorway. Her face was flushed, her hair come a little undone,
and she was wearing a dress sprinkled with blue cornflowers.
"I always get too excited when I play my piano!" she said.
"Miss Harriette's developing some photographs. Of me,"
Sophie said, and fixed a curl she imagined was falling.

No one knew where Sophie had come from—not from
Desideer, though. Miss Harriette found her in some town
somewhere, an orphan girl, and took her as a companion.
Sophie had an eager smile, but it made Obie want to back off;
seemed like she was wanting something, but never knowing
how to ask.

"Miss Harriette's got a letter from my sister," Obie said,
and looked out at the trees again; a leaf fell, another crossed
it mid-air.

"It just makes me want to cry that Ada's left Desideer,"
Sophie said. "When I get married, I want to stay here
forever, I love it so much. Oh, it just makes me want to cry."

Obie thought that she did not look like she wanted to cry,
for she was smiling eagerly at him, and sat down at the other
end of the glider.

"I'd like to get me some land in Montana," Obie said.

"Oh no, you too? What's in Montana, for heaven's sake?"

"Nothing, I guess," Obie replied. "Just lots of it."

Sophie put her hand over her mouth and laughed; Obie
noticed that her teeth stuck out when she smiled too wide,
and thought she was probably over-conscious of it. "All those
cows to herd around, all those Indians to escape from, and
plains of cactus and sagebrush to ride over. Seems like it'd be
nothing but trouble with all that land." When Obie didn't
respond, she fixed her curls and began again. "Is there really
a desert as far as the eye can see?"

"Sure," Obie said. "Why, you could stand in the desert and turn all the way completely around and never once see another soul, just sand as far as the eye goes. Or maybe you'd see a wagon train crossing, or some Indians fixing to attack, and you just watch 'em real close, and then..." Obie jumped and spun around, pulling his hands up along his hips, then letting loose with a two-handed volley: "Pah! pah! pah!" Sophie shrieked and grabbed her stomach and reeled back in the settee. Obie kept firing—"pah! pah! pah!"—until she was a heap in the corner of the glider. He blew on his fingers, and sank back against the railing opposite her. They were both a little breathless. Sophie opened her eyes and drew herself up straight, brushing at her dress as if all the ruckus had mussed up the fields of cornflowers. She poked a small pink shoe out from her dress, and ran it around the porch floor.

"I'm drawing someone's initials," she said and laughed pantingly behind her hand. It looked to Obie like a tongue darting out and licking the ground. He pulled handfuls of leaves from the bushes at the porch railing, picked them apart, and dropped them to the porch floor; he wished she'd stop and go inside now. She was over-excited, her thin chest rising and falling.

"How is it to live alone?" she asked. "I don't know anyone who lives alone except you. Widows and old maids usually get themselves a little kitty for comfort. You got a little kitty?"

"My daddy drowned 'em," he said; it wasn't so, but he liked saying it.

"I never even had a daddy," she said and looked toward upstairs in the house. "No momma either, after a little bit, and no daddy ever, never. Just being a companion to Miss Harriette. That's my life. And now she's thinking of going all the way to Paris, France. Maybe sell the house, you know that? Oh, I don't know. I don't know." She was wringing her hands. Obie looked at the house, drew his belt tight, shrugged, and rubbed his eyes. "Gosh Obie, I'm twenty-five years old. I got to do something besides..." She looked around her; looked at her hands. "You don't know... you don't know."

Obie watched her closely, his fists opening and closing. Tears slid along her cheeks, she clutched her skirt. Obie felt near to breaking something with his hands just to distract her, maybe slap her face, make her stop letting all this out.

"You ought to keep still now," he said, and ducked inside the house. After a moment, Sophie followed him in and played a piece at the piano that sounded like things tumbling into the sea. Miss Harriette was coming up from the basement, peeling off the India-rubber gloves she wore when she used chemicals.

"Got my letter from Ada?" he said.

She smiled, and reached in her pocket for it.

"Read it to me?" Obie leaned his forehead against the window, watching the leaves fall one by one. Would Ada be at a window now? He could see her at a window, looking out at an ocean, a lonely look on her face, thinking about what to do.

"My dear Obidiah. I know how you don't like being called by your full given name, but you are a man, and it's not fitting for you to be called by your boyhood name. We're still living in a hotel in Los Angeles. What a big city this is! There are fifty-seven churches alone! There's Child's Opera house, where we saw Primrose and West's Minstrel Follies, which featured thirty actual Negroes. It's always sunny here, every day nothing but sun. I certainly am glad to be roving around Los Angeles, all right, even though it's congested with people. It is invigorating just to be in the midst of it all. I'll bet there isn't another place in America—in the world, maybe—where the citizens are so full of their own possibilities. I love being part of that.

"So far I've seen Mexicans, Indians, and Chinese people, heard Spanish and French and German spoken, and been mistaken for a Swede by a man looking for his mail-order wife. I've seen real cowboys, too, and naturally think of you whenever I do. They've got half-shut eyes, and they don't shave very often. Emmett is a sweet and kind man, I have discovered. Right now he's making plans about buying us a big piece of land on the ocean. Some day he plans to have his own wine vineyards, and a big ranch, too, cows and sheep, though, to tell you the truth, I'm not sure he knows the difference, city boy that he is. I hope you'll see your way clear to coming out here some time. There are a thousand and one opportunities for a boy like you in a city like this. And of course you'd have the advantage of already knowing me and Emmett so you would never be a stranger.

"I wish it could be like it was, Obie, but things just change. I don't understand why any better than you do. Maybe you might like to come see us for just a visit, if you don't want to come to live. You are often in my thoughts. Your loving sister, Ada."

He turned and took the letter, held it up to the light, then lowered it again, folded it carefully, and handed it back to Miss Harriette. "You keep it for me," he said. Miss Harriette nodded, and left it on the piano top.

"Now why not stop all this nonsense and go and see her?"

"Her husband don't want me to come," Obie said, shrugging.

"How do you know that?" Miss Harriette asked. "She says he's a kind man."

"I don't need to go galloping all over the world just because she goes and gets married!"

Sophie stopped playing suddenly.

"Seems to me the world's getting awful big if a man can't even go and see his own flesh and blood," she said, and ran from the room. Miss Harriette watched her silently for a moment, then turned to Obie.

"You've grown up to be a fine-looking young fella, and you best start behaving like one," she said.

"I just want people to leave me be," he replied.

Miss Harriette clasped her hands together tightly in front of her, mad enough to slap him. "Ada wants you to go out there. And you know you want to go. Why are you torturing that poor girl with your orneriness?"

Obie fingered Miss Harriette's lace curtain; it felt to him like dirt sliding over his palm. "She left just like he left."

"Who did?"

"My so-called father," he said in a light mocking voice. "Stayed around long enough to get a good look at his future, and 'so long Jack.'"

"I won't have self-pity," Miss Harriette said. "I simply won't have it. I believe you're hanging all this stubbornness on Ada's lack of proper enthusiasm about getting you to come. She is willing to take you. You can't deny that."

"He don't want me there."

"You're a grown man," she said. "You should know how to take better care."

It scared him, this being a man. He was nearly big as one, he knew, a mite on the skinny side, though he thought he'd fill out once he was into his twenties; he did a man's work at the stable, at a man's wage; he'd had thoughts about girls, bad thoughts, thoughts a boy couldn't have. He thought of

Sophie. Why, I should've just slapped her and been done with it. She wanted me to, anyone could see that.

He stood up straight, and shook his clothes around him. "I got my future all planned, don't you worry none." He made a slight bow to her, though he never let his eyes leave hers. As he left he scooped Ada's letter from the piano, and trailed it through the air; it looked like a white bird frantic to land.

Chapter 8

Emmett sat at the hotel bedroom window, listening for Ada's return but loath to hear it, too, for what could he tell her? That he'd misrepresented himself? That, far from being the picture of virile manhood he appeared, he was weak and sickly, a potential invalid? He'd been able to fool himself—and her—but after what happened this morning he could no longer maintain the charade.

He had taken a streetcar downtown to Avery Benson's office, and on the way back was assailed by a recurrence of his familiar fatigue. He could not rise from his seat, even as the streetcar went past the Saint Elmo Hotel, past the railroad station, and all the way out to the end of the line in East Los Angeles. He rested for a few moments, chewing on calcium tablets, then looked up to see a broad vista of tall grass and wildflowers and fresh mint, hazy, purplish mountains in the distance under an impeccable blue sky. The Los Angeles *Times* had called this section "a howling wilderness"; but how calming was the sight of it! This was the California he'd come for, this was what he wanted, and the time of playing tourist seemed like shameless indulgence. It's the city that's distracted me and brought on this spell, he thought.

He got off the streetcar to walk a bit before heading back to the city. There were a few houses—squarish white boxes—and as he got close to them he saw the people who were drawn to this place: men with the translucent skin and high flush of the tubercular, old women whose hands were twisted with arthritis, men propped up in wheelchairs against the buildings, canes across their laps, frail men on crutches, children lashed into braces. Like the grotto at Lourdes, he thought, choking on the laugh; all lured to Southern California by the promise of a miracle cure. The hope he shared with them seemed to lessen the possibility; the coincidence was grotesque.

No, he decided now, he would say nothing of his morning to Ada. He heard her coming in the door of the suite, and hesitated to greet her, as if his thoughts were etched on his

face where Ada could not help but read them. But then she
appeared at the doorway to the bedroom, flushed and excited, her hands raised to him, palms open. Look how her eyes
light when they see me! Look how she smiles! Her lips were
warm on his, her cheek hot and moist.

"Emmett, I've got news!" she exclaimed and pulled away
to see his face. "I'm going to have a baby!"

Her skin glowed as if a layer of affection had been peeled
away and a deeper one revealed. She's left home and family
and job to marry me, to travel two thousand miles with a man
she hardly knew because he had a dream she believed in.
And now to have a child with me. That was the kind of man
he wanted to be, would be; a husband to inspire a wife, not
one to burden her. He made a vow on the blessed head of his
unborn child that healthy or... health be damned!—he'd
fulfill her faith in him. This child was his link to the future; he
would go on, it was guaranteed. He pulled Ada close again.
"This makes all the difference in the world."

Obie stood in the shadows just outside the door of Schulsky's
Haberdasher on River and Third, waiting for the store to
open. The awning was being rolled back next door at Addison's
Barber Shop; a pink-faced young man emerged trailing a
cloud of lilac talc as he crossed in front of Obie and entered
Rayburn's Oyster Saloon on the other side. Women in bonnets and shawls walked by, heads swiveling and nodding,
faces mottled with shadow and sun. A buckboard horse drank
at the watering trough. Across the street in the sun, two
young salesmen in boaters and striped blazers were testing
out their line of chatter on the young girls that passed by.

Mr. Schulsky was barely visible in the dark recess of the
back of the store, but Obie's eye caught a flash of movement
and he ducked to protect his face, then laughed uneasily and
looked around, shrugging, and moved closer to the door. His
hands were sweating and cold, fingertips icy; a line of sweat
kept forming at his hairline. He wanted to laugh, to run
alongside the river, grab a few big apples. Got to get out, he
said to himself, as if to bolster his courage.

He moved through the shadowy doorway into the store,
and crouched behind a stack of Dobson hat boxes and a
gentleman dummy in evening clothes with puffs of white silk
for a head. Across the street at Tye's a gent in yellow trousers
and a derby consulted his pocket watch and looked up,

shaking his head as if the sun was the one who was off; he said something out of the side of his mouth that made his companion, a slow boy named Toby Owens who Obie knew in school, throw back his head and laugh a big silent laugh.

"Damn sun," Obie whispered out of the side of his mouth and threw back his head. He waited another moment, then rose from his crouch and closed the door silently. He pulled a blue handkerchief from his back pocket, wiped off his hands and face, and walked toward the back.

The store was deep and narrow and high. Glass-topped counters ran along both sides, showing collars and cravats and bolts of cloth. Shelves climbed to the ceiling, and a big ladder on wheels reached the top ones. He wrapped the blue handkerchief across his face, and patted the bulge in his pocket. Mr. Schulsky came out from behind a drawn curtain.

"You turning gunslinger, Obie?" he asked; his spectacles caught the light like two silver dollars pressed to the eyes of a dead man.

Obie felt his scalp'd been peeled back; he pulled the handkerchief down to his neck. "Just sporting," he said.

Mr. Schulsky nodded but didn't move from his spot. "You wanting something?"

Obie hesitated, then blurted out, "Want me some nankeen trousers, Mr. Schulsky. And make sure they got a neat crease. And I want a tooled leather belt, and suspenders, and a canvas shirt, and a red kerchief."

"Thought you told me you was going out to be a salesman, Obie."

"Me? I got better things to do than slick pomade on my hair and parade around selling ladies' garters," Obie replied. Mr. Schulsky nodded again, lips pursed, running his thumbs under his suspenders. "You better get me a pair of Wellingtons, too, and a planter's hat." Mr. Schulsky took one long, last look at him, then, then shrugged and climbed the tall ladder. "Already got me a Colt Derringer number one," Obie said quietly. He took the gun out of his pocket and turned it over in his hand. "You ever seen one like this?" he whispered. Sweat broke out at his hairline again, he felt flushed and nearly faint; he hefted the gun once more and, with a sound catching in his throat, jammed it back in his pocket. "If you follow the Orenoke on the map you get to the Mississippi, you know that?" he said loudly. "And then all the way out west. River to river to river."

Mr. Schulsky had pulled down a few boxes, and was routing around behind the counters to dig out a few more, piling them all up at Obie's feet. "Where'd you get money to pay for all this stuff?" he inquired, red-faced from the exertion.

Obie touched the gun in his pocket. "Ada's been sending me for to come out to California." He pulled the boxes across the floor, and dressed behind the drawn curtain. A few minutes later he stood in front of the long mirror transformed. "Need a better gun," he muttered to himself, turning this way and that. "Can't you see me riding out on the range? Dodge City, or Cheyenne, or some place real western. Maybe have my own spread, with my own cattle. Already got a brand all drawn out on paper." He leaned on the counter, and drew on the back of Mr. Schulsky's receipt pad: OW. He grinned up at Mr. Schulsky, and went back to the mirror. "Cowboys live a great life on the open prairie. Always riding out past the horizon, where another day's waiting for them. And they have campfires, and other cowboys for buddies, and everyone's loyal and lives by the code of the West." He narrowed his eyes and crouched, nodding.

"Let's put a leather vest on you," Mr. Schulsky said, and helped Obie into it. "Now you look like the genuine article."

Obie walked toward his reflection, then turned and walked away, more and more pleased with this image of himself. "Someday I'll show up at Ada's front door." He narrowed his eyes again and backed off from his reflection, one hand on his Derringer, the other on the brim of his hat, spinning this picture of himself into the future. "Howdy, ma'm, I'll say. But I won't say who I am. Just stand there and then..." He closed his eyes. "The mystery stranger in the white hat."

"Fifty dollars," Mr. Schulsky said.

Obie looked at him for a long moment in the mirror; the man's face was lopsided, enough to make someone turn away and run. Obie put his hand on his gun and faced the real Mr. Schulsky. "Can't," Obie said. "I'm going to need it."

Mr. Schulsky's hand lay palm up on the counter, and Obie brought the gun butt down on it like he was driving a nail in a board. When Mr. Schulsky screamed, Obie slammed the butt against the side of his face, and Mr. Schulsky, gurgling blood, slid down behind the counter.

Obie stood still for a long moment, listening, then quit the store. A storm was coming up, he could tell by the bright white sky and the clattering of the branches along the river

where his roan mare waited, but underneath the wind and
the clatter was a horrible, mean white silence. He stroked
the Derringer in his pocket. "Good thing I got you," he
murmured, and felt all right about going.

He kept his head down on the ride through town, didn't
see anyone for his concentration on the roan mare's neck,
chuckling to himself all the way, shoulders jumping up and
down with the great joke of this town, these people who
didn't know how to treat anyone except for same danged rules
they invented for the purpose of suiting themselves and their
notions of what was the what-you-do. He knew something
about these people that they didn't know he knew. Probably
didn't even know it themselves; they thought they were so
close to God, thought they were sitting on His right hand,
knew just what He'd be saying if He had the voice for it.
Quiet down, Obie! that's what they think He'd be saying.

He had a thought of knocking down a row of men on the
steps of the post office building. One two three four, "pah!
pah! pah! pah!" When he got to Carl Chang's Laundry, at the
edge of town, he stopped the horse and turned around in the
saddle for one last look. It's smaller already, he thought, and
felt he'd gone a thousand miles. And then another thought
echoed loudly behind that one: no one knows me.

He shrugged elaborately, dug his heels into the horse's
flanks, and was off west.

Chapter 9

The sky was swollen and ominous, and every day and night there was a splashing, thick rain. There was no escape from the stuffiness of the hotel. Ada lay stretched out on a settee, lazy with the damp heat, her hands resting easily on her stomach, feeling the infant move inside her, watching the rain glisten in tiny silver drops from the gambrel roof of the hotel. "Have you heard the new Chamber of Commerce slogan?" she asked Emmett. "If it isn't native, just bring it to Los Angeles, and we'll make it native." Emmett's laugh was short and polite, and he continued to pace from sofa to window to mantle, drumming his fingers on table tops and listening to his shoes squeak. He extended his hand out the window beyond the protection of the eaves and drew it back with a palm full of rainwater. "The Sunshine State." Ada leaned back and breathed deeply of the fragrant air, exhaling in a long satisfied sigh, her eyes closed, listening for something unseen, unseeable, the noise of the upward urge. She had a continuing sense of wonder at the secret of growth and the natural process of it working through her own body, as though a witness to a gradually unfolding miracle yet somehow not quite the agent of it. Her body was as full as the earth under these full rain skies. When she thought about the women in Desideer as child-bearers, her feelings for them loosened and enlarged. But, having known this miracle of expectation and growth, she wondered how they could have strayed so far and grown so hard. Had it made of the rest of their lives a disconnection? A cheat?

"Dear Ada, I see that married life is treating you fine. As for me I am taking off out of this place. Gave notice at the stable and everything. My destination is west as you could probably guess. My aim has always been to be a cowboy and now I am going to be one. Got the gear and all. One of these days I will show up on your doorstep and you will not know who I am. I will be so different. The mystery stranger in the white hat. Your brother, Obie."

She patted a scented handkerchief on the back of her neck and showed the letter to Emmett. "It's hard to imagine Obie on his own like that, out of Desideer. He was such a baby," she said. "He didn't want me to go, you know. He was afraid to be alone. But... oh, I feel bad about this. I promised him Christmas in California but maybe he didn't believe me."

"Obie'll do just fine on his own," Emmett said. "He's nineteen years old! He's not a baby. We'll make it up to him later. When the baby's a few months old and we've got a house there'll be plenty of time." Ada nodded, though she was picturing Obie that last day, riding after the train. She was glad for the knocking at the door, glad Chester Puhls got in the way of the sight of Obie riding after the train.

"I know this probably seems like a crazy time to come calling," Chester said, half out of breath, "but I couldn't wait till morning, not with this news."

Emmett beckoned him into the parlor, where Chester stretched out on a plush chair and tassled hassock. Ada brought in a plate of pastries from the Italian bakeshop on Figueroa. Chester scrambled to his feet to present her with a much-thumbed copy of *Ramona*. "You'll notice," he said delicately, "that it's been personally autographed by Helen Hunt Jackson herself."

"I wouldn't have thought you'd be a fan of this book," Ada said skeptically.

"Oh, I love a sentimental read," Chester replied expansively. "What Californian doesn't want to know about the glorious days of the missions? The padres swinging church bells and calling out for the Indians to come to church. Yes, yes. Mission country stretches along the coast for hundreds of miles, strung out like a rosary, 'Course, most of them are working ranchos today. Can you imagine the old Franciscans walking the coast from mission to mission? Umbrellas on their shoulders? Just like in *Ramona*." He swiveled his head from Ada to Emmett with a big friendly grin slapped on. "Makes you feel like you're living in ancient history."

"Didn't you once say that California was nothing but *recent* history?" Ada asked.

Chester, embarrassed, shrugged; shameless, he said, "Man's entitled to change his opinion."

"Facts aren't opinions, Mr. Puhls."

"Ada," Emmett said, "I think Mr. Puhls came here to tell us something."

Chester coughed into his hand, glancing through lowered lids to see if Ada was going to throw the book on the floor, but she merely passed it to Emmett, who, Chester was relieved to see, murmured in appreciation.

"The Malibu Ranch," Chester said, pleased to see that they both looked up at him. "You've heard of it?"

"Of course we've heard of it," Emmett said.

Chester pursed his lips and looked down to set the crease of his trousers straight. "I was wondering if you'd be interested in buying it."

Emmett let the book slip from his hand; Chester leaned down and handed it back. "Careful," he said.

Emmett said nothing, his hands palm up on his knees, his head moving slowly in disbelief. "The Malibu," he said in a hush.

"Twenty-six miles of oceanfront property," Chester said. "Twenty thousand acres, give or take a hundred. Cattle and sheep already grazing and waiting for a new owner. Fresh water supply from the Malibu Creek. Grapes on the vine. Orange trees, almond trees... You don't mind if I help myself to one of these little pastries?"

"The Malibu Ranch, Ada. It's... it's..." Emmett turned back to Chester. "And you're saying it's for sale?"

Chester nodded. "Just found out the Kellers're moving to Santa Fe to live with Mrs. Keller's sister. Don't think they can handle the place any more, is my guess."

"You mean you've spoken to them?" Emmett asked.

Chester looked at Ada and slapped his hand on his thigh. "How do you think I got my suit so wet?" he asked. "I rode all the way out there, and back here tonight, instead of waiting for the morning like any other land agent'd do, that's how."

"Did you tell him about us?" Emmett asked. "About how we've been looking for a place just like the Malibu? And now—"

Chester took another bite of his pastry. "Told him all there was to tell, and more. There's just one little problem. Keller's from the old school of Alta Californians. A real isolationist, too. The place hasn't got a decent road on it. But if he thought there were deals being cooked up over his ranch, he'd never sell."

"But there aren't any deals," Emmett said. "I just want to buy it. Tell him I'll buy it!"

"Emmett!" Ada exclaimed. "Don't you want to see it first?"

Emmett glanced at her as if he'd forgotten she was in the room, and without responding, turned back to Chester. "You're sure he wants to sell it at the price I want to pay?"

Chester nodded and pursed his lips over another pastry decision. "Oh, by the way, I told him I was Mrs. Newcomb's brother," he said. "He's touchy, like I said, about land agents and deals. The family connection relaxed him."

"My brother? Why did you—"

"It's all right, Ada," Emmett said and turned to Chester. "My wife actually has a brother, you see, so it did seem a little . . ."

"You being in a family way is going to help things, too," Chester said. "Him and his wife never had a family, just them two. You know how those kind of folks can be. You just tell Keller you're expanding your family, and expanding your horizons, too." He took another bite of his tart, and sat back proudly. "I kind of like the way I put that. Feel free to use it on Keller. I bet he goes for it."

"But I'm curious, Mr. Puhls," Ada said. "Why isn't the railroad buying the Malibu? I thought what they wanted was to buy up the coast. And they could certainly pay more."

Chester bit into a cherry tart. "Keller'd never sell to the railroad. But even if he was willing, the situation's all changed around. For a long time everyone thought there was going to be a harbor built at Santa Monica, just a few miles down the coast from the Malibu. The South Central Railroad built their own pier out there, see, so the South Central Railroad naturally wanted their tracks from the north and their tracks from the south to meet at the pier where this great harbor was going to be built. But the Mendell Board just gave their recommendation to getting the harbor built at San Pedro instead. South Central don't need the Mailbu coast if it can't have a harbor for its pier. What you do is, you buy it from Keller and if and when the railroad ever does want it, you sell off just a tiny bit of it to lay the tracks, and you make back the price you paid for the whole thing."

"But the Malibu's completely untouched, isn't it?" Emmett asked.

Chester shrugged. "Can't afford to be sentimental about things like that. Not in modern times. Land out here's to be sold, bought, built up, and sold again."

"Shall we feel free to try that one out on Mr. Keller, too?" Ada asked.

"Better not," Chester said equably. "Now, here's what you do. You go out there together, tomorrow, and talk to him yourselves. Tell him about that expanding family, et cetera. What I mean is . . . "—his hand hovered over the pastry plate, then snatched a final apricot tart—" . . . he's expecting you."

The air on Wilshire Boulevard was rank and still. Birds shrieked, crickets trilled, flies buzzed incessantly. The protective canvas sun cover of the carriage made the air even closer. The sun came through a high haze which thickened as they neared the ocean, softening the rough edges of the road, making rocks and scrub brush shimmer and the ground intensely white. Emmett's paper collar was disintegrating in tiny shreds at his neckline; he had the woozy sensation of being pulled under water.

Ada sat impassively beside him, one hand on her stomach, the other waving a palm-frond fan. She wore a light cotton dress whose looseness emphasized her condition, and a sun bonnet with ribbons resting on her neck.

The Wilshire Boulevard transformation into Nevada Avenue was the demarcation point for Santa Monica's border, but the sun and the heat and the whiteness of the sky were relentlessly the same, all primary colors bleached out and burning. An occasional bank of fog floated past them, bringing the sharp smell of the sea, but the dampness brought no relief from the heat.

"Sometimes I think this famous California weather is the single most lethal element in the state." Emmett took off his hat and fanned his face with it.

Ada patted his hand gently. As her pregnancy proceeded, she felt closer and closer to the ground. Time marched at the exact speed of the baby's growth in her body, and she walked step by step on its path. "Try to be very still," she said to Emmett.

Emmett grunted the impossibility of this suggestion and dug surreptitiously into his pants pocket for his valerian and calcium pills. "Headache," he said, and swallowed them dry. He took them more often than he liked to think, but now his heartbeat slowed and the accompanying roar in his ears faded, and it was easy to resolve to take no more.

A stagnant pond on the side of the road threw off the biting stench of wild grapes rotting. Emmett wiped his face with a soaked handkerchief. He rubbed his eyes and squinted at the white sky. "I'm fine, I'm fine." He concentrated now on guiding the horse. The heat hung inside the haze, heavy as weight. Emmett pictured falling from the carriage and lying comatose till winter, the only respite from the heat a faint sea breeze.

The final blocks of Nevada Avenue approaching the ocean were rough and rutted from the rains of the last weeks; the sun was burning the fog silver. Emmett had sweated clean through his tweed suit by now. The insides of his boots were as slick as if they'd been bear-greased like the outsides.

Nevada Avenue ended abruptly at the northwest border of Santa Monica, on a flat sandy plateau above the beach; two low posts straddled the end of the road, strung with ineffectual rusted wire. A hand-painted sign was nailed crookedly to one of the posts:

   Malibu Ranch. No trespassing. H. Keller, prop.

Fog rose from the ocean and advanced toward them. The pier at Santa Monica appeared, snaking its way out to sea, its farthest curves obscured.

Emmett could see only enough to get the carriage down a shallow dip in the embankment and onto the beach. The wheels dragged heavily until they got near the water, where low tide provided a wide stretch of hard-packed sand.

"I wonder how you get there when the tide's high?" Ada said.

Emmett looked down at Chester's written instructions. "Follow the shoreline until we get to the stream. I wish we didn't have to meet Keller. Damn that Chester Puhls. I hate the idea of bargaining with a man over his land. I'd like to have nothing to do with Keller at all, never see him. I don't even want to know what he looks like. I don't want him appearing in my dreams. I want to think of us as the first people who ever lived on the Malibu."

Ada laid a restraining hand on his arm. "I'd still like to see it before we make up our minds."

Emmett grunted and they rode on slowly, unable to see more than a few yards in any direction. The waves moved with an ominous rumble just beyond the fog, appearing only as they crested to break and sweep up the beach, licking the hardpacked sand near the carriage wheels and slinking back down into the sea. Emmett peeled off his coat, hot clear through his chest, not exactly sure, now that he was actually on the property itself, why he wanted land at all. Growing up in a series of rooms, he never imagined open space to be this vivid; it seemed to him suddenly more burden than pleasure. All he wanted at the moment was a cool room and a soft bed.

A mile or so further on, they found the stream—wider than they'd expected—its current and the ocean's tide rushing together and pooling in a slow swirl on the beach. They tracked alongside it up the beach—the sand gradually gave way to an expanse of crushed beach grass—into the fog-drenched canyon. Sea gulls cried invisibly overhead; when two or three swooped down into the clear air, the gulls and the Newcombs were equally startled by each other's presence.

The carriage wheels moved more smoothly on the matted grass; silence prevailed but for the sounds of the stream rushing by and the gulls crying overhead. Fog clung to most of the land; the area they rode through was overgrown with stunted trees and brush, and long grass hung into the stream. They'd gone only a few hundred yards from the shoreline—though the distance seemed longer for the fog—when they came into a sudden clearing, edged by tall oak trees which led the eye to the bottom of a hill. The road could just about accommodate a carriage, though the horse had uncertain footing, slipping on the smooth dry stones, losing purchase in the cracked earth. The mist hung over the land, drifted in veils, revealed patches of dusky color and concealed them. As the carriage crested the hill, there appeared a white stucco wall. They rode closer, and an old man came out through tall wooden doors.

"Keller," Emmett whispered. He guided the carriage up to the doors, clambered out, and let the reins drop. The old man was wearing a white plantation suit which might have fit him when he was young, but he'd shrunk inside it. His white moustache drooped at the corners and his eyes turned down.

"Mr. Keller? My name's Emmett Newcomb." Emmett moved a few tentative steps forward, expecting recognition, but the old man ran surprisingly thick fingers over his moustache and said nothing. "I'm from Boston," Emmett said. "Massachusetts," he added, and took another uncertain step, then looked questioningly back at Ada sitting in the shade of the carriage.

"You lost? Don't get to see that many people out here, unless they're lost." His voice was deep and rumbling, as if he hadn't talked in days.

"We're not lost," Emmett replied with forced heartiness,

cursing Chester Puhls but relieved to elicit at least some
response. "We've come all the way out here from Los Angeles
especially to see you, as a matter of fact." He took a deep
breath and began again. "My name is Emmett Newcomb,"
he said, and, when the old man still gave no sign of recognition, said, "Chester Puhls spoke to you about us." Emmett
turned to Ada again, and she climbed out of the carriage. The
old man removed his hat, running his hand over a thick crop
of white hair.

"Oh, yeah, yeah, your brother told me all about you. Place
burn down, huh?"

"Chester told you that?" Ada said.

They followed Keller through the doors and into what had
once been a large garden; untrimmed and untended, it had
long gone to weed and rot. A gallery ran around the garden,
and rooms opened from it. Grass grew on the path between
the cracks in the stone; the white stucco walls were chipped
and peeling.

It looked to Ada as if no one lived here. No, as if the
people who did had just given up on it. Keller took them into
the kitchen, where two Mexican women were carrying bou-
quets of parsley and garlic. One of them poured out three
glasses of warm, bluish wine. The room was damp and
dough-smelling, and very simply furnished: besides the rough
pine table and benches they sat on, there were only a few
straw chairs and a straw footstool on the slick clay floor, a
small shrine with a plaster statue of Mary surrounded by a
gilt sunburst, and a hand-tinted print of Jesus on the cross.
The clay walls were whitewashed and wet-looking; two shuttered
windows opposite each other let in a faint ocean breeze.

Keller took a long swallow of his wine, and rolled the glass
between his palms. "Reason the Spanish *conquistadores* never discovered the Malibu, the reason the padres never built
one of their damn missions on the place, was because they
couldn't land their ships here. Shore line's too regular and
the sea's too rough for a big ship to drop anchor and tie up.
The sea don't open up the Malibu to the world, you see, it
closes it in. And the mountains close it off in back. That's why
I thought you was lost." He took another long swallow of his
wine, refilled his glass, and started talking again. He told
them how some of the religious artifacts in the room—a
crown of thorns, a silver communion chalice—were rescued
from a mission up the coast that had been abandoned by the

padres and picked clean by tourists. The house had been
built by his father, Keller went on, and he himself had never
seen a reason to do more to it than add a room here and there
over the years. Keller looked through the open doorway at
the garden, but it seemed to Ada he was seeing somewhere
farther off.

Emmett hardly listened, but nodded all the while Keller
spoke; he sensed the old man had to be encouraged to talk
himself out before the point could be broached. Finally, he
could bear the suspense no longer. "The reason we . . ." He
hesitated then shifted in his chair and began again, Keller's
sad eyes on him now. "We'd like to . . ." With a helpless look
at Ada he leaned across the table toward Keller, but could not
seem to say the words.

"What about us buying the Malibu, Mr. Keller?" Ada
asked.

Keller stood up to get another bottle of wine. Emmett
concentrated very hard on keeping his hands flat on the
table. "Sure, sure," Keller said with sudden anger, waving
the bottle at them. "So you can turn around and sell it to the
South Central for a handy profit. Strips of metal stitched up
and down the Malibu," he muttered.

"I'm expecting our first child, Mr. Keller," Ada said. "We
want to settle in and make the Malibu our home."

"We'd protect it with our lives if we had to," Emmett said,
a little wildly.

Keller laughed, though his face was tight and his eyes cold.
"Your lives! Oh that's good, that's good. Now I can rest easy."
His balled fist beat on his leg. "Your lives aren't worth all that
much. One shot from one rifle, and to hell with all your brave
talk, mister." he poured another glass of wine, and sat down
again. "Anyway, the Malibu's already spoken for."

"But we thought—"

"My vaqueros come with the ranch," Keller declared,
pulling his head up. "They've been through every period of
grief and joy this land has ever seen and, damnit, there is no
way I sell this ranch and make 'em lose their homes. There's
Quinones, the foreman, he runs the place, you'd need him
bad; there's a hundred vaqueros working the place. The
Malibu belongs to them. I just got my name on the deed, is
all. I'd give it to 'em free of charge but the courts'd never let
'em keep it."

"We'd keep them on," Ada said. "That's a promise, isn't it, Emmett?"

Before Emmett could say anything there was a high piercing shriek from behind a closed door at the dark end of the kitchen. "Sell it, Henry! Sell it!" The Mexican woman didn't move from the sink as Keller turned heavily and made his way through the doorway. There was a movement deep in the adjoining room's darkness, the batting of a bird's wings, scuffling, muttering, a basin kicked, silence. In another moment, red-faced and pulling at his coat, Keller emerged and shuffled outside. Ada and Emmett followed to join him on the gallery. The fog drifted above them in wispy shreds, the sun a fuzzy lemon glow that almost pierced through. Keller turned to look at the house for a long moment and sighed deeply.

"My wife was a preacher's daughter," he said. "Should never have married me. Her family warned her, told her it'd be lonesome out here. Hell, I warned her myself. Can't get too friendly with the Mexicans, seeing as how they aren't our kind of true Christians. Not many other people out here. None, actually. I never had the problem, myself, working out on the ranch every day, but... she never did take to the isolation. Her sister's asked us to move in with her in Santa Fe." He shrugged as if he had always understood it would end this way. "She'll be wanting to meet you," he said in a subdued voice, and went back inside.

Ada and Emmett walked a few feet away from the house and sat down on a stone bench. Ada understood now about the ruined garden; a chill passed through her; the baby kicked. Emmett's hands were pressed firmly to his knees, he breathed evenly, but he could not stop his heart from pounding. He leaned back and crossed his arms over his chest as if he would crush his heart in his coat and stop the wild feelings. "I used to dream about a place like this," he said, standing.

"He hasn't said he'd sell it," Ada said. She sat in silence, remembering the long trip out, thinking of how far they were from the city.

"We'd need a new road," Emmett said as he paced. "Don't worry about that."

"Emmett, please don't get too far ahead of yourself," she said, reaching for his hand. "It's not ours."

"But you do love it?"

"Yes, I love it," Ada said but knew impatience had made her speak.

"Chester said Keller'd sell."

"Oh, Chester!" Ada exclaimed. "If words were deeds, Chester'd own Los Angeles."

At that moment, Keller emerged from the house with what looked to be a child. Ada took Emmett's arm as they came closer. The child proved to be his wife, a tiny creature in a long white dress, gray hair hanging loose down her back as she must have worn it when Keller married her. As Ada and Emmett advanced, she moved closer to her husband, her bright blue eyes wide and wary; her hand on Keller's arm was chalky white with lavender veins.

"Missus Keller," Keller said hoarsely, with a mixture of pride and embarrassment. Ada could see evidence in her of the loveliness she must once have had, and none of the virago that had shrieked at her husband to sell. Mrs. Keller curtsied like an obedient child, and looked around at the walls that enclosed the garden.

"We're leaving," she said very quietly to Ada.

"Mrs. Keller's got family in Santa Fe, see," Keller said. "We'll be... going out there pretty soon..." He closed his eyes for a moment and nodded slowly. "Yeah, I knew you came out here to buy the place. Knew someone would, I guess," he added with a sudden laugh, then exhaled and his shoulders slumped. "But I just don't know about it. I just..."

"Please..." Mrs. Keller's voice was tiny as a bird's.

Keller patted her small hand. "My daddy bought this place in fifty-seven, twenty thousand acres for ten cents an acre," he said stiffly. "I guess I'll be wanting ten dollars an acre for it now."

"Two hundred thousand dollars!" Ada exclaimed. "That's twice what—"

"Railroad's offered twenty an acre," he replied.

Emmett felt all the days of his former life spill into the past like loose change from his pocket. He did not look at Ada to voice his decision. "Yes," he said, and felt a surge of emotion in his chest. "Yes," he said again, he liked saying it, he couldn't stop the smile, and rushed forward to pump Keller's hand. "You've got yourself a deal, Mr. Keller." Keller's arm shook lifelessly in Emmett's hand. "I guess we'll take a look around now, Mr. Keller. And when I get back to Los Angeles I'll have my lawyer get in touch with you and we can close the sale."

Mrs. Keller burst into a high-pitched staccato laugh; Keller squeezed her arm hard, and cut her off. She covered her mouth and wrenched her arm free. There was silence for just a moment. Everything seemed to stop. Keller looked at Ada and Emmett—Emmett was already straining to go, but Ada lingered one moment longer, drawn by something she would never forget—the endless sorrow on Keller's face as their future crossed paths with his past.

Keller took his wife inside. The moment ended. Ada followed Emmett out the doors to see the Malibu rise from the fog. As they walked through the doors of the garden the sun pierced through, the fog drifting past them into the canyon depths. Sunlight winked through leaves of ancient sycamores, dancing across the road like coins tossed spinning in the air. Green hills undulated into the distance as if a giant stirred beneath the surface. There were huge magenta boulders in tumbling lines down those furred green slopes, great rents in the earth from the rains had caused rivulets to flow into the great stream below. Brilliant shafts of golden light shot purple shadows across the canyons: hills against hills against hills. The strong smell of eucalyptus rose from the canyon floor, whipped up by the wind, which came in sudden whistling shrieks.

The fog had lifted along the coast, and the Malibu was arching in from the sea, embracing it, the mountains like the spine of a great slumbering beast curving down and dipping into it, stepping back to accommodate the waves. The sand stretched down the coast to Santa Monica, appearing and dissolving in mist, and for miles up the coast in a graceful crescent that ended at an immense jutting boulder which loomed proudly over the sea. The canyons themselves, in this late afternoon sun, seemed scooped of living, flowing gold; deeply etched crevasses and sloping hills flowed down to the beach of burnished sand that tumbled over itself into the sea. Gold leaf sculpted the inside curl of sleek, whale-backed waves.

Emmett's chest swelled with pride and wonder at the splendor and immensity of what was spread before him. "Ada, oh, Ada... this place is... it's everything I've dreamed about since Europe. And... I can say it now... I never really thought I'd ever find it, not really. But I have... I have..." He shook his head; there were tears in his eyes. "We'll have our own world here, away from everyone, away from railroads and... progress." Every moment now was vital, every mo-

ment to be aware of the essence of life, to see, to smell, to
feel.

Ada was touched by the depth of his satisfaction, moved
that this man had been so fulfilled; and wasn't this another
attestation of what love was? How far we've come together,
she thought. She felt steadied by the land now—it was worth
the looking for, worth the waiting—an infinite limbo was
concretized here and made substantial in majestic proportion.
She had her husband, she had her child on the way. She
watched the earth's subtle curve where sea met sky, the sky
lowering, deep, soft gray against the crisp, metallic sea, ever
advancing, ever retreating, now crawling up the beach and
peaking to slip back down.

They would simply be the Newcomb family, self-contained
and self-sufficient. There would be no leaving, no disrup-
tions. They would have each other; they would be enough.
They would be those people who lived out on that ranch by
the sea. You know the one: the Malibu.

Part 3

If there is a paradise on the face of the earth,
It is this, oh! it is this, oh! it is this.

—Anonymous Mogul inscription in the
Red Fort at Delhi

Chapter 10

"I want you to show me everything there is to show, Mister... Señor Quinones," Emmett said when Fernando Quinones presented himself at the house a few weeks after they moved in.

"I am at your disposal," Quinones replied formally and waited for El Señor to get ready.

Though dressed like the other vaqueros—a tilted kerchief bound his long black hair under a weather-worn leather hat, his wide-sleeved shirt was torn at the shoulder, his trousers reached the knee and skimmed buckskin boots, in which a long knife was held by a garter—he looked very different in every other way. He was taller than any of the others, especially in the saddle; his face was narrow, with a high-bridged Roman nose and pale eyes the color of the beach sand. The vaqueros who worked the rancho for Keller—who tended the cattle and the sheep, whose families worked in the orange groves and in the vineyards—were more than curious as to what actions the new owners would take. Despite assurances that the new owner had given Keller his word everything would remain as it was, they wanted Quinones to hear it first-hand. New to the land, the owners were bound to be curious. But would they stir things up? Would there be trouble?

He did not wish to appear curious, though his peering eyes managed to take in all the changes the Newcombs had already wrought in the house in the few weeks they had been there. Though they retained the basic shell of the Keller house, the insides were being transformed. A crew of workers—from the city, Quinones assumed—were scraping the old whitewash from every wall, and swabbing on fresh coats. Some interior walls were being torn down altogether. La Señora—big with child—was standing in the once-ruined garden of Señora Keller, directing the turning of the soil. A horse was brought out from the stables, and El Señor spoke a few last words to his wife, on her knees now, planting bulbs in the earth, and joined Quinones again.

Emmett mounted the horse clumsily, waved to Ada and turned back to Quinones. "Mrs. Newcomb is amazed to be planting tulip bulbs in January. There's no time to waste in Southern California. Sun three hundred and sixty days a year, I promised her that." He turned his gaze to the sea below, calm and steely blue; above the sky was bright, whitish, cloudless. My land, he thought with a quick grin, still surprised at the very fact of it—rolling hills the color of gold dust, purple in the shadows of the hills. "I've got a million ideas I want to start putting to use," he said to Quinones, and patted a bulge in his chest pocket. "Got a little notebook here; don't mind me if I stop to jot down my ideas as we go along."

Quinones drew his head back and peered at Emmett beneath the brim of his hat. "I will be glad to hear any suggestions you have," he replied warily.

Emmett nodded, as they started down the hill. He noticed that Quinones's hands, loosely gripping the reins of his horse, were in marked contrast to the rest of him: though rough and hard, they were surprisingly small and delicate, almost like a woman's.

As Ada watched them move off a slow smile spread across her face. Emmett was so happy since they'd moved to the Malibu, it gave her pleasure just to see it: such excitement he had for this place! She herself was not quite with him yet; the Malibu still seemed like an idea to her, no matter that the sea breeze cooled her cheeks, no matter that she curled her toes around the soil in her own garden and planted jonquil bulbs in mid-winter. For him it was a dream which had miraculously materialized; for her the land was still a stranger she knew would take some getting used to. The size alone was a little forbidding. Could put all of Desideer—including the outlying farmlands—in just the big canyon behind the house. Shaking her head, Ada sat down on the freshly turned soil in the garden, and turned her face up to the sun; the baby'll be here soon, she thought, and that slow smile of satisfaction spread on her face again.

The two men rode north along the beach. Emmett was exhilarated at the low, wide sea and the clapping of horses' hooves on the wet sand and the salt-sprayed breeze and the way the mountains seemed to step back from the sea and present the land to him. They rode to the top of Point Dume to look up and down the coast above the immense, implacable sea. Emmett imagined himself taking off into space, losing the ground, legs in the air, weightless, waving joyously, out of breath, touching hand and foot to rock and bush and plunging into the sea.

"You want to see the cattle?" Quinones asked, and, at Emmett's nod, turned his horse back to the beach. "I take you to Zuma." Emmett noticed that he spoke English with a barely discernible accent, and chose his words with the care of a diplomat.

Emmett rode after him, holding tightly to the reins, already sore in the seat, envying Quinones his ease in the saddle, and followed into a canyon pass and up the hill. When they emerged above the valley there were, spread below on the valley floor, a thousand head of grazing cattle. Their soft lowing blended into the sound of the sea's roar and the hum of bees hovering over a nearby field of clover. "It's like silence, this roar," Emmett said, inexplicably moved by this sound of his land.

"We take them to Oxnard to the slaughterhouse," Quinones said as they followed the rough road down the hill. Mounted vaqueros in leggings and chaps, with ropes curled over their saddle mounts, eyed Emmett cautiously as he and Quinones rode past. "In the old days there was a trade in hide and tallow; now the trade is in meat."

On the far side of the valley Emmett noticed two low hills that dipped down into a canyon, shimmering now in a pearly mist. The sight—and the smell of wild mint—made him think of a place in Amalfi. He stopped his horse and took out his notebook. Quinones stopped ahead and waited; a few vaqueros called to him, but he said nothing. A moment later Emmett rejoined him.

"I was just thinking that I'd like to build a footbridge between those two peaks there. People could walk from peak to peak, and avoid the valley altogether. Can you imagine the views?"

Quinones listened and nodded, but did not speak. Emmett finished writing and followed Quinones out of the valley and farther north to the vineyards: acres and acres of hillside land of deep blue-green leaves and plump purple grapes. "These grapes were imported from France," Quinones said.

Emmett nodded happily. "They look so familiar! I saw many vineyards in the South of France."

"They're shipped from here to the winery in the Santa Clara Valley," Quinones added.

Emmett nodded again and took out his notebook again. "What a perfect place for a cottage," he muttered. "With a terra cotta fountain lined in tile. I saw one in Morocco that's stuck in my mind all this time. I suppose I could import the tile myself, reconstruct the cottage right in this valley, right here, with the vineyards and the sea in the distance and..." He finished the sketch while Quinones watched impassively, then they rode farther north from the vineyards to the sheep camps in the hills, through fields of mustard, waist high, Emmett feeling he might be in Jerusalem: the golden color, the ancient smells, the sense of forever. I could be riding backwards in time, he thought.

The sun was white now, the land glaring and bleached to the bone. "What solitude," Emmett said as he looked at the shepherds on the hills. "What does a man become, I wonder, pared down to his essence like this?" The shepherds didn't approach Emmett or Quinones, but only stared from a distance. "It's just like Crete," Emmett said, "but exactly." He squinted and imagined Greek shepherds squeezing wine from a goatskin sack and tearing off hunks of bread for lunch. The only false note in the scene was hearing one shepherd call to another in Spanish. "I'd like to bring some poplars in, plant them up here. More cypress trees, too." He laughed. "We'll have the place looking like Greece pretty soon." He made some further notes in his book before they left. "Ought to have those shacks rebuilt," he said. "Some white plaster houses built into the side of the hills, maybe."

Quinones nodded impassively, still saying nothing, but he gripped the reins very hard; his small hands were white-knuckled under the burnished skin. But Emmett was effusive. "The Malibu just goes on and on and on, doesn't it?"

Quinones pointed to a low peak in the near distance. "That's the western border, that line of trees. And from there northwest to a configuration of bounders—"

"And who's on the other side?" Emmett asked. "Does the Malibu have neighbors?"

"Homesteaders," Quinones said with an impatient shrug.

"The way you say that word makes me think you don't like them."

Quinones looked away again; he did not like to be read. "We have worked things out over the years." He turned now to Emmett. "You must remember that it is the Malibu that stands between the homesteaders' land and the sea, between their land and the beach road to the Santa Monica and Los Angeles marketplaces."

Emmett squirmed in the saddle. "But you say you've worked things out?"

"For now," Quinones said, and Emmett was satisfied.

At the bottom of the hills where the sheep grazed were the set of pens where the shearing took place. The men there used small scythe-like razors to hack off the wool. The sheep struggled and cried out; blood from small nicks flew everywhere. After the shearing they were dropped into a steaming stream of sulphur and tobacco. Quinones noticed Emmett's repulsion. "It kills the parasites," he explained.

Emmett nodded. "Isn't there some other way that's less cruel?"

Quinones was surprised for the first time. "We do not sentimentalize our sheep."

They rode back along the beach without speaking until they got to Paradise Cove, where Emmett stopped. He seemed out of breath and pale, but Quinones did not ask him anything. Emmett reached into his coat pocket—more notes, Quinones thought—and took out two pills. After swallowing them dry and breathing deeply for a few moments, the color returned to his face. It was then that he took out the notebook.

"You know, I've had an idea for a small pier of my own. I'll be importing a lot of things from Europe, and it seems such a waste to have to bring everything to the one in Santa Monica, when we've got the perfect place right here." He looked around at the cove. In addition to having a deep, flat beach, it was secluded by an outcropping of rock and a reef that calmed the waters. "It's the only real possibility for one on the Malibu, despite what Mister Keller thought."

Quinones shrugged. "If you say so."

"Your opinion?" Emmett persisted.

"I have no opinion."

They started riding again, slower now, the pace set by Emmett and by a tug of silence that was finally acknowledged by both men. Emmett could not get Quinones's last words out of his mind.

"Have you worked on the Malibu for very long?" he asked.

Quinones's eyes looked straight ahead. "I grew up on the

Malibu. My father was foreman for Señor Keller. When he died I took over."

"I wondered how a man as young as you came to be foreman."

Quinones turned to Emmett, and regarded him coolly with pale, hooded eyes. "My father told me everything there was to know."

Emmett sensed a threat of some kind in the words. "I'm sure he did."

They continued in silence, and stopped only at the bottom of the hill that led to the house. "I really ought to learn Spanish," Emmett said. "Everywhere we rode today, the men looked at me with such suspicion. If I spoke their language, I suppose—"

"The life of a vaquero on the Malibu has not changed much in a hundred years," Quinones said abruptly. "Most of these men you saw are descendants of vaqueros who were themselves descendants of vaqueros, whose lineage can be traced to the first vaqueros of Alta California up from Mexico while the land was still under the rule of the Spanish king." He paused for a moment and looked at Emmett. "If I may be frank? The careful eye with which they watch you is that of a native viewing a foreign conqueror."

"But I have no intention of taking anything from them," Emmett said. "I paid a lot more money for the Malibu than I probably should have. I'm depending on you and the vaqueros to run it at a profit."

Quinones nodded, relieved at least to have elicited these words, but he could not help retain his doubts. He remembered too well all the stories his father had told him about gringos and their plans for the Malibu; never mind that Quinones was half gringo himself—it was something he wanted to forget, which he never forgot.

He left Emmett at the bottom of the hill, refusing an invitation to the house. Let the distance be kept.

They named the baby Cornelius Wilder Newcomb after Ada's mother; he was delivered in their bedroom by a Mexican midwife living in the vaquero camp. Emmett stood by Ada's side, and watched her nurse the infant. The light coming through the curtains of the room bathed Ada and Cornelius in a patina of gold. Bowls of red tulips stood by her bed.

"In Desideer," Ada whispered, "I'd be wading through dead leaves about this time of year, feeling for apples with my feet instead of having a roomful of cut flowers."

Through the open terrace doors they saw a bank of high clouds move across the sky. "I used to think clouds were God's breath made visible," Emmett said. "They still make me see things." He came and sat on the other side of the baby, and took Ada's hand. "You make me see things, too."

Ada shook her head and laughed, and looked down at the baby. "You embarrass me."

"I thought women liked compliments," Emmett said.

"Did your mother tell you that?" Ada asked, looking up at him, "or did you learn that during your famous trip to Europe?"

Emmett laughed too, and leaned forward. "Wait till you see what I've had built for you. A gazebo, just like one I saw in Sorrento. I don't think Señor Quinones approves. He'd like me to keep my hands off the place altogether."

"The Malibu belongs to you," Ada said.

"I'm not sure Quinones thinks so," Emmett said, and pressed Ada's hand to his lips, to his cheek. "What's really important is what our baby thinks of the Malibu." He put his finger in the baby's hand; the baby grabbed it and made a tiny peeping sound. "He's perfect, isn't he?" Emmett whispered.

Ada smiled lazily. The air was very still, the silence palpable as fine dust. "This day reminds me of August on the plains," she said. "Without the heat or those buzzing bugs. But that same . . . wholeness."

Ada felt wonderfully exhausted, her body aching with its own fullness. The baby beside her, all flailing arms and tiny clutching fingers, drew her and Emmett closer together; no longer simply man and woman, but mother and father; for the first time Ada felt they were truly related, bound for all time. The intimacy and joy of their physical union had been made tangible, alive. What peace, she thought, what peace.

Emmett held his breath: the sound of a bird, of a cow lowing; in the distance, the faint echoing beat of the sea. "I used to dream about a day like this," he said. He turned to Ada, tears in his eyes. "You know what we are? We're the Newcomb Family." His chest swelled with pride and wonder at the splendor and immensity of what was his. All of life seemed focused here in this room, on this ranch. "Oh Ada!" he cried. "Everything is so . . . so . . ."

"Isn't it?" she said as he gathered them both in his arms. "Isn't it just?"

Dear Ada:

This will be my last letter from Desideer before Sophie Simmons and I depart for Europe. The imminence of our trip has forced me to write. I have been putting it off for months. I am afraid I must convey a piece of distressing news. In your last letter you said you'd had no news of Obie since he left Desideer. Sad to tell, I am not surprised. On the day he left town, your brother "relieved" Zeb Schulsky, the haberdasher, of a suit of cowboy clothes, then pistol-whipped Zeb instead of paying. Zeb's got a big dent on the side of his head now, and two of the fingers of his right hand are useless. I convinced him Obie was heading for California to stay with you, so no criminal charges were pressed. My guess now is that he's scared, and ashamed to come to you. I don't know why that boy had to go and make such a mess, but without you around he just sort of went haywire. He read your letters asking him to come, and I urged him to go and see you, but he kept insisting that you didn't want him when you said you did. Can't teach sense to someone who doesn't have a natural feel for it.

"We are leaving for London the first of March—"

Ada crumpled the letter in her fist. Oh for God's sake, Obie, for God's sake! She brought the letter to Emmett in his upstairs study, stood at the terrace doors and watched the sea while he read. By the time he finished, she was sunk in the brine of guilt. "I left him when he needed me, and here's what happens, here's the result of my selfishness."

"But you had to leave Desideer for yourself," Emmett said reasonably, and did not add that he was part of her leaving too. "He knew that, didn't he?"

"Yes, yes," Ada said miserably. "I had to get out of there, but he probably thought I wanted to get away from him. I told him to come, I told him, but..." She paused, and turned her face back to the sea; she looked at Emmett and was calm again. "To tell the real truth, I was relieved to leave him there, relieved not to bring him along. There, that's the truth of it. As much as I told him to come, I was relieved that he stayed."

"They're both the truth, Ada," Emmett said.

She was pacing now from one end of the terrace to the

other, angry at Obie, and impatient with herself for that anger. How lonely he must have been, how scared. But just when everything in her life seemed balanced and holding steady, he had to throw himself, and everything else, too, so out of whack.

"I have to look for him," she said. "I have to bring him here."

"Could be he's on his way, maybe seeing the country first," Emmett suggested. "Not everyone is in the same rush to get here that we were."

Ada nodded, but had barely heard him. "How do you get in touch with someone when you don't know where they are?"

"An advertisement in the personal columns," Emmett said.

Ada stopped pacing and looked up, surprised at the good sense in this idea. "I could run an ad in the personal columns of the . . . hundred biggest newspapers in the country. He's bound to see one at some time, maybe not right away, but I'll keep running the ad. Some day he's bound to see it, and then . . ." She hesitated. "What should the ad say? I have to be very sure of the wording . . ." She closed her eyes to see Obie, to speak to him directly. She saw him coming toward the train the day she left; she opened her eyes to stop him.

"Dear Obie," she said. "All is forgiven. Please come home."

Chapter 11

As the months passed, Ada's confidence in herself and the real rightness of what she had done struck her again and again: Emmett, the baby, this ranch, all of it, so... she hesitated, even to herself, to think of it as "perfect." That was a word Emmett might use, and she knew he usually meant it to describe how something on the Malibu conformed to that grand dream of his. For her, the Malibu continued to remain out of her grasp. She would stand on the hill in front of the house and look at the sweep of beach, the swell of the ocean, or behind the house at the canyons, sculpted of light and stone and reaching, stretching into the distant mountains and disappearing in fog: and all of it the Malibu. The Malibu. But it was still too large, too insistently endless, to hold in her mind all at once. She had to reach for it herself, stretch herself out to encompass it all. "I've got the smallness of Desideer in me yet," she'd said to Emmett with a rueful twist of her mouth. As soon as she could leave Conny with one of the Mexican girls, she began to explore the Malibu on her own.

Ada took the buckboard down the winding hill from the house to the stream below, and spent the morning digging for clams where the creek pooled on the beach. She piled the clams into the buckboard, tied the horse to a tree in the shade, and walked upstream into the canyon to gather wild columbine and chokecherry for the house. At the end of an aisle of sycamores, just out of sight of the house, she saw another buckboard whose horse had just stopped near the stream.

So infrequent was the sight of another person on the Malibu, who was not from the vaquero camp, that Ada laughed aloud. The Malibu was many things, but it had not yet seemed like a place which invited chance meetings; at the very moment this one presented itself, Ada realized how she'd missed the company.

"Hello there!" Ada called, and set down her basket of wildflowers to walk on ahead.

A woman sat in the buckboard and nodded as Ada approached. "How do." She was dressed like a man, in a blue wash shirt, leather vest, and denim pants, and a battered old hat square on her head with a knot of rawhide under the chin. She put out her hand like a man might to a gent he was aiming to know. Her hand was dry and hard in Ada's. Above them the trees shifted in the breeze, a raven swooped and disappeared in the overhang.

"My land's just north of here," the woman said quickly, with an abrupt gesture of the head. "Back there, see, where that low ridge is."

"But then we're neighbors!" Ada said. "My husband and I have the Malibu."

"Mrs. Newcomb?" She inclined her head, then lifted it and looked up, past Ada at the Malibu, then back at her. "Well, I been hoping to meet you. Veeda Weller's m'name."

"I knew there were farms in back to the mountains," Ada said, "but the Malibu seemed too big to have such a cozy thing as a neighbor." The skin on the woman's face was weathered and aged, the lines scored deep by sun and wind. Ada raised a hand to her own face, wondering if this was what living out in the sunshine did. "I didn't expect to meet another woman out here," she said. "I can't get used to how big it all is." She gestured vaguely around her and smiled. "I come from a small town."

"We had a little farm outside Mason City, Iowa," the woman said. "Frosts eight feet deep lasting through March, so me and Mackie, my husband, built us a Conestoga wagon, and across the plains we come." She shook her head. "Can't hardly believe I'm the fool did that. All that loneliness, maybe a hoot of some animal you never got to see, lightning stabbing at the ground." She hugged her bony chest and squinted. "We was always being beat down by something or other. If it weren't a merciless, sharp-edged sun, it was the rain didn't stop for a week, or biting sand winds in the desert. Mackie had to shoot one of the horses once on account of its hooves going frostbit and useless."

As she spoke Ada was struck by the notion that she knew this woman; something so familiar... All the poor women in Desideer look like this, Ada thought, but that was not the cause for this uncomfortable sense of familiarity. There was even a slight resemblance to her own mother in the woman's narrow face... there, yes, that's it, that's it for sure. But there was something else, too, which she couldn't quite place.

"The Santa Monicas was as far as we could come," Veeda was saying. "'Cause by the time we got to the coast all the rancho land grants'd been made. 'Cept that back there. Agent told us we had water rights, good roads, and fertile soil. He didn't tell us the Indians already give it the name 'stone canyon'. Had us our little boy with us then, died in the Sierras on the way out. Can't have no more. Heard you had a little boy." She shrugged. "Some folks get what they want, some get what they deserve." Misery was splashed across her face, her features pinched tight against it. Ada said nothing now, shocked at how the woman's story had turned so suddenly bleak. "Mind if I just fill up my water bags?" At Ada's continued silence, she added, "Malibu Creek being on your property, is why I'm asking."

"Oh! Well... the water's free, of course. Please..." Ada gestured fussily, flustered, for the woman to take what she wanted.

Veeda nodded, and hauled the empty canvas bags down from the buckboard to the side of the stream, then stooped down and lowered one into the water. She looked back at Ada while it was filling.

Ada watched the woman for a moment longer, until Veeda's pained smile made her feel that her mute witness mocked the woman's work.

She wanted to say "I'm the same as you, I'm a girl from a town just like your town." But am I? Ada wondered. Am I any more that girl when I've got the Malibu?

She turned back to the way she'd come. "I'll be seeing you!" she called out to Veeda with forced heartiness.

Veeda looked up again with a squinty little smile. "I'm sure of it," she said. "We're neighbors, ain't we?"

Ada backed away, the pained self-conscious smile on her own face now. But the Malibu belongs to Emmett, she thought as she turned away. He's the one with the true connection: I'm still a visitor here.

Christmas of 1894 was celebrated on the Malibu with Clara Sweet and Avery Benson, and while Emmett showed Avery the stables, Ada took Clara on a tour of the house. "Most of the things come from Emmett's trip to Europe." Ada explained the antimacassars and Oriental rugs, the Victorian wicker, the divans, the large and exotically patterned and mirrored pillows, the straw chairs from the bazaars of Constantinople.

"Emmett's sister Elizabeth and her husband John sent this bed that Emmett kept stored in their attic," she said of the elaborate four-poster in their bedroom. "He actually slept on it in an inn in Amalfi." Ada was proud of what had been accomplished as she showed Clara along the gallery that ran alongside the garden. What had been in the Kellers' day a ramshackle series of dark, wandering rooms was now bright and airy. The living room opened onto a terraced dining room, and beyond that was the newly tiled kitchen, with harnesses of garlic and ropes of purple onion strung from the beams. Ada's pride was the garden. "I cut back most of what was dead," she told Clara, "trimmed the rest nearly to the roots, turned the soil over, and planted catalogue seeds, and then some bulbs. I'm just getting to understand how the weather works out here, and how to use sandy soil, and how much rain to expect, and how much fierce heat. Those Santa Ana winds are a disaster, aren't they? All the topsoil gets blown away; I've never seen anything like it! Emmett's almost finished building a redwood water tank on the roof, see, so we can water the garden even in the driest of dry spells. I even planted poinsettias—makes me feel like a real Californian. We eat oranges from our own groves, and sip wine from our own vineyards." As they wandered back into the house, Ada said, "I sometimes feel wicked here." She ran her fingers along the back of the tufted chaise longue. "All these beautiful rooms, all to ourselves. My whole house in Desideer would fit into our bedroom here."

They joined Avery and Emmett in the dining room decorated with gooseberry and red squaw bush that Emmett and Cornelius picked in the chaparral. Juniper mistletoe hung over the entrance. The two maids who had worked for Mrs. Keller served dinner. Ada cooked rose pudding, and made mint jelly and orange preserves from ingredients found on the Malibu.

"The turkey is the only thing on the table that didn't grow right here," Emmett said, expansive with the occasion.

Clara fed nuts to Cornelius, who sat on her lap. "I think this red squash matches your hair, Conny," she said.

"Oh, his hair'll turn brown any day now," Ada said. "I had red hair, myself, when I was three." She heard the tension in her throat, and went over to ruffle Cornelius's hair; it was just like Obie's, she couldn't help thinking, but exactly. She shivered, and went to the other side of the table. "We just got a Christmas package from Emmett's mother," she said. "Mittens for Cornelius, a scarf for Emmett, and a flannel nightdress for me."

"I wrote and told her last year that it was eighty-four degrees on Christmas Eve," Emmett said, "but she doesn't seem to believe Christmas is possible without cold hands."

Ada's mind drifted back to Desideer. Trees would be bare there now, a tenacious leaf or two still clinging to that old maple across the road from their house. And soon there'd be snow, if some hadn't fallen already. Early snow in Desideer gave the world two distinct sides: an upper side—branch tops, roofs, buckboard backs, horses' manes—covered in snow; and an underside—tree trunks, porches, horses' bellies—bare and cold till the deep winter winds whipped snow everywhere, and everything was white. Any spot of color after that—winter berries, the depthless maroon eyes of a roan mare, a man's red beard, Christmas candles in a country house window—was a surprise to the eye. Moonlight would turn the world blue, sunlight make it achingly white.

Emmett had spoken to her, and to his questioning look Ada said, "Oh I've just been thinking about Desideer. My home town," she added to Avery and Clara. "How I longed to leave it, how I wanted to get out and never see it again. And I suppose I never will. Not that there's much reason to go back. My brother Obie's long gone, haven't seen him in . . . my God, it's more than three years now. I keep expecting him to show up any day now, but . . ." She shivered a little, and wrapped her shawl around her shoulders.

"I think most of the people out here are far from where they started," Avery said.

"Every one of us is trying to dig in," Emmett said, then recounted his Christmas as an eight-year-old, a memory of candlelight, huge amounts of sweets and iced cakes, kisses from great-bosomed aunts who smelled of violets, and tipsy uncles who smelled of port.

Avery and Clara each told a Christmas memory in turn. Ada asked questions about Los Angeles: what were people doing in town, what new buildings had been built, and were there as many immigrants in the real estate offices and saloons on Spring Street.

She missed the excitement of the city, but more than that

she missed the opportunity for contact with other people. She had begun to get the strangest feeling lately, that she was drifting on the Malibu. Emmett was busy, the baby did not absorb her attention the way he had in his first two years. She thought of herself as she was in Desideer before Emmett came: wild, restless, yearning. She felt, in the face of that memory of herself, privileged and lazy. "If you've got an itch, scratch it," Cornelia used to say. Ada steeled herself, and made a silent promise.

Cornelius squatted at his father's feet. Emmett bent to pick him up; his hand felt immense and rough as a tree on the fine and delicate skin of his boy. Emmett was awed by the child, by how relentlessly present he was, how he changed and grew from day to day. It was as if Emmett's own movement into the future had been affirmed and assured.

Ada protested when Avery and Clara got ready to leave. "We get so few visitors," she said, but the drive back to Los Angeles was a long one; no matter that the night was warm and the sea breeze mild. Emmett excused himself, and went upstairs to put Cornelius to sleep while Ada walked out to the carriage with their guests.

"He certainly is his father's son," Clara said.

The night was very still, the moon so bright it drained everything of color, but the low stucco wall was washed a cheerful rose, its unbroken length studded now with pots of goldenrod and poinsettia; bougainvillea vines hung from its top like a fringed shawl thrown across a chair back.

And yet to Ada the whole picture seemed draped in sadness, even the beauty seemed sad to her. Christmas away from home, she thought, and thought again: but this is home.

"You ought to come to town and see for yourself what they're doing," Clara said. "Tearing down hills, damming up streams. Paving roads. Still more streetcar tracks, a new railroad depot grand as a cathedral."

"We've got to move our office next month," Avery said. "They're tearing down our building to make room for a new Hall of Records."

"Oh, you're lucky to have the Malibu," Clara said. "And I'm not the only one who envies you. Lots of talk going on in Los Angeles about the Malibu. With Santa Monica growing in leaps and bounds right to your borders, and that pier doing daily steamship business and bringing the whole world to

Southern California, instead of just the whole country, word is that these Newcombs of the Malibu bear watching."

"People are watching us?" Ada said. "Talking about us?"

"Here's a perfect example," Clara said. "There's a Mrs. Belanger—"

"Her husband's a client," Avery said. "I'm working with him on buying some acreage in the San Fernando Valley. Dry as a bone, but—"

"Yes, yes," Clara said dismissively. "Mrs. Belanger knows we know you, knows we've been out here to the Malibu, and how she pumped me for information! 'Mrs. Belanger,' I said, 'the well's run dry.' She told me she heard the house was a monstrosity, and how dare you snub her she wants to know."

"Snub her?" Ada said. "I don't even know the woman."

Clara shrugged. "Don't matter to her. 'As decadent as an oriental parlor,' she told me, and wanted to know if it was true you wore your hair loose, like an Indian. You've even been written up in the social pages of the Santa Monica *Chronicle*."

Emmett came outside in time to hear this.

"The last thing I want is to attract attention," he said. He looked south along the coast. The Santa Monica pier snaked out into the sea, the city's lights on with the sun gone down. "Maybe we ought to think about building a new house farther up the coast. Actually, I've already made a few sketches..."

"I don't think we have to worry about people bothering us," Ada said. "The Malibu is private property."

"You're right. I'm not going to worry." Emmett looked away from the pier. "If it bothers me, I'll turn my back and look north."

"I wonder how the Kellers are doing in Santa Fe," Ada said idly.

Avery and Clara mounted the carriage. Their horse's Christmas bells jangled loudly.

"Oh, I thought you must have heard," Clara said. "She died, poor thing."

Ada suddenly saw Mrs. Keller, long gray hair and pale skin, clutching her husband's arm that last day, and pleading with him to sell so they could get away from the Malibu. Oh, how she'd wanted to get away. Ada shuddered; this was not the time to hear such tidings.

"Poor thing," Clara said. "I don't think she ever even made it out of the state of California."

With mutual promises of return visits, Avery and Clara left. Emmett went into the house; Ada stayed outside and listened to the carriage going down the hills and out to the beach. She remembered how Mrs. Keller had looked that day the Malibu released her. Long after Avery and Clara had gone, Ada could still hear the faint jangle of the Christmas bells, a very small sound that went a very long way.

Obie rode a boxcar into Roline, Nebraska, on a cold night with a high, cow-brown night sky that bulged with snow. He left the train and took himself walking the town till he saw a poster for *An Adamless Eden*, Lily Clay's all-female company of lady artistes in exotic specialty dances and tableaux, depicting "The Greek Slave" and "In the Chamber-Maid's Chamber," performed nightly at the Crystal Pistol saloon. Since leaving Desideer Obie took women where he found them: on the train when they were alone and scared of the prairie blackness swimming on the other side of the glass; in saloons, a girl in a red satin dress for the silver in his pockets; once a mute girl in a wheat field, once a widow lady. For a while they took his mind off Ada, but after it was worse. Except it was thinking about Ada made him want to go after them all anyway. He was crazy about having a sweet pink hand running all over him.

The brown Nebraska sky threatened to fall apart. The streets were emptying fast, and soon Obie found himself bathed in the yellow light of the stage at the Crystal Pistol, applauding the "Sleepwalking Ballet of Madame Godiva." The next lady was introduced as the sensation of Tony Pastor's in New York City, "Miss Topsy Miles!" She stepped into the light. Obie stood up. She was wearing a dark red velvet dress with a green rose at the throat. She sang "Father, Dear Father, Your Little Girl's Crying." She walked across the stage; a pink leg shot out from a slash in the red velvet skirt. Obie was pulled back down in the seat, but he knew she'd seen him. Same big gray eyes as Ada, same pile of thick dark hair, same slow smile, like only I know it, like the one she give me just to me.

"... and each night she's crying, crying for you..."

Oh, Ada, you been lonely too, I know. I know, I always know, but it hurt me so when you left, that's all I could think about. Never thought how you didn't want to go, how you been missing me, crying for me.

"   . for tears shed alone at twilight   "

She stretched out on a pink divan, and rested her cheek on her hand, a pink leg bared through the slit in her gown. Her eyes passed Obie's, her lips came together—Obie gaped— she smiled, she pouted. She blotted a tear with a lace hanky, and poked it down her dress.

". . . and each night she's crying for youuuuuuu!"

He waited for her afterwards in the little mud room next to the stage; she walked out wearing the red dress, and came right to him.

"I seen you," she said. Taking his arm with a great laugh, she led him through the beaded curtains and onto the dance floor at the Crystal Pistol Saloon. The other artistes of *An Adamless Eden* disappeared for him.

"I love you," he said to Topsy; she murmured that she did, too, and buried her face in his shoulder. Obie let out a long stream of air that he'd been holding in since Ada left him. "You smell like apples," he whispered.

"Come to my room," she said into his ear.

Obie held on tight to her, his Gladstone bag stowed under his arm, frantic she might get away again. Snow had started to fall, powdering the raised wooden boards of the sidewalk. The snow made things sound like they were happening somewhere else.

They reached her room and brushed off the snow. She embraced him. "I'm all alone in the world," she said with a little pout, and sat on the bed to peel off her stockings. "Can you help me, please?"

He sprawled on her, pushed his mouth deep inside hers, talked the words out loud . . . I'm scared, Ada, I need you, Ada . . . you're with me . . . oh . . . oh . . .

He kept at her all night. "I love you. I love you," he said, each time he took her, until she rolled away to sleep. He watched the darkness fade into her flesh until the sun licked her back to rosy pink. When she awoke he took her again, then he slipped off the bed and, with great excitement, reached into his Gladstone and got into his Levi's and boots, placing one foot on the edge of a chair for her to admire.

"What do you think of that? One hundred per cent mule-ear leather. Got myself these brand new pair of Levi pants, too, copper rivets. Ain't they a peach? And a blue bandana, and chaps with a Cheyenne leg. First time I wore 'em all."

"You look pretty as a poster for a Wild West show, dearie," Topsy said lazily.

Obie ran the barrel of the Smith and Wesson under his nose, smelling the sharp clean smell of Benzo's Oil, the sleek metal like a sliver of ice drawn across his lip.

"Oh, this is a beaut, all right," he said. "Look, it's got a break-down hinge, see? Just flick it with your thumb, all six empties get kicked out the barrel. Man who invented it used it to commit suicide."

Topsy looked at the gun and stretched. "Seems like kind of a waste to have five more bullets."

Obie squinted at his reflection in the mirror and nodded his head slowly, his eyes meeting Topsy's in the mirror. He drew a bead with the pistol and it fired.

The bullet shattered the mirror; Obie's image trembled, Topsy bolted upright in bed. His gun was still drawn, eyes narrowed and mouth open wide as cracks broke out on the mirror, silver lines racing away from the bullet hole. One jagged piece near the bottom slid out, carrying an image of his hip and, in the background, her shoulder, then all the pieces on either side—a pale lip, a white knuckled hand, the edge of a window curtain—fell in a crackling heap on the floor. Neither Obie nor Topsy moved, as if the bullet were still alive in the room.

"You're a damn fool," she said finally and jumped from the bed to pick up her clothes.

"You got to have a sensitive touch," Obie said, frowning at the gun. "No, don't put your clothes on."

"We leave today for California, where it's sunshine all the time," she said, slipping her lace camisole over her head. "When they say 'all the time', do you think they mean to make us believe it's twenty-four hours a day?"

"But you don't have to go," Obie said. Topsy didn't answer, but Obie saw her haste.

"You're not leaving me here alone," he said. "No more of that. Either I'm going with you or you're staying here."

"*An Adamless Eden's* only got ladies, you fool," she said and looked out the window at the falling snow. "Going to like where there's sun all the time."

He felt something turn over inside. "You was never here with me like I was with you," he said in a low, accusing voice. "Haven't felt a thing for me all along. Here I been loving you and trusting you with my secrets—"

"It was a grand night, dearie!" Topsy said. "But it don't give you rights."

She was doing it again, it was happening all over again. "My sister's living out there in California," he said.

"Mm, I'd die for a blood relation," Topsy said. Fully dressed now, she gestured to the door. Obie stepped back from it, shaking his head.

"No."

Topsy pursed her lips, closed her eyes to be kissed. "Kiss me bye-bye, dearie."

The gun blew a streak of white light through her chest. She staggered like she'd been shoved back in a crowd, her eyes open in astonishment; hands clawing at the air, she bumped into the iron bedstead. A gurgling sound came from her throat, and she sank slowly to the mattress, to slide down, down the white chenille bedspread, a wide streak of blood to mark her descent.

Obie fell to his knees and slumped against the bed. His knee touched her upturned palm, and he leaped to his feet with a yelp. Oh, I done it now, he thought, I'm in for the full measure this time. He grabbed his Gladstone bag and quit the room fast, running into a blinding gray snowy morning on the plains that made the gunshot no more than a crack of lightning in the next county.

Never meant it, never did. And I never meant for to be wearing these clothes till I saw Ada. He followed the railroad tracks out of town, and crouched at the windsafe side of a boulder till the westbound Atchison, Topeka slowed for the curve, then jumped onto the heavy sliding door of a freight car, and crawled inside. The morning sky was bright with falling snow, flakes whirling up as the train passed by. He called out Ada's name; his voice sailed out across the plains. He was determined to follow its course: he'd shouted due west, and there he'd go.

Chapter 12

When Avery Benson moved his offices the following year, he sent out to the ranch the original deed and assessment for the Malibu. Ada brought them, along with the week's mail, down to the creek where Emmett was supervising the construction by three workmen of the second in a series of footbridges, copies of ones he'd seen in Sorrento. Two other men, from Sprague's Nursery in Santa Monica, were planting three-foot poplars in neat rows along the banks.

Emmett nodded at the papers, and handed them back to Ada. "I saw these when I signed the purchase agreement," he said, and turned his attention back to the bridge.

Back when they bought the ranch, all the legal ins and outs of the purchase had seemed irrelevant to her—indeed, neither her signature nor her presence had been required at the closing. Up until this moment of reading the documents, she had known nothing of their existence, much less their significance. She leaned back against a sycamore tree, read Avery's brief explanatory note and, astonishment mounting, went over the papers herself.

"Emmett!"

Cornelius, sitting on the stream bank, tossing pebbles and watching the water circles spread and disappear, turned at the sound of his mother's voice, and shielded his eyes from the sun to watch her.

"Did you know that it was actually through an error in a clerk's penmanship that the ranch came to be called Malibu at all? Malaba, Malabo, and suddenly Malibu. Look how that one error just gets continued on!"

"I hope using wood on these bridges is the right thing to do," Emmett was saying, half to himself, while the workers continued. "Stones are so heavy on the banks here, although..."

"Oh I didn't know this!" Ada exclaimed. "Keller's father bought the ranch from a woman! A Frenchman's widow. Her husband bought it from a Mexican immigrant and . . . let me see . . . he got it by applying for it as part of a royal Spanish land grant." She looked up, and was caught unexpectedly by

117

the staring green eyes of her son. Startled, she turned to Emmett. "It's like finding out about your ancestors," she said.

Emmett was concentrating on his original sketches of the bridge. "Mmmm, hmmmm."

Her eye caught Cornelius's again. "Don't stare like that, Conny," she said, a bit more abruptly than she meant to, but she couldn't bear the way he stared at her; those green eyes so like Obie's, that same needy stare.

Cornelius turned back to the stream; by leaning forward just a tiny bit, he could see his mother's and father's wavery reflections in the water.

Ada was looking at the documents again. "Wait a minute, wait a minute. Did you know how the original boundaries of the ranch were determined? By throwing a pile of stones to the ground as the starting point, then measuring the distance from that point to a point a man would reach by riding until sunset, sighting one natural landmark to another, orange groves to boulders to stream mouths to configurations of trees. For heaven's sake!"

Emmett looked up from his sketches, satisfied now and laughing. "That sounds all right to me. Orange groves to stream mouths. I like that. What about you, Conny?"

"I like that," Cornelius said to his father's reflection.

Ada was usually reassured by the bantering affection between her husband and her son, for it relieved her of the pressure to be to Cornelius what she sensed she could not be; though now, when they seemed to take sides against her, she was less amused.

"It's not very precise," Ada said.

"No, but it is colorful," Emmett said. "I like the spirit of it. It seems right for the Malibu."

"What if there were to be a dispute about a property line?"

He turned to her with a sigh. "Why is it so important to pin everything down? Nature isn't precise," he said with a wide gesture at the land around them. "It's untamed."

"But nature is absolutely precise," Ada said. "It's people who make a mess of things."

Emmett looked at his wonderful little bridge. "Are you trying to hurt my feelings?" he asked. "I haven't made a mess of anything."

"I didn't mean that you had," Ada said, impatient that he would not see the seriousness of her point.

"Then let's leave the borders as they are."

"But I don't want to change anything," Ada insisted. "All a border does is say that the land stops here, and—"

"You've got the markings on the deed. They've served just fine for two hundred years—"

"But that's just it," Ada said. "Two hundred years ago it may have been all right to stake the land out by riding till you dropped, but these are modern times, Emmett."

"We haven't had any troubles, Ada. I don't see why you're ringing the doomsday bell."

Ada sighed, and looked from the map in her hand out toward the beach. Him and his bridges! He would forget that the Malibu was real if she let him. But she would not let him. "You can see, even with the naked eye, how the stream pools closer to the canyon mouth than the map indicates," she said to Emmett. "The sea's been eating the shore away in the last two hundred years."

"Must be pretty hungry, eh, Conny?" Emmett said; he knew when his son was listening. Conny, pleased, nodded without turning around.

Ada saw she would get nowhere with him, and thought she would no longer try. "I'm going to measure the land," she said. "I won't bother you with it. I won't get in your way. I'm going to learn how to take readings with a compass and sextant and really see where our borders are."

"Just seems like months worth of unnecessary bother."

"I think I'll do more than just the borders," Ada continued. "I think I'll indicate the canyons, too. I don't even know the names of most of them."

"The pilings for the pier at Paradise Cove arrive next week in Santa Monica," Emmett said. "I've got to be there to supervise getting them across the beach. I've rented plough horses and drivers . . ."

"I don't need you for this," Ada said. "I'll ask Quinones. He proably knows the names of every rock and tree on the whole ranch."

Emmett sighed and shook his head. "He makes me feel like a visitor on my own place." He stepped onto the little bridge, testing his weight. "I don't want to know where the land stops," he said, a smile widening at the bridge's strength. "I like the idea of it just going on and on." He ran off the bridge and pulled Cornelius behind him, pointing with delight at the rows of young poplars wending their way along-

side the stream. Cornelius looked back at his mother, scowling,
and held tight to his father's hand.

"You know, I think I will use stones for the next one,"
Emmett said. "We'll reinforce the banks here. I remember a
stonecutter in Sorrento . . . if I can just remember his name . . ."

Ada watched him for another moment, impatience growing
in her. Would he never stop trying to alter the ranch, she
wondered. Did he ever see what was really there at all? Did
he even see her for what she really was? She thought of their
courtship, and how surprised he had been at some of her
behavior. But he'd fallen in love with me before he'd even
met me, fallen in love with my photograph! And now here he
is, building bridges and planting trees, reconstructing a dream
of a ranch on a ranch that already exists! And here am I, no
more than peripheral, no more—though no less—than a wife.
No, she thought, in my own estimation of myself I'm a lot
more than that.

After a few months of preparation, Ada set out to start the
measurements. The sea appeared calm that day, though enormous swells made it beat like a pulse on the shore. Two
brown sea lions brayed in the waves. Gulls soared overhead,
black against a whitish sky, white against the sea. Ada took a
deep breath, her long skirt hitched between her legs so she
could ride straddling, and made off up the shoreline. Saddlebags held lunch and notebooks; a compass was strapped to
the saddlehorn.

Her face was flushed with the excitement of going out on
her own; for the first time she would be putting her mark on
the land, or rather, delineating the deed's own markers that
made of a rambling piece of property a ranch called the
Malibu.

She passed, shortly, through Paradise Cove, where construction of the pier was in progress. Emmett was striding
back and forth in the surf between the first set of pilings and
huge stacks of lumber for the dock itself. He waved briefly to
her, but they did not speak; Ada knew he preferred that she
not measure the borders, and so she kept the project to
herself.

She was not pleased with his attitude, nor, she suspected,
was he pleased with hers, but this rift did not stop her. He
never told her not to do anything, nor would he ever, she was
sure of that. She was sure, too, that the rift was temporary;

he could not fail to see the benefits of her work once it was completed.

She stopped just past the cove to record the first reading and to mark a line between points in a roughed-out map. It would be a slow, painstaking process, and she knew she could not expect to cover much ground on any one day. But it did give her a chance to learn the Malibu, rock by rock, hill by hill, and that seemed at least as important as the border lines.

The first canyon she charted out was Zuma, where the vaquero camp was, north and west of the hill upon which the house stood, in a shallow valley behind the Zuma Beach grazing land. The canyon floor here was wide and flat, with room for a rough road and a small corral for horses, which gave out onto the pasture lands. Ada stopped her horse and simply gawked at the rows of simple white houses—shacks, really—almost a town in itself. Though she'd been here, it was a long time ago, when she first came to the Malibu and was given the grand tour.

She had not noticed the beauty before: the timelessness of the houses set into the hillsides, the bleached-out, ageless rocks and sand, so like Emmett's loving descriptions of similar settlements along Mediterranean hillsides. Nor had she noticed the squalor before, the poverty of the houses, the shabbiness of the people's clothing, the paltriness of their food and livestock. She had been a tourist before, had seen what a tourist sees, and no more.

Now, with her compass and notebooks, there was a purpose to her visit.

The women of the camp began to gather together as they noticed her. They stood in the harsh sunlight, wrapped in black shawls, long black skirts dusted gray at the hem, brushing bare, hard feet, regarding her with open suspicion and curiosity. Ada was determined to allay their suspicions, to befriend them.

She rode her horse a little closer to them. *"Buenos dias."*

The women looked at each other, Ada heard them muttering. They nodded as if by communal consent, but none made a move.

Ada essayed a smile and looked around her. *"Donde esta los niños?"* she asked, curious as to why there were so few children.

A ripple of interest and relief seemed to go through the assembled women at Ada's having spoken more than a greeting in Spanish; one woman detached herself from the rest, and beckoned her inside her home, away from the glare of the sun.

The door to the hut was wooden; goat hides hung across it. "*Bienvenidos*," the woman said.

As Ada entered the darkened interior, she was reminded of the original kitchen in Keller's house, but the simplicity of that kitchen had been due to neglect and the peculiarities of Mrs. Keller; the simplicities here were due to poverty, and there was no way Ada could overlook that.

The woman served Ada a cup of not very cool water, and gestured Ada to sit on the single stool. The only other hut furnishings were a primitive cot, covered with goat skins and a few coarse blankets, wooden utensils and clay plates and bowls on a shelf, and a small table. The air was dry and close with the smell of old cooking oil, though there was no hearth in the house.

"Where do you cook?" she asked in Spanish.

The woman laughed and wiped her face against the heat. "Outside," she said.

"And is there enough to eat?"

The woman shrugged. "Plenty of oranges from the groves . . . wheat . . . rice . . ."

"And clothes? Clothes for the children? And books?"

Again the woman shrugged.

Ada wondered if Emmett knew the extent of the poverty of these people, and decided he could not, not possibly, for he was too kind to know and do nothing about it. This, then, would be her part in the Malibu, for how could such beauty remain if such poorness was stamped so indelibly on the landscape?

"You make a list of things you need—anything you need— and I'll see to it that—" She stopped speaking when she saw the woman's rigid attention at the door.

Fernando Quinones appeared, slightly out of breath, poised expectantly, as if something needed immediate correction. There was a joke Ada had heard about Quinones from the maids that worked in her house: the man spent so much time in the saddle, he would walk a hundred yards to his horse in order to ride seventy-five yards back.

"La Señora is lost?" he said in a tone so formal that Ada lost the easy feeling of the joke.

She stood up, smiling at the woman. "La Señora is taking the measure of things," she said.

"Perhaps I can help," Quinones said impassively.

Ada couldn't tell what he was thinking, his face half-hidden under the shade of his wide-brimmed hat, and what she could see was an expression that came from a lifetime of squinting in the sun. He held open the door in an undeniable gesture for Ada to leave. Ada turned to the woman and took her hand. "I promise," she said, and strode past Quinones.

The other women of the camp, their children, and a few of the vaqueros were waiting outside. Ada paused for a moment, shading her eyes from the glare of the sun. One vaquero led her horse to her. Ada mounted, and could tell from the murmuring this provoked that they thought she had no business straddling it like a man; indeed, had no business being here at all.

Quinones emerged after her, mounted his horse, and drew it up to hers. "May I help you now?"

She regarded him with the same skepticism with which he regarded her; neither got the other to drop the gaze. Finally Quinones touched the brim of his hat in a gesture of *"adios,"* and backed his horse away from her. Ada turned, and started down the plain toward the beach, furious that she had let Quinones bully her into leaving the vaquero camp, determined still to do what she had promised. Emmett was right; Quinones made you feel like a visitor on your own land. But she had made a promise to those vaquero women, and she intended to keep it, sorry now only for Quinones's interference in what should have been a simple offer of aid.

By the time she reached the beach, he'd caught up to her, but Ada had no chance to accuse him, for he spoke even as he stopped. "What do you want from my people?" he demanded. "What kind of promises do you make to them?"

"Only ones I intend to keep, señor," Ada said.

"We are better off without promises," he said.

"Are you better off without sheets and blankets and dry goods, without proper clothes and books for the children of the camp?" she demanded.

"Let me . . ." Quinones hesitated before he continued. "Let me tell you something. The Indians once owned this land. But they were stupid, they believed promises that were made to them by the white friars in the missions."

"I thought the missions saved the Indians," Ada said.

Quinones smiled ruefully and shook his head. "With the blessing of the white man's god, the missions made slaves of the Indians. Used them like mules, for the strength of their backs. They ran to live in peace in the hills, but the mission padres said no, we must save your souls for Jesus. They worked in the padres' orange groves, they shoed the padres' horses and branded the padres' cattle, and slaughtered them too. They had never seen a cow until the missions came. They got diseases then, bad diseases. They died, thousands, thousands. Not many newborn. When the missions lost the land, the Indians lost everything. The old ways are over. Gringo whiskey finished them off good."

Ada shook her head when he was done, her anger spent. "My husband hasn't driven you off the Malibu. Your lives are the same as when the Kellers were here. He's kept his promise to you. And I'll do the same."

Quinones had an odd, pained expression on his face. "*Gracias, señora. Muchas gracias*, but . . . leave us alone." He tipped his hat, pulled his horse about, and was gone. Ada gripped the reins of her horse and pulled about too, furious at the way he had talked to her, at how he had refused her offer of aid—which she was determined to give despite him—at his lack of respect. But, as she rode back to the house, the expression of pain on his face kept appearing in her mind.

Obie crawled out the window and along the ledge until he could swing his legs down onto the next floor's outside stairs. He stopped for a moment to listen in the quiet to the thundering of his blood. The excitement and the terror was always like this, every single night since Ada left Desideer. There was no moon tonight and he was glad of it. He could never sleep in the dark anyway and now, since Topsy, there was the law that could see him in the day. Used to moving at night, he could keep a close eye on all dangerous possibilities.

A whole network of men were after him, he was sure of it. That hair oil salesman that spoke to him was Pinkerton for certain. That fella with the fake moustache kept too close an eye in that train station a few weeks back. Everyone had an eye on him, waiting to spring the trap. He had to get off the train in Sepulpa, Oklahoma, when he spotted the local sheriff talking to the conductor. He waited till folks were boarding the train, then stole a horse and lit out of town. He lived on the run, sleeping in dry creek beds, riding at night, holed up once in an abandoned farmhouse, sick with fever. Met the Kid on the western tail of the Panhandle, lucky.

Obie dropped onto the stairs below, gripped the handrail, and sidled down with a rhythmic scrape of his boots on the steps. He walked in the shadows toward the rooming house, didn't make a sound, his hand clamped on the bulge of bills in his pocket to show the Kid that he could pull his own, a worthy partner. Kid to the Kid; he picked up his pace. The Kid was waiting.

The Kid wasn't much older than Obie himself, but to hear what he'd done Obie would've thought he had to be thirty or more. "Been on my own since I was eight, made up my name, don't even know my born one no more, 'cause two gunmen came and killed the family. See this scar over my eye? Gunshot wound. They thought I was dead, too. Stole to get by. Had so many notches on my first gun I had to ditch it, it cut my aim." Obie met him in a whorehouse, and they buddied up quick, traded life stories. Obie never had a friend before, and told him all about Topsy even, the mistake of it, and how he had a price on him now, he guessed. They listened night after night for a month to each other's stories, eyes wide open in the dark of the rooming-house room; made it seem to Obie like there was a future waiting for him.

He didn't like those shadows moving in the shadows of the bank building across from the rooming house. Same shadows in the shadows as last night. Take this dough and go, he thought, take the Kid, take the dough and go. He edged his way out to the back stairs and along the walls of the halls to get to the room without being seen. The Kid was watching the streets through the window; there was a funny greenish light coming in through the curtains. The Kid looked startled to see him, and jumped away from the window like it was hot.

"You got it all so fast?" the Kid whispered; the scar across his eyebrow gave him a skeptical look. "You couldn't've got it all."

Obie was excited that the Kid doubted him, must be a fast take, he thought. He lifted his jacket to slip out the wad of bills. The Kid caught Obie's wrist before Obie could lower his jacket.

"Where'd you get the buckle?"

Obie shrugged; he was planning on keeping that for himself. "The guy was wearing it when I took the cash. I took it off him."

"How?"

Obie said nothing, but smiled slow; let the Kid's mind do some of the work.

The Kid froze. "You shot him?" He looked toward the window; he seemed to breathe the words in.

Obie swallowed hard, proud and flattered at the Kid's faith in him. "You really think I'd shoot him?"

"You're crazy," the Kid said and jumped to the bed to pull his boots on.

"Where we going?"

"You kill a guy, and you're asking that? I'm getting out of here!"

Obie watched him in silence for a moment. He started feeling a little dizzy.

The Kid peered at him in the dark. "You're really crazy, you know that? Killing a guy when the law's already after you."

Obie had a sick flame in his belly. "What do you know about it? I didn't say I killed him!"

The Kid tried a laugh that went nowhere, and edged away from Obie. "You said..." He came close to the door. "I got to go, Obie."

"Don't go call me by my name!" Obie whispered fiercely.

The Kid looked at the window again. "I got to go, I got to go."

Obie groaned. "Look at yourself. Scared of me, huh? I thought you knew all about this stuff! You talked like you was on shooting terms with Billy the Kid himself! Damnit, you're just another mean kid, that's all. Damn!" He dropped onto the bed and stared hard at the dark. He heard the Kid stuffing bills in his pants pockets, heard him shuffle away, stop at the door... deep breathing... and the door closed after him.

Obie was still for another minute, watching the dark move— another mean kid, oh damn, damn!—then lurched to the floor in front of the pale green window. He watched the Kid sidling away through the shadows like a snake, in and out of the light to the bank building across the way. Other shadows moved, a glint of a match being struck—a face!

Obie stood up, scared now. A dog howled. He touched his new belt buckle, and then the door behind him burst open.

Obie squinted, unused to light after nights and nights in the dark, and dropped to his knees at the side of the bed, but it was too late to disappear. There were two of them, all gunned up, and the Kid behind, sniffling, scared.

The cuffs were on him now, it was all over.

"Don't be mad at me, Obie," the Kid said.

Chapter 13

"Dear Mrs. Newcomb. In regard to the matter with which you have retained our services, we have the following to report. We have circulated the photograph of Mr. Obidiah Wilder (and are returning it forthwith, although copies exist in our central files in Chicago) to train conductors, hotel managers, boardinghouse keepers, law enforcement officers— all with little success, I am sorry to say. As you have indicated yourself, the photograph is not a recent one, and the subject may have altered his appearance considerably since it was taken. All avenues, of course, have not been pursued. It has been our practice to continue on a search for years, if necessary, though this decision ultimately rests with you. Of course, if Obidiah Wilder has done wrong, we will find him. 'A guilty conscience is a detective's best friend', as our founder was known to say. We await word from you as to our future participation in this case. (signed) Millard Lerner, for the Pinkerton Detective Agency."

Ada studied the photograph that was returned with the letter. It was the familiar silver nitrate print; a skinny fifteen-year-old in a tight black suit—his neck straining under his first Celluloid collar, hair slicked down—standing next to a dusty potted palm. He was still a boy in the photograph, and Ada thought he was probably taller than Emmett by now. Still skinny too, I'll bet, you'd want to give him a square meal. She had had only one letter from him in the seven years since he'd left Desideer, and this Pinkerton letter now only told her that his disappearance remained effective. Emmett liked to say that she'd just lost track of him, but whatever the words were, the situation was the same. How long does a boy stop off on his way to getting found again? The country was so big, there were so many ways to get lost.

She found her family in the garden, Emmett showing Cornelius his sketch for a cantilevered bridge over the twin peaks at Paradise Cove. "See, we strap water pipes underneath the bridge, and connect them to other pipes that lead to the creek, and then up to our water tank on the roof

Then, if we had to, we could irrigate the orange groves and water the cattle in those long spells without rain."

Ada squatted down next to them, the detective's letter in her hand. "Nothing." Emmett patted her hand encouragingly as Ada sighed. "I was just thinking how Obie and I used to be as children. Could I really have known him as well as I thought I did, if he could disappear this way?"

"Where's Uncle Obie?" Cornelius asked.

"Sailing the seven seas," Emmett said, and Cornelius laughed, then stopped, looking in the direction of the ocean, considering what seven of them might be.

Ada watched Emmett and Cornelius as she often did, feeling far away from them, the two lost from her in this particular kind of bantering that always excluded her, which left her as alone as she'd been back in Desideer.

"Is he coming here to see us?"

"Someday, sure," Emmett said.

"Can he ride a horse?" Cornelius asked.

"Yes, he was a good rider," Emmett said, "like you, Conny."

"Did he have his own horse?"

Emmett laughed. "Yes, but not until he was older than seven. Not until he was ten, isn't that right, Ada?"

Ada's eyes watched Cornelius consider this, and she turned to Emmett, conscious of the effort to control the anger in her voice. "Conny's hair never did change color like I thought it would. Just stayed that bright, bright red." Same skin as Obie's, too, she thought, so white it seemed to quiver. No California baby, his skin'd burn for sure without Ada's protection. "My brother never had his own horse," she said, the anger bursting through her control. "No horse, no nice house, no—" She thought of the boarding-house life he might be leading: a room with a bed and a chair, meals taken with strangers; she turned away, embarrassed now. "I'm going to keep running my advertisement in the personal columns. I know it's only a matter of patience. The right newspaper at the right time. Someone who knows him is bound to see it, even if Obie doesn't himself." She stopped, shook her head. "But does he have friends? Do people know him?" She held the photograph in front of her like a talisman that would produce her brother in the flesh if only the right person could set eyes on it. "There's really no reason why he shouldn't have come out here with us," Ada said. "I've never felt right about it."

"He'll come," Emmett said, and took her hand. "You'll see. Someday, when you least expect him."

"I used to think so," Ada said. She unfolded the letter and looked it over again. "If he'd just write, just write and tell me he's... Oh, his face that day we left Desideer ... like it'd burst through the skin... his eyes... I should have had them stop the train, and taken him with us right then and there. I turned away from him instead." As she looked at the photograph, one thought nagged at her: "But he knew we've come to California, he knows we live on a ranch called the Malibu." She crumpled the letter. "I just hate thinking he's dead. Oh, it's bad when someone won't let you make up to them."

She wrote a letter to Millard Lerner at the Pinkerton Agency and told him to continue the search. She would not be able to close the book on her past until she knew.

Ada moved the map out of their bedroom and onto the terrace, where she could spread it on the ground and work on all parts of it away from Emmett's disapproving eye. Until now, he had been polite about his lack of interest in her project, and she had no wish to provoke anything stronger. She continued taking compass measurements, increasing the lines on the map.

She felt stronger than she had in years, the notion of purpose drove her forward, and the purpose was one she came to believe in more and more strongly. Whereas Emmett saw the Malibu as a landscape upon which to recreate a dream of a Mediterranean paradise, Ada—as her map grew in detail and the borders became clearer and more precise—saw it for precisely what it was.

Her rides took her inland now, adjusting and readjusting her course, stopping, recording. Some days were so fog-drenched she had to put off the rides. At least two days of every week were spent on teaching Cornelius his lessons, three mornings the garden took her time, but the map on the terrace, she was sure, would be finished before the rains next winter. She arranged for bolts of cloth, boxes of books and linens and vegetable seeds to be sent to the vaquero camp. Word of thanks was conveyed through the women who worked at the house; no word at all from Quinones.

She made the final inland border line at the southwestern edge of the rancho by early autumn. The old deed indicated that the border was marked by a grove of sycamores and, yes, here they were, at the base of a grassy hill, tall, white-barked, their great leaves arching over an aisle of perfect stillness. Malibu creek ran nearby; Ada dismounted and drank the water, icy and shocking as prairie snow. A pair of tiny birds pecked at the leaves; a buff-colored rabbit hopped into the clearing, regarded her for a moment, still as stone, and hopped out. The sense of the mountains so near the sycamore grove was nearly overwhelming; Ada was fascinated with the power of such dominance. A warm breeze blew across the valley with the scent of brine and clover.

She walked the horse through the trees, and as she entered the compass readings in her book, a buckboard appeared at the far end of the aisle. A voice called out to her, and an arm was raised in salute. Ada remounted her horse, and rode on to what she now realized was the end of her property line, and stopped a few feet from the buckboard. It was occupied by a woman and a child. The child was six or seven, no older than Cornelius, and shy, sloe-eyed, wearing a dress closer to a rag.

"Morning," the woman said.

"Morning," Ada said.

"Name's Cassie Hinderman. Me and my husband just bought this piece of land back here."

"A new neighbor," Ada said. "I'm Ada Newcomb. Where are you from?"

"We started out in the state of Michigan," the woman said.

"Michigan! I'm from Michigan!" Ada exclaimed. "You ever hear of Desideer on the Orenoke River? It's near Cashman."

The woman nodded though she seemed too tired to be surprised. "We used to have cousins in Cashman. Owned a tavern near the mill. Name of Farnsworth."

Ada laughed and put out her hand again. "We know lots of people in Cashman come down on the riverboat to Desideer. Isn't this something? Isn't it?" She turned and looked back across the canyon floor to the rising hills of the rancho, golden now in the sun, the sky feathered with high thin clouds; she was suddenly very happy. "Living out in Michigan is sure a sorry memory when you've seen this."

"The past's the past," Cassie said.

"I'm Phoebe!" the little girl shouted.

"I've got a little boy about your age, Phoebe," Ada said. The child's stare was so intense, Ada was disconcerted.

"Never mind her," Cassie said to Ada. "Her shyness gets her. She don't see that many people one day to the next."

Ada once again had that disturbing sense of something familiar she'd had when she met Veeda Weller. What if Emmett had never come to Desideer? she thought. What if I'd just gone and taken that steamship downriver or the railroad across country and met another man, a poor man? A farmer, let's say, who'd heard about the golden land of California. I was ready for it, I would've come with him, and that could've been me, she thought, her eyes on Cassie, or Veeda, or any of those women homesteading behind the Malibu. A hard, mean life; struggle, accommodation.

"I could bring my little boy here, and you could have a playmate, Phoebe. Would you like that?" The child continued to stare.

Cassie looked down at her and sighed. "Oh, she's lonely all right. So hard to get her to see the other homesteader brats. I can't teach her much neither, don't know more'n the abc's myself. Can't be trekking out every day to take her into Santa Monica. Wouldn't, even if I could. I get the idea they're not partial to canyon brats in the city. But I heard there's a teacher who comes visiting and gives lessons."

"When she comes," Ada said. "If she does."

"Does she manage to reach all the kids?"

Ada shook her head. "I've been giving my boy lessons myself," she said.

"One teacher, coming once a month—*not* coming once a month—can't do much," Cassie said.

"I'm a teacher," Ada blurted out, though she never expected to hear herself say these words again. "I mean, I was. Back in Desideer. And . . . there must be a dozen or more children back there. And the vaquero children, and . . ." Here was a chance to right all the wrongs forced upon her by Dr. Blaisdell and the church elders and the church ladies of Desideer who adhered so rigidly to an outmoded idea of education. Here was a chance to teach the way she wanted to teach, to encourage freedom of thought in her students.

"I've always wanted to have another school," she said, "providing it could be the right kind of school, provided I could teach the way I wanted to."

Certainly Cornelius would need schooling soon, and it was a chance for him to be around other children. She knew what a life without playmates could be like. And it'll get me going, too, something worthwhile for me to do and do right this time. She was getting excited about the idea, and prepared a speech to present to Emmett.

Cassie pulled her head back and stared at Ada as if she were measuring her. "I'm curious about something," Cassie said. "How is it a woman like you wants to be a schoolmarm?"

"A woman like me?"

"A woman whose husband owns the Malibu Ranch," Cassie explained. "Seems like teaching school's the very thing a woman gets married to get out of doing."

Ada shook her head, remembering how she had had to humble herself in Desideer to keep her job. It'd be different now; it'd be hers and hers alone.

"I know what you mean," Ada said. "But I never had the chance to do it right before. I think it'll be different on the Malibu."

"Hope so," Cassie said.

She turned away from Cassie, looking at the sweep of the canyon floor to the hills of the rancho. "You can't really own something like land, can you?" she said, half to herself. "You just sort of make a bargain with it and the land is ... like a silent partner. There's no real proprietorship, I don't care what the deed says." She laughed and looked at Cassie. "Or what my map says, either."

Ada felt ashamed again of the Malibu's plenty. Having grown up with so little, she could not be unaware of the discrepancy. She was determined now to prove herself worthy of this beneficence, to pass her luck on to those who needed it.

"I want them to learn as much as they need to be independent," she told Emmett. "To have their minds open."

"You'd better not tell their parents all this," Emmett warned. "I'm only half-joking, too."

Ada shook her head. "That's the way it was in Desideer. But it'll be different here. There's no First Methodist Church to get in the way, no righteous Reverend Dr. Blaisdell for the parents to be afraid of."

"That's true," Emmett said.

"I want the vaquero children to come, too. It doesn't seem fair to have strangers come and not—"

"I've kept on every vaquero and his family that worked for

Keller," Emmett said. "And probably a whole lot more than that just came on the ranch when they heard there was a new owner from the East who was bone ignorant about running the place. No reason I should provide an education for their children."

"You still have fantasies of a completely unspoiled land, don't you?" Ada chided. "Malibu Primeval."

"I prefer the Age of Romanticism, actually," Emmett replied.

"You'd like it if no one ever set foot on the place, wouldn't you?"

"Well, what if I do? No, Ada, I'm not joking either. I hate the sight of trespassing. Wagon tracks, campfire remains."

"They're mostly tourists who don't realize this is private property," Ada said, and Emmett grunted his assent. "Cornelius needs the companionship," she added.

"You said that already," Emmett replied. "Where were you planning on building this school?"

"I hadn't . . . well, I suppose near the spot I met Cassie at today. It's almost at the very edge of the Malibu."

Emmett nodded. "As long as they won't have to cross my ranch to get to it."

"Your ranch?" Ada said. "Or ours?"

The Malibu Pier at Paradise Cove, finally completed, was two hundred yards of pier pilings and wooden slats jutting straight out into the ocean, surrounded by masses of floating fan-shaped red seaweed. It was dwarfed by the mile-and-a-half-long pier at Santa Monica, just down the coast—visible on a clear day from the end of the Malibu pier—but, as was Emmett's original plan, it enabled smaller ships to come directly to the Malibu. "Ultimately," he told Ada, "we'll be self-sufficient."

On the day the first steamer arrived with a cargo of tiles and a species of Bolivian tree for transplanting, Emmett arrived at the pier with Cornelius, and together they watched the steamer dock.

"I said you could have your own horse when you were eight," Emmett said.

"I'll never be eight," Cornelius said.

"Oh, yes you will. And then nine, and then ten, and then twenty and thirty. You know what you are, Conny? You're the future of the Malibu. Do you know what that means?"

"That I get a horse when I'm eight?"

Emmett laughed. "That's right. And someday the Malibu is going to belong to you. All the beach and the hills and the pier here and—"

"And all the horses?"

Emmett took the boy's hand. "I want to show you something," he said, and they walked onto the pier toward the cargo steamer. "How old did you say you were?"

Cornelius looked up at his father; didn't he know? "Seven."

"Sure you're not eight?"

They stopped on the pier just as a gangway was being lowered from the deck cargo section. Emmett felt the tug of Cornelius's hand as the horse appeared on deck, a two-year-old Argentine mare, dappled gray and brown with a fine black mane.

Emmett knelt down next to Cornelius and held him while the horse was led down the gangway by one of the vaqueros. The boy's body under his hands felt like a bird trying to fly. "Happy birthday, Son," Emmett said.

Cornelius broke free of his father's hold and ran to the horse; the horse lowered her head, and Cornelius ran his fingers through her mane and down her nose. Emmett came up behind him, and took the reins from the vaquero to lead the horse off the pier and onto the beach, where another vaquero stood in wait with a new saddle. When the horse was ready, Emmett mounted, and pulled Cornelius up in front of him, and they started to ride. The morning fog lifted all along the coast. The beach stretched down the coast to Santa Monica—a wink of the city and the pier—and for miles and miles up the coast to Ventura County.

"The Ocean of Peace, sweetheart," Emmett said and rode the surf line with his son and felt anew the boundlessness of it, the earth's subtle curve, the sky a deep, soft gray against the crisp metallic sea.

They were on the beach, a few miles from the house, when Emmett felt that familiar bottomless sinking in his stomach, the dizzying sensation of falling through himself. He managed to stop the horse and tie the reins to a root growing out of the side of the hill, then slide to the sand. "A little rest," he said to Cornelius. "Find some seashells for momma."

Cornelius looked at his father; he wanted to laugh, pull his father up. But he walked toward the water, murmuring to himself. "She hates seashells."

Emmett tried to breathe evenly. His pills were back in the

house. He'd been well for so long, so long. Oh hell! Blackness poured in waves at the edges of his vision—was Conny safe at the sea's edge? Conny!—he dragged himself to a sitting position, and tumbled backwards endlessly, endlessly. Roads appeared in his mind, roads splintering into more roads, downhill, down, downhill to a bridge over a lake, the lake was black and glassy—it cracked! He was riding across the lake, but it was a field of tall grass, and then not a field at all but sky, endless sky above the sea, and the pounding beat of his blood in the ocean.

When he opened his eyes the shadow from the hill had turned the skin on his hands purple. He took a deep painless breath.

"Conny!"

The horse was nudging him in the back. Emmett looked up; Cornelius was astride her. Emmett had never seen the boy's eyes so green, the green of the sea. Emmett stood up slowly, feeling the life in himself again; he hugged his son, glad the future was alive.

Dr. Theobald Rowe, tall and narrow as a stork, his neck liberally splashed with heat rash, was impassive during the examination. His office on Ocean Avenue in Santa Monica was on the top floor of an elaborate Victorian rooming house, and gave out onto the Arcadia Hotel; during the whole time Dr. Rowe probed and pondered, Emmett kept his eyes on a young woman in the outdoor restaurant below, swirling a parasol and looking quite ridiculous and dear.

"I'm aging just like my father!" he'd told Ada with a rueful laugh, but there was more to it that he didn't tell her. The medicines he bought did no good—no medicines had ever had a lasting effect—but now he was no longer convinced of the health benefits of California. Damn it! There were days of bright sunshine in which he hoped he would never have to leave his morning bed. Spirit's the thing that counts, he told himself and told himself again and again, but a voice deep inside—the spirit itself?—announced with alarming regularity that the spirit was nearly useless in this new land where body was all. The books that had been such boon companions to him in his youth had left him with a pointless residue of dreams and desires. What are the simplest things? he wanted to know now. How can I make anything truly mine? How may

I possess one thing, one thing I can touch, one that will live forever?

Dr. Rowe concluded the examination; to Emmett's questioning look he said, "It's more than simple fatigue. I think you know that."

The girl with the parasol threw her head back and laughed. "I had rheumatic fever as a child," Emmett said, "pneumonia twice, not to mention . . . oh, what does it matter? What can I do about it now? Anything?"

Dr. Rowe shrugged and turned his back to lay down his stethoscope; there was no use arguing when the patient was right, his slumped shoulders seemed to be saying. "Do you sleep well?"

"Sleep? Well . . ." Emmett looked out the window again; the girl was sipping a soda.

Dr. Rowe was murmuring, stooped over a case filled with bottles. "You say you've tried nearly all of these?" he said, and then rose, a bottle in the palm of his hand as if conjured there. "Sudorific? Ah, yes. Promotes sound sleep, made of crawley root and pleurisy root, lobelia and skunk cabbage." He bestowed the bottle upon Emmett with a smile of encouragement, then burrowed among the bottles again, emerging with another. "Nerval nerve powder?" he asked, and nodded happily. "Skullcap, valerian, catnip, cayenne, and coriander. Mix it myself. Tranquilizes irritable nerves without deadening the sensibilities."

Emmett pulled down his cuffs clean from his coat sleeves, and forced himself to look away from the girl. He put the two bottles in his coat without looking at them. "I'll take them," he said.

"You couldn't be in a better place," Dr. Rowe said. "Sunshine and fresh air are your best medicines. Breathe, that's the best of them all. Breathe in the sea air, and go on about your business."

"Doctor, I've lived by the sea for the past eight years."

Dr. Rowe looked away, embarrassed and ashamed now. "There's nothing else to do, really. But you have time, certainly . . ."

Emmett remembered the first view from the hilltop in Cannes, the seeds of his dream. He could see the rainbow on the sea spray as it was then, smell the sun on his flesh, feel the sand cool and silken through his fingers, red and yellow flowers and tall grass blowing in the wind. "It's difficult to

plan for the future when..." He did not finish, but thanked
Dr. Rowe, took a last look at the girl in the restaurant, and
left with a small bow that reminded him of the ones he used
to make at the conclusion of the dancing school sessions he'd
been to as a boy.

As he rode back to the ranch along the shore, his vision
went inward to a time when the future was still a series of
infinite possibilities. There would be sunshine and clear air,
skies by Raphael, sheep whitening grassy slopes, mission
bells and olive branches, pomegranates and figs, walks in
waist-high wheat, carriage rides along the shore at dusk, a
simple life without this storm of emotional details. He thought
of his Boston childhood, a city boy's beginnings, days
remembered as dark—walnut-paneled walls and staircases,
mahogany furniture, and that great looming mantelpiece of
amber marble set against deep red walls, the fireplace like a
yawning mouth dabbing itself politely with a brass peacock
grate, damask drapes covering linen liners over shutters on
the windows so that no light entered to fade the carpet or
illuminate the dust; his own room a fortress of books and
carved oak dressers, a massive bed imported from Frazier's in
England; and hushed tones, polite speech, table manners,
and decorum at the expense of deep breaths and high color;
and so much darkness, so little space even outside the house
but the park on the flat of Beacon Hill, a neat square of trees
and houses next to his own, and on all four sides of this park a
limited horizon, the sky only a square of blue or gray directly
overhead.

He climbed the hill to the house slowly, relishing each
revelation of late afternoon sun on the land, and finally
on the sea, rising, rising. He'd never known, until the
Malibu, what it was to live where the horizon soared to
the edge and spilled over the visible curve of the earth.
I don't want to lose it, he thought, but how can I hold
on?

"How do the eucalyptus trees live without water?" Ada
wondered aloud when Emmett joined her on the bedroom
terrace. "You'd think they'd have to live on their own tissues,
and eat themselves up."

Emmett put his arms around her and held her for a
moment. This is real, he thought, and turned his head out to
see the ocean. The sun was split by orange and purple clouds
flattening out in sharp rippling reflection on the ocean.

"Master of all I survey, isn't that so?" he asked, and Ada murmured that of course it was so. "I love you," he said, and they both watched the ocean until the sun sank and the colors grayed.

Part 4

An age employed in edging steel
Can no poetic raptures feel...
No shaded stream, no quiet grove
Can this fantastic century move.

—Philip Freneau

Chapter 14

Ada picked the site for the school building at the edge of the sycamore grove where she'd met Cassie Hinderman. It seemed sentimentally appropriate and aesthetically pleasing, nestling in the shade of two ancient sycamore trees. In its proximity to the border it was convenient for the homesteader children who would be her students, and close enough to Zuma Canyon to let the children of the vaquero camp come, too. And it would satisfy Emmett's desire to keep people from trampling across the ranch.

Emmett had kept himself absent while the schoolhouse was being built; it was clear to Ada from the first that, though she might get no further opposition to her plans, neither would she get any help. And it's all right, she thought, as she watched the schoolhouse being built near the sycamore grove; it makes it mine all the more, mine for sure and no one else's. For even now the memory of her days as a schoolteacher in Desideer was enough to make her face burn with shame and frustration. She was determined that this be different.

A half-hour before the children would arrive for their first day of school, Ada opened the double doors of her new schoolroom and regarded it critically for a moment, comparing it with that first classroom in Desideer. The room was a simple rectangle with tall windows and doors which would remain open in most weather so the children would never feel the restricting confinement of the classroom. There were no traditional desks or benches; instead, Ada sketched to her own design wide octagonal tables, sturdy enough to withstand a child's rambunctiousness yet light enough in weight for two four-year-olds to carry across the room. Each child had a wide bench of his own. There were a series of small washstands along one side of the room, and space for each of two dozen pupils to keep his own soap. Cupboards filled with materials of learning and play were ranged along the two long walls; an aquarium stood on top of one, potted plants from Ada's garden on others. Blackboards were hung low enough for a three-year-old to reach, and no pictures would be hung

143

on the walls that had not been selected by Ada and the children themselves. There was even a baby grand piano in the corner.

Much of the school day would be spent outdoors: the children would each have a four-foot-square plot of garden to tend, each to grow flowers and vegetables. Ada would play music to them as they dug in the earth. For rainy afternoons there was a wood stove and cords of oak and buckthorn, reminiscent of those in the old Desideer classroom.

She would achieve harmony here, she felt; her life—schoolroom to schoolroom—seemed suddenly complete. Yes, I was right to do this, right to oppose Emmett and insist, because now I belong on the Malibu, too. I've made my place.

Standing at the doorway, looking out at the sycamores and waiting for the children, Ada thought how far she'd come, thought of Obie, lost to her now. The memory of his face continued to pain her, but the pain had dulled. She wondered from time to time if she had indeed betrayed him in some way, but she could not answer the question; doubt was her punishment. His presence was closer now in this classroom than anywhere else on the Malibu.

She moved quickly to arrange the room for her pupils: music sheets placed on the piano, lesson books in neat piles in the corners. The walls would be covered with the children's own pictures. She started to write on the slate the lesson she had never been allowed to finish in Desideer—"heard melodies are sweet..."—when the doors behind her opened, and she paused, chalk in hand.

"But those unheard are sweeter," Quinones said.

Ada looked out the window; his horse stood alone. "You didn't bring the children of your camp," she said, and thought he's as stubborn as I am.

Quinones shook his head. "They will learn what they need in the camp and on the Malibu."

"But you had an education, didn't you?"

Quinones looked out the door as if he would leave that moment but turned back to her. "Not in a school. I learned everything on the Malibu."

"Not your English," Ada persisted. "Someone had to teach you English. You speak it too well."

Again he looked out at the plains that would take him back; Ada knew she had struck a responsive chord. The muscles in his jaw were clenched; Ada wondered for a moment if she had better not know any more of his life, but Quinones had begun to speak, and her doubts were realized in what he said.

"I tell you this because you might hear it in rumor, and I would rather you know the truth of it from me. Also, it will tell you why I don't bring the children." He continued quickly, as if to stop Ada's response. "Mrs. Keller was very lonely when she came out here with Mr. Keller. Los Angeles in those days was a small town a long way off, and no roads to speak of. Santa Monica was a few bathhouses on the beach. On the ranch was just her and her husband and the vaqueros. Mr. Keller was busy, naturally, and Mrs. Keller turned to the vaquero camp for companionship. She learned Spanish, spoke it fluently. My father even taught her some Spanish songs. They became lovers, I was born." His shrug said it was inevitable. "My father was too good a foreman to let go. Easier to sacrifice a disloyal wife. Keller let my father raise me. Mrs. Keller had to sneak away to see me. Keller knew, he let her sneak off. It was... it is over, at any rate."

So this explains the pain in his face, this is the reason for his sorrow. And his anger, Ada thought. She wanted to speak, but an apology would be an insult, sympathy a sop to her own guilt. "Maybe someday..."

His pale eyes were hard as pebbles. "I want nothing you can give me, señora. I told you so you would know the truth and ask no more questions. Just let us do our jobs..." He started to go, and Ada moved swiftly to the door to block his way.

"You're not being fair," Ada declared hotly, angry at being misunderstood. "Haven't I kept my part of the bargain? Didn't I do everything I promised to do?"

Quinones stopped and nodded. "You have been generous, yes. But there is one thing you cannot do, señora." He turned to her and touched his hat in a gesture of *adios*. "You cannot give me back the Malibu."

Before she had time to reply to what he'd said, the children began arriving: on horseback and mule, in wagons and one-horse carriages: Cornelius himself on his Argentine mare, Cassie Hinderman's Phoebe in her buckboard, Lemuel Diebenthrop, Noah Prescott, the Bass twins, Nell and Luisa Smith, the Woodley boys, Bobby Hart, Rebecca Lockridge, and Johnny Small.

Quinones mounted his horse and rode off across the plain. Ada watched him for a long moment; the irony of their respective positions was not as easy for her to accept as Quinones might have thought, for it was a situation that would never, could never be amended. It was not in the realm of possibility for him to get satisfaction.

But the children were squealing for attention; the day began and Quinones's claim was put aside.

It had been particularly dry the year before, and this year was not much wetter; the last year of the last decade of the nineteenth century might prove to be the most parched in Southern California history. The Italianate fountain Emmett had had sent from Fiorrenzi and reassembled in the garden was reduced to sputters, and finally drained. His plans for an artificial miniature Lake Como were put aside indefinitely, though tiles to line its bottom continued to arrive in crates at the Malibu Pier. Though the fortune inherited from his father was large, Emmett knew it would not last indefinitely. Yet he continued to spend it as if it would.

With the tiles imported from Morocco, and marble brought in from Carrara, plantings brought from North Africa and olive trees from Jerusalem, Emmett was constructing a duplicate—with minor amendations—of a cottage he remembered from the hills of Positano, this one to be in the hills north of the house they lived in, with a view of the sheep flocks. The finished cottage was to be a surprise for Ada, and he asked her not to visit the site until the construction was complete.

Emmett planned a series of cottages at various places on the Malibu: one at the vineyards, another on Point Dume, another on the beach below Paradise Cove. In the final selection of sites he rode across the beach and up the coast, into the canyons, taking trails he had not traveled for months; the settings had to be just right.

Signs of trespassing were distressingly frequent, all the more so since the lack of rain seemed to have made the evidence more serious: fires were an ever-present danger. He followed wagon-wheel ruts across pasture land, saw orange trees prematurely picked. One day, on the approach to the crevasse that led into Bieule canyon, he saw buzzards flying in slow circles above and ahead. They scattered at the sound and sight of Emmett riding in. Emmett followed them into the canyon, where the birds shuddered in midair and returned to where they had been. He followed deeper into the canyon, the terrain nearly impassable. His horse stopped, skittish and nervous, and Emmett saw the reason. On the ground a few feet away, the decapitated body of a cow lay in sand drenched black with blood. The head sat on a rock a few feet away, flies crawling from the eye-sockets. The carcass had been hacked and trimmed and skinned, and the skin lay drying in the sun, the charred remains of a campfire nearby.

The vultures hovered; Emmett felt the heat of their flutter. One perched brazenly on the bones, and pecked. Emmett dismounted and threw a rock. The bird shuddered and rose again.

He walked his horse further into the canyon: another cow hide, another, a pile of them. He stopped at a gulch deep in shadow and peered down, then scooped up a fistful of scrub brush, set a match to it, and threw it into the dark: the bones of a dozen more cows became visible, shreds of black meat still on the bone.

When questioned, Quinones was surprised at Emmett's shock, and said he knew all about it. "Travelers, maybe, or hunters, thieves, homesteaders." He shrugged elaborately. "I cannot say for sure. But it was the custom in the old days that if a passerby killed a cow for food, he only had to leave the hide."

"This isn't the old days," Emmett said. "I want it stopped."

"The señor doesn't understand the realities of the situation," Quinones said. "It is an unspoken agreement—"

"I understand enough," Emmett said. "Cattle killed, campfires left burning in this drought. One piece of trespassing at a time doesn't seem too awful, but this is different . . . all of this together . . . it feels dangerous." He shook his head. "I want you to keep people off the Malibu. Tell it to the vaqueros. Tell everyone. The Malibu is private property. I don't have to put up with this kind of disrespect."

Quinones nodded. "There will be trouble."

Emmett laughed mirthlessly. "There's trouble already."

I went across the river and I lay down to sleep/When I woke up with the shackles on my feet.

Ever hear that song, Ada? The men sing it here all the time. The window of my cell is a square of yellow on the wall. Leg irons clank in the cell next door, but I keep my back to

it. Rather get it that way, surprised by a coward for the boots
on my feet, than have to look at anything in this hole.

He ran in place for hours at a time in the winter, wringing
his hands to keep them warm. His mind emptied out, he ran
himself into a trance, away from the jail and the cold, but
then he would stop and it would all happen again, the slow
unfolding of events, like a dream he couldn't awaken from no
matter how hard he ran.

Prisoners curled up around the bars to keep close to the
wood-burning stove. Two boys froze to the bars; guards had
to hack off their hands to get the bodies out.

Dear Ada... though I know I will never send this letter
nor even write it down. Nothing to write on but old newspapers used for wiping up the muck. I am whispering my letter
to you in the dark, sister Ada. I hope you are listening with
your heart, Ada. That is the thing that keeps me going. If
they ever find out I shot Topsy, that is the end of Obie. But
Ada, see, shooting her was like breaking through a wall of
noise, put up my gun hand and everything got still.

He grew lean and close to the bone; there was no excess on
him, not even his real name; he dreamed of his guns in their
holster, a moneybelt strapped inside, a tight pair of gloves,
nothing that couldn't be run with or dropped.

"What you in for?"
"Five years."
"What'd you do?"
"Trusted a mean kid."
"That ain't no crime, bub."
"I took something from a guy."
"Oh, a thief, huh? Coulda fooled me."
"Oh yeah?"
"I thought you was a killer."

The stench in the prison rose high and rank in the spring
thaw. The cell floors turned sticky and foul with streams of
human waste. Obie set his body hard to the task of physical
toughness. No one on the outside knew just how lean and
hard and mean he could get. Whenever thoughts of Ada
made him edgy and fixing to bust, he ran up and down for an

hour, the other prisoners jeering at him—but hell, he thought, we're all crazy here—and he laughed right back at them. If he ever got out of this place, he wanted to be ready for anything. And wouldn't that Boston dude of a husband like to meet up with a down-to-the-bone boy like me? He was determined to rid his body of soft spots; be a sight different coming out than I was coming in, for sure.

Obie heard talk about Butch and Sundance and Jesse and Jim Colter and Bill Bonney until he was sick of hearing about dead people's lives.

I'm thinking about a woman I knew. Oh, she's so sweet, she has the nicest curve to her back and so warm between the legs, so much moving, I can just hold on and go. Oh, Ada it's bad I'm bad to be doing this what I done, what I do here, oh Ada you forgive me, huh? Ada? You forgive me?

There was a newspaper at his knee, yellowed edges, the Kansas City *Star* two years old. He knelt, it tore, the words grabbed out at him.

—Obie, all is forgiven. Please come home.—

The dust motes on the very air stopped floating, he could see beyond the cell across the plains and out to the west, half expecting to see Ada coming toward him, and he peered through the window, but there was only the yard and the shadows and the smell of himself.

Imagine it, a message from her broke right through this wall of world surrounding me. His fingers pulled at his lip. He was shaking.

—Obie, all is forgiven. Please come home.—

"Getting hanged a week come Thursday. You?"
"Never."
"Stay here? Ruther die."
"Someone's waiting for me outside."
"You ain't got no one waiting."
"Yeah. Someone."
"In hell, more'n likely."
"No. California."

*   *   *

Your husband keeps you there and keeps me away, for sure
as shooting he don't want me there seeing how he holds you
there, knowing I'd tell you the truth. Don't have to take but
one look at that puss of his to know I am one boy sorely and
surely in the way.

Ada kept him company, encouraging him, singing to him,
running her cool hands on his face, whispering secrets in his
ears, making him laugh. There was only one home, and that
was with Ada. He kept a picture of her alive in his mind, and
apologized a hundred times for what he did to that girl. Ada'd
forgive him, no worrying that.

She was like the north point of a compass; he knew that, no
matter how many years he stayed away from her, he'd go to
her some day, and so he had a goal: no matter how long he
sat, he was always on his way to Ada.

Her advertisement fell apart, he had only his memory of
it—All is forgiven. Please come home. He saw her saying the
words. Please come home.

He looked up at the small cell window: a square of bleed-
ing red.

We couldn't have gone west together, Ada. But I'll come on
alone now. I'll make it all OK. Break out, head west. The
mystery stranger in the white hat is coming to stay.

Chapter 15

The sea was wide and low this evening, the beach narrow; waves began their heave in sonorous motion, and swelled, ending with a brutal smash. Ada, in silver satin that seemed sculpted out of moonlight, and Emmett, in midnight blue cutaway and high white collar, were skimming along the shore road in their Tilbury gig on the last evening of eighteen hundred and ninety-nine. Their destination lay veiled in mist: the Pier Hotel in Santa Monica, and the Chamber of Commerce banquet that would ring in the bells of the new century. And what a century it promised to be! Wages for the average worker were up to twenty-two cents an hour. The newly invented horseless carriage sold for fifteen hundred dollars. Seventeen out of every thousand people owned a telephone. New York was the most populated state; California, less than a hundred years old, was twenty-first. Life expectancy for the average American was forty-seven years; for the average Californian, fifty. Californians were optimistic and self-confident to the extreme: they did not simply hope for the best, they assumed its imminence. If a man didn't prosper, they insisted, it could only be out of sheer perversity.

Ada ran her fingers lightly, repeatedly over the folds of satin; she had not been dressed so extravagantly since her wedding in Miss Harriette's heirloom gown, but tonight's was her own, made for her, and she'd laughed when she'd put it on earlier this evening, thinking of what the church ladies of Desideer would make of so much shoulder exposed, of such grandness.

"It's a perfect night," she said.

Emmett turned to look back at the Malibu: pale blue in the mist, a gauzy gardenia-colored moon rising behind the mountains. The house lights were on; Emmett pictured Cornelius as they'd left him, his books ranged around him on his bed, his watercolors on his bedside table at the ready, head leaning on the pillow, his eyes drowsy. He turned back to Ada.

"I can't believe you really want to meet these Chamber of

Commerce people," Emmett said. "All they do is mimic other so-called civic leaders, in Boston or New York. And all *they* do is imitate their counterparts in Europe."

"I don't want to know the terrible ones," Ada said. "I want to know the extraordinary ones."

"Well, it's understandable," Emmett said, half to himself. "You're speaking from lack of experience. But I—".

"I never claimed to be a woman of the world. I went from Desideer, Michigan, population eight hundred and five, to the Malibu Ranch, population three, including Cornelius." Ada was a bit exasperated at his attitude. From the moment they'd received their invitation he had not wanted to go; now, on their way, he continued to oppose her and her idea.

"Ada, a senator and his wife lived next door to us in Boston. I grew up with their children, ate dinner with them a hundred times. You can't talk with your mouth full, or reach for something if it means showing your shirt cuff."

"This isn't Boston," Ada replied, feeling she had to defend these people she had yet to meet. "A new society is bound to create new kinds of behavior."

"Just as arbitrary as the old ones, I'm sure."

"For God's sake, Emmett, I don't get off the Malibu from one month to the next, and now you act as though I'm a social butterfly!" She had not meant for her temper to explode this way, but her patience with his isolationism was running short tonight. Usually she did not mind, but tonight she would not stand for it. She held her head steady, refused to look at him, to see his expression, whether fierce or shamed or stolid.

The Pier Hotel loomed at them suddenly out of the evening mist. Built on pilings, and jutting out over the sea, it was a monument to Victorian excess, resembling, from the perspective of the beach, the feverishly decorated birthday cake of a spoiled Bavarian prince. Just before he'd have to take the carriage underneath the hotel, Emmett turned it up the beach and into the line-up of carriages on the pier itself. There were sleek phaetons with fringed canopies, high-topped country wagons, open stages with decorated side panels, whitechapel carts with black oilcloth bonnets, landaulets, and a French vis-à-vis, plus dozens of snorting, steaming, pawing horses and the grooms whose job it was to keep the beasts watered and serene. There was even a brand new custom-built automobile, choking and sputtering and sending out billows of smoke.

"As long as we're here, Emmett..."

Emmett nodded, and took her elbow in his hand to guide her. "As long as we're here," he replied, and they left their modest Tilbury gig and entered the hotel.

On the main floor was a reception parlor and the hotel office, a small dining room for the public, and the ladies' billiard room. Directly opposite the entrance was the gilt elevator, which Ada and Emmett rode to the sixth and top floor. The hum of distant thunder became the chatter of many human voices, and, as Ada and Emmett stepped off the elevator into the salon, the noise became a din. The guests for the evening's celebration had congregated here, doffing cloaks and top hats, before taking the stroll down the hallway into the banquet hall. There being no private rooms to accommodate the ladies, a great deal of rearranging was being done in public, and movement was much restricted. Each gentleman was given a boutonniere whose ribbon bore the words "a new century" in gilt letters; each lady bore a corsage about her wrist.

"Buy oil, land and grain," a man said to his companion. "Sell pigs and cows quick!" The liquor business, to hear one fellow tell another, was reeling; pharmaceuticals flourished. Ada heard someone's aunt from somewhere say that if she wanted darkies she'd just as soon stay home in Macon, where at least they spoke English—"of a kind," the lady added.

"It's just like the parties I've read about on the Santa Monica *Chronicle*'s social pages," Ada said.

A woman waved happily at them as she approached. "The Malibu people!" she exclaimed. She wore a watered silk dress as padded as a horsehair sofa, heightening the resemblance with generous lace bibbing on the bosom. Her face was broad and ruddy with strong horizontal lines; though long past her girlish prime, girlish curls poked down over her forehead.

"And they said you wouldn't come!"

"Who did?" Ada asked.

The woman shook her finger. "I'll never tell!" she piped and shook her head. "I'm Augusta Washburton," she said breathlessly. "Mister Washburton is with the Chamber of Commerce and I'm with Mr. Washburton."

"Ada and Emmett Newcomb," Emmett said with an ironic bow that Ada could see delighted Mrs. Washburton; he certainly remembers the way to do this, Ada thought.

"Let me take you to the dining room," Mrs. Washburton said. "We're at the same table, you see, and I've been appointed unofficial guide." She took them each by the arm, and walked them down a hallway lined with enormous terra cotta umbrella stands, antler coat racks, tusk and hide divans. "Have you both read *Ramona?*" she asked as they walked. "I consider it a civic duty to get people to read it. You feel you've stepped into the past. And so many people think California hasn't got one. Mmm. Spanish boys with olive skin and black curls. Chapels and devout priests. Cows and sheep, ancient oaks. I've followed the mission trail myself. It stretches along the coast for hundreds of miles. Strung out like a rosary."

Ada nodded; she remembered Chester Puhls using the same words to sell them on the Malibu.

The banquet room was lit with a series of ivory candles in wall sconces, and brass sticks on each table. There were fifty tables, at least, each seating a dozen or so. "Six hundred of our finest citizens," Mrs. Washburton said.

The decor was an uneasy combination of the machine-made furbelows and fripperies of the French style of the 1850's and the ponderous, puritanical Elizabethan oak made popular by the Centennial Exposition. An uncertain match to begin with, the room was further internationalized by stamped Spanish leather walls and a Southern Plate rail which ringed the room two-thirds of the way up the wall with rows of platters, plates, steins, pitchers, and bric-a-brac. Over each table hung a German leaded glass lamp.

"The decorator makes annual trips to Europe," Mrs. Washburton said, indicating the room, "and adds."

The decorator had also installed huge stained-glass windows that looked out onto the sea; as the sun sank, shafts of color careened across the room and provided the guests with an illuminated vision of a pre-Raphaelite damsel in a swoon over the pierced heart of a stag, whose lower anatomy was turning human.

"Ladies and gentlemen?" Mrs. Washburton said querulously as they approached their table. "May I present Mr. and Mrs. Emmett Newcomb? Of the Malibu Ranch?" The other guests at the table turned to look, embarrassed and surprised, as if they'd been interrupted in their gossip of us, Ada thought. Mr. Morris Lynes, circulation manager of the Los Angles *Times*, looked to Ada like a precocious boy despite the cosmetic aging of a bearish beard, combed from the center outward like a matched set of unfurled flags, and a somber, ill-fitting suit of black serge. Phillip Washburton, their guide's husband, was on his right, the vice-chairman of the Santa Monica Chamber of Commerce; he smiled quickly, proud of his expensive new dentures, Ada could see. "Santa Monica welcomes you!" he piped. Next to him were Senator and Mrs. Buford White. The senator was pale and small-chinned; his wife wore egret feathers in her hair. Ada thought she looked mean and silly. The senator rose, bowed, and, when Ada and Emmett sat down, resumed his own seat. Interrupted in conversation with Mr. Washburton, he now turned back to him. "My question is whether the whole state of California is worth the five million dollars it would take to build a new harbor in Santa Monica!"

Mr. Washburton, as civic spokesman, visibly reddened but his voice remained cool. "I think you'll see here tonight just how worthy our state's worthiest are."

The senator's wife fussed with her face as the egret feathers besieged her from above. "Brillat-Savarin," she said in an adenoidal voice for all to hear, "declared that the number of guests at a dinner table should always be even, but we've got lucky seven and one empty chair."

Mrs. Washburton leaned across Mr. Washburton to address the senator's wife, indicating the Newcombs. "These folks here have got the right idea. Instead of living in the city, like the rest of the diehards, they live out on the beach. They've got that Malibu Ranch we've all heard so much about, isn't that right, folks?" Before Ada or Emmett had a chance to reply, Mr. Washburton was already blustering.

"Well, nothing wrong with the city that a little ocean air won't cure," he said. "That's why Santa Monica's thriving so. A city on the beach."

"I think the major curse of the city is too many invalids," Mrs. White said. "Whenever I get out of my carriage during this visit to your city, I'm reminded of Lourdes. Don't you agree, Mrs. Washburton? Mrs. Newcomb? Don't you think of Lourdes?"

Mrs. Washburton smiled cheerfully. "Oh yes! Absolutely!" she said, much to her husband's chagrin.

Ada shrugged. "I've never been abroad, so I couldn't say."

"Never been?" Mrs. White raised her eyebrows to the senator. "They come here to die," she went on, ignoring Ada, "And that's not a very good face for Santa Monica to show, is it? I'd like to know who all these people are."

"Immigrants, transients, and foreigners," Mr. Washburton said with a dismissing wave of his hand.

"Don't get me started on foreigners," Mrs. White said. "You learn a few words of their language, to be pleasant, and they think you're making fun of them! The Mexicans, the Chinese, oh my Lord, how do you stand it? I heard of a group of Polish people who live here communally. Can you imagine the kind of settlers they attract with that kind of gypsy behavior? One of them is an actress, Madame Modjeska. Quite famous in Poland, I've heard."

Ada opened her mouth to speak, but thought better of what she might say, and simply smiled at the senator again and hoped the man had enough sense to ignore his own wife.

The table was set with three plates per person, two forks, three spoons, two knives, a crystal tumbler and two wine glasses, napkin rings, butter balls, casters, a cut-glass rest for every knife, finger bowls with doilies beneath, a horn spoon in the open salt cellar, and an epergne of fruit at each end of the table. Dinner was served at that moment, though a chair at their table remained unoccupied.

"Most of the indigestion of today started with the Puritans, who allowed no laughter at their tables," Mrs. White said. "Our meals should be scenes of uninterrupted merriment. Bright conversation," she added, "is the best of all sauces. Brillat-Savarin again. And a good supply of that is worth a hundred delicacies."

There was a flurry of interest, muted murmurs of delight as the food was served, and a quick succession of safe conversational topics raised, saluted, and summarily passed on until another, equally benign, took its place. Much of the conversation was the news and gossip of the day: Belle Starr, did Ada know? had been shot by her own son after she'd whipped him for riding her favorite horse without her sayso; had Ada read *Welcome to Whistlewood*, the new novel by Bessie Joan Taylor, this one a tender saga of a young woman's love for a Canadian mounted policeman after she and her baby have been stranded in the snow near his cabin in the north woods: "breathtaking in a very adult manner," was Mrs. Washburton's cautionary recommendation; also the hazards of elevator travel, which Ada had already seen satirized in *The Wasp*; the Mexican problem and the Indian problem. Various health cures were bandied about over raw oysters, succeeded by great literature over chops *macedoine*. Mrs. Washburton piped *A Bird in A Gilded Cage* for the senator's wife's personal delectation over chicken zephyre with peas.

"My mother once told me," Mrs. White declared, "that the reason table manners were invented was to deflect attention from eating. Chewing was always thought to be vulgar, you see. Inevitable, I suppose, but vulgar. Bared teeth and grinding jaws..."

"Some of my own acquaintances chew their food endlessly," Mrs. Washburton said to Mrs. White. "I find it not real refined."

But for the lavishness of the banquet hall and the extravagance of their clothes, these people could have been the good citizens of Desideer, Michigan; certainly their conversation and opinions seemed to Ada no less petty and contrived. She looked at Emmett with an expression of mock despair: and the evening had just begun.

She was about to suggest they leave soon when there was a rustle of activity at the dais, and the diners' attention went to the man who had assumed the position of dominance merely by standing up at the center of the long table. Ada shifted in her chair to see past Senator White. The speaker, in his tight-fitting tails and starched shirtfront, was of a robustness which Ada thought age would graduate to imposing. A clear reading of his features was thwarted by muttonchops and moustaches balletic in their twists and curves. His eyes raked the diners with an expression Ada saw was at once impatient and amused, and the crowd ceased to speak. Ada settled herself comfortably; something told her that this man might be worth listening to.

"N. F. Gass," Mrs. Washburton whispered.

The man so named cleared his throat, smiled at various people and began. "The survival of Southern California is our goal," he said in stentorian tones, "the goal of all us new Californians." He indicated with a quick movement of his eyes the others at the dais table and those hundreds at other tables around the banquet hall. "Railroad men like myself, newspaper publishers, oil magnates, real estate lords, investors in grape vineyards, owners of herds of cattle and sheep, bankers, lawyers, journalists, merchants. This is America's last frontier. This is where America'll attain her greatness, I promise you." Ada had heard this kind of latter-day boosterism, but this man, this N. F. Gass, seemed to be taking personal credit for the vision.

"Things are starting to move West, instead of the other way around. California's the future. You write down those words, and tell me in a hundred years time if I wasn't right."

"That's called progress," Mr. Washburton whispered to Senator White.

"If tearing up the land for personal profit is your idea of progress," Ada remarked drily.

Mr. Washburton glanced sharply at Emmett. "Your wife, sir!"

N. F. continued. "There never has been a really great city without access to water. Look at New York and Chicago. It's true all through history. Look at the British, look at the Greeks. Much as we all love Santa Monica, good weather alone can't make a city great. We've seen what can happen when prosperity runs amok, we've seen the dark side of the moon..."

Oh, this speech again, Ada thought, disappointed in its lack of originality. Surely everyone in the room knew Southern California's recent history; they're the ones who've made it, for God's sake! she thought.

By 1899, ten years after the boom, real estate offices—co-printers with the railroads of the very books and brochures that had once littered Emmett's sick bed—stood empty, painted names chipped from the windows. Properties that once changed ownership doubling and tripling in value were distinguished now by swooning fences dividing one plot of sand from another. Hundreds put their money into a new city called Fertile Plains of Eden, which turned out to be a thousand acres of yucca, cactus, and scrub brush smack on the desert wall. Fancifully named towns like Morocco, Ramona, and Ivanhoe stood empty, bizarre sign posts of broken deals and dashed hopes. Ada had heard a story which, true or not, had come to symbolize the end: A young bachelor disappears from the Hotel McWilliams; when a child-faced woman and a pale-faced child come for his belongings, the lurid, familiar story comes to light: desertion, swindle, wild hopes and folly, and a drunken desperate dive from the tower of Hazard's Pavilion. In other versions, household treasures were peddled to pay court fees on border disputes; or sons and daughters were impressed into domestic service and worse to meet mortgage demands on land their parents couldn't live on and couldn't resell. Fantasies of paradise and quick profits were shattered, ground underfoot, and blown out to sea.

Salesmen, once roused from beds to show land by lantern light, slept till noon. The solution to the problem of Southern California's future was suspended like an alchemist's formula, one ingredient shy of the real thing, for the land was stripped of illusion, no longer golden but parched.

"Whole blocks in the downtown of Santa Monica are available," N. F. was saying. "All a man's got to do is build on the corner, and the block's his. The Whitworth block alone's got the Jackson Hotel, the first Methodist Church and Gillooley's Pharmaceuticals." Ada had heard this, too; the descriptions of eucalyptus trees lining Ocean Avenue, Oregon Avenue's recent pavement, and the fountains on the circular crest of the railroad depot.

While he spoke, Ada looked at N. F. Gass. He was obviously pleased with himself, a hint of a smile at the corners of his mouth giving away a mocking superciliousness toward everyone in the hall. Ada doubted he took anyone's opinion as seriously as he took his own.

"'Course, most important of all, as far as the future of Santa Monica and the whole southern coast is concerned, would be the harbor," N. F. was saying. "I believe so strongly in Santa Monica's future..."—And here he paused for dramatic effect—"...that I built this new pier and this very hotel out of my own pocket. Now, any town that can call up that kind of faith deserves Federal support, wouldn't you say?"

An outburst of enthusiastic applause greeted N. F. How people love to be told how brave and grand they are, Ada thought. She sat with her hands clutched in her lap. The arrogance of the man! She watched him as he left the dais amidst much handshaking and backslapping. His color was very high; this attention excites him, Ada thought, and thought it vulgar to court and flatter people the way he did. He made his way past the dais and, for an uncomfortable moment, Ada thought he was coming directly at her, but he veered just slightly, and ended up behind the empty chair at their table.

"Wonderful, N. F., grand," Mr. Washburton said.

Senator White nodded without much enthusiasm. "Can't deny the town's got a future."

Introductions of the dinner guests were made, and N. F. nodded once in a sweep of the table. Ada noticed a flicker of interest when his eyes met hers, a hesitation to pass her by as quickly as he did the others. Why me and not the senator, she wondered. Emmett, she saw, noticed nothing, sandwiched between Mrs. Washburton and Mrs. White; his boredom was embarrassingly apparent.

N. F. Gass was served all the courses he'd missed, while the rest of the guests waited. Ada felt no impatience, too amazed that he commanded such power. It was this power which had built the hotel they ate in now, and the pier on which it stood.

Though his manners might be atrocious, he ate quickly and efficiently: food is simply fuel to him, Ada thought. She watched him nodding, and listening, and looking with sardonic amusement, as if he thought everyone assembled here was a fool. I won't have him look at me like that; she could not refrain from attempting to wipe that expression from his face. "Mr. Gass. Since you're president of the South Central Railroad and chairman of the board of the North Pacific Steamship Company, both of whose terminals would be on this new harbor, isn't it true that you'd control all the trade on land and sea between Southern California and the rest of the world?"

"Mrs. Newcomb!" Mr. Washburton exclaimed.

N. F. Gass shushed him, and nodded to the others at the table to assure them he was in command of the situation. "I admit I have more than a little to gain by this good deed of mine," he said. "Still, everyone in Santa Monica's bound to get his share, too."

"You mean, the men who've bought Southern California and pay to keep her going have no intention of letting anything mess up their plans."

N. F. leaned back and drew deeply on his cigar, sending smoke billowing around his head, then sat up straight and shooed the smoke. "Remember Los Angeles years ago?" he demanded. "That little pipsqueak of a place? Railroad made Los Angeles, same as the harbor'll make Santa Monica."

Ada shook her head. "I think it's your own future you're talking about, Mr. Gass. Not California's."

He drew on his cigar again, and returned the headshake. "Never trust a man who doesn't have his own interests at heart. But in this case they're one and the same. I've never tried to hide that. Wouldn't be possible. We've locked destinies, me and California."

"In that case," Ada said. "Pity poor California." She stood

up, and walked alone across the floor and through the stained-glass doors, outside onto the balcony cantilevered over the sea. Her heart was pounding. She felt her face and shoulders flushed.

A moment later there were footsteps behind her. "My compliments on a provocative exit." Ada turned to see N. F. Gass standing in the doorway; she looked beyond him, but his bulk blocked her view. She wished she had something to cover her bare shoulders. "Your husband's gotten himself into a conversation about Europe and the Malibu's future."

Ada nodded. "We've had that conversation ourselves."

"Social occasions like this can be pretty tiresome," N. F. said, and Ada found herself unaccountably laughing in recognition. N. F. nodded at her through a veil of cigar smoke. "Women don't usually speak their minds the way you did in there."

"My husband's embarrassed by me, I'm sure."

N. F. smiled. "I'm sure he's no such thing."

Ada shrugged. "I'm from a small town in the Midwest," she said, "and I have no manners."

"You do all right, " N. F. said, and laughed. "All the first Mrs. Gass understood was how to make me look good by consistently spending as much of my money as she could in the shortest time possible on the best stuff that was available to buy. I am not joking, either. I married the woman for her skill at it."

"Women have different things on their minds than men," Ada said. "But I don't know as I'd take that as a sign of their capabilities."

"'All men are created equal,'" N. F. said. "Nothing about what all women are created like."

Ada shrugged. "I think if women mattered to you, you might understand them better."

"Like you, for example?"

"Me?" Ada turned away; she knew he shouldn't have said that, that she shouldn't let him. The conversation was barreling away from her.

As if to dispel any notion of impropriety, N. F. looked out to the sea. Below them on the beach, workmen were setting up the midnight fireworks display. "You know what the history of our country is? Someone getting there first. We're a frontier people basically, isn't that so? Didn't you come out to California because it was less touched than any place you knew?"

"My reasons for coming here are personal and complicated," Ada said, feeling herself more in control by this reticence.

"Complications are apt to slow you down."

"What's the point in moving forward just for the sake of it?" Ada said.

"Why, it's the natural order of things. A man wants to make his mark. If you lie still long enough, you could get buried alive!"

Her heart was pounding again and she hesitated, not trusting herself to speak. N. F. drew deeply on his cigar and regarded her for a moment in silence. "I could use your cooperation on something."

She looked at him closely. "What could I possibly do for you?" She had the urge to pull the cigar from his mouth.

"I'm determined to make Santa Monica a world harbor. But it's taking the government a darned long time to make up its mind who to give their money to. How opinions do waffle when money's at stake! A government inspector comes out and looks things over and he reports that San Pedro is the clear choice for the harbor. Another one comes and says the same thing about Santa Monica or Redondo Beach." He turned to Ada now. "What do you think ought to be done?"

"What does my opinion matter?" Ada asked, wondering how their conversation had veered in this direction. "I have no influence on the government's decision."

"You think not?" he leaned toward her, and laughed in his throat. "We've got tracks all the way down the coast from San Francisco, and all the way up from San Diego. Our natural aim is to have them meet in Santa Monica. You can see how desirable a connection that would be. How it would make Santa Monica's getting that five-million-dollar harbor an inevitability? If the South Central can guarantee the government a rail line clear down the coast, that would be just the thing to tip the scale in our favor. And all that stands in our way is a twenty-five-mile strip of beach called the Malibu."

Ada felt she stood on the edge of something dangerous and vividly colored. "You want to run railroad tracks along the Malibu?"

"There are millions of dollars at stake. The five million is just the beginning. You'd share in them, of course. Don't be too hasty in your response."

The flush left her face and neck; she looked down at her

satin gown, feeling overdressed and absurd. "You think I'm as big a fool as everyone else, don't you?"

N. F. didn't reply for a moment. "Perhaps not," he said.

"And you came out here to bribe me!"

N. F. shook his head. "To tempt you," he said, smiling.

Fireworks exploded from the beach below them. The sky was lit with stars and pinwheels of red and blue and white lights. The glass doors swung open, and people swarmed out onto the balcony, calling out to each other and to the people on the beach below.

"The twentieth century! The twentieth century!"

N. F. bowed slightly to Ada, head up, eyes on hers, as if to mock the conventional gesture. "I'll leave you with your thoughts," he said.

A trumpet blared in the banquet hall; raucous laughter surrounded her. Glass crashed, then her name was being called, and she looked up to see Emmett waving and coming toward her. Just beyond him, N. F. Gass was holding a glass of champagne in the air.

"The nerve of the man! The nerve!" She raced inside, and felt safe only when her arm was linked with Emmett's.

Chapter 16

The completed cottage nestled on the side of the hill where the sheep grazed. The continuing drought had left the land bone white, and the cottage walls of stucco took on the pale colors of their surroundings: from the glare of high noon white to the rose of sunset. Cypress trees were planted around the cottage, and a garden, not yet in bloom, stretched up the hill in back. A wide terrace ran around three sides of the cottage, with an ocean view from the widest. Hammocks were strung in the shade; the shuttered doors to the inside were left open all day long.

The first week spent there was idyllic, the days hot and bright under a sky perfectly, uniformly blue, the nights black and clear, lush with the smells of flowers and sun and the queer baby bleating of the sheep below them on the hill, punctuated by occasional outbursts of laughter from the shepherds.

Cornelius rode his horse around the hills all day—Ada remembered how Quinones had once been described as being part of his horse, and this applied to her son, too. Ada thought back to herself and Obie as children. They had played so much harder than her own son; it required so much more effort to get away from their surroundings. She wondered, too, now, if her own mother had ever sat in some warm place beside her husband and taken simple pleasure in her child at play.

"Conny's a born rider," Emmett said, stretched out in a wide string hammock on the back terrace.

"Mmm," Ada replied, but she could not enter as fully as Emmett into parental gratification: not with this boy, she thought, for no matter that he was her own, her only, he bore the signs of his uncle Obie as a stigma Ada could not overlook. She tried, had tried, and continued to try, but she had never yielded her heart to him the way Emmett had, and it kept them apart, for she knew that it pained him to see, and that in a way he could not acknowledge—even, perhaps, to himself—he did not forgive her for it. But he loved her, and this was what made it so difficult to bear. Was this the Newcomb family, then? It was, it was.

"Careful of the trees, Cornelius!" she called out, as he guided the horse in and out of the growing cypresses. "Don't knock them down!"

"He's too good a rider for that, Ada," Emmett said. "Go easy on him."

Ada shook her head to hear the tightness in her own voice. "I'll go make something cold to drink," she said, and walked around front. Just before she entered the house, she heard the muted sound of horses coming up the hill: Quinones and two other riders, one of whom Ada recognized as Veeda Weller. Loath to unsettle Emmett, Ada walked off the terrace to meet them.

Veeda had grown red-faced and bony, her features pinched together as if smelling something foul, dressed in an old calico print worn limp and nearly white. Ada wondered if her own mother had appeared to the people in Desideer like this woman: skinny and sour and a little dangerous. Funny, though, the woman's weaselish face might, at age sixteen, have been thought "adorable." Veeda smiled, slow and crooked; Ada was a little afraid of her. "Thought we was going to get friendly, me and you," she said. "Veeda Weller? Remember? This here's Mackie."

Next to her was a tall, emaciated man with long, restless hands at the reins of his horse, his body pulled back in reluctance. He was all hollows and smudges around the eyes and mouth, as if many nights had been spent drinking in the dark. Ada thought of Felix, her own lost father. Quinones was behind them, and now Ada saw that his pistol was drawn on them.

"What's happened?" Ada said. "Has someone been hurt?"

"No one's been hurt *yet*," Veeda said, anger mottling her face still further.

Quinones shook his head at Ada. "Stealing cattle," he said grimly.

"He's lying," Veeda said. She rode closer, her eyes on Ada, looking up at her hair then down at her dress, nodding all the while, her lips curled in on her teeth. "I see your little boy riding that nice horse," she said in a low voice and laughed, then straightened up and smiled again. "Nice boy," she said. "Heard about your school, too, Mrs. Newcomb. Wish my little boy was alive, so I could send him to your school."

Mackie pulled his horse around next to Veeda. "Can't prove no one stole nothing," he said hoarsely. "Just trying to get to Santa Monica. Crossing the Malibu to get to the shore road, that's all."

"They were in Bieule Canyon," Quinones said, "leading a cow by a rope."

"That true?" Ada asked; much as she felt sorry for Veeda, her stealing cattle did not seem unlikely.

"Drought's taken half our stock, and the half that's left is skinny and parched," Veeda said. "We need the blood meat bad this year, worse'n most. My husband here's got liver trouble, ain't you, honey darling? Doctor told him he's gotta eat red meat, ain't you, Mackie?"

Mackie muttered that it was so. "You gonna arrest us for that, or what?"

Ada felt backed into a corner, her generosity challenged. She had so much; dare she deny these people?

Ada shook her head. "No, of course not. But you can't... you can't just steal a cow and not..."

"We was gonna leave the hide," Mackie said and looked at Quinones for corroboration. "Ain't that the way?"

"Not any more."

Ada turned to see that Emmett had come around the terrace to hear. He was walking toward them and shaking his head. "Sorry about this, folks," he said stiffly but politely. "I told my foreman here. That policy's been changed."

Veeda grinned at Emmett. "You're gonna have to keep a sharp eye if that's so, Mr. Newcomb." She looked at Ada, and laughed. "All right if we go now? C'mon, Mackie."

Ada watched them move slowly down the hill and finally disappear around a bend. She was reluctant to turn to Emmett; something in his tone, the easy dismissal of the Wellers, disturbed her.

"Make sure they go all the way," Emmett said to Quinones, and Quinones turned and followed them down the hill.

"I told Quinones to keep an eye out for trespassers," Emmett said. "Keeping an eye out doesn't do much to keep them off, though."

"They're not exactly trespassers," Ada said, hearing the defensive tone of her voice. "They're like most of the homesteaders. They have to cross the Malibu to get supplies from the city markets, and to sell what they grow. Some of them don't even have fresh water on their property. You should hear the stories their children tell me in class."

But Emmett was no longer listening. "There's only one thing to do," he said. "To keep people from coming on the ranch in the first place, I've got to put up gates at the roads."

"You were going to fix the roads!" Ada exclaimed. "Now you're going to close them? Then what are the homesteaders supposed to do?"

"There are other roads," he said. "There's the Las Flores Canyon road; not more than a hundred yards of it are on the Malibu. They could use that. There's the Bieule Canyon Road, and the Trancas Canyon road, too. That's plenty, it seems to me. We'd be eating up the land with any more of them. It's not our responsibility to provide passage for our neighbors when they kill our cows and steal our water."

"But the homesteaders don't do these things!" Ada insisted. "I know these people. I teach their children. They're just poor people trapped with the mountains behind them."

"Ada, don't you see that—"

"No reason you couldn't run fences along all the borders of the Malibu, and keep out everyone if it came to that," she said, trying to control the rising anger in her voice. "Do you have any idea how dry their land is? This is the third year of the drought. They haven't had rain since—"

"Neither have we, for that matter."

"But Emmett, how can we deny poor people some of our riches? Water doesn't belong to us just because the creek is on our property. It's free. It should be free to them, too."

"I don't begrudge them the damned water!" Emmett shouted.

"But you're accusing all of them of trespassing and slaughtering our cows on the basis of this one example."

Emmett looked around at the land, aware again of its fragility. "All right, as a group, I'll give them the benefit of the doubt. They aren't personally responsible, all right? But as long as people cross the Malibu whenever they please, unguarded, unescorted, there's going to be trouble. I just don't see how I can leave the roads open."

"You *are* blaming the homesteaders!" Ada insisted.

"And I say I'm not! But even if they never set foot on the Malibu, what about tourists on the mission trail? What about travelers? Or thieves, professionals?"

"I don't see any proof it was the homesteaders," Ada said.

"It doesn't matter, don't you see? Ada, it's been going on in small ways for years. Since we bought the Malibu. Since before Keller owned it. Little things, campfire remains, fruit trees stripped, grasslands with wagon wheel ruts, but this..."

Ada could not face him and listen to this talk: more isolation, more denial of the real world. How could she break through that romantic haze he lived behind? Was it even possible?

The sky was too intensely blue, as if another lurked behind it. A land breeze brought the smell of canyon roses.

"The thing of it is, Emmett, that woman today could have been me. I mean, I could have been her. I could have been any of the homesteaders' wives if it wasn't for your money." The inequity of their positions was as unsettling as catching a glimpse of her own reflection in a distorted mirror. Fortune had come upon her so quixotically; couldn't it just as randomly turn its back on her? What preparations could be made? What precautions taken?

Emmett sighed, shaking his head. "Maybe I don't understand the needs of these people the way you do. Maybe I don't empathize the way you do. But it doesn't matter who did it, only that it got done."

The ocean murmured in the distance; Emmett came and stood behind her, his hands on her shoulders.

"I have to plan for the future, don't you see that? I can't just wait for worse things to happen. I have to plan, to be prepared."

Ada jumped away from his touch; at that moment he was the enemy, he was all the rich people who ever deprived poor people like she'd been once.

"Oh plans! plans! plans! Am I to hear nothing for the rest of my life but your plans?"

Emmett drew back from her, shaking his head. "This is bigger than the homesteaders," he said quietly. "This time I'll get a court order keeping people out. I'll put up gates across the roads. I'll padlock them. I'll—"

"What about my school?" Ada asked. "Are the children to be locked out because the school is on the Malibu?"

"The children have business here," Emmett replied.

"And their parents? They won't let their children come if they can't. And I don't blame them. I blame you!"

They glared at each other in silence, their essential differences locked and unyielding. And finally Emmett looked away, and Ada felt mean and hard for staring him down. What do I win if I lose him, she wondered, but she could not bring herself to soften her victory.

The sun was dry and harsh on the day the first gate went up; summer had begun to fray nerves; its persistence past tomorrow, past next week, bore down heavily on people's patience.

The fall days retained the lingering afternoon aura of a long summer day. All breezes died, and the desert winds returned. A butcher in Los Angeles complained that his pork rind crackled when the temperature reached a hundred and four. Heat from brush fires in the foothills of the Santa Monicas made the lowlands shimmer and writhe. The land looked mean and poor, bleached-out and harsh in the glaring sun. The sea breeze on this particular day died with the dawn, and the heat hung heavy as steam. A swarm of bees buzzed nastily above the field of clover, the scent of honeysuckle so strong Emmett felt nauseated.

Ada sat impassively on a dappled mare next to Emmett on his black stallion. Since the decision had been made, she and Emmett had barely spoken. She was tired of his plans, tired of taking a back seat to a dream when very real things needed their attention. She had told him again and again that they couldn't fence people out, but Emmett was unmovable on the subject.

Two vaqueros were digging post holes on both sides of the road, where the land sloped steepest.

"A man'll be able to cross the gate on foot," Emmett said, "a horse, probably not; a wagon, never." He did not look at Ada, for he knew she disapproved. He threw a leg over the saddle horn, and took out his pipe, but one draw turned his stomach; affecting a calm he did not feel, he knocked the pipe on the fence post, and dismounted to grind the live ashes under his boot heel.

One of the vaqueros hauled the gate out of the buckboard and leaned it against a tree, while the other piled dirt into the holes around the posts. Emmett put on a hat and looked out at the road behind the gate, which continued onto foreign terrain, winding through tall shoots of dry yellow grass that shimmered in heat.

"I think we'll be all right now," he said, and turned his back on the sight.

A rumbling sound attracted Ada's attention, and she looked

to see an enormous cloud moving on the other side of the fence. For a moment she thought it was the very heat made visible, the dry earth cracking, heaving up and exploding with the pressure. She watched with alarm as two riders emerged from the forward thrust of the cloud, seeming to pull it across the road behind them; hoof beats sounded like an endless peal of thunder. They came to a straggling stop a few yards from the other side of the gate. Their horses shuffled restlessly under them; dust rose in clouds around them, made them seem like they'd floated up the hill.

It was Cassie and Lucius Hinderman. He was dressed in canvas chaps and leather vest; Cassie, in a battered hat, looked like a plains woman prematurely aged, skin leathery and ancient, the iodine color of an old Indian.

Lucius advanced. His eyes were frightened and belligerent at the same time, as if he anticipated a fight he knew he'd lose. He said nothing, but edged his horse until he was in position to read the sign on the gate.

NO PASSING THROUGH THE MALIBU RANCH IS ALLOWED.
NO CAMPING UNDER PENALTY OF LAW.
SHOOTING AND HUNTING FORBIDDEN.
BY ORDER OF COUNTY BOARD OF SUPERVISORS.

"Not very friendly," Lucius said.

"That's as far as you go, I'm afraid," Emmett said.

His voice sounded thin and strained. Ada was almost afraid to look at the Hindermans. The only other sound was the shuffling paddle of horse hooves.

Lucius raised his long-legged frame out of the saddle and thumbed his hat back off his face, squinting in the sun. "Our cattle're pretty thirsty." He wiped his forehead with the back of his hand; the palm looked tough as saddle leather and scarred with rein burns.

Ada's eyes went from one to the other, but saw neither of them; she shot a quick glance of reassurance at Cassie, tried to tell her with her eyes that she herself did not want this fence.

Cassie edged her horse forward, and tipped her hat to Ada, then spoke reasonably. "How're we supposed to get to the shore road if we can't cross the Malibu?"

"This gate is to keep out trespassers," Emmett said.

"I ain't no trespasser!" Lucius Hinderman said.

"Someone's been damming the creek," Emmett said.

"We're all thirsty these days," Lucius replied. "Had to shoot two of my longhorns this morning."

"My rights are being violated all the time," Emmett said patiently. "Campfires burn out of control. My water's drained away on me. There are wagon wheel ruts on some of my finest pasture lands. Fruit trees get stripped bare. Someone else's cattle and sheep are eating my grass, while my own are being killed for food by I don't know who. That's the reason for the gates." The vaqueros hefted the gate and hooked it onto the posts; the gate creaked shut, echoing sharply across the plains; the lock clicked.

"He doesn't mean you're responsible," Ada said, but heard the emptiness in her words; now even Cassie turned away. "Not you personally."

Emmett put a restraining hand on her arm. "This is very embarrassing and useless."

"We just want our rights, is all." Lucius Hinderman rose in his saddle, muttering. "And I don't want no damn Mexican taking me by the hand when I cross, like your vaqueros been doing."

"This road is private property," Emmett said. "I've got a court order from the Los Angeles Board of Supervisors that says I have the right to put up gates on the roads that are on the Malibu."

"All we want's the shore road," Lucius said. "It's public."

"But you've got to cross the Malibu to get to it," Emmett explained. "The law is on our side, I'm afraid." He drew the court papers from his pocket, and held them out to them. "You can read it right here."

"You think 'cause you're a rich man you're closer to God and the law and every damn thing!" Lucius Hinderman said. "Well, you've got poverty in the soul, if you can shut folks out like this!"

"I've got the right to keep people from destroying what's mine!" Emmett replied hotly.

Lucius turned his excited horse in a complete circle. His eyes and cheeks were red and sore-looking. "There's got to be more roads, not less of 'em. And better ones, too."

"We've got the right to do what we have to do, to keep people from trespassing on our land," Emmett said. "The Board of Supervisors says we have the right."

Suddenly there was a gun in Lucius Hinderman's hand. No one moved; there was silence. Ada's heart pounded in her ears. The moment seemed frozen to her, a tableau of hostility and opposition; she felt they might stand there forever, but then there was movement, without her being absolutely sure who started it.

"This is just the beginning, Mr. Newcomb," Lucius said. The Hindermans disappeared in the same cloud of dust they'd come in.

Ada's allegiance was clear to her now; sides had to be taken, and she was with her husband. The Malibu... Emmett was the Malibu... the Newcomb family was the Malibu... the Malibu had to be saved. But...

"Sometimes I hate the Malibu," Ada said. "The way it's taken us over. Everything is the Malibu. Every thought is connected to it, every decision..."

"Ada, I know we're right. We must protect the land... if we don't... well then..." He looked at her, suddenly stricken, the color draining from his face. His chest hurt; there was a blank behind his eyes. He wanted nothing more at that moment than that everything go away. His head dropped back, he closed his eyes, and blackness poured in.

Emmett's recovery was as gradual as his attack was swift. Ada continued to give Cornelius his lessons as if he were not the only pupil in the schoolroom. "They'll be back," she told him, "when their tempers cool." The children's gardens needed weeding. Cornelius missed Phoebe Hinderman; he'd ridden his horse to see her, but had been rebuffed by her father. Ada was right about the homesteader parents; once the gates had been locked they refused to let their children get to the school. Emmett, from his position on the sun porch day bed, was adamant. And Ada, as adamantly, refused to close the school.

"I was forced to do what other people wanted me to do in my school in Desideer," she told Emmett. "But I won't be pushed around now. Not by you, or them. Not here, not in my own school, not on the Malibu. No, never again."

From beyond the mountains the Santa Ana blew hot and dry air from the desert, sweeping down the canyons and along the canyon floors, drumming seeds and pods through the chaparral.

They stayed in the cottage for a few weeks, the breeze cooler this high in the hills, but they couldn't escape the sight of lambs lying dead on the hillside below, the ewes bleating, milkless. Ada had the sensation of being suspended in time, waiting for something unknown to break this waiting apart.

"It's like this all over the countryside," Emmett said. "I heard about a rancher in Ventura, shot all his range horses rather than watch them die."

The hot wind was strong enough to uproot trees, yet the sky remained an unnervingly intense blue; the expected showers didn't follow.

"I heard branches snapping in the wind this morning," Ada said. "Sounded like rifle shots."

"Quinones says the drought is so bad that the pasturage of alfalfa is going to cost more than the cattle are worth. But... can I just let them die? Quinones has no sentiments about the cattle. You know how he is."

Ada nodded, but said nothing. Quinones's past was never something she and Emmett had discussed. She doubted Emmett even knew. But ever since the onset of Emmett's illness, Quinones had been running the ranch operations. "Still," Ada said, "if Quinones says that cattle have to be sold..."

Emmett nodded and grunted his reluctant assent. Ada said no more; sentiment about the ranch in these summer days of the heat wave had to be put aside.

The wind in the hills grew fierce, and they moved back to the main house. In lieu of horseback riding, Emmett took to checking the house, alarmed at the low level of water in the roof tank. For his first time back in the saddle, a few weeks after their return, he rode along the pipe line to see if there was a leak anywhere. The pipes, he saw, were all in place and functioning, but the creek itself was very low, its pebbly bottom showing white and dry in places. He followed it upstream, into the depth of the canyons, and found, near its mouth at the base of the mountain, but still within the Malibu boundaries, a dam of rocks and mud that diverted a section of the stream off the Malibu. Emmett turned to look at the land behind him. People wandering over the ranch, he thought wildly, blades and appetites sharp enough to decimate the herd and destroy the crops. No, that couldn't happen, it just couldn't be allowed to. It belongs to me, damnit! The land is mine, and I've got to protect it. He got down on his hands and knees and with furious pawing and kicks, broke up the dam.

* * *

By early August Los Angeles's water consumption exceeded the inflow into the reservoirs; water famine threatened. Cattle from the San Joaquin Valley to San Diego died of thirst; thousands of carcasses littered the countryside. Quinones and the vaqueros tried walking the cows along the beach from the dried-out Zuma Canyon pasture lands to Malibu Creek, but the dune sand was too soft for them to make easy progress, and the harder sand was so close to the water they shied from the waves.

Ada was worried about Emmett's health; alone together, the outside would shut out, their isolation was complete. It began to unnerve her, how completely she depended on him, and him alone.

"Emmett, why don't we go to Boston for the rest of the summer?" Ada asked.

"We can't leave the Malibu now," he said. "Anyway, when I left Boston I left it for good."

"How about a trip to Desideer?" Ada suggested. "Cornelius? We could buy an automobile and drive it there."

"An automobile!" Cornelius looked to his father. "What about my horse?"

"Of course, there's not much left to see in Desideer," Ada said, as if to stifle her own idea before Emmett did. She thought of her recent letter from Karen Sewall of Desideer, telling her that the little house had collapsed last winter in the famous blizzard of '02, and, incidentally, had anyone informed Ada that Miss Harriette Austin had died last spring in Rome? Would I be here today, Ada'd wondered then, if Miss Harriette hadn't believed in the wideness of the world?

"Wouldn't it be incredible if Uncle Obie's gone back to Desideer?" Cornelius said. "A secret rendezvous on the roof!"

Ada remembered their last meeting on the roof, just before she got married, and what she'd promised him their future would be. She shook her head and turned away from her son. "Your uncle Obie felt about Desideer pretty much the way your father feels about Boston."

"Father says maybe Uncle Obie went to sea as a sailor," Cornelius said. "He could be in Madagascar now. Think of it. All that way across the ocean. Did he really have red hair like mine?"

Looking down at the top of Cornelius's head, Ada was struck, as she often was, at his resemblance to her brother.

Obie'd been smaller at twelve, but Obie hadn't had a tall man like Emmett for a father. Had she even seen Obie at his full height, she wondered, leaving as she had when he was still a growing boy? Cornelius's face was erasing the memory of her brother's, like a fine tracing that obscures the original.

But even if Emmett had wanted to go to Desideer, Dr. Rowe forbade him to leave the Malibu. "All my life, you medical men have looked over your bifocals at me and shaken your heads," Emmett told him. "'You can't, you mustn't.' And I fooled every one of you."

Ada knew Emmett would not be well again, though she agreed when he said it was nothing, and applauded his imitation of Dr. Rowe's storklike walk. "If doctors had their way I'd sit at the window and watch the ocean while they run roads all over the Malibu, and railroad tracks across the shore." He laughed, but Ada saw panic dart across his face, like an animal startled by a sudden bright light. He would not fool her or the doctors this time. Or himself, either.

Emmett was rereading the poets he'd once read as a boy, when all his thoughts were of a destiny yet to be fulfilled. "And here I sit," he muttered angrily, "and here I sit." He had lost weight; the skin around his eyes settled against the bones. Ada was afraid for him, afraid that the thing held in limbo these hot summer days was Emmett himself; like a fever that had to peak and break or . . . Ada watched him sleep some nights, running her fingers restlessly across the pillow. He slept fitfully, a book open on his chest. He turned and turned, a finger at his cheek as if there were something he was trying to recall.

Ada dreamed one night of a field of scarlet poppies blowing in a fierce shrieking wind, and woke up startled. The hot desert winds blew sand everywhere, even with the shutters kept closed; a fine film of it gilded all objects. She got out of bed and walked downstairs, the floors gritty under her bare feet; the garden was blue on black under a half-moon sky. The wind rushed sand along the gallery; a whistling, a hushed, shushing sound. And then there was another sound above it, a whimper, low and steady, pleading.

Nothing's happened, Ada assured herself, but she quickened her pace to follow the sound. She cut across the garden, and through the doors. The door to the stable was unhinged, and

creaking in the wind. Ada was relieved, and went to shut it,
but the sound came again—closer, steady, agonized—from
inside the stable. She lit the lantern that hung just inside the
door, and for a moment saw nothing but shadows careening
into the rafters, and heard that sound ... and then movement
on the right. She jumped, startled ... Cornelius's horse was
bound to the door of its stall with barbed wire. It had been
blinded. Blood streamed from its eyes. Its ears were cut off at
the skull. Not yet dead, it moved its head, lowing in pain.

Numb, not thinking, Ada took a tack knife from the wall,
and moved toward the horse. It raised its head at the sound
... Ada paused for only a fraction of a second before slitting
its throat: the head dropped forward as the blood poured out
onto the ground, splashing her robe.

"My horse!"

Ada turned, the bloody knife still in her hand. "Oh,
Conny." The boy sucked in a fast breath, eyes on the blood
pulsing from the horse's neck. Ada threw the knife into the
hay, and embraced her son.

He stood rigid under her arms. "You killed my horse."

"But I had to, Conny," she explained. "You see what they
did to her ... how they hurt her ..."

"I see what *you* did, how *you* hurt her."

There was blood on her hands, blood on her robe, on
Cornelius's shoulders; the barn was stifling, hot with death.
Behind her the horse kicked once, and was still. Cornelius
looked up at Ada, his green eyes full of accusation and hate;
she was suddenly exhausted.

"Don't look at me that way, Conny." She held his shoulders, but he turned his head away. "Never mind, never
mind," she said, more to soothe herself than him. "We'll bury
her tomorrow, and then we'll find out who did this."

Cornelius broke free of her grasp. "I know who did it!" He
looked at his horse once more, and ran out of the barn.

Ada turned to look at the dead horse too, at the clumsy
gash she'd made, at the pool of black blood on the barn floor.
She covered her eyes with her hands, but nothing she did
could blot out the image of hate on her son's face.

Chapter 17

Obie hated the pitch and roll of a boat, but there was something fitting and right about coming to Ada on a steamer, just like we used to think we was going to escape Desideer, straight downriver to Cashman and further, a whole line of rivers criss-crossing the country and out to sea, across the world.

Stretching out his legs on the deck of the *San Mateo*, he was finishing the journey begun all those years ago when Ada stepped on the train with the husband, and left him.

"Pretty wild, Los Angeles, humm?" There was a rustling next to him, and a pink palm flashed open; the man laughed to let Obie know he was regular. "I'm a newspaper reporter out here from New Jersey. Ben Kingsley." He kept his hand out till he saw Obie wasn't taking any. "Work for the Newark *Star*," he said with a shrug. "Story I'm working on's about all these people who come to Southern California from New Jersey. Folks back home're dying to hear the latest. Everybody's got a story, see, if you know the right way to look at it." He pulled his head back and peered at Obie. "Where you from?"

Obie pulled his hat further over his forehead; just the gleam of his green eyes showed, and his mouth set in a tight, determined line.

The man laughed. "I always think that when a man doesn't talk much, he probably has something he really wants to say."

Obie ached with the need to press down hard and make a permanent imprint. "I want to see a newspaper. You got a newspaper?"

"Los Angeles *Times* OK?" the man said.

Obie grabbed his arm. "Give it to me."

The man wriggled his arm out from under Obie's hand, shaking his head and laughing. "You got a persuasive way of putting a thing," he said and surrendered the paper. He smiled again, thin-lipped, as if he and Obie shared the joke.

Obie turned away and rifled through it until he came to the personal columns.

Oh my heart, it's there.

—Obie, all is forgiven. Please come home.—

The ship was close to shore now, a strip of pale beaches, and faint mountains way back. Obie stared hard, looking for some movement. As the steamer came closer to land, he thought he saw a house on a hill. His heart beat fiercely; he thumped on his chest with his fist to stop it. He ran nervous, quick fingers over his face, pulled at the beard he'd grown in prison; just one thing left to do.

He hoisted his Gladstone bag, ran downstairs to the washroom, and propped the bag against the door, then laid out the equipment he'd bought for this purpose. He started cutting, and in ten minutes the beard was gone; in another five he was clean-shaven. Then he put the scissors to work on his hair, taming that red wildness, getting it down close to his scalp, a bright red fuzz. He scrubbed everything, rubbed his face hard, rubbed the years off hard, hard, until the face that stared back at him in the mirror was the boy she'd left twelve years ago.

He ran up on deck again, and fell into the line of disembarking passengers. The pier was empty and still, a ghostly gray-blue in this pre-dawn time. There was a chill in the air; where's the damned heat, the damned sun, Obie demanded. Where's the damned sun!

He moved along with the crowd, head down, seeing boots and dress hems, steely shadows and splintered wood. "Malibu?" he whispered to a man. The man shrugged. "Malibu?" he asked another, who didn't hear him, and Obie wanted to haul him back and make him. "Malibu?" he asked. "Malibu?" and someone pointed a fat hand into the gray morning mist. Obie heaved his Gladstone bag onto his shoulder, and started out along the shore. Me, Ada. Get yourself set.

He smoked all the tobacco he had left in the pouch during the walk. He could roll a perfect little white bullet with one hand and give it a licking good kiss closed, smoking the only thing that kept him going. He dragged his feet through the sand, then off the beach when he came to a gate, and up into the hills.

He ran on until he found a stream, then followed it across a plain, and slowed down finally to take a rest in a grove of sycamores. He leaned into the dry stream, and pressed anxious fingers into a lone muddy spot. Howdy ma'm, he'd say, the mystery stranger in the white hat...

... coming to the door, knocking on the door, and waiting for her footsteps, and there she'd be, in his arms, head to head, the smell of apples, her cool touch, and he'd press his face to her face and she'd understand it all without him saying a single word...

He got the sour taste of tobacco from his mouth by chewing a few blades of yellow grass.

He heard a sound of a horse behind him, and moved further into the grove of sycamores; birds swooped by his shoulder. The sky was getting light, like a dark glass bowl slowly filling with milk.

Ada appeared on a horse. Obie crouched down, ready to spring from the balls of his feet. Rides like she has a purpose, like she's coming down the road to our house, look at her, a little smile on her face 'cause she's going to meet her boy, 'cause I'm in the house waiting for her with a bowl of red apples! Look at her, still pink in the cheeks. Oh, Ada!

She rode past where he'd concealed himself, and he ran after her a short way until he emerged at the end of the grove and saw Ada going into a small white building. He followed, struck by how like their mother she'd become, the way Cornelia'd looked to him when he was a boy. Something had happened then between him and Ada; what was it made him so mad at her? She was still his Ada though, after all.

He looked through the window at her... A classroom!... and all the years in between just flew away. Look at her, the same, the same. Her eyes look easy, though, she looks slower, too, not like she was set to fly away like she once did. Still puts her hands on her hips when she's thinking. Still those wide gray eyes.

Seeing her there in the schoolroom just stripped away the years for him, like peeling an onion and getting right to the nub of it. Her hair was still that dark reddish color, and thick still, and he was glad she hadn't done anything fancy to it like he's seen in places. She was still leading with her chin, too; he smiled slyly to remember busting her one once. So many ways she was still the same.

Another horse was coming up to the building. Obie's smile froze in anticipation of the husband. The figure dismounted and came into the room, too small for a grown man, more like a boy. Yeah, a skinny boy, rubbing his face. He watched the boy walk sleepily into a sudden shaft of sunlight that set up

his red hair. His hands uncovered his face, and Obie caught
the color of his eyes too: green, like mine.

...Ada's long fingers raking through his red hair and
coming to rest alongside his neck, the boy squirming
away...No! Obie's throat got tight. His boot heels were
sinking into the earth.

He was burning up; every swallow sent fire into his chest.
His face felt big and hot, he wanted to scream until it
stopped. There was the smell of dry, rotting wildflowers, like
the inside of something dying.

He backed his way through the garden, his eyes burning
on the pair inside, back to the sycamore trees.

There was a stirring, a flapping: hundreds of blackbirds
hovered over him.

The image of Ada rubbing that little boy's head jabbed at
him, like a big angry fist between the shoulder blades: keep it
moving, boy.

Ada coming pointing her finger at me, punishing me for
what I done.

Why'd you never write me, Obie? Why'd you never let me
know where you were? It's too late to come back now. You
were a bad boy, now you've got no place here with us. I've
got me a new boy, starting over with him fresh, and I got a
grown-up man with money who took me out of that place we
used to call home, and bought this big ranch just for me. No
place for you on this big ranch, and no more living on the
roof for me.

He felt cut up, like small animals had been clawing at him.
The insides of his eyes grew red and burst, and grew red
again. In his mind, Ada still beckoned to him, but her voice
was distorted, like she was breathing the sea into his ears.
Everything between the time she was a schoolteacher in
Desideer and that schoolroom here was what stood between
them. He strained, his head bullied with blood, but he
couldn't quite get what she was passing on to him, only the
feeling that he had to tear down this block of time, and
muscle on through to Ada. The only way for them to be
together now was to take down everything that was in the
way.

His chest pounded and felt hot again, his belly heaved;
staring hard, swallowing, scared, his chest so full and hot he
thought a balloon of blood'd come bursting out of his mouth.

But you said all is forgiven, please come home.

And then he was sobbing, his body wracked from deep inside.

... like I never even was ... like I never even been born.

The world was as bad as he knew it was. It was so hot and dry that the hair in his nostrils felt brittle as July hay; the night had a heart of dry ice. Sycamore leaves clattered above him. He grabbed a fistful of late-blooming purple succulents, and crushed them. The sky was ink-black at night, like dark, perfumed glass, and open as a yawn that threatened to suck him dry. *What right's the Malibu got to torture me like this?* He thought about how Ada looked.

The sun was rising; it would scorch today. The narrow canyon floor and the chaparral turned the color of hot butter. The hot wind tortured his eyes; he wrapped a neckerchief across his nose and mouth against the sand and seeds blowing. There was no one at the school now. A door had been blown open by the wind.

He set a branch across his knees, and wrapped tumbleweed and scrub brush around it, piled the dry wood in a corner of the room. When he finished making the torch, he set it against the wall and started on another one. *Better get myself set to run. The wind and the fire together's gonna take this room fast.* He squatted, and laughed softly to himself. *Obie, please come home.* He grabbed the torch, struck a match against his boot heel and brought them together. The tumbleweed fell apart, and the flames bit at his hands. He jerked them away, but sparks flew at his shirt. He leaped back; flames rushed at his face. *Obie pulled away.* A whoosh of fire roared up behind him, wood so dry it burned without another sound. He tumbled onto his back and rolled across the floor, struggling to regain his balance. Obie felt himself shaken, shaking inside, snapping his neck back and forth; behind him, so close, so close, the fire, reddening the walls on the sides of his vision; it felt like he was coming loose, all his parts, all at once. He stumbled back, teetered at the edge of the flames, watching himself from the outside of it, thinking of a river. He saw Ada reach for him through the wall of fire, and disappear in a streaming blur of yellow white.

The fire was all over him now. Tears hissed down his face. He turned and turned as white heat enveloped him; he turned and turned, and the flames punished his skin. He turned again and again, covering his face; his eyes, his hands

were burning, he heard the wind in the heat. What is it?
What're you telling me! The wind was the heat, the wind was
the fire, the flames rose around him and made no sound at
all.

Emmett was riding in the drying stream bed on his weekly
check against damming when he smelled the smoke. He
paused—even a campfire could go out of control in weather
like this—then took off toward the source; as he rode into the
hot wind, there was more smoke; the silence was eerie, and
he was chilled under the heat: the chaparral, he knew, was
dry enough to burn without a sound.

The wind blew hot as flame now, as he rode. But was it
only hot wind? He held out for the final answer until he saw
the heat waves shimmering above the sycamore grove. Smoke
obscured the sky as he rode through the grove and saw what
was left of the schoolhouse: a sheet of flame exposed the
structure of the building, its blackened skeleton. As he
watched, it fell in on itself, a great blast of heat drumming at
his face; sparks flew into the trees, whipped out into the
fields; dry, they went up, hungry flames licking wildly in
every direction at once, the hot wind urging them on toward
the sea.

He had a wish to rush in and embrace the flame, extin-
guish it with his own body, but he knew he had to move. The
schoolroom was gone. He wrapped the reins tight around his
wrist and rode off.

Smoke obscured the way back. He tried to form a picture
in his mind of what the canyon floor looked like between the
school and the house: brush and weeds and dry yellow grass,
the big sycamore, and a row of smaller ones. Head down,
hands gripping the reins, he rode into this mental image.
Behind him the fire consumed the school, the sycamore
grove, the fields; he felt its heat and imagined the flames
immense. Muddy shapes swam in a flood of tears.

He fell from the horse when he reached the house, his
breathing strangled. There were footsteps running along the
gallery floor, and he struggled to his feet.

"Emmett, what is it? What's happening? There's smoke in
the canyon. I can even smell it up here."

"The schoolhouse..." he choked. "Burning...burning..."

"The schoolhouse? They burned the schoolhouse?" So this
is it! This was the fever breaking!

Emmett had never seen a look of such hate on her face.

"Ada, there's no time. The fire's spreading. The wind's taking it everywhere! Send everyone down to the beach. Get Cornelius to take the horses down. Then get in the buckboard and wait for me. The land's so dry, the fire . . ." He ran along the garden walks and into the house.

Ada ran behind him; there was everything in every room she needed to save, everything in every room precious— there, that photograph; there, those books, those primitive paintings on bark, the baskets, the woven rugs—she wanted them all, and she could take nothing.

Emmett ran to the second floor, and from there to the roof. He leaned against the redwood water tank, and looked out across the Malibu, pressed his hands to his mouth to stop from crying out in rage and despair.

The sky above the mountains had a greedy, fevered glow; the undersides of clouds shimmered like hot coals, as if hell lurked below. The wind pushed the sour smell of burning brush from the canyon; ash veils floated up from the bottom of the hills.

"They'll pay for this," Ada said at his side.

"Get downstairs!" Emmett said. "It's too late to do anything here."

Smoke and hot ash swirled in strong gusts of wind around the house. Emmett looked down, and saw Ada run into the garden, pulling peonies and lilies and roses and geraniums from the ground, filling her arms with all her doomed flowers.

"Get in the buckboard!"

When she ran from the garden, he released the safety on the water tank, and put his hands into the rushing stream of it. As the water flooded the garden, he closed his eyes and remembered riding in the cool ocean breeze along the shore of the Malibu. He ran to his study, and grabbed all the blueprints and plans he'd made for the bridges and tunnels and pipelines and cottages and pulleys. He looked out his study window:

The flames had crested the mountains, a low wall of flame as wide as his stretch of vision, a continuous sheet of flame unrolling low and ominous and steady, the whole face of the mountain burning, paradise become a living vision of hell.

For one long moment he did not move at all, but closed his eyes and imagined never moving again; just stand still, and he'd be gone with it. He imagined the flames enveloping him and ending it the right way.

A live spark bit the back of his neck; he opened his eyes: a spark had set the curtains on fire. He jumped away and ran down the stairs back through the house and garden and to the buckboard. "Let's go," he said, and climbed in, exhausted, as Ada picked up the reins and started down the hill.

"Cassie Hinderman, all of them," she said bitterly. "I trusted them. I believed in them."

Emmett leaned against her. "There's nothing to do now." There was a hot lick of pain in his chest and down his arm; it hurt to breathe. The light was fading behind his eyes, a great yawning darkness exposed.

Ada used the switch over and over on the frightened, reluctant horses, until they reached the bottom of the hill. The tops of the trees were smoky; long, dry grass crackled as the wind drove the fire along the creek. The buckboard finally broke free of the smoldering brush, and the horses dragged it onto the beach.

Gulls soared and shrieked overhead, white underbellies burnished rose gold by the fire, and rode the wind out to sea. The buckboard horses trembled, whinnying, terrified.

"I want to be close to the water," Emmett said. Ada drove the buckboard closer, and Emmett slipped from the seat to rest on the wet sand. The coolness at his back seemed to penetrate him, numb him, and move on through. Thick smoke blew in strips across the beach and out to sea. Ada loosened his collar; he let her take charge.

A feeling of dread washed over her; she watched his chest rise and fall, waited for the rise again, and the fall.

The beach was obscured by smoke now, the sky black with odd shoots of fire-reddened sun. The ocean lapped out of the smoke at their feet, yet seemed miles away; it was inconceivable that such flame could be so near such water.

"So quiet," Ada said. The silence was like a vacuum, an enormous rush of heat and air which absorbed other sounds and was ominously quiet itself.

"Listen," Emmett said.

Ada shook her head. "I don't..."

"The cattle."

Indeed, when Ada knew what to listen for she heard their insistent, angry lowing, the demand to be alive. Quinones suddenly appeared out of the smoke, and jumped off his horse to kneel on the sand next to them.

"I'm all right," Emmett said. "Tell me what's happened."

Quinones looked at Ada; her glance told him all. He looked back at Emmett. When he spoke, there were tears in his eyes.

"The cattle are saved. We ran them down to the beach. They're terrified, they can't see, but they're alive. Our camp is . . . gone. All of it . . . the fire raced through the canyon. We don't know if everyone . . ." His voice broke. He swallowed hard and continued. "The sheep are . . . they were trapped in the hill, ran to the top instead of coming down . . . the shepherds, I don't know . . . the vineyards, gone . . . all of it."

"Cornelius?"

"He's taken the horses to Paradise Cove." He wiped his face and stood up. "We save what we can save," he said, mounted his horse, and was gone.

Ada wiped Emmett's forehead with her handkerchief. He pressed her wrist to his mouth.

In the distance the flames broke over the last hill and hovered, hesitating, teasing, then swept down like a bear claw and took the house. Emmett raised up at the sight of it going; the last light of hope faded in the flare.

"It'll all come back some day," Ada said. "We'll rebuild the house on the hill . . ."

"I've saved my plans," Emmett said. He paused, eyes closed, then opened them quickly, pointing to the notebooks and tubes of paper lying on Ada's flowers in the buckboard. Ada tried to hold him up, but he slipped from her grasp, and she finally let his head rest on her lap as she knelt in the sand beside him. His eyes were open, a waxy shine on his cheeks. "I feel I'm on the ocean," he said, laughing to himself. The sun bled through the smoke. The sea was red. He closed his eyes, his smile faded, then he grabbed Ada's hand, and his eyes flew open. He pulled her closer; there was a metallic taste on his tongue. "Promise me you'll keep the Malibu, Ada. Promise me you'll bring it back."

"As if you weren't going to bring it back yourself," she said. "As if—"

He shook his head and gripped her hand tighter. "No, Ada. Promise me. Promise."

"Stop it, Emmett!" she cried. "You're exaggerating." She held back, she didn't want to admit to what his question implied, not yet, not yet. But the naked plea in his face couldn't be denied. "I . . . I promise," she said finally.

The panic left his face; he looked peaceful, calm, twenty-eight again. She imagined for an instant that he was a young man on a swing in front of her schoolroom, none of it even begun. It was an illusion she could not sustain; their life together was already slipping into the past.

He looked at her face now: her mouth parted, eyes opened wide, guileless, but plaintive, too, the look of a woman who watches her husband off to sea. Their eyes met for a moment.

"I was remembering you at your schoolroom door that first day," Emmett said. "Such a sweet, determined smile. Like you were moving into the wind. I loved you right then, did you know that?"

A chill went through her; she held his head.

Emmett sighed. His head dropped deeper into her lap. His breathing was shallow. "I had such plans," he said. "There's so much left to do." His eyes fluttered, closed. He pressed her hands to his face, warming them with his breath. His own hands slipped to his chest. She held him until his last breath turned cool on her flesh.

Part 5

The first man who, having fenced in a piece of land, said, "This is mine," and found people naive enough to believe him, that man was the true founder of civil society.

—Jean-Jacques Rousseau,
*Discours sur l'Origine et le Fondement
de l'Inegalité Parmi Les Hommes*

Chapter 18

For long weeks he was no one, not a name, not a man, but something that burned in hell, all dreams of flame, of people without faces, of flesh melting, seared with salt tears, of bones dry and cracking, powder to ash. But if it all burns, what still feels the pain?

With consciousness—of light and dark, of weight, of voices, of the place—came the realization that it was all beginning again: he was alive.

"Do you know your name? Can you say your name?"

His face felt forced back into a grin; he thought: Obidiah Wilder.

. . . running from the schoolhouse, the wall of it collapsing down his back, his hair burning, his face and his hands, his poor hands pulling off face skin and burning up worse than anything . . .

He awoke in agony, in salt tears and sweat.

Oh God, God, I remember everything.

Only in sleep had Ada not lost everything. The moment before she opened her eyes each morning she imagined the sky bright blue, the wind up, the bougainvillea clattering against the sides of the house, her garden ragingly in bloom, Cornelius riding his horse on the beach, and Emmett, Emmett on the beach, in the hills, riding up from the pasture lands, by her side, in her arms. She thought of Desideer, too, of Obie and the apple orchards and the long blue sweep of the Orenoke River. And the day Emmett Newcomb came and sat in that schoolyard swing against the gray autumn sky, handsomer than any man she'd ever seen.

The past, the past, I'm drowning in it.

"Emmett."

With a chill she heard the sound spill across the hotel bedroom. She opened her eyes; so the days began.

Cornelius moved rigidly through the hotel rooms, his eyes half-closed, suspicious and angry. Ada felt her own loss mirrored in his and magnified, and so, distorted. The gulf between them was revealed all too nakedly, and Emmett, once the bridge between mutual estrangements, was now a chain of grief that made them wary, strangers bound by a pain too intimate to bear for long.

He reminded her more and more of Obie—a secretiveness, a wildness alien against the background of a city. She hardly recognized her thoughts about him: he felt out of place in her own mind. It was once the three of us: the Newcomb family of the Malibu Ranch.

Emmett's sister wrote frequently: brisk expressions of sympathy, and voluptuous outpourings of grief, tinged always with blame for Ada's having kept Emmett away from Boston, even from their mother's funeral. Ada did not tell her that he wouldn't leave the Malibu.

There were inquiries about her own health, and the obligatory invitation. Perhaps a brief visit for the Christmas holiday? Easter? Independence Day? A veil obscured Ada's inner vision when she tried to plan the future. Emmett's specialty, she thought jealously. "We have such plans for him—Cornelius—Choate now, Harvard Law later—all the things his father missed," the sister said.

Ada was surprised—though she could not conceal to herself her relief—when Cornelius accepted his aunt's invitation; in less than a week all the arrangements had been made, his suitcase packed, and he and Ada waited in the hotel room in an uneasy silence for the carriage that would take him to the railroad station.

"When I get to Boston, Aunt Elizabeth and Uncle John have promised me a long ride in their new automobile. It can travel up to ten miles an hour. You've got to wear dusters to the ground, and goggles to protect your eyes from the dust." He stopped in front of the mirror and tightened the knot of his new tie; he sighed, his shoulders slumped. "I'd rather have a horse. I'd rather be on the Malibu. I wish everything was the same . . . Oh, Mama!" he ran to her and dropped to his knees, his head buried in her lap. Ada patted his head and looked around the room but could find no object of comfort on which to rest her gaze. When does this end, she thought.

"I wanted to see the Malibu once before I went," he said.

"There's nothing left to see, Cornelius."

He nodded and wiped his eyes, then stood up. "What will

you do?" His voice had hardened; already he sounded like a young man.

Ada didn't reply for a moment, her mind remained bare of invention. "I don't know," she said. "Join you, maybe." She had a restless urge to pick up and go, go somewhere, anywhere. And soon, too, before she sank into the ground of her own heaviness.

After he was gone, Ada looked around the familiar rooms uneasily, as though they reproved her for remaining alone and empty-handed; for surviving alone. There'd been nothing to unpack, everything had gone in the fire. I won't stay here long, she thought.

She started making forays out of the hotel room. The streets everywhere were wider, traffic heavier, congested with automobiles. Instead of sheriffs in the saddle, there were uniformed police bicycling along Broadway. The women in the streets looked fierce and determined in boyish jackets and skirts that showed the ankle, and let them stride along with purpose. The population of Los Angeles had doubled since the Newcombs had stayed there over a dozen years before. A hundred thousand people, and they all seemed to be on the streets at once. The electric railway lines carried people into the city to work from as far away as Whittier and Newport. Tourists by the tens of thousands gave Los Angeles the aura of celebration, even to its residents. The wilderness which once had been the end of the railway line was now a nest of oil riggings. Downtown streets were studded with honky tonks, Bible thumpers, and side shows. A balloon a hundred feet long floated over the city with a sign lit up to read "Hockmeyer Beer."

Ada felt like a tourist herself; her clothes were new and strange, she traveled alone in groups to see the Ostrich Farm in Pasadena, the carnation ranch in Venice, the cliffs in La Jolla. She stopped her practice of placing ads for Obie in the personal columns; it was a fool's mission. After all these years her brother was simply, utterly gone. She had lived through the fire, through Emmett's death and the Malibu's destruction. She was becoming the true daughter of loss.

She tried to replace what she'd lost in the fire with store-boughts, but sometimes, shopping, she would pick up a simple household object and see Emmett's hand on it, and tears would flood her eyes.

With a deep, regretful sigh, she packed her trunk for Boston.

"The smartest thing," Clara Sweet said. "Grief is a wound that only time can heal."

His feet and hands and face got the worst of the fire, though there were scar trails down his back and legs that looked like flame itself. The skin on his feet and hands couldn't seem to stick on; it'd heal bright pink, then start draining some fluid and turn gray and drop off, and underneath would be raw skin flecked with fresh blood, and the whole process'd start again.

But it was his face that was hardest of all to take. The skin healed so tight that any kind of expression felt like someone came up to him from behind, grabbed his face, and yanked.

The hospital room of Sisters of Mercy was long and narrow, two rows of ten beds lined the walls, with enough room on the sides and at the foot for the nuns to pass by.

When the bandages came off his face, the light stabbed his eyes. In the flood of tears he saw a ghost. The nuns at Sisters of Mercy put cool, wet towels on him and read to him from the Psalms: "There is no soundness in my flesh because of thine anger; neither is there any rest in my bones because of my sin."

"Sister?" The ghost moved to his shoulder; he felt a light pressure there where he wasn't burned. "Newspaper."

He shook his head as she turned the pages and showed them to him, and grunted when she came to the personal columns.

The fine print was too small for his hazy vision, so she read it to him. Obie shook his head at the sound of all the lonely folks in the world making their little noise.

It wasn't there. No more "Obie, all is forgiven." No more "please come home." She knows. And if she don't know, one look at me'll tell her for sure.

He leaned back and closed his eyes. The nun closed the paper and said good night. Obie stared through his eyelids at the candle flame on the table next to him, eyelids bursting with blood, and he was at the fire again . . . running from the schoolhouse, his hair burning, his face on fire and his poor hands stamping it out and burning too . . . oh, God!

He pressed his palm against the candle flame, and the long room went dark.

* * *

A few days before she planned to leave, Quinones came to see her. He said nothing for a long time. Each sat in a stiff-backed silk brocade chair; Quinones, in his leather hat, neckerchief, rough shirt and pants, made the ornate hotel furniture look overwrought.

"Telephone in every room," Ada said. "Full electricity." She turned a table lamp on and off, then sat erect again, hands pressed on her lap as if she were about to run. "Before I know it I'll be out of here and . . ." She felt giddy. There was nothing to say, and they continued to sit in silence. But Ada felt the presence of the Malibu more strongly than she had since she was there, and when Quinones began to speak she put up her hand to stop him.

"I don't want to talk about the Malibu," she said. "I'm going to Boston. I've packed and . . ." She ended uncertainly.

"The vaqueros are eager to work," Quinones said, as though she had not spoken. Ada shook her head. "They have lost their homes, too."

"I know that, but . . . more than our homes were lost."

"I have seen chaparral fires before," Quinones said. "They are part of the cycle of the land. But the land comes back. Already—"

"I don't want to know about any of this," Ada said. "The Malibu was my husband's dream, and now he's dead. The dream is destroyed, and there's nothing to go back to for me. I hope you'll understand that, and explain that to—"

"The Malibu is not a dream, señora," Quinones said. "And it is not destroyed. It is hurt, badly hurt, but we are eager to bring it back. You promised once that you would help . . ."

"I know that, but things were different then."

"Señora, if you don't come there will be no more Malibu. Land developers want pieces of it. The railroad wants to run tracks along the coast. Without someone to protect the Malibu, it will truly be destroyed. The fire is nothing compared to what men will do to it."

Ada shook her head and looked away; she felt she was losing the Malibu all over again. "You're making it difficult for me to leave."

Quinones looked hard at her. "I mean to," he said.

Ada stood up and stalked across the room until she found herself in front of the mirror. Yes, yes, I see what everyone sees. Black dress, black lace at the wrists, and a garnet

brooch at the throat. The widow Newcomb. The grief was
getting familiar, comforting as Cornelia's old shawl, something she sat down to dutifully, like the evening meal. She
mourned now because she didn't know what next to do:
courageous mother, brave widow, and now? She squinted to
blur her reflection, and imagined herself as she was when
Emmett Newcomb appeared in her life. What had she been?
What had he loved? How had he once put it?—"like you
were moving into the wind."

Well, I'm not twenty-three years old any more, she thought,
I'm thirty-five, and I've been walking with the wind at my
back too many years. But that prairie girl is still in me.

She turned away from the mirror to Quinones. "Wait for
me while I change my clothes," she said. "Then get me a
horse. I'm going out to the Malibu."

She was greeted as she rode with nothing less than the
persistent and relentless presence of death. Mist rose from
the sea as if the water boiled, the color a cold snake-green. A
scalloped edge of white against black ran along the shore
where the salt sea licked the ash. The sun was high and faint
beyond the mist. The land seemed uniform muddy gray in
the early light, acres and acres still covered with a moist filmy
ash. As the mist rose, the hills were revealed black and
scabrous, the contours in sharp, bare outline against a clear
sky, seared remains of the fire.

Spring had come, and Malibu Creek flowed again, healthy
and alive through the charred remains of bushes and wildflowers.
Ada turned into the canyon; ash gray prevailed, charred
stumps of trees and bushes lined the stream banks. Some
trees and shrubs stood as they once had, but blackened and
skeletal: she leaned from her horse to touch them, and they
fell apart against her bare hand. Her horse was restless; she
rode on, a spectral figure in white.

Her heart pounded fiercely as she clicked the reins and
rode up to the house; the sea stretched out slick and brilliant
below. Where the house once stood was now rubble, the sand
and clay walls fallen back into the hills. Only the outline of
the adobe walls was still visible, arching toward the canyon.
Ada dismounted, and walked alongside the remains of the
walls. The sun glinted on something: the brass pull of the
great mission doors melted over a stone. Ada bent and
weighed it in her hand, then stood and crossed the threshold.

She moved quietly down what had once been the vaulted gallery, past blackened rooms and the shattered glass of the tall windows, and up the stairs that once led to the second floor and that now led to nowhere, her feet moving through a cloud of ash. Then into what had been the kitchen, and the sudden surprising click of her heels on a perfect yellow tile. With every other step came the soft squeaking crunch of charcoal. Their bedroom had collapsed into the terrace below, their iron bed twisted by the flames into nightmarish exaggeration of itself, even to the veils of blackened gauze that clung to it. The smell of ash was rancid with a faint underlying sweetness that made Ada nauseous.

It's over. It's gone. Quinones lied to me, she thought, to encourage me, but I can't lie to myself. There's no way to bring this back. Not now, not next year. And how can I hold off the railroad or the land developers or anyone? She moved a few steps around a pile of beams which had once held up the living-room ceilings, and stopped.

It was impossible. It couldn't have happened. But she remembered that the last thing Emmett had done as the fire was consuming the Malibu was to release the water in the redwood tank and flood the garden.

And now, against a background of cinder and ash, the garden was coming into bloom: her roses and geraniums, her peonies and lilies, blood red, brilliant crimson red. She knelt at the base of the garden, charcoal crunching softly under her. She swept the charcoal aside and dug furiously with her hands: charcoal and ash and sand and dirt, and then, suddenly, earth, moist and rich, the roots slick, alive. She crouched among the blooms and in the midst of the ashes, and buried her face in Emmett's last gift to her.

Chapter 19

"But Ada!" Clara Sweet exclaimed when Ada came to Avery's office and announced her decision. "What do you know about running the ranch?"

Ada shrugged, impatient. "Not much, I admit, but—"

Clara cast a worried glance at Avery. "Well, then?"

"Well, then, I'll have to learn," she said. "Did you know that Quinones and the vaqueros have been out there since the fire? They never left the ranch at all. They're sleeping out in the open, or under tents they've rigged up out of old blankets."

"But Ada, they aren't . . . I mean, you'd have to be their leader, you'd have to be responsible for them."

"Quinones is their leader," Ada said. "He knows how to run the ranch. And I have every intenetion of being responsible."

"Ada, I don't think you have any idea of what you're getting yourself into," Avery said.

Ada sat down on the Chesterfield sofa. "I won't be warned off, I'll tell you that right now, so you'd be doing me a service to let me in on all of it. I don't want to be protected."

Avery sighed, and nodded to Cara. "Get the Malibu folder," he said, then sat at his desk and faced Ada. "You know, since you bought the Malibu a lot has changed."

"The Malibu hasn't changed at all," Ada declared. "That's the whole point! To keep it as it was!"

"I agree," he said as Clara placed the folder in front of him and resumed her seat at her own desk. "But maybe not in the way you mean. You've seen the changes in Los Angeles since the days you first stayed at the Saint Elmo."

"The city's spreading like spilled ink," Clara muttered.

Avery cleared his throat. "It's spread out to Santa Monica, and right to your borders. People want in. Here . . ." He held up some papers from her file. ". . . offers to buy the vineyards, offers to lease beachfront property for vacation homes. The state highway commission is getting interested in building a coast road right through the Malibu. Here's an offer from Doheny's Oil Company. They've found oil down in Long

Beach, and now they won't be happy till they've plugged everywhere. I've even heard people talking in the courthouse building, saying you don't have the water rights to Malibu Creek, that you own only the creek bed itself." He placed his hands carefully on the pile of papers. "You're in a lot of people's way, Ada."

Ada looked away for a moment. "The poor widow Newcomb," she said and turned back to Avery. "I'm not so easy to get rid of. Let's keep going with that pile there. What else?"

Avery pressed his lips together, and glanced again at Clara; he pointed to the next piece of paper. "This is the homesteader petition for free passage across the Malibu."

Ada looked it over, saw the names of the people who'd sent their children to her school. "The nerve of these people. The nerve of them!"

"They have a lawyer, who's prepared to sue on their behalf for you to remove all the gates on the Malibu roads. The possibility of a court case is very likely, unless some kind of amicable settlement can be reached."

"They've already removed the gates by burning down the ranch. Now they want free passage. The irony of the situation is a little grim." Ada handed back the petition. "There'll be no amicable settlement."

"Don't be too hasty, Ada," Clara said. "Some of them are in a pretty bad way. The fire got their land, too."

"More irony," Ada said. "Since they're the ones who started the fire."

"There's never been any proof who started the fire," Avery said.

"Oh, they may not have meant for it to go as far as it did," Ada said, "but it started in the schoolhouse. Who else would start a fire there?"

"I can't go along with that line of reasoning," Avery said. "You're drawing a conclusion based on inference. I couldn't take that into a court of law."

"I don't have to prove it," Ada said. "I'm just not going to settle their petition. As a matter of fact, the first thing I intend to do on the Malibu is fence it in."

"Ada! They'll take you to court in a minute if you do that," Avery said. "And they'd have a case, too. The only access to the shore road is across the Malibu."

"Let them take me to court, then! I'll be vindicated. You'll see."

"Oh, Ada, no," Clara said.

Avery shook his head and picked up another paper from
the file. "Here's something not so easily dismissed. The
Malibu's become well known, in the years since you bought
it, as the last twenty-six miles on the southern coast without
rail service. The South Central is getting very impatient—
they say the 'people' have a right to rail service—I've been
routinely appealing their claim to lay tracks, but it looks like
the government is swinging its support to the railroad now.
The South Central has to have that last twenty miles to
complete its coastal route in order to get the harbor appropriation for Santa Monica and not San Pedro. This has been
going on for years, you know. The South Central is not likely
to take no for an answer. Not now."

"You mean it'll be easy pickings, now that the Malibu's
been burned and there's just that poor widow Newcomb to
defend it."

Avery looked down, embarrassed. "I suppose that's part of
it, yes," he admitted.

"Keep the appeals going," Ada said.

"But what for, Ada? On what grounds?"

"Because the land is there," Ada said. "Because the Malibu
is waiting for me." Avery shook his head again. "Are we done
here now?" Ada asked. "Well, we'll have to be, for the
moment. I have to get out to the ranch before the rainy
season; start setting up some kind of temporary shelters for
everyone—and myself. The cottage survived the fire but I
couldn't live in it . . . not now . . . not yet."

Avery stood and came to sit by her on the Chesterfield sofa
he'd brought with him from the old office. "Ada, are you sure
you want to do this? Wouldn't you be better off sticking to
your original plan to go to Boston? You could live very nicely
there."

Clara came to sit on her other side. "A gentleman from
Sarasota, Florida, was interested in buying the Malibu vine-
yard land, with the idea of building a health spa. Mr. Benson
could get a very nice price."

Ada still said nothing, and Avery went on. "I've had one or
two requests to lease parcels of the land for private beach
clubs. The best people as members. You might give some
thought to that." Ada nodded; Avery continued. "You could
derive an income from the sale of the pieces of the ranch, and
still hold onto some of it. You could live very comfortably in
Boston on the sale of—"

"And do what?" Ada demanded. "Become a professional widow?" She stood and drew on her gloves. "After the fire I thought the Malibu was destroyed, and everything else seemed gone with it. But..." She looked from Avery to Clara. "Don't you see? Emmett's dead, and I'm alive, and the ranch is still there! Oh Avery, Clara, you just don't leave a place like the Malibu to the land developers and railroad builders. You don't leave it to your neighbors. You take hold and you protect it. Land's getting eaten up so fast. Plugging holes to drill for oil. Rerouting rivers, rearranging the earth to suit a highway or a set of railroad tracks. It seems like a mass craziness. Feasting on the land like the supply was endless. But land is always going to be less and less. And they know it, too—these so-called leaders of industry—but it doesn't matter to them. With all the talk of California's future, they're still working on the short view. The only future's in a place like the Malibu and the only chance to save the Malibu is to keep people off it. You've never lived there. You don't know what it gives, what it needs. Just... just don't oppose me, Avery. Clara? Will you promise me that? Will you be my friends on this?"

"We like to think we were your first friends in California," Clara said.

Ada smiled. "At this point, you may be my only ones."

Paradise Cove had escaped much of the devastation the rest of the ranch suffered, the pier untouched by the fire, and the small steamer docked there now resuming its regular service. The first shipment to arrive was the tents, and for the next days the cove was a mass of flapping canvas sheets and the clacking of poles as the tents were assembled. Ada's tent was set up on a low rise toward the back of the cove; spread out below were the tents now occupied by the vaqueros and their families. These temporary living quarters looked to Ada like the beginnings of a small coastal city. Foodstuffs came in on the same shipment: dried meat and vegetables, sugar and flour, beans. Cooking fires burned from sun-up to dusk. Babies cried, dogs barked, a guitar was strummed; Ada felt that life had returned to the Malibu.

The first rains came right after the tents were up, and the land that was scorched lifeless, black, began its slow return. Astride a horse, now, wearing men's trousers, with a pistol in the waistband, and under an India rubber coat against the rain Ada, along with the crew of vaqueros, began the slow, painstaking process of erecting the fences along the entire border of the Malibu, using her own survey map as a guide.

She tried not to dwell on the destruction, and for weeks would not visit the schoolhouse—or what might remain of it—refused, too, to visit the site of the vaquero camp or the bridges over Malibu Creek which Emmett had built. But she knew that the fences would soon reach that part of the ranch, and so she rode up the creek one day to see what was there.

The bridges were gone but for the stone foundations on either bank of the creek. She could hear Emmett's voice talking about the original bridges in Italy; closing her eyes, she could see him striding onto the bridge, testing its strength. The creek itself flowed through the burned-out canyon like a vein of healing water; it gave Ada renewed confidence in the recuperative powers of the land. But when she got to the school there was nothing that the blackness of her imagination hadn't already shown her. It might never have even been there at all, so totally were all its traces removed, but for one thing: the round black belly of the wood stove which had never even been used. The sycamores were crumbled around blackened stumps; Ada's view was unobstructed in one direction all the way back to the hills; in the opposite direction to the flat plains beyond the Malibu.

Oh Emmett, Emmett, you were right about it, right to be afraid of other people on the Malibu. And for the first time she was glad he hadn't survived to see all this devastation. She choked on a sob; no, I won't go soft now, I can't. I won't.

The sound of a horse distracted her, and she turned to see Quinones coming up beside the creek. It was his practice to give weekly reports of the ranch's progress, and today brought her the news that half the cattle would have to be sold. "There is little pasturage that did not burn," he said. "The rains will produce more—eventually—but meanwhile the cattle get thinner, and their price goes down. If we sell half now, the other half have a chance, and our loss is not so great as it would be if we held on to them."

Ada reluctantly agreed. As Quinones was about to leave, they both noticed a group of people watching them from the flat plain beyond the Malibu: two adults and two children, sitting in the back of a buckboard, sitting motionless, staring.

"I can't stand how they watch me," Ada said. "Every day I

see them or other people all along the places where the fence goes up."

"They did not expect that you would fence them out," Quinones said. "They did not expect that you would return to the Malibu at all."

"They have you to blame," Ada said. "If you hadn't come to see me that day in the hotel, I might be in Boston now."

Quinones shook his head. "When I see how you work for the Malibu, I know in my heart that you could not have left. If you had, you would have come back. The Malibu has its hold on you now, I can see this."

Ada looked at him and smiled. "You know, I think this is the first time you've ever approved of me," she said, and laughed to see Quinones look away to cover his embarrassment. "But you're right. I could never leave here now." For the Malibu had indeed been reborn. The animals were coming back: she saw three mule deer one day, a half-dozen ground squirrels and opossums and brush rabbits; hawks circled the mountain ridges again; a pair of golden eagles resumed nesting in Las Flores Canyon. She looked out at the hills now: old roots had successfully resisted the fire, and festooned the blackened hills with wild morning glory; seeds buried deep enough to survive the heat began to bear mistletoe and holly and Christmas berry bushes. Her gaze brought into view again the family in the buckboard, still staring at her. She shivered involuntarily. "It's that patient silence that's the worst thing," she said to Quinones. "You just know they're about to break." She looked at them once more then turned away. "Let them break, then. They won't break me."

"Dear Cornelius:

"It looks like my trip to Boston is going to have to be put off for a while. There's so much on the Malibu that needs my attention. As I told you, we're all living in tents, so a visit from you on your summer vacation is probably best put off until I get a house built. That is my next project, but now there is plenty of time—all year—until your next vacation. I've made one change on the Malibu I think you'll like. At Mr. Benson's insistence I had a telephone system run in from Santa Monica. Mr. Benson said that with all the lawsuits coming up against me, the least I can do is be available. The lawsuits are mounting, I'm afraid. Mr. Benson has even hired a law clerk just to keep track of all the appeals and writs and court dates and I don't know what all else. You'd better hurry and get through Harvard Law School, so you can come back and help. Your father always said you were the future of the Malibu. I just want to make absolutely sure the Malibu gets to have a future."

Her first telephone call was from Avery Benson, informing her that the homesteaders' petition to compel her to open the ranch roads was finally being brought to court. "I'm not going to dignify their behavior even by appearing," she shouted into the strange contraption. "We're almost finished fencing in the ranch, besides, so I can't really spare the time. Anyway, no court's going to let them on my land. It's an impossible claim. It's illegal. From the very moment I came back to the Malibu I have known I was in the right. I hate the idea of a court battle, but I know I'll be vindicated."

The last stretch of fence—at Las Flores Canyon—was only a few hundred yards long, from the mouth of the canyon out onto the beach to the high tide line. The rest of the fencing—and the natural barriers of ocean, mountains, canyons and hills—had effectively closed the ranch to the world outside. She missed Emmett right at that moment: he felt so much a part of a gentler past as she so relentlessly moved into the future.

Houses had to be built for the vaqueros and their families; this tent living could not go on much longer. She wanted to build a new house for herself, too, and so the final day of work on the fences was simply another day, and no cause for celebration.

The process of erecting fences on the beach involved sinking postholes in the sand, unraveling the immense bales of barbed wire, and wrapping each post, then cutting, dragging it through the sand to the next post, and the next.

There were, as usual, a few people watching her from the public beaches south of the Malibu. There was always someone watching, not always the same one, either. Today, Ada noticed, two of them on horseback disengaged themselves from the rest and came toward her: their heads came together as they stopped. Ada watched them watching her, their arms gestured toward her and away; finally they came forward. Ada's hand went to the pistol tucked in the waistband of her trousers. She had known this moment would come, and had even looked forward to it, the way she anticipated the crashing of a wave before the sea could be calm again. Ada advanced cautiously on foot. The Hindermans stopped a few feet in front of her: their horses pawed the ground.

"We just come from court, Mrs. Newcomb," Lucius Hinderman said.

Ada clutched the gun in her pocket; would she have to use force to get them off the Malibu now? Wait! Did she have the right? Or did they have the right to be here? Had the courts given them the right? She was appalled at how quickly doubt had stepped in.

"You won," Cassie said, spitting the words out like they had a bitter taste. "Law's on your side." Ada felt their eyes on her, hard and unforgiving.

"Maybe you won in a rich man's court," Lucius said, "but that ain't the only place wars get fought."

"I don't like threats, Mr. Hinderman. Can't you say what you really mean?"

"You make us criminals!" he cried. "To take our produce to the markets, to get ourselves some damned water—we got to break the law. Your law!"

"There's only one law," Ada said.

Lucius hit his leg again as he spoke. "Only it applies to rich people a little more, don't it?"

Cassie pulled his hand down and rode closer to Ada. The two women regarded each other in silence for a long moment. "We was sorry about your husband."

Ada narrowed her eyes and set her jaw hard. "You have no right to say that."

Cassie dropped her gaze. "About those fences, now?" she asked quietly. "Maybe we could make some kind of friendly arrangement. Maybe start up the school again. My Phoebe still—"

"Mrs. Hinderman, I know who's responsible for burning my school!" Ada paused to let the weight of her words be felt. "Even if you didn't intend to burn the Malibu along with it—"

"Me!" Cassie exclaimed.

Ada nodded. "You, one of you. It doesn't matter which one."

"I didn't burn your school," Cassie insisted.

"Don't worry," Ada said. "My lawyer says I need proof, but

the only proof I have—the fact that I know it's so—isn't good
enough for a court of law. And yet you dare to sue me for free
passage! Well, now I'm just making sure that no one sets foot
on the Malibu to cause any more destruction."

"You must be crazy, Mrs. Newcomb," Cassie said, "to think
I'd do something like that. You seen our place? You seen
what's left of it after the fire? Why would I burn down the
Malibu?"

Ada smiled grimly. "I didn't expect an apology," she said.

Lucius rode up to join his wife, and took her arm. "Stop
talking to her." Then he looked at Ada. "None of us
homesteaders is sitting with this," he said. "We're keeping
our lawyer, and we'll sue you till we get our satisfaction. We'll
get our rights."

"You gave up your rights when you started trespassing and
killing my cattle and knocking down my gates and setting
fires—"

"We didn't set no fires!" Cassie cried.

Ada hesitated for a moment then ran up the beach to the
vaqueros' buckboard and took out the sign for the fence:

THE MALIBU RANCH. NO TRESPASSING.
USE SHORE ROAD ONLY AT LOW TIDE.

The sound of her hammering it into the final post resounded
across the beach. Cassie rode up to her and read it. Ada
reached into her pocket and drew out the pistol. "I consider
you trespassers on my land."

Cassie sat straight up, and backed her horse to her husband; they stared at Ada again, then moved off slowly down
the beach.

Ada took a deep breath of sea air, a little giddy. I'm right,
she thought. I'm right, and the courts know it, and I know it,
and now everyone knows it. She looked up the beach and
into the canyon, but there were no witnesses to her triumph,
no one to congratulate her. She got onto her horse and
clicked the reins and took a long, long ride along the sea.

Avery Benson sent her a copy of the judge's decree. The
wording was mercilessly unambiguous, and she thought of
the frustration the homesteaders must have felt when they
heard the judge pronounce his decision:

"According to the law, if Mrs. Newcomb allows the use of
her land by anyone else, she might just as well open it to the
world. Under the principle of 'prescriptive easement', if an

owner has not attempted to halt public use of his property in
any significant way, it would be held as a matter of law that he
intended to dedicate the property to the public. Mrs. Newcomb
had not then and has not now any such wish or intention.

"The mere fact that the roads on the Malibu have been
used by persons without objection from the landowner prior
to now does not make these roads public. The fences in
question are reasonable and proper means of protecting the
defendant's land from trespass, and useful for proper enjoy-
ment thereof. They were built by Mrs. Newcomb in good
faith, with no intention of appropriating or inclosing public
lands or preventing lawful access thereto. In connection with
the fences and natural barriers on the west and north, they
amount to a substantial inclosure of privately owned lands,
and the crux of the question, then, is whether the defendant
can use reasonable, proper, and appropriate means to inclose
her own property without violating federal statutes. In my
judgment she can. The canyon roads have not been built by
the government, or given to it. The United States has no
implied right of way. If the canyon roads were made public
they would chop the ranch up into fragments, and damage its
value without compensation."

Ada knew that this decision did more than keep people off
the Malibu; combined with the very real presence of the
fences—though they were sabotaged, torn down, and rebuilt—
it effectively kept Ada sealed inside.

Chapter 20

In the months that followed the court's decision, letters in support of the homesteaders poured into Ada's Santa Monica postal box: members of the Highway Commission and the Board of Free Trade, the Board of Chinese Laborers and the California Booster Association, various merchants with interests in a coastal road; over a dozen different companies that manufactured automobiles asked her why she was trying to keep them from making a living in Southern California.

A Santa Monica *Chronicle* editorial called her situation "a fight to the last ditch to prevent progress and selfishly maintain the sanctity of her ranch"; Mrs. Newcomb herself, it read, "sheds crocodile tears, and treats homesteaders like timber wolves." Ada sued the newspaper for fifty thousand dollars, a sum she claimed commensurate with the damages done to her reputation. The editor stood behind his reporter; the judge did not, and awarded Ada damages that amounted to a bit less than her court costs.

Regard for the Malibu went down in direct proportion to the development of the areas surrounding it. Santa Monica encroached on her southeastern border, and with the railroad making half a dozen daily excursions from downtown Los Angeles, the beach all the way up to the Malibu line was dotted with bathers. Debris washed ashore as far north as Paradise Cove. At the Ventura County line to the north, and the Santa Monica line to the south, the South Central Railroad was poised, breath held for the go-ahead to come through.

Paperwork kept her at a makeshift desk in the tent more and more of the time, but she managed to ride once a week with Quinones on a general inspection tour of the ranch. What the two of them saw was often disheartening; campfires burning in Bieule Canyon again, a whole line of orange trees untouched by fire now stripped bare, the creek dammed again and the water siphoned off the Malibu.

"We found a dozen cattle with other brands grazing with our herd," Quinones said.

Ada nodded, and made a note of it in a little book she carried around with her just for this purpose. "Did you hire those extra men to patrol the fences at night?"

"Yes, and I gave them rifles, too."

"I'm keeping a careful record of all of these things," Ada said, indicating her notebook. "The next time someone brings me to court, let them try and argue with this. They want proof, here's proof." They covered only a few miles in each day of this inspection, and Ada's notebook filled with offenses. "What gets my goat is the way I'm the one being portrayed as cruel and unreasonable. Look at this! Look at what they do! Who's the victim here?"

The tents at Paradise Cove came down a few at a time as the stucco houses were rebuilt on the old site in Zuma Canyon. Ada continued to conduct business from the tent site; she liked living there, facing the ocean at the ocean's level, "cheek to jowl with the elements," as her mother used to say. And there were fewer associations with Emmett here. But after one winter of heavy rains and another of cold weather, she was forced, despite her fear that Emmett's presence hovered over it, to move back to the cottage above the sheep meadow.

And Emmett's presence was indeed strong—it was the very reason she had avoided the cottage for the past three years. But rather than being haunted by it, Ada found herself comforted instead; she missed him, but no longer grieved. She sometimes sat in his hammock and thought through a problem as he might have, sometimes enlisting his advice by imagining herself to be him. And she was not so alone.

She and Cornelius corresponded, but he hadn't been back from Boston since he first left the Malibu. For one thing, Ada told herself, Christmas vacations from school were never long enough to justify the train ride across the breadth of the country. She could understand why Christmas vacations were out, and so accustomed herself to the idea of only seeing him in the summer. But the first summer he had just been enrolled in a new school and Ada agreed with his aunt Elizabeth that it would be best if he wasn't taken out just yet, not when he was so far behind the other boys. Just before the second summer Cornelius wrote that he'd been invited to

spend July and August with a family in Newport, Rhode
Island, and would that be all right with her? Ada wrote back
that of course, yes, he must go with his friends and that yes,
of course she'd miss him nevertheless. During the third
summer Ada was so involved in the road cases, she asked that
Cornelius put off his trip so she wouldn't spend his whole
vacation in court. The fourth summer he spent in Boston,
taking brush-up Latin and Greek for fall entry into Harvard.
She wrote that she looked forward to the day of his return: "I
can't always manage the Malibu alone, Cornelius. A young
lawyer is the ideal role for you." She thought: a young scion
of the new Malibu. It would be Cornelius, she remembered
Emmett saying, who would escort the Malibu into the future.
But she was no longer sure she knew the boy who signed his
letters "love, Cornelius." She was too proud to insist he visit
his home; and though she missed him very little, she could
not help but resent him for not wanting to come sooner. The
memory of the Newcomb family of their early Malibu years
had long since become simply a fact on the ledger of the past.

Ada stood at the door of the cottage and watched the
one-horse carriage making its way up the hill. The presence
of the pistol in the deep pocket of her skirt allayed her fears,
but no one should have gotten this far into the Malibu. There
was always someone using the prerogative of the low tide line
and riding along the shore; there was nothing she could do
about that, as long as they kept down there and didn't stray
onto the Malibu sands. Yet, every time someone rode by, the
sight stuck in the corner of her eye like a cinder, and
bothered her till they were gone. Who was this coming up
the hill now? She kept a close eye on the carriage as it came
toward her, and was quite surprised at its occupant.

She hadn't seen N. F. Gass since the 1900 celebration at
the Santa Monica Pier Hotel, and the years had made just the
change in him she might have expected. He'd let his whiskers
get overgrown, and it made him look just a little wild. He'd
become stout, too, but every new pound seemed to be
inhabited; there was no excess. As the carriage came closer,
he waved a beefy hand and smiled; he seemed to be assessing
her, admiring and laughing at her all at once. Ada ran a hand
over her hair, and straightened the collar of her shirt. She
remembered the offer of money for the Malibu N. F. Gass
had made on the terrace of the Pier Hotel; oh, how I wanted

to wipe that satisfied smile off his face. The same smile was on his face today.

The carriage stopped near her. N. F. Gass doffed his hat and got out. "My deepest sympathies for your loss," he said.

"My husband's been dead for three years, Mr. Gass."

N. F. smiled pleasantly, and bowed as if Ada had accepted his condolences with a curtsy.

"How'd you get up here?" she asked.

"I can pay your guards more than you can, evidently."

Ada looked away before he unsettled her further. Her skin felt feverish hot; got too much sun today. She looked down the hill and thought of the guards, and was alarmed.

"I was working in my office at the hotel on the pier, and thought I'd come and take a good look at your place again. Always liked the Malibu as a piece of property." His glance took in the modest cottage without much interest, then moved down the hill. "Doing much good, fencing the place in?"

"The trespassing's worse than ever," Ada admitted. "It's like a nightmare. Roads raking down the canyons and across the ranch. Gates sawed in half, padlocks shot off. They uproot fence posts, they empty their guns on the 'no trespassing' signs. I can only cover so many miles of the ranch each week. By the time I revisit a place, a month or more's gone by and it's all begun again."

"People are eager to get places these days."

"And they're evidently willing to destroy the very ground they travel on."

"You're getting quite a reputation," N. F. said. "You get your name in the papers, and you're not even trying. That's a real accomplishment at a time when getting their names in the papers is what most of the citizens out here are doing as a full-time occupation. 'Course, you're not trying to sell anything. Or are you?"

"I'm just trying to preserve my ranch," Ada said. "I'm immune to flattery."

"I didn't think the woman'd been born that didn't like a compliment."

"You never did have a very high opinion of women."

"Maybe not," he said. "I heard you carry a gun, Mrs. Newcomb. That true?"

Ada slipped it out of her pocket, eyes on his, and hefted it in the palm of her hand, as if testing its weight. She'd learned to use it by practicing on tree stumps in deserted canyons at dawn; she had never used it on anything that breathed.

N. F. narrowed his eyes. The smile was gone. "Woman like you don't need a gun," he said darkly.

"I wouldn't have one if I didn't need it."

N. F. nodded, staring at the gun. "Maybe you're right. Guess I'm not the only one who wants the Malibu. The Highway Commission's got some bright ideas about a road ripping up across your beach. By now you must've had offers from Doheny's oil company. And land grabbers who—"

"I guess you and the South Central Railroad would know all about land-grabbing," Ada said.

N. F. smiled appraisingly at her. "Funny how particular the law can be, though. At some point you're going to have to give."

"Are you the one who's going to tell what that point is?"

"I'd like to be around when it happens."

"You'll have a long wait," Ada said. "I'll take on all comers, and I'll beat them, because the law is on my side."

N. F. moved his hat back on his head. "I admire your confidence, Mrs. Newcomb, but let's face certain facts. California's on my side."

"I don't believe the state of California can be bought as easily as one of my guards. Maybe ten, fifteen years ago. Not now."

N. F. looked hard at her and didn't speak for a moment. "You mind if I light a cigar?" He said this even as he took one out of an ebony case and lit it, puffed, drew and looked at her again. Ada thought he was doing this elaborate charade just to make her wait for him. "Why not make it easy on yourself and all of us? If you let me have the rights to shore land for my railroad tracks, instead of me having to take them from you, I'll throw my weight behind you in your fights with these other people. You're going to lose, Mrs. Newcomb, and I think, deep in your heart, you know that."

"I judge the situation by the law, not by what I feel in my heart, Mr. Gass. And I'll wager you do the same."

N. F. Gass laughed. "I like you, Mrs. Newcomb. I really do." He sighed and shrugged. "Well, I tried asking in a nice way, didn't I? Can't anyone say I didn't behave like a gentleman."

He smiled, and slid a packet of papers from his pocket. "This here is a court order saying that the public can't be denied rail transportation between the northern and southern boundaries of the Malibu Ranch, which is the only stretch from north to south on the coast that hasn't got them." Ada looked at the papers, but made no move to take them. "You still don't quite get the point," he said. "Eminent domain—the right of the government to take private property for public use if it sees fit. With compensations of a financial nature, of course. The government's on the side of the people. It's issued condemnation proceedings on the shorefront property of the Malibu Ranch."

Ada read the papers now, while N. F. Gass puffed calmly on his cigar. She looked up after a few moments. "Now, now," he said good-naturedly, "don't look so stricken, Mrs. Newcomb. The South Central—I mean, the people of Southern California—are only entitled to the land the tracks are on, plus fifty yards on either side. You'll still have lots left."

"And you'll finally get what you want, Mr. Gass," Ada said. "An uninterrupted line of railroad tracks from San Francisco to Santa Monica." The entire situation seemed suddenly to be nothing more than a scheme to humiliate her, "Why didn't you give this to me right away?"

"Might not have had such a good time if I told you right away," N. F. said, looking past her at the Malibu. His eyes swept it, mountains to canyons to the beach and sea beyond.

Damn him! And damn Emmett, too, for dying and leaving me with everything started, everything dreamed up and all of it still to be paid for or saved.

"I always hated this place," N. F. said finally, and got into his carriage. He guided the horse in a full circle until he was facing Santa Monica again, then leaned out to Ada and put on his hat; he was smiling now.

Ada telephoned to Avery Benson right after N. F. Gass left, then rode to the vaquero camp and enlisted Quinones. By dusk the three sat on the small porch of the cottage and looked down the hills, wondering, each of them, if this was the end of the Malibu Ranch.

"What I'm afraid of is that the railroad coming on the ranch is only a preview of what's going to happen in the future," Ada said grimly. "It's not just that the tracks are going to destroy the beach, but that, for the first time, control of who comes on the ranch will be in someone else's hands." She paced, stopped, turned to Avery. "Isn't there anything I can do?"

"From a legal point of view," Avery said haltingly, ". . . no . . . not now that the courts have granted Gass the right."

"We could appeal again," Ada said. "Take him to court, stall for time until we think of something."

"Ada, the fortune Emmett left was considerable—I say *was* because it's certainly diminished since the fire. You can't just keep on pouring money into the Malibu and not make any. The Malibu is your main asset, but it's taking all the rest— your cash, Emmett's investments and securities—just to maintain it. These court costs mount, you know. The legal costs for the fence suits alone forced you to sell all your shares in Pacific Mutual Life Insurance."

"I have no choice but to liquidate whatever I need to save the land."

"Ada, once the South Central lays railroad tracks across the Malibu, your rights of prescriptive easement will end. That means the road case will be reopened, the homesteaders' case, the highway commission—"

"But why should the government say yes to the railroad?" Quinones, silent up till this moment, stood and spoke. "Doesn't private property count for anything in the state of California?"

Ada looked hopefully at Avery, but he simply shook his head. "The South Central is one of the corporations that paid for this state in the first place, I'm afraid. Ada, when Gass told you that California was on his side, he knew what he was talking about." He reached into his briefcase and drew out a newspaper. "Story about Mr. Gass's plans in today's Los Angeles *Times*. Let me read you something from it. 'The progress of the South Central's railroad tracks along the coast is only temporarily halted by factors still under negotiation.'"

"That's me, I suppose," Ada said. "A factor still under negotiation."

Avery held out the paper to her. "There's also a map of the coastline from San Diego to San Francisco, marked with the South Central's proposed route."

Ada looked at the map; heavy black crosses like surgical stitches were drawn all the way along the shoreline, including the twenty-six miles of the Malibu, "as if it were just another stretch of land." Ada threw the paper down in disgust. "But I can't just give up on it now!"

"We'll salvage what we can," Avery said. "The government will see to it that substantial financial reparations are made. This might be a blessing in disguise."

"I remember Emmett talking about the future of the Malibu beyond himself and me, even beyond Cornelius. Would he ever have believed that the price for keeping the Malibu would include the destruction of huge pieces of it?"

There was a silence among the three people now, and the dry, harsh sound of the wind rustling the newspaper.

"Damn!" Ada said. "The South Central wants a railroad, and they get one. For 'the people.' Greed, greed, greed. Who'd believe it? I might as well build one myself for all the protection from it I have on the ranch. At least that way I'd be the one in charge, at least it'd be my own railroad and my own tracks and... Maybe we should bomb theirs... oh, damn!"

There was silence again; the sun was setting in a long lick of gold on the distant sea. "I've got to be getting back to the city," Avery said quietly and started stuffing papers into his briefcase. "I'll talk to the South Central lawyers tomorrow and—"

"Is it possible?" Quinones asked Ada. "Is it possible to build a small railroad on the Malibu, your own railroad?"

Ada hesitated. "My own railroad..." She turned to Avery. "Is it?"

Avery laughed and shook his head. "Your own railroad? But you're joking, aren't you?"

"Just... just think about it for a minute," Ada said. Her mind raced down a path, half expecting to come to a thudding stop but, no, the thought continued, on, on... "Avery! No judge would let two sets of railroad tracks go through the same piece of property, would he?"

"Well, I..."

"It's just common sense that if there already was a railroad through the Malibu, the South Central's claim to build another one would be thrown out of court. Avery?" She was almost laughing now. "Is this crazy, or do we have a chance?"

Avery cleared his throat, stalling for time. "It sounds logical, I admit. Even possible, but..."

"But I would obey to the letter just what the condemnation proceedings against me called for. Look." She held the condemnation papers, reading from them. "A set of railroad tracks between the southern and northern borders of the Malibu. One set, not two. And it would be mine."

"It would still be a chance," Avery said. "If the courts upheld Gass's first claim after you'd done all your work, you'd be left with—"

But Ada hardly heard him now. "And I'd serve condemnation proceedings on him this time. How I'd love that."

El Valle square was crossed with paths of cracked tiles in bird and flower patterns; between them a dozen banana palms and stunted pepper trees grew out of the sand; worn stone benches from the early days of the pueblo faced a bandshell—relic of the square's brief life as a marketplace before the Gold Rush—where the nightly entertainment now was most likely to be a gunfight or a stabbing. The heat was a permanent resident; no breeze stirred the air. The square smelled of cooking oil and frangipani, stale beer, and the meatier scent of dried blood.

Obie found his way here from the Sisters of Mercy by moving deeper and deeper into the city; alone, surrounded by the open air, he felt exposed, nerve endings flayed by the sun. He wanted only to hide in the denseness of population.

Men drifted through pools of yellow light in the square to smoke cigarettes in the shadows of the banana palms; a lone guitar repeated the opening bar of "La Loma." Old Mexican women padded silently by, their heads wrapped in black rebozos. Vendors sold manzanita roots for fuel. On one side of the square the houses clung to the steeply sloping Fort Moore hill.

For the first few days, the whores were the only ones he ever spoke to. After the first weeks the other habitues of El Valle Square, and especially the Hotel McWilliams, let him know by a little nod that when it came to life lived close to the bone, they knew he knew. After a few months they hardly saw him; he was simply there, a fact, like midnights at twelve, and so what?

Nights hummed with static electricity, pierced with the poignant cries of the sweet-potato vendor far off near the railroad station. The yellow light from cooking fires and the sticky smoke that clung to the skin made people feel sick. The residents of the square had known hunger; some of them were no strangers to dressing in the dark with the rent due at dawn. More than a few had felt their wrists grabbed by a sheriff for the bulge in their saddlebags that shouldn't have been there.

If you wanted to find a man to throw a brick through the window of a gent's store who owed you, he'd most likely be in

Hot Sally's; if you wanted someone to pick someone clean, he'd be in the Hotel McWilliams bar, practicing.

Obie waited till sundown every night—no one'd ever seen him in the day—then came out of his rented room on the second floor of the McWilliams. His hat was pulled low over his face, dark glasses in place, never mind it being night, shirt collar up against the pinched neck-skin. The outside stair let him in the alley behind the hotel; he lingered there in the darkness before going into the bar. He liked listening to the high-pitched chatter on the streets, especially of the Mexican whores. He liked to see them light their black cigarettes, and blow blue smoke through puckered mouths. Hot and restless, he liked watching them lure strangers into these tiny rooms on the top floor of the McWilliams.

Inside the bar, the bartender brought him a bottle of rye and a day-old copy of the Los Angeles *Times*. Obie slapped down his four bits, and went back upstairs and sat with them in the dark. He hated the burn of the rye going down, but he wouldn't change it; he didn't want anything to make things smoother. The first swallow of rye burned; the second one burned, too, and he was glad. The room was black in the corners and deeper blue everywhere else, except by the window, where a sickly yellow haze from outside penetrated the curtain. He sat on the narrow bed, in the darkest corner, farthest from the window. He sat quiet and still, hands clutched around the rye, the newspaper pressed to his side, thinking about breathing, about the fire in his gut, listening to the sound coming up from the streets, and knowing that outside of hell itself this was sure the right place. He lit a candle on the bedside table; the small yellow flame threw dim shadows around the room, made the place look like it had the fever bad. He lowered his head under the brim of his hat, and adjusted his dark glasses. He drank one long pull from the bottle, gasped, downing it, and took another.

His hands hurt something fierce. He drew off his gloves, rubbed in Cloverine salve, and the stinging on his palms lessened, but the skin kept peeling off in hunks; slow-welling blood rose to the surface. He relished the stinging, savored it; all he had left to have a feeling for was this burning pain to prepare him for life in hell. Only right thing about it's at least I don't have to touch my own face. He slid the dark glasses down what was left of the bridge of his nose. His eyes didn't burn so much in the dark; neither did the skin on his face. No matter that the fire was long past: the fire never stopped for him.

There was a soft knocking at his door, and it opened. The yellow light from the hallway spilled in; Obie put his arm over his face. "Shut it," he hissed. When the door closed, he opened his eyes and lowered his arm. Used to the dark, used to silhouettes, he beckoned her to him, and lay back on the bed, in deep shadow and watched her come closer. "You looked scared, señorita. Don't be scared. Didn't your friends tell you? I'm just a bad man, that's all. You know about bad men, don't you?" She giggled, and sank her weight on the bed at his feet. He picked up the bottle of rye, again and again, and by his fifth pull at it he was whispering fierce truths to her in the dark: ". . . till I got shoved out of the way by certain folks just too eager to make their own end of it and forget me, push me out of it, leave me with the damn leavings to lap up like I was some damn pussycat and glad for it. But I fixed 'em good, fixed 'em good. Burned up the whole damn place, and now there's no chance of Obie coming home 'cause she'd know just by looking at me what I done." He took the bottle and fumbled it to his mouth, took another pull. "I'm an old cowhand from the Rio Grande!" He slammed his hands on the bed, and laughed when she bounced, then gasped in shock at the new pain in his palms. ". . . Malibu ranch . . . damn, damn . . . and now I'm out, I'm out, down, down and out at the Hotel damn McWilliams. Damn!" He stood up, wavered and sank back on the bed. "Her land . . . who took a back seat? Who always took a back seat?" He stood up unsteadily and again tumbled back. "She owed me!" He was whimpering as he slid off the bed to his knees, but his face was immobile, a mask of passivity.

He pulled himself back onto the bed and edged his way into the shadows at the head of it. He jabbed the girl with the side of his boot. "Unbutton." He puffed out his chest to indicate his shirt. She leaned over him. He felt drenched in the sour smell of her long wavy hair—pomade and sweat and smoke from the cigarettes of a thousand men. "Turn away," he said when his shirt was open, and when she did he lit a match to the other candle on the bedside table, then leaned back into the shadow. He pulled at her arm and she turned back; the candlelight showed the pockmarks she'd covered with powder, her mouth greasy and bright red, a tiny pink tongue poked out like an animal testing the terrain. He

pulled her head down and whispered fiercely. The girl nodded, reached for the candle, then hesitated; Obie sighed,
disgusted and impatient, and squirmed on the bed. He was
truly excited now, her hesitation, her hand so close to the
candle, and soon the exquisite licks of flame on his chest
while her other hand did its work inside his pants. He
watched her unsteady fingers grasp the flickering candle and
hold it over his chest. A drop spilled, tingling, another; he
cried out, and his chest lifted as if to meet the pain. Then she
hesitated, again, the flame was flickering.

"Go on, go on, do it. Do it!"

But she leaped away, frightened, and the candle fell onto
the bedspread and started burning. In the instant between
the moment it went up and the moment Obie clapped the
flame dead, the girl saw his face in the flames, and gasped,
holding her hands over her mouth and throat. Obie saw, and
made no fast move to cover himself. Slowly, then, his eyes on
the girl, he put on his hat and his dark glasses. The flame out,
the room plunged back into the darkness. The girl was
crossing herself and mumbling frantically: "Dios, Dios." Obie
made a move toward her and she leaped back. He stepped
into the darkness near the bed, nodding, nodding.

He knew what she saw: a man whose face showed the
horror and sin of what he'd done right there on the outside, a
man's face turned inside out by the sheer terror of being him:
the scream on the outside, the scars and the glassy ridges of
flesh stretched white and red, and stitched together rough,
the nasty blue welts that wouldn't go down, the swelling, the
infections. "Won't die from it, neither," he said with a mean
laugh, and thought: I'm past dying, I died already in that fire,
and what's left's nothing nobody even wants to put out of its
misery. "Go on," he said. "Beat it."

He pulled off his shirt and let it fall to the floor, tripped on
it, and stumbled into the wall. His body was white, still, and
smooth, no different than when Ada left. He looked out the
window and squinted at the moon, his flesh dyed now a pale
blue. He was sliding down, down fast and sure. I'm a bad
man, he thought this every day, and going straight to hell if
I'm that lucky. I'm dead is what; just got the walkies, is all.

He got to his feet again and stumbled in the dark room to
the middle of the floor, swaying, eyes closed just to show
himself how it didn't matter where you were when you
couldn't see. His vision was failing, eyes burned too bad, no

more'n a swimmery sight of things, all wavery under slow balmy water. Any light, tears flooded his eyes; the light was repentance and punishment. He thought how nice that old roof was, old roof, he thought.

He slid down along the wall, and half-fell onto the stack of newspapers. He slapped his hand on it, and felt a tickling trickle of blood slide down his wrist. He held yesterday's newspaper up to the moonlight. Long used to looking at personal column messages, it didn't surprise him that since the fire her name began to appear in the other pages of the paper as well. Know her as good as if I was there by her side. "...ten thousand acres burned...started in the Malibu schoolhouse..." That's how he learned how it happened, and he'd squeezed his left fist tight to grab the feel of skin cracking inside the leather glove.

"The late Emmett Newcomb..." Never was my doing he died; the hissing of the thought was cool and blue as the moon. Well, that's the end of it, he thought. That's the end.

Then: "Mrs. Newcomb Moves Back to Malibu." "Mrs. Newcomb Builds New Houses on Malibu." "Road Suit Brought Against Owner of Malibu." "Mrs. Newcomb Builds Fences on Malibu." "South Central Sues for Passage Across Malibu." And there tonight on page four: "Mrs. Newcomb Fights Battle to Build Own Railroad." Obie moaned, and let the paper fall onto his lap. He watched the moon rising over the Hot Sally saloon at the far end of la Calle de Los Negros.

He didn't sleep, not something he recognized as sleep at all, but a kind of rising and filling the room out to the darkest corners, aching all over with the expansion: the whole room an extension of the burns on his face and hands, his eyes burning; he closed them and they stayed on fire. Now even the darkness hurt him. His mind was flaming hot inside; he gritted his teeth against the pain. Ada, it's you. Ada, hold still, stand there, no more trains. Her face swam up out of the pain, quivering behind a sheet of flame, and he felt if he could just pull her through and onto the other side of the flame with him, pull her through it, into it where she could burn with him.

"No, Ada, no! This time the train's not leaving without me." He moaned. "Oh Ada, I want to die with you. Ada, die with me, please, please, Ada."

Chapter 21

Ada filed her application with the Los Angeles Board of Supervisors for incorporation as the Malibu Railway Line, Ada Newcomb, President. She spent the next months trying to find an engineer to lay the tracks. The first few told her they already had more work than they could handle. Another few complained that the job didn't pay enough for what they'd have to do. Some came drunk to speak to her, some didn't show up at all.

"Just come from Fairbanks, Alaska, working on a roadbed in the oil fields. Seen nothing but snow last six months, be glad to get back in the sun." Pete Schuyler had white-blond hair, and a long narrow face with heavy eyelids that made Ada think half of what he was saying wasn't quite true. Though he was specific about his background—"I'm a native Californian, yes ma'm, daddy was a forty-niner, mother was a whore"—he was vague about his previous experience, referring to viaducts and spans and flying buttresses.

"Like to take a look around," he said. "Take a week, maybe, and map out a route. See what I see, see how you like it."

"A week! A week seems like a very long time."

Schuyler tilted his hat back off his head. "I see you don't know much about laying railroad tracks. You see, there has to be a kind of marriage of the tracks to the terrain, a kind of—"

"All I know is that I'm in a rush," Ada said.

"But you wouldn't want to start this project till the spring, anyway."

"The spring!"

"Can't do much work in the sand when it's raining, Mrs. Newcomb."

"But I haven't got till the spring," Ada said. "Circumstances are such that I . . . I have to have it finished soon."

Schuyler took two days instead of the week, and returned to the Malibu with a stack of notes and a tentative route for the tracks. "I'll show you," he said. "Let's ride."

The sea looked thick as pea soup in the shallows as they rode along the shore. Just the smell of the salt air reaffirmed Ada's convictions about the Malibu.

"The track'll skim the top of the hills right here," Schuyler said as they rode past two rolling hills a few hundred yards back from the water.

"Oh, but then you'd be able to see the train from the beach," Ada said. "I want it hidden."

"Can't do that," Schuyler said. "Unless you want to blast tunnels through the hills." Ada opened her mouth to speak but hesitated and said nothing; Schuyler continued. "OK. The tracks come down the side of the far hill, and swing out onto the beach there—" he pointed to the vee between the hills "—and hug the base of the hills for a few miles still—"

"Your plan is to lay tracks on the beach?" Ada slowed her horse and hung back to cast a narrow-eyed look at the prospective track line. She clicked her reins, and caught up with Schuyler. A few miles further on, they rode up off the beach and stopped to look across a flat plain backed by rolling purple hills and golden mountains beyond.

Schuyler moved his finger in an arc toward the horizon. "Right along there."

"But this is prime grazing land," Ada said.

"Oh." Schuyler turned his head. "Well, you could keep them on the beach—"

"I don't want that!"

Schuyler shrugged. "You're sure you really want this train to come across?"

"I hoped you'd find ways of concealing it," she replied.

"Conceal a railroad and miles of tracks?" Schuyler shook his head, and they rode onto Paradise Cove, where they stopped again at the base of one of the twin peaks rising above them. "A bridge from the southeast peak to the northwest peak."

"Oh yes, were you able to study those drawings I gave you?"

Schuyler took out the drawings. "I did, but you're not really serious about this bridge being built here."

"Why not? My husband had some very good and beautiful ideas for the Malibu. Before the fire he—"

"I'm not saying it isn't pretty," Schuyler said.

"Well, then?"

Schuyler jammed his foot into the base of the hill, then

eaned down and scooped up some earth. "Didn't your husband ever put his hands on the sand in these peaks? A strong
wind blows it away, changes the whole terrain, for God's sake.
Support beams would have nothing to set in. Add that to the
weight of a locomotive and... well!"

Ada took Emmett's sketches back from him and rolled
them up tightly. "Never mind, then."

"The location's basically right, Mrs. Newcomb, but the
bridge needs to be lighter. Let me show you the plans for a
wooden viaduct I built in Portago, New York." He took some
old papers out of his pocket and smoothed them on his knee.
Ada gave them a cursory look, and shook her head.

"I'm looking for someone who'll do it my way," she said.

Schuyler folded his papers and stuffed them back into his
pocket. "I'm sure you can buy anything these days in Los
Angeles, Mrs. Newcomb. No reason you shouldn't be able to
buy someone's opinion to suit your own." He turned his horse
around to leave.

"What did Mr. Gass offer you to turn me down?" Ada
called after him, and Schuyler pulled his horse around back
to her. "I know this project's got a reputation," she said. "So
I'm not surprised that you're afraid."

Schuyler scratched his head and laughed and rode back to
her. "You're in a funny position, Mrs. Newcomb. You know
that everyone's been paid not to take this job, or they've
been threatened that they won't work in California again if
they do, or they aren't fit to hire. All except me, and you're
making it pretty impossible for me to stay on."

"Couldn't Mr. Gass meet your price?" she asked.

"My price is five thousand dollars. Mr. Gass offered me
ten."

"Then you're on my side."

Schuyler shook his head. "I'm on *my* side. I just don't trust
people who overpay me."

All the usual Malibu sounds—of the wind and the sea, a
horse's neigh, cows mooing, gulls crying—were like blessed
silence compared to the noise that wracked the sky once the
work began.

Schuyler raided the tea houses and rice parlors of Chinatown
for a work gang, promising them twenty-eight dollars a
month—Ada couldn't spend more, she said, and they wouldn't

do it for less. If Ada won, he told them, there'd be more
tracks to lay, jobs that might last as long as three years.

Once more the tents were set up on the beach: one
functioned as a bathhouse, another as a company store where
the two hundred men could buy dried oysters, bamboo
sprouts, and abalone meat.

The workers themselves, in uniform black pajamas, hardly
spoke at all, the only human sound Schuyler's voice shouting
orders as he walked his horse alongside the line.

The rails were shipped into Paradise Cove, and a makeshift
street of wooden planks was built on the beach to slide the
rails across. Immense barrels of gravel were rolled along this
same wooden street, the gravel packed in tightly against the
sand from the line beginning at the mouth of Las Flores
Canyon. One set of men dug long, low pits, another packed
the pits with gravel, a third laid the wooden slats into the
gravel in a ladder formation, the next pulled the rails themselves on the slats, and a final crew drove in the spikes.

Quinones kept the rest of the ranch running as he usually
did, and Ada tried to keep her own attention on it, too, but
there was an urgency to the track-laying that occupied her
mind even when it did not require her time or presence.
Trespassing did not cease; she saw its grim evidence in full
brazen display wherever she rode, no matter that she had
won the right to fence in her property and maintain her
gates. Whatever doubt she'd had about the inequity of her
situation over the homesteaders' was dissipated at the sight of
gates torn down and wagon-wheel ruts dug into her pasture
lands, of fences cut and grazing land used by homesteader
cattle, of a half-dozen of her new sheep poisoned, and the
capture one night of two men with dynamite and a firing
device in their satchels. Miles away on her weekly check of
the ranch with Quinones, Ada still heard the sound of spikes
being pounded into the rails like the bells of doomsday, their
harsh metallic clang brutal under the clear blue sky and high
hazy clouds. She thought that the vibrations must go right to
the center of the earth.

Schuyler worked in what had been Ada's old tent, in
Paradise Cove, leaning over a long trestle table, plans and
sketches laid out or pinned to the canvas flaps.

"Listen," Ada said. "Today's Los Angeles *Times*: 'N. F.

Gass, President of the South Central Railroad says "Harbor or no harbor, interference or cooperation, there will be a complete coastal rail system before the century is ten years old. The will of the people shall be served."'" Ada threw the paper down. "Oh, what a bag of wind!! 'Harbor or no harbor.' He's lost the harbor appropriation unless he can get the north-south coastal route, and he can't because I've stopped him." She laughed a little wildly, then a chasm of doubt yawned in front of her, and she clutched Schuyler's arm. "Oh, Pete, have we stopped him, though? Is it really possible to do this?"

Schuyler patted her hand reassuringly. "The thing is, a full-sized engine is going to be too heavy to get across the bridge the way you want the bridge, or it's going to come sliding down the hills in the first rain." He took his pencil to Emmett's sketch. "We've got to simplify the design, Mrs. Newcomb, get it as light as possible without sacrificing strength." He crossed out some lines on the sketch, drew in others. "The embankments would wash out in the first bad rain if we used all the concrete your husband indicated here. We use wood instead, except on these central beams. Now don't groan, Mrs. Newcomb. You know what the South Central would do in this case? They'd take down the hill."

Ada watched him alter Emmett's design with swift, confident strokes of his pencil; it was all she could do to keep from clamping her hand on his wrist.

"I save you ten dollars a foot on this bridge by using timber, and not steel," he said.

"Really? Well..." She could hold it back no longer. "Stop. You'll have to... make some other adjustment. I mean to keep my husband's design."

Schuyler looked at her and shook his head in dismay. "You're determined to have this fall out from under you."

"But don't you see why I have to keep it Emmett's way? Just erasing his ideas... I can't. I just can't do that."

"I understand," Schuyler sighed and looked at the drawing again. "Does it say anything in the condemnation proceeding about the size of the engine?"

"No, I don't think so."

"We could build from the original design, and lighten the engine instead of the bridge, I suppose."

"Oh, that's a wonderful idea," Ada said.

"Don't expect a modest denial from me," Schuyler replied
and leaned over his drawing board again.

If Ada had once been perceived by social journalist Han
Fisher as "a lonely beacon of reaction in the wilderness o
progress" in her consistent refusal to open the Malibu for th
"good roads," this same intransigence began to be irritating
as a thorn in the heel even to her supporters. A feature is
Sunset Magazine appeared detailing Ada's "reclusive monop
oly" of the coast, and quoted N. F. Gass: "Towns to the north
and south of her go begging for a coastal route." Letters to
the editor of the *Times* asked if it was legal for one person to
own so much land—"and if it is it shouldn't be!"—and wen
on to question the very existence of a ranch left over from th
days of Alta California. "What is the use of such a place in th
twentieth century?" one letter asked.

The change in the weather began to alarm her. The sky wa
white through mid-afternoon, with a faint milky halo of sun;
week later high clouds were gathering out at sea, and a chil
dampness stayed in the air. The fog sometimes did not lift a
all, and even the heat of the sun did not pierce it. Along the
mountain ridges hovered long tubelike clouds. The air wa
very still; there was something in it that absorbed all sounds
When the workmen stopped for the day, the silence wa
awesome.

"How'd you ever come to work on the railroads?" Ad
asked Schuyler when they came back to his tent after a
inspection of the rails. "I never did check up on you
references, you know."

Schuyler smiled and leaned his elbows on his knees. Ad
leaned forward too; sometimes, in this weather, it was hard t
hear your own voice. "Got my start at Promontory Point
Utah, in 1869," he said, "the year they joined the rails eas
and west. That was a day I won't forget. 'Course, I was only
the cook's boy at the time, but I was there, watched 'en
hammer in that last spike. It wasn't made of gold, you know
that was a story a newspaper man dreamed up." He closed
his eyes as if he could see the whole scene before him. "Tha
first train barreling through—the sound of it! And the cheering!
He opened his eyes and slapped the work table, his eyes li
up. "I felt like I was in on the beginning of some kind o

greatness. Fell in love with the railroads right then, right here."

"When I was a little girl, I fell in love with the river that ran through our town. Thought that'd be the way to see everything. My picture of America was rivers flowing into rivers flowing into rivers. All I ever wanted to do was jump in and get swept away."

"Where'd you want to get swept to?"

"Never thought about it. I didn't think much about the future at all. That was my husband's territory—California as the land of the future, the Malibu as the future of California."

Ada watched the ocean outside the tent: still, but cowed under the fierce gray sky; ominous swells barreled up the beach and sucked deep gouges in the sand. Thunderclaps pealed above them.

"Have you ever built anything else besides railroads?" Ada asked.

"What'd you have in mind?"

Ada stayed at the opening of the tent, looking out. "I'm going to build a house some day," she said, half to herself, a spoken vow to the memory of Emmett. She turned to Schuyler. "My son can't very well come home if there's no house, can he?"

"Kids don't mind that," Schuyler said.

Ada pictured Cornelius's face and shook her head. "No, we'd need a big house."

"I'll build your house for you," Schuyler said. "I'd be proud to do it."

"Would you?" Ada said and turned to him. "Because... you seem to... to have a feel for the kind of land the Malibu is. I wouldn't want someone who didn't have a certain feel for it." Schuyler nodded, but did not speak. "Maybe when you're done with the railroad we could talk about it."

"You're talking about the future, you know," Schuyler said with a shy smile.

"I know I am."

"Fine with me."

"You know, the only things Emmett saved from the fire were all his ideas for the future. The bridge was just one of them. Another was a big house on the hill. Oh, the plans he had for the Malibu..." She was looking at the ocean again, as if the unknown could be written there.

Schuyler didn't say anything, but this time his silence

made Ada turn to him. His head was down, shoulders
hunched, she couldn't see his face. "Sure, I'll look at his
plans," he said finally, "Why not?"

Rain had threatened for so long—the workmen rushing to
finish the last stretch of tracks—that when it finally arrived it
was a relief, like a fever finally broken and the worst over.
But the worst, Ada feared, was far from over.

She and Schuyler traveled slowly alongside the track bed,
the rails glistened dully in the cloudy rain sky. Gravel not
only filled the road bed, but packed the shoulders next to it
and tumbled in little clumps down the hills on the sides of it.
"The water's already collecting on the bed itself," Schuyler
said. "Pretty soon it'll loosen the gravel, and that'll loosen the
tracks, and that could send the locomotive tumbling right of
it. I'm going to have to do something I said I wouldn't do."

"What's that?" Ada said.

"I'm going to have to dig channels into the hill all along the
track bed."

"Dig into the hills! But—"

"I know, I know. But there's no other way. With the
channels dug, the water'll drain off and be absorbed into the
beach sand."

Ada looked at the low hills and imagined them dug up,
scored with ruts. "I save the land by destroying it."

"No, no, don't look at it that way," Schuyler said. "You...lose
a little to save the rest."

The engine arrived in two sections in the cargo hold of a
steamer docked at Paradise Cove, but the sea was too rough
even in the cove to unload safely. Ada joined Schuyler on the
pier; they held to the railings and watched the ocean in
silence. The rain came down in steady sheets, falling soundlessly
into the sea. The steamer glistened in the rain as if it had
been silvered.

"Almost done," Schuyler said.

Behind them the land looked like a dream, half-hidden by
the rain. Ada looked at the bridge spanning the cove peaks,
short sections of lumber over a lacy grillwork frame. It looked
like a drawing in a child's story book; she thought she could
see it swaying in the wind.

"Will it really hold the locomotive?"

"It'll hold this one," Schuyler said.

"If you can get if off the boat."

"I'll get it off."

"N. F. Gass asked me to come and see him tomorrow, says he's got some news for me."

"Oh, I'll bet."

"I'm too curious not to go," Ada replied. "Maybe he's changed his mind, maybe he doesn't want to come through any more. He sees we've actually built the roadbed and the tracks...I'm curious, that's all."

"You know that all he's going to do is make an offer like the kind he made to everyone else who tried to have anything to do with Malibu."

"I have to go into Avery Benson's in Los Angeles anyway."

"I'll watch the fort till you get back," he said. "The tracks are holding their own with the channels dug, but I wish this rain'd finally come to an end. Just get the locomotive onto the tracks and then business as usual on the Malibu, I suppose. Guess I'll just be on my way..." He shrugged, looked sideways at Ada, and back at the sea.

"There was a time not so long ago," she said, "when no one came on the Malibu at all. Amazing what I've had to do to save it. Emmett was lucky not to have seen it happen this way. Except for the fire, his dream of the Malibu has stayed intact. I think what's happening now is worse than the fire, though. At least the land came back from that. But if he'd lived to see his dream run over by—"

"Damnit!" Schuyler cried, "I built these railroad tracks and I built the bridge and I found this locomotive and I'll get it off this boat today and on those tracks and across that damned bridge, you see if I don't. I've heard enough about your husband's dreams!" He raised his arms in frustration and turned away. "Oh, never mind, never mind." He turned to her and then away again. "What I'm trying to say is that...oh hell, Ada, never mind, I can't talk like this, makes me feel like a kid." He looked down at his hands, then up at Ada; his heavy-lidded eyes were open wide. "Never even called you Ada before, and now—"

Ada shook her head. "Please don't say any more. Please."

"But I want you to know. I want you to come somewhere with me. San Francisco, you ever been there? San Francisco..." His words trailed off, his hands hung open at his sides.

"I have to go to Los Angeles," Ada said dully.

Schuyler laughed. "I don't mean right now this minute, Ada. I mean—"

"But I can't leave the Malibu," Ada said. "Not now."

"Ever?"

"I don't know, Pete." She stared at him, he waited for her. "I appreciate what you said, but . . ."

Schuyler turned away. "You don't have to say anything. I was just talking. Just words, is all. Pay 'em no mind."

Ada touched his arm. "But I . . . I can't even promise I'll think about it now. I can't ask you to wait for me. I don't know if the ranch will ever be settled enough. I like you, Pete. Oh, God, I like you, but—"

He turned to her and pulled her to him, pressed his mouth to hers. Ada felt herself going soft against him, molding her body to his. For a long, long moment, she was lost in him; then she broke away, stood up straight, took a step back.

The rain had tapered to a fine mist that gave form to the silence between them. Schuyler pressed his hands on the railing, shoulders hunched up to his ears. Ada brushed damp hair off her forehead.

"Pete . . ."

Schuyler shook his head and kept his eyes on the ocean. "I know. You have to go."

The carriage stalls at Santa Monica's Pier Hotel were empty when Ada arrived for her meeting with N. F. Gass. A sullen barefoot boy tied up her horse, and accepted her nickel with ill-disguised contempt. There were two steamers docked at the pier, wreathed in a light, rainy mist, but the hustle of the pier's early years was absent.

Ada entered the hotel, thinking about the last time she'd walked through the revolving doors and taken the gilt elevator to the ballroom: it was the eve of the twentieth century, there was music and dancing, a birthday-cake evening, never to be repeated in her lifetime.

N. F. was waiting for her when the elevator doors opened onto the dimly lit hallway. He was dressed in a somber gray suit that blurred his outline, but she saw that he was thinner, diminished since the time he'd come to see her in the cottage. "We're closed for the season," he said, by way of explaining the dim lights. "I keep an office back here."

Ada followed him in the same corridor she and Emmett had walked down to get to the ballroom; the sconces were unlit, the paintings obscured, the furniture draped in sheets. N. F.'s office was small and dark, with a window that showed a foggy, gray sea. As he moved across the room Ada wondered if he was ill.

"The governor has assured me that the rain'll stop any day now," he said. "The sun is shining in the state capital, no doubt." He sat down heavily at his desk, and poured a glass of sherry from a crystal decanter. "Californians have about the least patience for clouds as any people I ever met. We're spoiled, wouldn't you say so? Wouldn't you say we're spoiled?" He slid the glass of sherry toward her, and smiled. "We met in this hotel, Mrs. Newcomb, do you remember?"

"The night everyone talked about the future of the state, or the state of the future, I'm not sure which."

N. F. laughed. "I suppose I made a speech, too. I was always making speeches in those days."

Ada laughed too, then stopped herself. N. F. was silent. She picked up her glass, sipped the sherry, put it down, then looked around the small office. "Is this the first year you've been closed for the winter?"

N. F. followed her gaze around the office, and turned back to her. "May I say something, Mrs. Newcomb? We'd get a lot farther a lot quicker, you and me, if we stopped being at cross purposes and got together on things."

"I agree," Ada said.

"What I'm proposing is a merger. The South Central will take over the construction of the tracks across the Malibu, assume all the costs, and we'll incorporate together as the South Central/Malibu Railway Line. Think about it, Mrs. Newcomb. We could own the coast."

Ada did not have to think at all.

"Yes, I know how you'd treat the land, too. If it was in your way—move it, take it down, plow it over."

"I'm not sentimental about the Malibu, if that's what you mean. I see a job needs doing, I get the job done."

"Sentimental! You think that's what I am? I just see a day past tomorrow, that's all. I'm a realist. You look at a thing and only see what's convenient for the moment, what suits your immediate purposes."

"Look, Mrs. Newcomb. You're not going to be able to finish that toy railroad you've started, and then where'll you be? No more money, no railroad, and no court to back you up. I'm proposing a contractual arrangement in which our mutual needs are met."

"I've already got the rights to do what I want to do," Ada said. "There isn't anything you have that I need."

"It's true that you have the rights now. But what about the

next time? Can you afford to build a highway when the Highway Commission comes to call? Can you continue to repair fences for as long as people tear them down? How many more lawsuits can you handle in court?"

"The kind of contract you have in mind is one where the losing party has more to gain." She started to rise. "You know I'm winning, Mr. Gass, and that's the truth."

"I'm talking, Mrs. Newcomb, about mutuality. A contract that will relieve you of the agonies of continuing this railroad. Just on sheer nervous virtuosity you may be able to pull off these first few miles of tracks, but you've got to add five miles a year, or you lose the franchise. Are you prepared to do that? You must admit to our superior experience. Come now, Mrs. Newcomb. We'd call it the Malibu Railway line, if you like. You'd continue to own it, what do you say to that? In your own name?"

"What kind of contract are you talking about?"

N. F. smiled and flung back the flap of his jacket. "Marriage, Mrs. Newcomb," he said. "Now don't be hasty in your response. There's profit in this for both of us."

He was smiling the same smile of confidence he'd shown her in 1900; oh these men and their confidence, she thought. "You think I'm going to win!"

N. F.'s face darkened and he stood up. "I think that you ought to stop being a fool. If you lose you lose everything."

"And if I win, you lose everything."

She walked to the door and turned to face him one last time. "You know what, Mr. Gass? You're not smiling."

Oh, wouldn't Schuyler have loved to be there and see me, Ada thought on her way out of the hotel. Throwing N. F.'s offer right back in his face. Just like he once did. Birds of a feather, she thought, and couldn't help but smile. Maybe I could go away now; just for a little while, just for a week. It's true, I haven't seen San Francisco. But... there was the first train ride, she thought, and another lawsuit regarding the fences that she had to attend to. Oh yes, and Quinones was impatient to buy some new horses for the vaqueros.

When she got back to the cottage, there was a note from Schuyler: "The locomotive is assembled and on the tracks ready for your first run. I myself consider this a job well taken and a job well done and now I am off to Alaska again, longing for the cold. I hope our last conversation was not too embarrassing for you. It is a fulltime lifetime occupation, running the Malibu, but if it can be done by anyone, you're the one to do it. If you ever want to build that dream house of yours, you just let me know. Best of luck in the future, Pete."

Ada held the note for a long moment, and wondered if either of them had done the right thing. Yes, she thought finally, both of us. But I couldn't do anything different. I'm right, I'm right. The Malibu is me, and Pete—no matter what I feel for him—is only a man. She read the note again, then opened her hand and let the wind take it.

Chapter 22

The headline of the Los Angeles *Times* read: *Mrs. Newcomb Wins Battle for Railroad:* "The Malibu Railway Line, built by its President, Mrs. Ada Newcomb, was declared the winner of a battle against the South Central's claim for a coastal rail line of its own. Judge Olden of the Superior Court of Los Angeles referred to California law that prohibits the South Central—or any other railroad—from condemning land for a right-of-way that would parallel an existing, operating line. The Malibu Railway Line, with its locomotive and five miles of tracks, constitutes that existing line. When interviewed by this newspaper, Mrs. Newcomb stated 'To be vindicated in your beliefs is a great satisfaction indeed. It restores my faith that the courts are meant to serve people.'"

The terminal itself was marked with nothing more elaborate than a large flat stone with a bench of bent willow, and over it a sign that read "Malibu Railway Line." Avery Benson and Clara Sweet sat on it and sweated in their city gabardines. A photographer from the Los Angeles *Times* begged a photograph of Ada. "My readers want to see the woman who stopped the South Central!" Flash powder exploded as he took a picture of Ada getting into the engineer's cabin and adjusting herself in the leather seat.

The locomotive stood on the tracks, black and bold, massive, dwarfing the sand and hill behind it, glinting wildly in the strong sun so that Ada had to shield her eyes. Yet was smaller than she had dared hope, its cab not much bigger than one of those automobiles she'd seen all over the streets of Los Angeles. The cab had a tender for wood, two leather seats, and behind it a flatbed twenty feet long, which Schuyler had said would be adaptable to either passengers or freight; its sides read: "Malibu Railway Line."

A few Chinese workers were gathered around the train, polishing, oiling. Crowds from Fisherman's Village were lined up on the far side of the fence. She sat down on one of the leather seats and put her hand gingerly on the gearshift.

The smell of leather and oil and smoke sent her right back to the train platform in Desideer, and then along all the tracks from there to Los Angeles.

She waved to Avery Benson and Clara Sweet. The man from the *Times* got her picture once more. Behind him Quinones mounted a horse and rode down to the beach, to ride alongside the train and meet her at the Zuma Ridge depot.

The sky was the bright startling blue that had colored her arrival in Los Angeles twenty years before.

She took a deep breath and closed her eyes. The tracks stretched back in her mind far beyond Las Flores Canyon, back across the desert and the mountains and the plains, back across seasons and time and death, back to Desideer and then forward again—from her last day in Desideer at the depot, watching Obie sucked into the distance as she sped away, hurtling across America with Emmett on the first great journey of her life. This will be my second journey, she thought, and, like the first, she marked it as the end of one thing and the beginning of something else. She leaned out the side of the car to wave goodbye; on her left the sea was icily brilliant. Ahead the tracks glared like blades in the sand. She put her hand on the engineer's stick and waited one moment longer. Then she took a deep breath and slowly pushed the gear ahead.

The pain of coming out here was worth it to him, now that he was sitting on top of the hill, his arms wrapped around his chest, back pressed against a big rock. Hold out my arms to her, catch her to me, and we'll be together. He hugged himself tighter. Like it's supposed to be, like it was meant to be. His chest was hot; he remembered riding to the top of the hill in 'Desideer, watching her train make the final curve and disappear, lost and gone forever to him, standing and watching, doing nothing, letting her go.

He squinted up at the sun, sharp as needles in his eyes. Little spots all over his face felt wet and boiling, others soft and spongy. Any hotter, it'll just melt right down my shirt. His scalp baked under the wide-brimmed black hat. When he touched something, the pain in his hands shot to his shoulders.

He shifted to a shady spot on the other side of the rock. A dozen cows were eating their way up the hill, their tails flicking like they belonged to something else. The heat

settled on him. His bones felt bleached out, like dog bones
he'd seen in the desert. He tried to remember being cold in
the cold: there was all those winters, all that snow and red
cheeks and shivering, shivering and wearing every piece of
clothes indoors and out, chilling cold, white and icy, shivering
cold ...

He jumped up, sobbing with the intensity of the heat
bearing down on him. He paced around the hill, craning his
neck to see the locomotive. Paper said today, paper said
noon, and the sun couldn't be higher than right now. Why
don't they get started? He used his hat to fan his face; the
sweat chilled on his cheeks and made his shoulder flesh
quiver.

He closed his eyes again, saw himself as he used to be, not
in the sun or the cold, not with Ada, though it was a time she
was there with him. Poor kids we was, so skinny, so hungry
and like as if we hadn't got the plainest notion how to get fed.
I thought I was so bad back then, bad boy, bad boy.

When he opened his eyes the locomotive was rounding a
curve up from the beach, disappearing around the next curve
in the canyon. And suddenly, as if hitting pure air after
breathing mud, he started running down the hill, scrambling
down the side of the hill, never minding his hands as they
pulled at bush roots and scraped over rocks. He fell hard on
his left arm and felt something crack, a pain shot into his
side, but he kept scrabbling, numb now, until he reached the
bottom of the hill.

... turning it all around, make every minute disappear
from the time I let her disappear till now, till now ...

There it was! The train bearing toward him over the
bridge, coming fast, chugging steady as it climbed over the
bridge, down the slow curve on the other side. He leaped
onto the tracks, running fast, hands outspread to stop it.

... don't leave me, don't leave me ... panting, tongue dry
and swollen ... don't, don't. There she is, Ada, look at me!
Oh Ada I hurt, I hurt so bad, Ada, just let me break it and
spill it out.

He stumbled; a bone cracked in his ankle. He screamed.

... Ada! Ada, oh Ada, I love you so. I'm here, cool again,
the wind, Ada. Ada! Don't leave me—

When Ada recalled the incident in the future—and she
would for the rest of her life—her mind could not help but

stretch it out: his face, scarred livid red, green eyes swimming, delirious, all the brighter for the redness around them, the mouth misshapen into a terrified scream. But why? What had he been trying to do?

The locomotive had moved easily, though noisily, at the base of the hill along the beach. Ada admitted to herself more than a proprietary pleasure, a hedonistic one, too, though she couldn't help but notice the black smoke, little as it was, smudging that perfect Southern California sky. The train ascended from the beach right after crossing Malibu Creek and began the long slow ascent to the bridge over Paradise Cove. She waved to Quinones riding horseback on the beach. One hand rested easily on the throttle, the other on the gear shift. The air smelled of flowers, the sea, the heat. This is good, she thought.

What was the exact moment she noticed the figure on the hill watching the train? She thought: I've seen this before, as if the image had frozen in her mind and suddenly come unstuck. The train dipped around a curve and, the turn made, came up higher on the hill, and the figure disappeared. Oh yes, she thought, it was like Obie, twenty years ago, the day I left Desideer with Emmett. When the train came around the turn, Ada, sure she had imagined the figure, was surprised to see it reappear now, running down the hill. She watched with growing curiosity, as if awake at her own dream. Obviously a trespasser; one of the homesteaders? She wasn't about to stop the train to find out now. The figure stumbled, scrambled onto the railroad tracks; Ada sat up straight. The figure ran with abandon, arms and legs wild and ungainly, and too fast, with no ability to rear itself back.

She screamed too late—an open-mouthed wail on the figure's face—Ada shut her eyes. She gripped the handle as if she might fly away, and was jolted by the thud of the body bouncing off the train, before she pulled the train to a screeching stop. She couldn't move for a moment, dizzy and frightened, then jumped from the car and made her way back to him. A black gloved hand was poised on a rock, the body twisted away from it.

He wasn't dead. There was a pinkish bubbling at his mouth, bloody spittle formed a bubble and popped. The heat was intense on the hilltop, the wind stilled. Ada half-crouched over the man, repelled by his disfigurement, but drawn to the extremity of it. Suddenly he spoke. Ada crouched closer. "Don't go," he said.

Ada shook her head but saw his eyes were closed and found her voice. "I won't go. I'm right here. We'll get help for you."

He lifted his head, tried to open his eyes, but they winced closed, tearing, tears pouring from them, Ada never saw tears flow so. She looked around but no one was coming; hadn't anyone noticed that the train had stopped? Where was Quinones? She looked back at the man again. He was holding his stomach now, blood seeped through his fingers.

"I'll get help," Ada said and started to rise.

"No!"

"But you're hurt, I—"

"Ada!"

She stopped, turned and knelt again. "You know me?"

"Don't you recognize me?"

She stared at the ruined face as the man opened his eyes again and she saw them, glittering green in a sea of tears. Her hands flew to her face, she shivered. "Oh, my God."

"I knew you'd remember."

She stared at his ruined face, her body was trembling, she wanted to scream herself awake.

"Ada?"

She braced herself against a rock at his side and leaned closer to him. Tears poured down her face; his breath blazed in her ear. "Forgive me?"

Ada nodded, unthinking.

"Say it!" he hissed, his body half rose, he grabbed her arm, blood, blood everywhere.

"I forgive you," she sobbed.

Obie leaned back and sighed. He didn't lift his head again when he spoke. "For burning down your school."

Ada stared, her tears kept coming.

"Say it! For burning down your school!"

"For . . . for burning down my school."

Blood seeped out of his ears, he groaned, his chest heaved in a sob. "Say my name," he whispered.

Ada opened her mouth, breath barely moved the sound. "Obie."

He smiled, his smile an agonized scream; his eyes opened again, winced, flooded with tears, and closed.

Quinones crested the hill on horseback and dismounted next to Ada. He looked down at the body and drew in a sharp breath. "Do you recognize him?"

Ada shook her head, her mouth set tight against tears. "There's not much left."

"I'll call the sheriff," Quinones said.

"No," Ada said. "Just get someone to come back here and take him. But...I want him buried on the Malibu."

She stared at her brother's ruined face. Who had he become between the day she left him and the day he came back? The mystery stranger in the white hat. She covered his face and stood up, and suddenly realized, with a sickening pang akin to horror, that though he had asked for her forgiveness, she had not been able to ask for his.

Part 6

This is the end, O Pioneer—
These final sands
I watch you sift with meditative hands,
Measure the cup of conquest.

—James Rorty

Chapter 23

Ada's mind could not rest during those hot dry summer weeks. She woke exhausted at dawn, and knew she had not really slept. Try as she might, she could not put to rest the grisly memory of Obie's death. The image of his ruined face visited her in dreams, formed and reformed itself out of configurations of bright sunlight and wind in juniper bushes, formed and dissolved with the crashing of waves on the gritty shore, until she forced herself to confront that image directly. Then, the horror of it at least manageable in her mind's eye, she was prey to all the guilt and despair she'd put off thus far: How can I make sense of this? What did it mean that he came back in such a state? What had his poor life been?

She dreamed often of Obie, and stirred from these dreams with pounding heart to relight the bedside candle and make notes about the ranch until the candle burned down, and she continued even then, feeling her way down page after page of paper. In the morning her bed would be covered with pages of her enormous blind scrawl. Nothing made sense unless she wrote it down.

She hired another Pinkerton man to retrace Obie's life back from the moment of his ignominious end on the Malibu. Months later the bare facts of her brother's recent past were delivered to her, neatly spelled out on a simple sheet of paper: the McWilliams Hotel, the hospital in Los Angeles. And so it had come to this end; there was no more to be known.

She shared with no one Obie's confession of responsibility for the fire; indeed, she told no one who he was. If Cornelius were home she might have told him, but for now she had to hold it inside. It gave an unsettling edge to all past and present homesteader lawsuits; it had made of her, she felt, an unwitting cheat. But there was no way to retract her accusations except to open the ranch roads, and that, she knew, was out of the question.

Her sense of the world outside the Malibu was of an

inexorable wave pushing at the fragile dams of her borders, bolstered only by wire fences and some easily broken laws.

She was eager now for Cornelius's arrival, for someone to share the ranch, someone who belonged to it as she did. She put aside all feelings of doubt about Cornelius and the reasons on both their parts for their long separation. They needed each other now—at least I need him, she admitted ruefully—and, most importantly, the Malibu needed him. He's my son, she declared to herself, with something like the fervor with which Emmett had talked about Cornelius. We're the Newcomb family.

On the day Cornelius was to arrive at the Malibu for his first summer since the fire, Ada waited impatiently in the cottage, but finally mounted her horse to ride down to the beach and meet him halfway, binoculars in hand to catch the earliest glimpse. They would be the Newcomb family again, at least until he went back to Boston in the fall.

When she got to the beach, she stopped her horse and raised the binoculars to her eyes. The beach south of the Malibu was dotted with picnickers and fishermen, and out of this group an automobile was heading toward the fence at Las Flores Canyon. The sight of it was comical: shaking violently, throwing its passengers wildly from side to side, the front lamps like two crossed eyes. But the sparks and smoke belching from its rear, and the tiny drops of gasoline no doubt left in its wake, were not in the least comical. As the automobile cruised along the beach at low tide line, Ada saw that it showed every sign of ignoring the "no trespassing" sign and riding on past the fence.

She dug her heels into the horse's flanks, and rode along the shore to intercept it; as she neared it she could hear its passengers singing "Come away with me Lucille/in my merry Oldsmobile!" Just as the machine passed the fence and set its wheels on Malibu sand, Ada forced it to a halt. The smoke settled with the dying sputter of the engine.

The driver jumped out onto the sand, doffing duster and goggles and cap. When Ada saw who it was she had an instantaneous, undeniable—though she would try to deny it—impulse to turn her back, to hide, to let him search and never find her, to deny their connection if found, for it was as if her brother had not really burned in the Malibu fire, had not thrown himself in front of the train, had not been buried

n the Malibu, but had simply stayed in Desideer after she
eft, then taken the train to California as originally planned,
nd here he was, standing on the beach in a Panama suit,
esh-faced, red-headed, green-eyed, nineteen.

"Mother!"

Ada got off her horse and embraced her son stiffly. "You're
o tall!" she managed to say.

"I couldn't help it," he said with a laugh. "Am I as tall as
ather?"

"Oh, at least as tall," she replied, and heard with dismay
he accusation in her voice.

"And I've got red hair like Uncle Obie, too, I know. You
ught to hear the ribbing I take at school. Carrot top, fire
op. Aunt Elizabeth and Uncle John can't imagine where I
ot it from. They think it's something I should grow out of.
Mother, I want you to meet someone." He took her arm and
eered her back to the automobile. The other passenger
opped down onto the sand and opened her duster.

She was a doll-like creature, wrapped tight as a package in
 white linen dress that barely reached her ankles and a white
afari hat with an elaborate veil.

"Mother, this is my friend, Rose Adore."

"We meet at last," the girl said, in a voice so deep it
ocked her tininess. Her features were obscured by the veil,
ut her mouth was painted red and pushed forward like
omething about to burst.

"I'm glad Cornelius has brought you out to our ranch, Miss
dore," Ada said. "The Malibu is quite a relief if you live in
oston."

"Oh I live in Los Angeles," the girl said. "And I'm not a
ranger to the Malibu, Mrs. Newcomb. As a matter of fact, I
sed to live right behind it."

"You did?" Ada said. She tried to see the girl without the
eiled hat and the elaborately painted mouth but the disguise
as impenetrable. "I don't recall the name though. Adore,
ou said?"

"We've been having a little joke with you, Mother," Cornelius
inked at the girl. "Rose Adore is only the name she uses in
er work. She's an actress in the motion pictures."

"I'm Phoebe Hinderman, Mrs. Newcomb," she said and
fted the veil. "I went to your school on the Malibu. Conny
nd I have been corresponding for years."

Ada hesitated for a moment. "Yes, I remember." She could

see her now, skinny and shy, standing behind her mothe
Cassie; yes, those small fox eyes were unforgettable.

"The Malibu's completely unchanged, Mother!" Corneli
exclaimed as he looked up the coast.

Ada watched him. Was it possible he didn't know the bitt
fights that had taken place—that continued to take place
between her and Phoebe's parents? Was this his idea of
joke? She looked at Phoebe Hinderman; she knew.

"You were right not to let me see it after the fire
Cornelius was saying. "I would have remembered it th
way." Hands on hips, he struck the attitude of surveyc
discoverer. "I even like your famous railroad. It's so modern

Ada turned to Phoebe again. "The last time I saw yo
parents was in a court of law, I'm afraid. But I imagine yc
know all about our differences."

"Mother, don't be rude," Cornelius said. "Phoebe and
don't care anything about that."

Phoebe smiled at Cornelius and nodded. "One generatic
shouldn't have to carry on the squabbles of the last, isn't th
so, Mrs. Newcomb?" There was an expression of amuse
detachment in her eyes that Ada didn't quite trust.

"What do you think of this, Mother?" Cornelius slappe
the automobile affectionately. "It's called a Ford, Model '
Named for the man who made it."

"Not one man, Conny," Phoebe said.

Cornelius laughed in a way Ada had never heard. '
mean," he said to Ada with a smile at Phoebe, "a group
men make each one on a kind of line-up. Get in, Mothe
we'll drive up to the cottage."

"You can't drive this machine up there!" Ada said.

"Oh, you'd be surprised what this can do," he said.

"I mean, I don't allow these machines on the ranch."

"I told Phoebe we could—"

"But you should have asked me first."

Cornelius cast an embarrassed glance at Phoebe. "B
Mother, it's—"

"If I allowed these machines to—"

"It's an automobile!" Cornelius said. "At least you can call
by its right name!" He walked away, to stand at the water
edge with his arms folded across his chest.

"It was my idea, Mrs. Newcomb," Phoebe said quietly. "S
you have only me to blame. I wanted to bring it out, and I'
afraid I threw a tiny little temper tantrum. Poor Cornelius

he cast a forlorn look at him. "He has trouble saying no to
ne."

Ada was embarrassed now at the demonstration of her son's
ntimate connection to this girl. "If I let one of these automo-
ile machines through, another one would come after it, then
nother and another. All running their soot and oil and smoke
umes across the beach."

Phoebe looked up the coast, squinting in the sun and
aising a pale white hand to shield those fox eyes. "Smell that
ir," she said, making a great show of breathing in and out. "I
ust love it here. I do. If I lived on a place like this, I'd want
o keep people away just like you do. Conny wanted to spend
he summer in a little house in Hollywood, but I told him he
vas being just plain stubborn."

Ada glanced at Cornelius's intransigent back. "Let me have
carriage come up and take you to the cottage."

Phoebe struggled with a suitcase in the luggage rack of the
utomobile. "Conny!" she cried. "Stop sulking this minute
nd help me with our bags!"

Cornelius trudged up the beach and drew the girl close to
im, nuzzling her neck. "Isn't she wonderful, Mother? I keep
elling her—our destinies are intertwined!"

Cornelius spent the summer on the ranch, talking with
Quinones and the vaqueros, riding around with a notebook in
is hand, just like Emmett had done.

Phoebe Hinderman, much to Ada's relief, was living on
une Street in Hollywood, and only spending long weekends
n the Malibu.

It was also a relief to Ada to watch Cornelius begin to
ssume his position as the future proprietor of the Malibu,
specially since the prospect of continued, accelerated oppo-
ition to her made the future seem harder than the past.
Letters of attack continued to appear in newspapers and
ound their way out to the Malibu. Open the gates, the
demands went, take down the fences and let people past. We
vant a coastal highway, entrepreneurs of all sorts shouted in
ditorials and interviews. The Highway Commission's plea to
un a road across the shore line was supported by hundreds
of local businessmen and thousands of owners of automobiles.

It was at the worst of these times that she regretted saying
no to Pete Schuyler. But he had been right about her, and she

knew it; she could not be shared while the Malibu was still hers. And so her loneliness continued.

On one of Phoebe's visits—inspired, she said, by Ada' never having seen a motion picture—she brought a copy o one of her own along with a projector, a screen, and the ma who produced it, a man surprisingly familiar to Ada.

"Made a few career switches since our last contact," Cheste Puhls said. "I suppose you must of heard." Chester, Ad thought, was considerably the worse for the years. There wa a swimmy, desperate look in his eyes that replaced what ha once been the eagerness of simple opportunism when h dealt in real estate. He nodded appraisingly at the cottag living room as he went about setting up the projector, stretchin the screen—a chemically treated white sheet—against th opposite wall, as if he didn't have quite the tight grip o things he may have had in his youth.

"You ever get to the nickelodeon shows? Right down th street from where your lawyer Mr. Benson's got his office there's one I own. This whole business started out as kind of rag-tag operation but there's a pot of money to be made o it."

"Hollywood's cornered the western market on the busi ness," Cornelius said. "And it's just got incorporated into Lo Angeles, so you can see how seriously people take it."

Chester made some adjustments to his projector, cranke the generator, and the film began. A title came on in th flickering lights: *The Sweetheart of the Trail.*

"That's supposed to be the Texas Panhandle, but it's actua ly Protrero Canyon," Cornelius said, as they watched th images on the sheet.

"I predict a big future for our Phoebe here," Chester said "'Rose Adore.' Thought that one up myself. I predict she'll b as popular with the public as Blanche Sweet in a few years."

Ada watched Phoebe's by-now familiar face doing unfami iar and altogether grotesque things. She widened her narro eyes, she tossed her curls, she was coy, all jerking shoulder and fluttering hands. It did not resemble any human behavic Ada had ever witnessed.

"Now that's what I call acting!" Chester said.

Cornelius, for his part, was enthralled with her image watching open-mouthed and slack with wonder as Phoeb fluttered her lashes or waved slim white fingers to all th

men, who were evidently enchanted by her. Next to him, the
real Phoebe sat, sunk deep in her chair, her fingers in her
mouth.

"You do see what's so special about her now, don't you,
Mother?"

"Oh Conny, stop!" Phoebe slapped him and sank deeper in
the chair.

Chester laughed. The film came to its conclusion with
Phoebe, in a circle of light, hands clasped to her chest, eyes
up, and the final title: "To heaven with papa."

Ada rubbed her eyes while Cornelius opened the curtains
and daylight filled the room. Chester sat down opposite her,
and put on a serious expression.

"I've got a proposition to offer," he said. "I'd like to use the
Malibu to make the film of *Ramona*. We can't pay you
anything, but we'd give you a piece of the profits. We've
come full circle, Mrs. Newcomb," Chester said. "I brought
you that copy of *Ramona* the night I came to tell you the
Malibu was for sale. You remember? That was the ground
floor for all of it, back then."

"Phoebe would be wonderful for the part of Ramona,
wouldn't she? With her dark hair?" Cornelius added.

"Conny! You're embarrassing me!"

"This is the ground floor again, Mrs. Newcomb. No telling
how far the motion pictures as a business could go."

"A motion picture of *Ramona* on the Malibu?"

"It's a wonderful idea, isn't it, Mother?" Cornelius exclaimed.

"Just look at your place, Mrs. Newcomb," Chester said and
gestured to the land spread out below them: rolling hills,
rows of cypress in the distance. Fields of goldenrod and
scarlet poppies. The sky reared above them, an immense flat
azure blue, solid and unvarying from horizon to mountain
ridge. "It's perfect. What they call 'timeless'. Just the way the
land's described in *Ramona*. Think of it, Mrs. Newcomb. The
mission past immortalized on film. Are there any olive trees
on the place, by the way?"

"Do we need olive trees?" Cornelius asked.

"We'll buy olive trees!" Chester cried.

Cornelius held Phoebe's hand, and turned to Ada. Ada
looked from one to the next, squirming with what she knew
she had to say. "Oh, I guess it's a good idea. I don't know
much about these things. But you see...the thing is I've
never allowed the Malibu to—"

"Oh, Christ." Cornelius dropped Phoebe's hand and strode to the window.

"Maybe you don't get the larger picture," Chester said. "I'd be putting Phoebe in the picture, and part of the profits would come back to you. I know you're in some kind of financial—"

"My financial affairs are none of your business," Ada said.

"Never mind, never mind. Leave her alone," Cornelius said. "There are other ways."

He helped Chester pack up his projector and flim, and went outside with him to load the carriage.

When she was alone with Phoebe, Ada said, "Are you using my son to get back at me?"

Phoebe laughed. "Mothers can be so blind," she said. "Don't you think it's just possibly the other way around? That Conny's using me to get back at you?"

Ada was struck as if by a cold hand with the truth of this. "You told me you didn't care about carrying on your parents' fight, and he agreed."

Phoebe shurgged. "Well, I don't want you to take down any gates for me, or open up any roads for me to use."

"Then what do you want?"

"Isn't it perfectly obvious? I thought you were shrewd enough to see through me all along. You'll be my mother yet, wait and see." She left the house, gave Cornelius a chaste kiss, and departed in the carriage with Chester Puhls.

A dry breeze blew into the room; sand whispered along the clay floors and piled against old Chumash rugs. Cornelius came up onto the porch and watched in silence as Chester and Phoebe rode down the hill. Ada came out and stood next to him. She thought of how she had once wanted to unburden herself about Obie to Cornelius, but the moment in which to do that—if it had ever existed between them at all—had long since passed.

"I'm sorry," she said.

"How do you think I feel when she goes off to work and only comes here on the weekends?"

"Why don't you marry her?"

He turned away and moved stiffly to the railing. "She already has a husband." He turned back angrily before Ada said anything. "Well, she had to get away from the place she lived in, didn't she? Didn't you do the same thing once?"

"I'm not taking a moral stand, Cornelius," Ada said. "But

I've had to keep a close eye on everything that happens on
the Malibu. I have to keep things simple. I had no idea you
were interested in this motion picture business."

"I'm not, particularly, so let's drop it." Cornelius looked at
her and nodded his head. "I've been doing a lot of thinking
about the Malibu this summer."

"Oh?"

"*Ramona* was just one of my ideas." He took out his
notebook and leafed through it. "The way I see it, a lot of the
land is just going to waste. Miles of beachfront property just
sitting there, not even used for grazing anymore since Quinones cut down the size of the herd. I had an idea that we
could lease some of the grazing land. Or sell off some of the
beachfront property. Just to a few people. Or lease it to them.
Have houses built, or let them build their own. Bungalows
are the coming thing for beach living, Mother. I've seen the
plans for the bungalows at Laguna Beach." He stopped when
he saw that Ada was shaking her head, then continued, a
little less expansively. "If the Highway Commission wins
their case against us, and the highway goes through, all our
land will come down in value. Now is the time to develop it,
Mother. The Malibu could become a greater resort area than
Santa Monica or Venice or any of them. But we've got to be
the ones to do it, or someone else'll take the ranch away piece
by piece and do it themselves."

"Nobody's taking anything away," Ada said.

"Thousands of automobiles are driving into California every
month. It's the biggest boom since the eighties, bigger than
the Gold Rush. Automobiles are the wave of the future if
you'll only realize it. You can go anywhere you want in
them—or you will be able to, as soon as the roads are
better—without schedules or timetables. There are people
opening up service stations and garages along the coast,
restaurants and hotels and shops. We've got a potential gold
mine in our hands, and you're sitting there with your fists
clenched."

"The Malibu land can't really support the kind of road the
Highway Commission is planning," Ada said. "Or what that
road will inevitably bring. The ranch is mainly sand, there's
no bedrock. Storm tides flood the beach. Heavy rains erode
the hills above where the road would run. You'd have land-
slides. It'd be a disaster. The land goes its own way, does
what it wants to do. It doesn't care that you've built an

expensive highway if it wants to flood. Cornelius, since 1907 the state of California has tried to force legislation through the courts so they can run U.S. 60 through the Malibu. I know there's public support for the road. I get hundreds of letters a month telling me just that. I thought that you, at least, might be on my side." ·

Cornelius was silent for a long moment. Then he said, "Maybe I misunderstand, Mother. But you've kept me shut out of all the ranch business. I should know more about the financial end of it, shouldn't I? I mean, if I'm to take my part?"

"Oh, I don't think you need to bother yourself with that right now, do you? After all, you're just here for a visit. You'll be going back in a few weeks."

Cornelius looked away. "Not necessarily," he said.

"What do you mean?" Ada asked.

Cornelius shrugged. "Only that I might not go back." He turned to face her. "It's just so boring, Mother. You have no idea. Remember what father used to say about Boston? Well, it hasn't changed at all. No wonder he got out of there. I'm only surprised he stayed as long as he did."

"I thought you were going to finish law school," Ada said.

Cornelius shook his head and met her eye. "No, I'm here to stay."

"Well . . ." Ada could not drop her gaze from his and what she saw there frightened her: he was her son, with her brother's eyes and his father's zeal, but he was a stranger. "I'm glad."

Cornelius shook his head again. "No, you're not, Mother. You're not glad at all." In the shocked silence that followed this truth, Cornelius paced away and back. Then he sat down again and spoke in a more reasonable tone. "I'm sorry, I'm sorry. I didn't mean that. I just thought, well, that it'd be nice to stay here a while longer. Spend Christmas here. It's been a long time since we spent Christmas together."

Ada looked down.

"But I can't stay here and not work on something," he continued. "Not be a part of the Malibu. I can't just be your son."

"Cornelius, I hate this, I really hate it. Why do you push me into situations in which I'm forced to say no to you?"

Cornelius leaned heavily against the porch railing. "I'm

just trying to make you see that it would be to our advantage
to develop the Malibu before someone else does."

"I'm quite happy with it the way it is. I'd be happier if
everyone would obey the laws and just leave me in peace. I
still haven't even had time to build a house with all that's
been going on."

"You haven't had the money, either."

Ada looked out at the canyon again, as if measuring the
distance she'd come and how far it was back to where she
belonged, but the trip was a trip through time.

"You can't keep yourself isolated out here forever," he said.

Ada remained seated. "I don't equate protecting the Malibu
with isolation."

"What difference does it make what you call it if it comes
down to the same thing?" He came and sat by her now, his
hands clasped together.

"Well, now I know what you'd do if the Malibu was in your
hands! You'd bring it in step with the so-called 'times'."

"No, Mother," he said. "I'd push it even further. Don't you
see what this place could become? There'll be jobs for
roadworkers, and increased monies for the businesses served
by the road," he said. "The orange groves will be made
accessible to new workers. Houses'll be built, new settlers
brought in. Think of the national prestige of such a highway.
The power it would give us."

"I'm sure Phoebe must be very pleased with these plans,"
Ada said. "After all her parents' years of being shut out—"

"You don't intend for me to have any say in the way the
ranch is run, do you? It's your way or not at all."

"You're only nineteen years old, Cornelius."

"I'm twenty, Mother, and father intended for me to carry
on the ranch. You just want to . . . you just want to drag it into
the past."

"I want to preserve it."

"You want to embalm it!"

She turned away and looked down at the hills. "I promised
your father I'd bring the Malibu back to what it was."

"I'm sure it was very fair of you to tell him what he wanted
to hear in his last moments, but do we really have to run the
rest of our lives by that gesture?" He was red-faced with
exasperation. "What you've done is enshrine the Malibu for
yourself, as a monument to how bravely you've carried on
without him."

"That's a careless and ungrateful thing to say."

Cornelius took a handkerchief out of his pants pocket, wiped his face, then folded it and stuffed it back; he did not face her when he spoke. "I'm trying to make you see that this is inevitable. It's not 1891 any more, when you and father can just say 'no trespassing' in a firm tone of voice, and expect people to slink meekly away."

There was something tremulous in his voice, as if he dared not say what he was saying. "When was the last time you were off the ranch? The world is moving, Mother, not standing still. You'd like nothing better than to declare the Malibu a separate state, and secede from the union. The Great State of Malibu. The Republic of Malibu."

"And you'd like to open the gates and have the world troop on through."

"You sent me away, Mother! You sent me away. And now you expect me to obey you and work for you, just like a hired hand."

Ada hesitated to speak; her protests sounded hollow even to herself. "Yes," she said. "I expect your loyalty."

Cornelius laughed to himself and did not answer. He stood looking out at the canyon. "Where's my horse's grave?" he asked in a small voice. "I went looking for it the other day, and couldn't find it."

Ada didn't answer; for a moment he was a little boy again. "The grave marker was lost in the fire."

Cornelius slapped his hands on the railing and spun around to face her. "Oh, the famous fire that destroyed the Malibu! How you love to make myths about this place!"

"Why do you hate me so?"

Cornelius was suddenly sobered. "I don't think that's funny," he said and turned away. He was silent for a long moment, then turned back to her and spoke in a flat unemotional voice. "I've tried to reason with you, and now . . . well, you might as well hear this from me as anyone else. I've been talking to a lawyer in Los Angeles. He thinks I've got a case."

"A case? What are you talking about? What kind of case?"

Cornelius shrugged and looked away. Ada stood up quickly. "Maybe you'd better go back to Boston and think about it before you say any more."

"I've been thinking about nothing else for years, Mother, and now that I'm here and can see what you've made of the Malibu—what you haven't made, I should say—I'm going to do something about it. I intend to take you to court and prove that you have so mismanaged and mishandled the business side of the ranch and its opportunities that a potential success has been pushed to the brink of financial disaster. I'm going to stop you from spending all our money on fences and gates and guards and ridiculous lawsuits. My lawyer has advised me of my rights."

"Rights? What rights?"

"Mother." He shook his head, then turned away. "I want control of the Malibu."

Chapter 24

The judge's chamber in the Los Angeles City Hall Building was high-ceilinged but airless, windows hung with heavy braided drapes, dust motes floating up shafts of sunlight. The judge and his stenographer sat at the head of a long table; at one side of it were Phoebe and Cornelius, heads together in conference, as his lawyer talked *sotto voce* to Avery Benson and Quinones. Ada sat opposite them, worried not so much because of the legal outcome—every court hearing thus far had gone in her favor; land was protected by laws, and it was as simple as that—but because her son was her opponent. Their only contact in weeks had been through their lawyers. Once he'd moved out of the cottage and into Phoebe's house on June Street in Hollywood, once he'd set his lawsuit in motion, there was no turning back, no bridging the emotional chasm that their disagreement over the Malibu had opened.

She looked across the table at him; until today, when they faced each other as adversaries, she had considered him only a rebellious child. Now her mind was filled with all that was left unsaid between them, all her words unheard that would define the Malibu: the true words, the right words, the only ones. But would all her talk of Emmett's dreams ever be able to link an old promise to a new idea? She feared now that she would save her land, and in the process lose her son.

Avery Benson resumed his seat, and smiled encouragingly.

The stenographer cleared her throat, the judge put on his reading glasses, looked up for silence, and began.

"The case before the court today is number 41743, Newcomb versus Newcomb. To be decided is whether the management of the Malibu Ranch is to remain in the hands of Ada Newcomb, or revert to Cornelius Newcomb."

The hearing itself was brief: in less than half an hour Cornelius's lawyer detailed for the judge the grievances against Ada Newcomb's management of the ranch that supported Cornelius's claim, piling documents on the long table: petitions by various civic and business groups demanding a coast road, petitions by homesteaders and automobile manufacturers, charts and figures citing potential revenues to the State. of California. He read the specific charges that Cornelius had brought against her: that she had irresponsibly and willfully squandered his father's fortune in lawsuits, gates, and fences, and refused to develop those aspects of the ranch which would make it pay for itself. In turn, Avery cited laws that upheld all of Ada's actions, demonstrated Ada's personal record-keeping of trespassing and all other legal precedents that had been set.

Ada listened to the familiar words; they had all been said before, in rhetoric more or less impassioned, in newspaper articles, by public speakers, in other lawsuits in other courtrooms by other judges. She and Avery had given but quick study to this case: how could her land be taken from her?

The judge nodded, head down, during all the presentations, then dismissed the court while he deliberated. The lawyers put their heads together once again, as Ada waited in the corridor.

From a shadowy corner, Cornelius and Phoebe were watching her. Now they approached her warily, Phoebe backing away behind Cornelius.

"I wonder how you justify what you're doing," Ada said before he could speak.

Cornelius sighed and held onto Phoebe. "You misunderstand me, Mother. It's not your defeat I want."

"Oh really? Then what do you want?"

"I want to save the Malibu."

"You want to save the Malibu. And how do you think you're going to do that?"

"The first thing I would do is make a deal with the Highway Commission," he said. "The sooner the road goes through, the sooner I can get the rest of my ideas going. As a matter of fact, a lot of them are really extensions of father's original notions of the Malibu as a kind of Mediterranean paradise. Bungalows on the hills facing the sea, a main road connecting them, like the Appian Way. Maybe a golf course, and a—"

"You really believe that you can save the Malibu by destroying it?"

Phoebe sidled up to him and pulled at his sleeve. "Conny, the judge is ready."

Ada and Cornelius looked at each other, alarmed. "The

Malibu's got to be opened to the world, Mother," Cornelius said. "It's inevitable, but you're blind to that."

"Cornelius, to open it up is to kill it. Don't you know what'll happen if you try to build houses on sandy hills? Or roads along the beach? Or—"

Cornelius shook his head. "You always talked about father's talent for the future. Well, take a good look at me, Mother. I'm the future."

Phoebe linked her arm in his, and they strode confidently into the judge's chamber; Ada waited a long moment, then followed slowly, Cornelius's words repeating in her mind: "I'm the future." She sat down heavily next to Avery Benson as the judge rustled his papers and looked from Ada to Cornelius before he spoke.

"Over the past twenty-odd years," he said, "Mrs. Newcomb has continually employed the courts as guardian to her private interests. But that can no longer be. Progress on the scale that is at stake here cannot be shunted aside merely to serve personal interests. Mr. Newcomb has demonstrated more than adequately that he has offered solutions to the Malibu's financial indebtedness, and that Mrs. Newcomb has refused each and every suggestion. In the light of her unmovable position, the court favors Mr. Newcomb in his suit for management of the Malibu Ranch."

Ada gripped the arms of her chair and stood up. Avery tried to pull her back down, but her stance was firm. "I'm not against the future good of the State of California." Her voice trembled with rage as she looked at her son. "But is the future only going to cannibalize the past?" She pulled out a pair of black gloves, and jammed her fingers inside. "Are each generation's treasures merely there for the next to ravish as they will?" She turned her back and left the room, strode blindly down the long corridor, thinking only of finding her carriage in the stables. The Malibu was in danger; she had to get home.

She came to a cul-de-sac and stopped, spun around, but the corridor bisected another and that another still; footsteps followed her, and Quinones appeared.

"I'm lost," she said breathlessly.

Quinones nodded—it was the second time Ada had seen tears in his eyes—and looked away.

"May I say something.?"

She looked up at him and laughed. "First time I ever heard you ask."

"I think your son's behaving like a bastard."

"I don't mind you saying it as much as I mind him behaving like one." She shook her head as if she could rid her mind of all thoughts of Cornelius, but anger was only replaced by sorrow and fatigue.

Quinones held her arm tightly. "You can appeal that decision," he said.

Ada nodded her head violently. "Oh, I intend to. I just wish..." The air went out of her; she slumped against him. "I just can't imagine the Malibu any different than it is right now. I can't imagine not standing on the hill and looking down at the beach and seeing what I saw this morning." She shook her head and thought of Obie, and the fire, and how wrong she'd been to blame the homesteaders. "I could have been wrong about all of it, couldn't I? Maybe I haven't seen what's always been coming. Have I been a bigger dreamer than Emmett, to think I could hold onto the things as they are? Maybe you just can't really own land at all. Maybe—"

"You should not talk this way."

"But where'll I go? What'll I do?"

"Your son is not going to throw you out," Quinones said. "It's not as if you sold the ranch to a stranger. He just wants to be in charge." His words did not ring true, even to him.

Ada nodded slowly, "The wave of the future," she said.

Quinones guided her toward the doorway at the end of the corridor. "What about that house you were once going to build?"

Ada looked at him and shook her head. "Oh, that was before. I don't think... I don't know..."

"I think you ought to build that house, señora."

She reached out and took his hand. "I didn't think I was going to need moral support. I didn't think I was going to need anything." She looked down and laughed softly to herself, then looked back up at him. "I'm going back to the ranch now. I'd like to go alone. I'm... I'm all right. But... you'll come later?"

"It's my home, the Malibu," Quinones said.

When she was alone in her carriage in the stable behind the City Hall building, Ada allowed herself one deep sob, and for a long terrifying moment saw the true black hole of despair; then she took a hard grip on the reins of the carriage and moved out of the stable into the street. Automobiles belched and spat bulletlike noises, frightening carriage and wagon horses and causing more congestion, it seemed, than they alleviated. Her horse shied as an automobile cut in front of her, and she made the turn into a less crowded side street which eventually joined Wilshire Boulevard, out to the beach. She watched the traffic around her, trapped by it, choked by it, and felt, no matter what Cornelius or the court said, that some ultimate, inevitable misery lurked at the very core of the parade. She guided her horse carefully through the city; she wanted to be back on the ranch before dark. As she rode she imagined the streets widening even more in the future, other boulevards created to join Los Angeles to the sea. There would be homes built along this strip of land, and shops and hotels and garages and service stations for automobiles. Already people were anticipating the day when the Pacific Coast Highway would be complete; as significant as the golden spike that joined the rails east and west, they were saying. A new frontier of travel, the travel of the future.

Early evening fog was rolling in by the time she reached the Malibu, but the air was clear and quiet. Soon this won't exist any more, ever again, anywhere. She rode slowly along the shore, acutely aware of the slap of horse hooves, the smell of the sea, the fine sea mist on her face, as if she had to memorize them against the time they would be gone forever and lost to her.

Ada got out of the carriage at the top of the hill where the original house had stood. Her hands were clenched tightly together—the beach below dissolving in early evening mist, the scent of lilacs drifting up from the canyon—and was nearly overcome with the sense of the Malibu as inextricably receding into the past: faded glory, old triumphs, wars waged, and battles won long, long ago. And she saw herself in years to come: a stubborn old woman, pathetic, disillusioned, unable to comprehend modern life, living alone in the tatters of a once-fabulous past, misremembered and misunderstood.

She stared at the beach, the graceful curves disappearing in the mist. She heard the regular beat of the waves on the shore, the pulse of the ranch itself. What will happen to it when I leave? Torn apart, gutted, transformed under an uncaring, impeccable California sky.

She sat on a rock where the outside wall had once been, and imagined Emmett's house as it might have been: wide canvas shades pulled across archways and snapping in the breeze, sunset shadows spilling across the floors, the colors deepening as the light faded until the sand-colored walls were silvered by the moon. The dream house of a boy brought up in a series of dark rooms, the promise made to him a long time ago, sealed but incomplete.

Oh, Emmett, nothing's come out the way you dreamed. My God, my God, it's over. She buried her face in her hands and wept.

A strange sound intruded; voices singing, tiny, tinny, far away; she got her binoculars from the carriage, and searched the beach for its source. Through the mist came two faint beams of light, wavering, unsteady, the voices trailing behind. As the lights broke through the mist, Ada saw Cornelius's Model T Ford; at the wheel was Cornelius in a straw boater, one arm thrown expansively around Phoebe, who wore a brimmed hat with red ribbons flying in the wind.

Ada remembered a day long ago . . . that first day she and Emmett drove a buggy along the shore, when, little by little, the Malibu was revealed to them: the most wonderful dream, wrapped in layers of mist, unfolding, unfolding . . .

She took the binoculars from her eyes and felt clear-headed suddenly. Nothing's changed in the way I feel about the Malibu, she thought. The beach may be torn up, but there are the canyons and the creek and the pastures and the cattle and the sheep, and if Cornelius Newcomb and the Highway Commission think it's going to be an easy thing to lay a road across my beach, just let them try.

She turned around just as a rider crested the hill. In a moment Quinones was at her side. "I want to build that house," she said to him.

She strode around the site in excitement, waving her arms to indicate walls and floors. "With a veranda wrapped around the hill so we can see the canyons and our sheep on the pasture lands. And flowers growing inside the house walls in huge sandstone pots. From the outside all that'll show will be tiny spots of flowers creeping along the ledges, like secrets spilling out. Inside, the rooms'll just sprawl, separated by low ledges sometimes, not even walls. From the outside there'll be a wall the color of the sand thrusting out to the sea, terraces set into the rocks and easing back along the canyon wall. The house will seem to rise from the hillside itself."

She squeezed Quinones's hands tightly. "We're the true owners of the Malibu now. You and me." She ran to the edge of the hill and looked down at the beach again, happy suddenly, as she watched the beams of automobile light thread in and out of the mist, bright red ribbons in the wind until they disappeared and the beach was clear again.

"I want to build it where they can all see it, so everyone who ever drives on that damned highway can look up here and see the house and know, they'll know forever what the Malibu was."